Ruby's Texas Ranger

Belles & Boots ~ Book 2

By Louise Crouch

Copyright © 2019 Louise Crouch

ISBN: 978-0-6484878-9-0

For more from Louise Crouch please visit http://loucrouch.wordpress.com/books

Dedication

To my family for their love and support

To my children for their patience

To my husband for saying yes

Table of Contents

Chapter 1

Jewel Daniels wrestled with her gun belt, tightening it another notch across her waist, tucking in her navy gingham so if she had to draw, she'd be ready. She sat back on the single cot and the springs squeaked as she landed on the straw stuffed mattress and tugged on her boots. The embroidered roses over red leather hugged her calves and soothed her soul. She didn't care that Calvin had mocked the only feminine item of clothing she owned. Her Pa had seen to it, with the little money that he earned as a farm hand, to buy his only daughter the prettiest pair of boots in Dew Springs.

Here in Delano, Kansas it wasn't only Calvin that mocked her, but any worthy gunslinger. It didn't matter, they soon found out a pair of rose embroidered boots didn't affect her aim.

Jewel ran her gaze over the poster that had hung on her wall since they'd arrived in Delano. *Calvin Hadley's Sharp Shooter Spectacular* written in big bold letters, had been plastered over a black and white caricature of Bryce Tanner aiming his Colts at a mob of bandits, their face concealed with bandanas. The bandits menaced *'Ruby Drawers'* the damsel in hooped skirts and a plunging neckline, who had been tied to a tree. It was the opening act of Calvin's show when the bandits hurled spinning knives at Jewels bound frame, the crowd shrieking and cheering as each blade thundered into the timber prop tree that Jewel would lean against. Jewel tilted her head, the artist had taken creative license emphasizing her chest, and her flowing curly locks, yet he'd been honest at least in capturing Jewel's expression of terror. Jewel still remembered that first opening night, eyes wide, figure trembling as she watched the spinning silver daggers hurtle towards her. It had been terrible and exhilarating at the same time and that feeling had kept her going for the last two years. Almost.

Jewel ran her eyes down to the casting comments, Bryce's name was at the top and then followed by each bandit, Hugo, Barty and Will, even the horses got a mention and then if Jewel squinted, she could just make out the last line, *featuring Jewel Daniels as Ruby Drawers*. Featuring! Jewel felt the heat rush through her limbs this time with poison. If Bryce could quit whiskey, cards or womanizing, then maybe, just maybe he could shoot half as straight as Jewel. His mouth ran faster than he could and he sure was handsome, so naturally everyone bought into the fraud, Bryce Tanner the best gunslinger Hadley's carnival had to offer.

Jewel snorted. Featuring Jewel Daniels! She had four stage lines to breathlessly gasp then escape Bryce's clutches before he smacked a kiss on her, only to duck into the curtained wings and pull out her own Colts. She hit every one of Bryce's shots, her dead accurate firing in total synchronization to Bryce's on stage antics.

She still remembered Bryce's expression when she punched him square in the guts after she hadn't been quick enough and his kiss landed. She laughed at the memory of him doubled-over gasping like a fish out of water, apologizing profusely that he'd leave *Ruby Drawers* well alone. Didn't stop him from trying off stage, despite the fact she married his boss, Calvin Hadley.

Calvin was a man that needed the stage to feel at home; that and a string of chorus girls warming his bed. Jewels anger simmered. She wasn't mad at Calvin as much as she was mad at her herself. Jewel pushed away her dismal thoughts. Today was the day she changed her fate and men like Bryce and Calvin wouldn't stand in her way.

Jewel took a quick glance at her reflection, tucked her ginger curls behind her ears and scooped up her overloaded saddle bags. She slung them over one shoulder and marched out of her room at Martha's Inn. She flipped a coin at the front desk to no-one and entered Maple Street.

Harpsichords and brass bands were drowned out by cat-calls to dancing girls and the flamboyant yet sporadic firing of vaqueros as they unwound after their latest cattle drive. She pulled her wide brim low over her eyes to shade the late morning sun, and headed to the stables.

Jewel inhaled shallowly, the scent of dogwood trees in full bloom clogged her nostrils. Spring was at a close and summer had just begun. A fresh start. A new beginning. But first a little hiccup named Calvin Hadley needed to be dealt with. She secured her saddle bags over the slate rump of her gelding *Rocio* and strode between the alleys to Polecat Ale House. The organ music reverberated through her veins as she swung through the doors. The odors of bruised perfume and soft powders competed with cigar smoke and sweat. Calvin would be upstairs, no doubt both hands filled.

"Now, where ya going in such a rush, Ruby?"

Jewel didn't turn to acknowledge Bryce Tanner where she knew he gambled in the far corner; always the same round table with his back to the wall. His gaze would flick between the doors, the stairs and the bar, his seat only three feet from the back entrance.

"Come ta warm my lap Ruby?"

"Kiss my go-to-hell, Tanner."

"Only if you say please."

Jewel's boot paused on the bottom stair, she met the steel gaze of Calvin's main draw card. His blonde strands tumbled across his upturned nose, a red bandana around his throat, a girl on either side of his chair. Lots of girls were more than happy the infamous Tanner warmed their beds, but his cheek bones sat a little too high, his grin too boyish, same as his sense of humor and his temper. Besides it would take a week to wash out the reek of whiskey he'd leave behind.

"You can't win for losing Bryce, you play those cards and leave the shooting to me," Jewel said.

The bar erupted with laughter.

"I'll win my girls back ya hear!"

"Sure Tanner," Jewel said as she winked to Bryce.

The bar erupted in laughter again only to be cut short.

"We playin' cards or yappin'?"

Bryce's poker competition had a voice like a tumbling scree. Lucky Chuck's humor was as short as Bryce's temper. His thick fingers stroked his grey dusted beard, two fingers, two knuckles short on his right hand. Charles Rogers Senior wasn't lucky, he was tough as a stewed skunk and lucky was what he called anyone who crossed him who lived to tell the tale.

"Hold ya pickles, I'm playing," Bryce said and tossed a hand full of coins into the middle.

Dancing girls dashed out her way as Jewel stormed up the staircase.

"Don't be rash, my darlin' Ruby!" Bryce called.

"I ain't your darling, Tanner!" Jewel snapped. Damn Calvin!

When Jewel finally left Delano behind, she'd bury her stage name too. Ruby would be dead and gone the minute Jewel rode across the Arkansas River. She hated the stage name the minute Calvin had given it her, but her skill had soon quietened the laughter.

"Not for lack of tryin'!" Tanner called.

The patrons sniggered, some chinked glasses only to be hushed when Lucky Chuck's chair scraped along the floor. Jewel set her sights on the last door on the right.

Jewel ignored the splintering timbers, the shouts and hollers as ale mugs went flying and Doves screamed. She ignored the cock of a pistol. Bryce and Lucky Chuck had history and even without his 'girls' Bryce was faster than double struck lightening. Jewel on the other hand, had been quicker. Well Ruby had been, not that any of Calvin's posters proclaimed it. Her name was there, on the lower left corner, partially obscured by a likeness of Tanner and a list of his exploits.

She squared her shoulders and cracked her knuckles. Although she came up to most men's chins it was the perfect height for getting right between their ribs and she wasn't above kicking them in the shins either. As she stood before the final door, she didn't even knock. The door flew backwards and Jewel stormed past the surprised half naked girl as Calvin scrambled to his feet.

"Ruby! What the devil are you doing?!" Calvin rushed to re-clothe himself as the blonde working girl scrambled to the doorway.

"You didn't tell me it was Ruby Drawers!" The girl called, her eyes flying to Jewels holsters on either side of her narrow hips, "Sorry miss," she stumbled into the hallway, her painted lips as crooked as her skirts.

Jewel shrugged her shoulders, "Where is it Calvin?"

"Why do you want it?"

"Cause I'm leaving."

"My love."

"Save it Calvin if it wasn't for whats-her-face out there, I had already heard Simone chatting all about you last week, and Collette the week before."

Calvin started to stammer.

Jewel cut him off, "I want what's owed to me and those guns will fix me a nice price." She tore into the second room to the left, opening Calvin's wardrobe and spilling the contents.

"Ruby is a part of Hadley's Sharp Shooting Spectacular, you'd be sorry to walk away on all of this! Where you gonna go anyway?"

"You should be down stairs, betting with Bryce. I'm off to try my luck in Kansas City I hear Buffalo Bills show is touring. You'll be seeing my face on one of them posters real soon."

Calvin laughed, "You'll have no luck there."

He buckled up his tailored pants and threw on a silk shirt. He had muscular shoulders, tanned, but the rest of him had gone to seed, thinning salt and pepper hair, a tiny pot belly. Jewel sighed, he was still a charmer with a sparkle in his blue eyes, the same sparkle that got Jewel into trouble.

"You can't leave, I forbid it, you're my wife -"

"Calvin, we ain't been husband and wife in more than name since the day after the wedding, now either you give me what's mine and I'll be on my way or I'll tether you to the back of *Rocio* and drag you down Main Street, to hell with the Marshalls!" Jewel rested her hands on her waist and tapped her toes.

Calvin must have realized the seriousness of her threat, "Are you asking for your wages, for the last two years, I've been a bit tight lately with the crowds...."

Jewel ground her teeth. How much had Calvin spent of her earnings on liquor and other women? "Just give me my winnings."

"I was keeping them as my insurance policy if Bryce Tanner decides to leave."

"I won them fair and square. Whatever deal you got with Tanner is none of my business. Besides Bryce ain't going nowhere." She wagged a finger at Calvin's wide nose, "When I'm gone you'll have to find someone else to take his shots for him. Someone who's happy behind the curtain, while the Drunkard fires blanks, now hand them over."

Calvin tucked his shirt tail into his belt, "You really are going?"

Jewel nodded.

"Always did think Delano was too small for you Ruby."

"Calvin."

"I mean Jewel," he sauntered closer to her, "You were always my favorite, my love," His palm reached for her cheek and she battered it away.

"Don't let me delay you any longer Calvin," Jewel rolled her eyes, "You're sheets are getting cold."

Calvin let out a chuckle as he strolled to his wardrobe and pealed up two slats. From underneath which he dragged out a small bundle of cash with two pistols, their barrels sparkled silver in the light that trickled through Calvin's heavy curtains, their ornate pearl handles glistened.

"You think you can get them past Bryce?"

Jewel let out a laugh. She couldn't wait to put as many miles between her and Calvin, Ruby and Delano. Two years ago, she'd chased adventure up the Chisholm Trail but she should never have left Dew Springs. Or at least not trusted the first man to whisper sweet nothings into her ear and slither in her heart amongst other things. Cattle were much easier than men.

"Watch me," she said.

Calvin handed over the two dueling pistols, "Good luck Jewel, I hope wherever you're running to, he finds you there."

Jewel winced. Like one of her bullets on show night, Calvin has struck her dead center. After a bottle of tequila she'd confided in Calvin about Dew Spring and what she'd left behind. Hoping the man with a jaw the size of Texas would follow her to Kansas. How wrong could she have been?

"He didn't then, he ain't gonna now."

"I think he's looking, but in all the wrong places."

Jewel nodded. Marcus Kearby followed his heart, right into the Texas Rangers.

Calvin dropped a kiss onto her forehead, "Take it easy and stay safe, darling. Happiness is more than you deserve. For everything, I'm sorry."

"Don't be sorry Calvin, it was short and fast, but an adventure all the same. Now stay out of trouble."

"Never!" Calvin winked and stepped back.

Jewel was tempted to put both guns in her holsters now, but walking around with all that sparkling in the Delano midday sun was not a clever move. The weight was both elegant and deadly. She didn't want to sell them, yet both weapons would feed her and cloth her enough to find her feet in Kansas City. She wrapped the bundle under her arm and strode down the stairs. She reached halfway across the saloon floor before Bryce called out.

"You taking my two loves?"

Bryce stopped trying to settle the upturned poker table, the cards spread across the floor, dancing girls bobbed and dipped to pick up the lost coins. Bryce Tanner was a sore loser, the minute the cards turned against him, he picked a fight.

Lucky Chuck was nowhere to be seen.

"You've got plenty of girls Tanner," Jewel pointed to his hip, where a Colt Dragoon hung low on his belt.

"Ah it's got no grace," Bryce caught Jewel by the arm.

"You ain't never treat them right, anyway Bryce." Jewel said.

"I could have treated you right Ruby." He's lips reached for hers.

But Jewel was quicker. She balled a fist and drove it under his ribs, he hunched over.

"And my name ain't Ruby!"

She stepped into the street to the cheers of the barman and what was left of the disgruntled crowd. She reset her hat just as Bryce caught up with her.

"Ruby wait," Bryce coughed as his hand rubbed his belly, "My brother is coming to town, stick around, you me and him, we can leave Calvin and his clowns behind, skills like ours shouldn't be wasted on Cowtown crowds, you'll see."

"Bryce, your brother's been coming to town since last year, I ain't waiting on you or your brother to make my fate."

Bryce put his hand on her shoulder, "You really are one of kind, Jewel." This time he leaned down and kissed her cheek. The whiskey tickled her nose, his three day old whiskers tickled her cheek, "Someday that man of yours is gonna realize it."

Jewel's breath caught in her throat, what had Calvin told him?

"Calvin will be sorry he let you go."

Jewel exhaled. Calvin? "Oh yeah, him." In her mind, she's seen a stocky dark haired figure and it sure as hell wasn't Calvin. Or Bryce for that matter. "He'll land on his feet. That man always does."

Jewel clambered onto *Rocio*.

"You take good care of Selina and Josephine!"

Jewel flicked the reins, letting the crowd swallow her. The midday sun was still climbing to its zenith, stirring up the scents of manure and sweat. She would cross the bridge into Wichita proper and find a reputable place to stay on the edge of the city limits. She may be the fastest gunslinger this side of the Arkansas, but she wasn't stupid. She would spend as many days as needed at the edge of Wichita, keeping her eyes and ears peeled for just the right kind of travelers to follow, maybe some Exodusters making their way north, or a caravan trader, a family hunting new lands. She would join them or trail them just out of sight to wherever north they were headed. She should never have left Dew Springs, but she'd be damned if she'd go back. Not unless Marcus Kearby dragged her back there himself.

Bryce Tanner stood on the porch of the Polecat Ale House watching the slinky hips of his friend saunter out of sight. Ah if only he had the patience, he could have wooed her a little bit longer. She was full of fire, she'd hiss and spit but he figured, the right man would get her to purr. Pity it wouldn't be him. Pity she wouldn't be here when Gabriel arrived. His older brother had sent a telegram; he reckoned he'd reach Delano in days. Surely this time Gabriel wouldn't be delayed again. He had an itch between his shoulders, and only the smell of gunpowder and blood would make it go away.

He had laid low in Calvin's circus of oddities, biding his time, waiting for Gabriel to take care of his business woes. Gabriel would be pissed when he found out he'd lost the girls to Ruby, but his brother had told him to do what he needed to stay alive, and gambling was what he needed to feel alive. Besides, the ginger haired dynamite, had won them fair and square, shot every target dead to the eyes.

He waited until her blue roan was completely gone before he stepped back into the shade. He was glad the girls had a worthy home, she'd shot all his targets for the last two years, making him the hero, the headliner, the Doves flocking to his side. Ah pity she'd miss out on Gabriel's next business venture. It'd be a gold mine for sure. Bryce ran his fingers through his hair and wandered down the side of the Inn, a barrel of water stood full to the brim, and the stuffy Ale House air and whiskey dimmed his wits. He dunked his head in the barrel, the water sending a rush down his spine and refreshing his nerves. Ruby had inspired him. If Gabriel didn't show this time, he'd ride out and find him. Bryce flicked his head back, his long blond strands, slicking against his neck, the water cooling between his shoulder blades.

"Hey Tanner."

Bryce wiped the water out of his eyes, taking a moment to remember that here in Delano he was supposed to be Bryce Tanner, not Francis Turner. It took him another moment to focus from the brightly lit street to the shadowy alley, but he recognized that voice.

"Howdy Chuck."

A spark ignited from the pistols muzzle, the ball striking his chest. He heard something crack, as blood pumped into his ear drums. Both hands went to his belt, coming up empty. Another weight slammed into his chest. He tasted metal between his teeth.

Gabriel would be pissed, he thought, just as another projectile slammed into his body, this time in his gut. He looked down at his hands that clutched his flesh. As if a wine bottle had smashed, dark droplets of claret splashed onto the dirt. The sun retreated, his shoulders shivered with the twilight chill that enveloped him. He sunk onto one knee, his other hand caught his fall. Pools of hot liquid welled behind his teeth and he spat. The parched ground absorbed the crimson spittle. Gabriel is going to be livid! Francis thought as the darkness took him whole.

Calvin Hadley stormed into his office, his teeth ground down on his jaw. Ruby gone, Tanner dead and *Hadley's Sharp Shooter Spectacular* was finished! And all in one day! Well he was nothing if not resourceful.

Two days had passed since they had found Bryce dead in

the street, and only yesterday when he worked out Lucky Chuck Rogers had skipped town. Witnesses had found him raiding Bryce's pockets before he legged it out of town. Well Calvin Hadley would pack his things, find a way to the Mississippi and try his luck on the steam boats. He wasn't a bad card dealer, and he had worked as a magician before Delano had ensnared his soul.

"Calvin, there's a Garrett Tanner to see you." Collette chirped as she opened the door to his office.

Calvin scanned his scant office space as he rushed to the double hung windows, tugging the bottom pane upwards to regard the busy street below. Could he jump and not break a leg? Calvin shook his head, maybe he just wanted to talk. Lucky Chuck would be caught and hopefully hung, if the rope didn't break and the bastard got away.

"Send him in," Calvin said as he buttoned up his silver waistcoat.

Calvin took a seat behind his unsealed timber desk, palms down to settle the wonky legs. He took a deep breath and tried to remain calm as Garrett Tanner and his cronies filled his office.

Garrett Tanner, stood 5 foot 11 inches, narrow shoulders, wide hands, and a hair lip. The man wore a pale cream shirt, with a doeskin cutaway coat and matching three button vest, his denims even looked starched. He pulled off his cream Stetson and took a seat in front of Calvin, resting his impeccable hat in his lap. He briefly ran a hand through his brown hair, wisps of grey to be seen around his temples. His eyes, the color of steel, same as his brother's, bored a hole through Calvin on the other side.

Calvin tried to sit still, the urge to shift, to cower, to turn away from that piercing gaze slithered into his veins and wouldn't dissolve. Calvin's vest buttons threatened to pop, his silk shirt two days old and damp under the armpits.

"Garrett, a pleasure to see you, although not in these tragic times, I am deeply –"

Garrett raised a single palm. He pointed over his left shoulder, to the brawny thug that rested there, three day old growth, chewing a cigar, dual pistols on each hip.

"Sampson, tells me that Charles Rogers Senior escaped Delano."

"He did, the Sheriff has assured me they are forming a posse–"

"And what of the girl?"

"Huh?" Calvin coughed.

Garrett pointed over his right shoulder, to the second goon. Dark hair plastered against his sweaty forehead, meaty jaw, broken nose. Both stood taller than 6 foot.

"Donnie tells me a girl, your girl, Ruby Drawers slugged my kid brother in the abdomen and stole his pistols."

"She –" Calvin started.

Garrett put his palm up again. The business man's nose was hooked, resting over his hair lip, with those grey eyes unblinking, Garrett Tanner reminded Calvin of an eagle. Calvin had to rely on all his experience in stage performance to make sure he didn't become the field mouse.

"If he had his pistols, he would have drawn and won."

Garrett Tanner didn't seem like he would take the news well that since they parted company, that Bryce had developed quite a drinking habit and quite a gambling habit, his aim had more than suffered as a result. Calvin didn't think Bryce would have won, but perhaps he would have gotten a shot on before Chuck finished him off. Maybe if he had his girls Chuck wouldn't have tried.

"She won them from him, in a shoot-out. I had no control –"

"Obviously. When I told you to guard Bryce as if he was your own brother, you thought I misspoke. You acted as referee for this shoot out, you let the girl win, your wife in fact, and you confiscated his only means of self-defense. It is almost as if you pulled the trigger yourself."

"Now," Calvin's neck heated, he raised his fist to point

and instead pushed his hair back from his sweaty forehead, "I didn't do no such thing. Your brother took that bet. He took far too many bets. Ruby won those guns, but she didn't pick the fight between Chuck and Bryce. Bryce did that all on his own."

"Are you talking ill of my recently departed, most beloved brother, Calvin Hadley?" Garrett Tanner leaned forward, his jacket opened to reveal matching gold and pearl inlaid pistols that rested either side of his rib cage.

Calvin cleared his throat, "I wasn't saying that, I was –"

"Defending your wife? It's only wild speculation at this point, that she and Charles might have set Bryce up, the Dragoon he had on his hip hadn't been drawn. That would also implicate you had a part in this. My brother wouldn't let his pistols out of his sight, in fact, the only way this Ruby Drawers would be able to keep them and her skin, would be if Bryce was dead."

"Now that's - Ruby's not like that - she –"

"From what I hear, she was jealous of his fame and scorned from his rejection. Where did she go Calvin?"

"Listen Garrett - "

Garrett held his palm up again and Calvin fell silent, "Before you answer me, I want you to think very careful about where you see yourself in the next fifteen minutes. Either in the post office filling out a telegram or filling out a pine box in Boot Hill. I am offering a bounty for the capture of the thief Ruby Drawers. If she won those pistols fair and square she can prove it." Garrett ran his fingers around the brim of his hat and put it back on his head, "If not she can answer to conspiracy to murder. If you do not assist me in this request," Garrett's deformed top lip pealed back at his words, "I will assume your complicity in Bryce's death." Garrett stood from his chair and replaced his hat neatly on his head, "Now where to Calvin?"

Calvin Hadley sat down in the Wichita Post Office, glad he thought to bring Tanner and his goons into Wichita proper where they had to hand over their guns at the bridge. It didn't seem to dim Garrett Tanner's malevolence. Probably Sampson and Donnie would just snap his neck.

"Description of Ruby Drawers," The Post Master asked.

"Ah 5 foot, 4, no 5 foot 6," Calvin said. He raised his hand up around his cheekbone height. Hopefully Jewel was already well on her way to Kansas City, but he'd do his best to make Tanner's job a bit more difficult.

"Hair?"

"Ah reddish but a bit light, I'd say um yeah, strawberry blonde."

He didn't dare risk a look at Garrett, would he believe a girl named Ruby had blonde hair? The entrepreneur didn't make a move.

"Build?"

"Ah voluptuous, curvaceous, ah if you know what I mean," Calvin winked and offered a laugh.

Jewel was as strong as a whip, but built like a greenhorn, she had slender hips, and an even slender waist. He had spent one night in her arms, surprised at how she hid her femininity, her perky yet ample breasts concealed in heavy gingham. When she wore a dress, she turned even Preachers heads.

"Outstanding features?"

Garrett leaned forward, "She'll be carrying or trying to sell matching .38 Colt Navy Revolvers, 2 ½ inch barrels, Nickel plated, with mother of pearl grips inlaid with silver. One engraved with Josephine, the other engraved with Selina."

The officer spent a moment jotting the information down and repeated it so it was correct, "Reward?"

"One thousand dollars."

"One thousand –" Calvin coughed into his fist. Garrett would have every man and his coon dog out tracking her.

"Direction of travel?"

"Ah Dodge City, she was off to Dodge." Calvin rushed.

One thousand dollars! It would take him a year or more to earn that on the River boats. Maybe he could shake Garrett and his goon's loose and head out after her, catch her on the trail and warn her? Tell her that he'd given her up? It was Jewel who left him!

Actually, now Calvin thought about it, he was the only one who knew Jewel was headed to Kansas City. If he caught up to her, he might earn himself a nifty reward. Garrett seemed mighty interested in Josephine and Selina. If Jewel could prove her skills, Garrett might be satisfied. Watching the older man's unblinking stare sent a shiver down Calvin's spine. Garrett had his own reputation, any debts owed, usually had to be paid in blood. But Jewel was a woman after all. Surely they'd catch Lucky Chuck by then.

Chapter 2

Jewel stood in the shade of the mercantile; her Stetson rested low over her eyes and watched the two men for over an hour as they crisscrossed Main collecting their supplies. She had no doubt what type of men they were and they suited her purpose greatly. With all the summer heat, not a lot of travelers had been heading North over the past two days. A family of Exodusters had kept to themselves and pushed off early yesterday but these two had instantly caught her eye. They walked with a certain kind of canter, a casual readiness that people would mistake for swagger. Their eyes constantly sized up those around, their denims were trail dirty, but their hands, callous free. Their hips swayed with the unusual absence that the regular weight of firearms brought.

Once, when a bar fight broke out, the taller of the two, named Abe had reacted a little too quickly. His right hand grazed his bare hip, fingers searching for the weapon that regularly kept him company. They wore no badge, but Jewel didn't need a second glance to know they were from Texas. Their slow drawl music to her ears. They had chatted quietly to themselves over the past few hours, Junction City their next post. Rangers! Jewel wouldn't have done any better if she waited all year. She would trail them to Junction City and find less conspicuous company to follow to Kansas City.

Jewel retrieved her pistols from the Marshalls office just before noon and headed out, she took a quick divert from the trail and waited in the underbrush.

It was well past noon by the time the Rangers moved out; their horses restless and eager to be away just like their riders. The dust kicked up from their hooves as they reached the open road, the wagon and cattle ruts had widened the Chisholm Trail so it was difficult for Jewel to keep up and stay out of sight. She had no doubt they would camp for supper and ride out at dawn to reach Newton. With that in mind she let the Rangers increase the distance, she would catch up.

As the sun set, Jewel climbed down from *Rocio* and walked on. He had been broken and trained by Cade Hamerton, so the horse instinctively followed steadily behind without direction. She stopped when she smelt their fire and *Rocio*'s muzzle nudged her shoulder. She ran her hand slowly down his nose as the horse snuffled in satisfaction.

The shorter man, Theo laughed and caught Jewel by surprise at her proximity. She retreated to a divot in the ground using the tall prairie grasses to conceal her location. Jewel spent that first night, tucked in her saddle bags, while *Rocio* slowly grazed under the Kansas stars.

This was the adventure she was supposed to be having. Her lungs filled with the air of the Plains, her belly half filled with jerky and beans, tomorrow's breakfast would be biscuit and more beans. Not like the last two years, sweltering in every town's sin, Delano's just the last, between alleys of boarding houses and saloons, the scent of whiskey and cigar clogging the air. She hadn't the heart to sell Josephine or Selina that first day, thought it pretty wise to hold onto them until at least Kansas City. She had a couple of dollars from Calvin and a jar of dried peaches and a fair amount of jerky. She would manage, besides it was a new beginning, Jewel promised herself no looking back.

Jewel rolled onto her back and regarded the constellations. She chided herself, but trailing two Rangers, had gotten her thinking. Would Marcus be looking up at these same stars somewhere, or perhaps he would be holed up in some Ale House with a few dancing girls of his own. Jewel snorted. Marcus was too damn honorable to have too much fun. *Rocio* snorted as well as if in agreeance. Jewel rolled onto her side and waited for the dawn.

The two Rangers, Abe and Theo arrived in Newton and passed straight through. It took Jewel a quarter of an hour to work out they had already left. Then again Texas Rangers would want to keep to themselves. They continued passing through each town and trading post, stopping just outside to rest up. The trail filtered through Jewel's soul, awakening muscles and joints she had forgotten about. The wide open Plains suited Jewel just fine.

The Rangers pace continued until they reached Abilene. After the cattle yards shifted further south and Wild Bill left some four years ago in '71, the town had matured. A regular peace had settled over the citizens.

This time as the sun set, the Rangers sauntered down Texas Avenue checking the post office first before taking rooms at the Merchants Hotel. Jewel kept her distance but took a room at the same two story timber Hotel. The outside was painted white with a raised porch and a single bay window facing the street.

She took receipt of her key and listened as the Rangers climbed the undressed timber stairs.

"I reckon he'll be sorry for leaving, what do you think, Theo?"

"He needed to slow down, but he'll have more than his hands full when he returns," Abe sniggered.

"When's his train due?"

The hotelier interrupted Jewel's eavesdropping, "Top of the stairs, second on the right, the dining room is still serving beef and beans and a peach cobbler if you're keen."

Jewel nodded, "Bath?"

"End of the hall, I'll send Jessie up," She held out her hand and Jewel handed over her quarter.

First she bathed before descending to the narrow restaurant, white clothed tables lined the walls with mismatched chairs, a few long benches near the front and sparse high backed chairs cradled an empty fireplace. Jewel took a seat in one of the high backed chairs, concealing her from the Rangers and ordered her first decent meal in three days. The Rangers sat to the left side, back to the wall, eyes on the doors. Jewel savored her beef and a jug of beer, while she listened.

"I reckon if there's no news, we'll head on to Kansas City, see if we can pick up the trail again."

"Ah pfft," the other one said, "The trail of that phony is well and truly cold since he left Chicago. We ain't heard any more of those forgeries getting around. I reckon Callaghan is sending us up there to tie up loose ends. Make us look like we've got something when we'll be twiddling our thumbs."

Jewel couldn't believe her luck. She chewed slowly, making plans for when she made the bustling city. Bryce's guns would have to go if she was to make a real run at it. Perhaps just one and she could keep the other to impress Buffalo Bill. Jewel's thoughts raced away from her, so much so that she missed the newcomer. He sat with his back to her position, his broad shoulders just in her peripherals. His dark brown hair stretched to his red checked collar, his denims clean, his boots chestnut. Jewel took another sip of her beer, the liquid almost spilled from her lips, when she heard the man talk.

"I heard word that the Turner Gang had turned south. Figured I might chase them down since I'm headed that way."

She rushed a hand to her mouth and swallowed, wiping her chin as she recovered. She turned her head slightly, using the figure of the waitress who took their order to break up her line of sight. He had at least three days growth across his cheeks, but Marcus Kearby looked like he had finally grown into his magnificent jawline. The man sat no less than ten feet away from her. His hazel eyes briefly scanned the room. She put her head down and listened.

"I'll send word when I reach Dallas if I get wind of them."

Abe whistled between his lips and dropped his voice so Jewel had to strain her ears to catch it, "That's all the Turner Gang are, wind on the leaves. They're probably all dead by now, no-ones heard of them since '73."

"They rob three stages and a gold train and don't spend a single drop? They're phantoms forget 'em." Theo said.

"What's the news from Wichita?"

Theo put down his mug and handed Kearby a wanted bill, "Some whore shot her lover, $1000 reward."

Marcus snorted and pushed the paper into his pocket, "I'll keep my eyes peeled. I'll push off in the morning at first light."

"I can't imagine Dew Springs has much to compete with this, but I wish you well." Theo raised his mug as did Abe.

"Same. Happy hunting in Kansas City."

"Ah it's a waste of our time." Abe scoffed, "Now if the rumors of the Turner Gang were true…" Abe whistled through his teeth, "Safe travels, Ranger."

Jewel heard the mugs clink and took her leave. She closed the door to her room just as the tears tumbled to her cheeks. The mattress caught her frame as she landed face down on the lumpy cot. Why now? Why here? She rolled over and kicked off her boots. He hadn't come for her, in fact he was returning to Dew Springs without her. The man who was supposed to be her first and last love, was down stairs, but could she face his rejection face to face.

The humiliation she thought long buried now doused her in ice cold shivers, her stomach clenched as she squeezed her eyes shut. Red-faced and broken hearted she left Marcus Kearby in her dust as she rode out of Dew Springs. It had been over two years, maybe she could march downstairs and ask him why he never came for her? She rolled over and stared up at the dark ceiling. It was pointless, she wouldn't humiliate herself again for that man. She had her own adventure waiting and she would be damned if she shed any more tears for that man.

The sun had well and truly risen by the time Jewel dressed and packed. Kansas City. A new future beckoned; one with her name on posters and loot in her pockets. She paid for breakfast and flipped the stable hand a dime as she made her way deep into the stalls. She saw Abe's tall bay and the Theo's pie bold was gone. *Rocio* had two new stall mates, a tall buckskin gelding whose neck swiveled to take in the new addition and a shy dun. Jewel nodded, her resolved strengthened that at least

Kearby would be safe. His ranch, the Crooked K would be well in hand. His Mama and Pa happy he was back. Well his Mama anyway.

Jewel froze as she saw a single hand on *Rocio*'s rump, the fingers tracing the Hammer and Lock of Cade and Evie's brand.

"Who do you think you are?"

A dark brown Stetson, the color of coffee rose from the other side, Marcus Kearby's toothy grin lit up the darkened stable interior. Her heart leapt into her throat as his hazel gaze slammed into hers. She snapped her lips shut, her limbs frozen unable to move.

"Miss Jewel Daniels, well what a pleasure!"

"Marcus, I thought -" Jewel caught her words.

"Where have you been hiding?" Marcus swallowed hard.

He tried to loosen the tightness of his throat and the jitters in his chest. The sound of her bossy tone had driven a spike into his spine and the sight of her petite freckled face had stirred long gone memories of dusted sunlit afternoons, covered in hay in a barn not unlike this one. He resisted the urge to pull back his hat and straighten his hair. God she looked good. Sun-kissed cheeks and those ginger curls that had driven him to distraction, blue eyes that alluded to a spirit that had burned too bright for him. As if a shadow pulled across his mind, he straightened his shoulders. They had been young, he had been foolish and Jewel had been too innocent and too encouraging.

"I've been around." She answered. Her pout tight as she twitched like a squirrel without a nut.

"Have you?" He tried to not sound accusatory, he had spent the last two years checking every sharp shooter festival and carnival his travels allowed, "Well I recognized the brand and I hoped it might be someone from Dew Springs, are you heading back too?"

Jewel pulled on *Rocio*'s saddle blanket, "Ah nope,"

"Oh," Marcus scooped up her saddle.

"So you're a proper Ranger these days, chasing stagecoach robbers and train gangs?"

Marcus draped the leather and tack over the blue roan. He shouldn't let her abrasiveness ruffle him. Dew Springs wasn't interesting enough to hold the likes of Miss Daniels. He had hoped to do her spirit justice, chasing down his own adventures, hoping he would achieve something of note so she would stop twisting her petite nose every time he followed the rules. After all she had left after a curt word to Cade that Marcus knew where to find her and that was it. Marcus Kearby was too square, too boring and too damn honorable for Miss Jewel Daniels.

"Something like that, where you headed now?"

He watched her eyes dim for a moment, unfocused until she stammered, one word, "Dodge."

"Dodge City? Who you riding with?"

Jewel snorted and dipped down to tie the belly straps, their hands met at the buckle.

"I don't need a riding party Kearby."

"Nonsense, your Pa would have a fit if he found out I let you ride on your own. Dodge you say, I can take you."

Jewel's head popped up, her cheeks suddenly reddened, "No thanks, I don't wanna delay you."

Marcus rubbed his nose and nodded, "You won't."

Jewel laughed, "You ain't got any better at lying Marcus Kearby."

"And you ain't gotten any better at recognizing a gentleman's offer when given," he said before he heard his own words.

Jewels cheeks darkened in color.

Marcus felt his cheeks match, "What kind of a man would I be if I let you ride on outta here on your own?"

"I like doing things on my own lately Marcus."

He sucked in air between his teeth, "That's all well and good around Dew Springs, but not around here, Jewel, it'll take us good on five maybe six days, how are your supplies?"

Marcus should heed his own warnings. He would be delaying his return to Dew Springs by taking this detour. He knew once he arrived home, his future would be out of his hands.

These last couple of years had been worthy of a dime novel, eating lean and living hard. The naïve Marcus Kearby that Jewel had left behind was now gone. He was owed one last adventure before he was forced to marry. He would savor these next five days like they were his last. So long as Jewel kept bristling like an alley cat he could keep his wits about him and his hands to himself.

"Marcus, I don't wanna trap you into some honorable gesture, I'll be quite fine on my own."

"You might be, but I'd rather be sure, than sorry." He left *Rocio*'s stall and saddled his own horse.

"What happened to *Cutter*?"

Marcus paused running his hand down the flank of his buckskin gelding, "Skirmishes with the Kiowa in Lost Valley." The wailing sounds of his gelding seared through his ears. The clang of the stall doors echoed his gunshot.

Jewels voice softened, "Oh that isn't fair Marcus, I'm sorry."

He stiffened his shoulders, "None of it is fair Jewel," He shook his head, hoping the scent of burning buffalo skin and human flesh would clear from his nostrils, "None of it. But this is *Scout* and he's another one of Hamerton's and just as keen." Marcus pulled his tack over his latest mount enjoying the deer hide coloring that quivered under his ministrations, "So what's taking you to Dodge City?"

He could hear her shuffling around in the hay, her rose embroidered boots itching to be away from him again; the simple cowpoke, the spare Ranchers son.

"Just business."

"Well that doesn't sound the least bit worthy of adventure. I'd have thought you'd be heading east to the big cities or even west to the gold. What business you got in Dodge?" He should mind his own words.

"What business you got with Dew Springs, Marcus Kearby?"

He swallowed hard, he knew it. Jewel had a way of turning things on their heads, his head to be precise, "Duty."

"Ranger duty?"

He heard the stall hinges creak; he'd have to be quicker next time, "Family duty."

"No doubt something honorable, Marcus."

He just nodded and moved onto his pack horse, by the time he rode *Scout* out to the sunlight, Jewel was saddled.

"I came by Rail, so I'll pick up a some supplies on our way out."

Jewel nodded as she let *Rocio* fall into step beside Kearby's taller gelding. The sun warmed her cheeks, and the sight of Marcus in his denims tickled her chest. His shirt sleeves had been rolled up exposing his roped forearms, his fingers curled around the reins. The rays danced off his dark strands, hinting at tones of copper and gold amongst the mahogany. He was as tall as most men as average height goes, yet his broad shoulders and thick thighs rounded him into a muscular morsel. Jewel never wanted to climb tall trees anyway. She tossed the thought aside. She should have protested more, refused his assistance to get her to Dodge. She thought he would balk at the distance and she could ditch him for Kansas City.

The embarrassment that colored her cheeks dissolved into an ache that burned under her ribs. Marcus Kearby should have followed her in the beginning so now he could follow her to Dodge. Heat rushed through her limbs and balled into her gut so fast Jewel had to inhale sharply to cool it. He owed her this time and if nothing else it would be an adventure. She would eventually find her way back to Kansas City. Marcus readjusted his dark Stetson, and smiled, his cheeks denting, the three day growth swirled delicately in the dimple in his chin. What was the harm in spending five or six days in this man's company?

A memory of a barn, sinking into the late afternoon shadows, slipped into her mind. Where her chest ached before it now stung. Jewel readjusted the reins, the leather warm and sturdy. She could depend on herself. Herself and her horse. Everything else was a daydream.

Chapter 3

Calvin ran his hand down the flank of his mount, the dun's withers shivered under his touch, the sweat flaking off to drift on the afternoon breeze. He needed to rest, his horse needed to rest. He had spent the last few days shaking off Donnie's tail. Garrett's goons had been as dogged as he thought but Calvin knew when to cut and run.

He had planned to track Jewel on the road to Kansas City, only leaving Wichita without Donnie or Sampson proved to be impossible. He had been forced to head towards Dodge only to leave the trail and head north as soon as he could. He had spent the next few days sleeping in the saddle, pissing on the run, and eating very little. His belly fat had trimmed but his shirt scratched against his flesh, his buttocks ached beyond reproach and the Great Plains had beaten him down these last few miles. He had to reach Abilene by night fall, or he would be dead.

The sun had scorched his skin to a husk and his mind melted into his shoulders. He switched between dreaming about the fortunes to be made along the river boats and handing in Jewel for Garrett's $1000 reward. Jewel would clear her name in an instant, outshooting Bryce was no easy feat and Garrett was not known as a sharp-shooter. The way he saw it, showing Garrett Tanner her skills was the only way to clear Jewels name. Most likely Lucky Chuck would be caught soon enough as he wasn't known for his horsemanship. If Calvin got Jewel to Dodge, he could keep the reward and they could both keep their necks. He just had to find her first.

Calvin pulled out his canteen and gave it a shake, the hollow sound hardened his resolve and he shoved it back in his rucksack. Abilene, he had to make Abilene by night fall.

Calvin threw an arm up to shade his brow as he squinted.

Tufts of dust ghosted across the horizon. Riders! He regarded either side of the track, rolling plains of wheat and grass, but not a grove to be seen. He pulled his brim down over his eyes, and pulled his stained collar up to his ears, dipping his head and waiting for the inevitable. His elbow tapped his hip, a Colt on the right, a Derringer in his boot. Calvin let his mount walk steadily forward. If there were riders, Abilene can't be far. He counted to twenty before he looked up again. The riders had slowed, taking their time observing him from afar. He let his shoulders slump, his bulk already wobbled in the saddle. The moments dragged out until Calvin heard the horses approaching.

"Howdy," came the gravel toned greeting.

"Howdy yourself," Calvin answered, "How far to Abilene?"

"Half a day."

Calvin lifted the brim of his hat, and took in the stranger. He sat proud in the saddle, a cattleman, a lawman or a bandit he didn't know. His gaze told the story of a long ride, but his clothing was fresh.

"Calvin!" A female voice snapped.

His gaze shot up to the second rider, "Who -"

"It's me Jewel," She spat. The blue roan edge forward as Jewel's blue eyes raked over Calvin's dust and sweat coated clothes, her brows furrowed, her cheeks heating, "What in the Devil are you doin' out here!"

Calvin pushed his brim back further and regarded his bounty. Jewel sat high in the saddle, her navy checked shirt almost creaseless, her denims dirty only at the cuffs.

"I could ask the same thing."

"Do you know this man?" the stranger asked as he pushed his buckskin horse in the distance between the pair.

He was of a height similar to Calvin, but thicker in the shoulders, his forearms tensed across the reins, his elbow tentatively connected with his holster.

Calvin straightened his shoulders at the tone, "I should ask the same of you, riding with my wife."

"Wife?" The cattleman swiveled in his saddle, his hazel eyes ignited under his brim, only to be dimmed as Jewel hung her head.

"Calvin Hadley, this is Marcus Kearby."

Calvin's throat rasped. The Texas Ranger! A pitcher of worms emptied into Calvin's gut. Did the man who haunted Jewel's dreams know about the bounty? How could he, Calvin had purposely mislead Garrett Tanner. The description of Ruby Drawers didn't even closely resemble Jewel Daniels in the flesh.

The Ranger's mount shifted closer to Calvin's, his eyes raked over his showman boots, caked in trail dust, ornate decoration but worn at the heels, his dirty trousers, the cut tight against his hips. Even Calvin's black seamed grey shirt had been made for ceremonies not cow trails.

"Calvin Hadley."

His own name sounded like a threat from the tongue of the Ranger.

"That's right. Jewel is my lawful wife, bound to me under our Lord, January 1874."

"1874?" Marcus threw another dark look at Jewel, the creases around his eyes seemed to deepen, "And what are you doing out here?"

"I'm fetching her," Calvin said.

Marcus regarded Jewel again. Jewel's gaze shot between the Ranger and Calvin's boots. Jewel flickered her reins and moved forward. Marcus shook his head and pulled his horse back.

Jewel clutched at her reins. What the Hell did Calvin think he was doing!

"Have you got any water?" Calvin shook his canteen.

"Yeah," Jewel pulled her horse alongside Calvin's and dismounted.

Her one-time husband did the same. She could hear his knees creak, the dirt crusted from his clothing and he wobbled against his horse before he gained his balance. She cast a glance to Marcus who had taken *Scout* off to the side. He leaned across his pommel and watched from a distance.

Jewel lowered her voice, "I know you Calvin, you didn't come racing on out here for me, out with it now."

Jewel handed over her canteen and watched as Calvin sucked the liquid down. His horse looked blown and the man looked just as rough.

"You've been riding hard since you left Wichita."

"I have." Calvin took another chug, wiping his chin with the back of his hand. "Bryce is dead."

Jewel clasped her mouth, "Lucky Chuck?"

"Yep, dead on. Shot him in the alley, the day you left, two days before his brother turned up."

Jewel put her head against the flank of *Rocio*. Baby-faced Bryce, his blonde hair always a mess, his cheeky side grin gone. Delano claimed another soul within its sinful streets.

"They'd have hanged Chuck by now if he didn't take off. They reckon he's headed to Indian Territory. In the meantime, Garrett Tanner wants to talk to you."

Jewel's head shot up, her eyes unclouded, "Talk to me?"

"Yeah, he needs to see how you beat his baby brother."

Jewel put her hands on her hips, and cocked her head to one side. Calvin was up to something.

"Have you still got Josephine and Selina?"

"What's it to you?"

Calvin through his hands up in mock defeat, "I told him you won them fair and square, he wants to see the great Ruby Drawers in action."

Jewel lifted the brim of her hat slightly, the afternoon Kansas sun hammered onto her fair skin, "And then what?"

"Look he's a businessman, from Kansas City himself. He's got connections. I wouldn't be surprised if he could introduce you to the Bill himself, at worst, he'd probably buy those guns right back off you."

Jewel regarded Marcus over her shoulder. The man was honor bound to return to Dew Springs. He hadn't come looking for her. He no doubt wanted to see her safe to Dodge, out of guilt and nothing more. It had been chance that brought their paths to cross. Would every day make her chest hurt like this? Bryce had always promised his brother would turn up, promised their sharpshooter skills were set for bigger things. Perhaps Garrett Tanner would help Jewel headline a poster. If not she could buy a rail ticket to Kansas City.

"He'll be in Dodge any day now." Calvin's voice took a softer tone. "Look Jewel, my show is bust without you and Bryce. I was heading to the river boats to try my hand there when Garrett Tanner walked in. What's the harm in meeting the man, showing him your skills and seeing where it leads?"

Jewel turned away from Marcus. He would no doubt accompany them to Dodge, he said he would, so the man would stick to his word. Jewel pondered her predicament all the while her ribs ratcheted tighter and tighter. She had promised herself a new future, one with adventure that she owed herself after wasting time with Calvin. One with fame and fortune, that she promised herself when she left Marcus behind. Was Garrett Tanner the answer to both? If it went south, she could sell Garrett the guns and head for Kansas City. What to do about Marcus? A lump thickened in her throat and she swallowed. What to do about Calvin? A thought blossomed in her mind.

"Alright I'll meet this Tanner fellow, but on two conditions."

Calvin jutted out his bottom lip and nodded.

"One, not a single word of this Ruby Drawers business do you hear." Jewel jabbed a finger into Calvin's chest.

Calvin winked.

"And don't even think you can get away with any Husband-this or Wife-that nonsense either. When we get to Dodge, before I meet anyone, you and I are visiting the Court and getting this dissolved."

Calvin through his hands up again, "Understood." He eyed Marcus Kearby over the rump of his dun. "What about him?"

"Nothing about him Calvin." Jewel snapped.

Marcus's elbows were crossed across his pommel, his jaw cinched tight.

"He's going to be a right gentleman you can bet on it."

Jewel resisted the urge to pull up her denims as she marched towards Marcus.

The Texas Ranger dismounted and leaned back, "Which is it?"

"He's going to Dodge, I said since I'm heading that way anyways – "

"He run out on you, or you on him?"

Jewel shook her head, "It's his business opportunity that's waiting in Dodge. You're free to head on back to Dew Springs – "

"Free?" Marcus leaned past Jewel's shoulder to watch Calvin slurp from her canteen, "I gave you my word –" Marcus sighed, his warm breath tickled her cheek.

"I know you did but I'm telling you, you're free to head on home."

Marcus's eyes raked over Jewel's face, his lips pursed as if to say something, before he turned and climbed into his saddle.

"Times must have changed. Nobody fetched the Jewel Daniels I knew."

What would you know, Jewel wanted to snap back. Maybe because you never tried, was her next insult. She let the fire reinforce the tightness in her chest. She felt the tears pool at her lids and she blinked them away. Picking up the reins of the pack horse, Jewel led him over to Calvin. After helping Calvin change the load she ordered him to mount up and prompted *Rocio* into a steady trot.

Jewel kept in front, Calvin behind, and Marcus bringing up the rear as they continued towards Dodge.

As the first arc of the sun struck the horizon, it turned the fields into rows of golden feathers, the clouds thickening with peaches and lilacs, the heat of the day shifting across their path and cooling the sweat on her skin. They detoured off the trail and headed inland to the streak of emerald that lined the banks of the Smoky Hill River.

Jewel let Marcus take *Rocio* and stake the horses out while she set about fixing a fire. Calvin knelt down at the river, and took off his shirt, he splashed the water over and down his bare back, his figure seemed leaner than before, the fuzz across his chest had grey's mixed in with chestnut. He slicked back his hair, before holding a finger to one side of his nose and snorting out the trail dust on the muddy bank.

Jewel's face contorted, only to find Marcus watching her from the side. She narrowed her gaze, and turned away.

"Up here," Marcus said, gesturing to the scrap of bush that would hide them from passing riders.

Jewel scrambled into the underbrush as Calvin splashed out of the river behind her. The scent of the freshly stirred earth mixed with elm filtered through Jewel's senses, the sweet woody flavors coating masking the musty odor of Calvin.

"Good idea!" Calvin chimed in, "I haven't had a hot dinner since Delano!"

Jewel winced as Marcus repeated it, "Delano? Is that where you've come from?"

"We lived there for near on a year now, ain't we Jewel." Calvin shucked his shirt back on his shoulders.

The side of Jewel's neck heated.

"We?"

Jewel couldn't look at Marcus and she didn't want to look at Calvin.

"What was your business in Delano?"

"Ah entertainment," Calvin chuckled. He sat beside Jewel's saddle bags and brought out a jar of peaches, popping one in his mouth before Jewel could protest.

"He's not very entertaining," Jewel managed before tugging the bags out from under him.

Jewel plonked them down on the edge of the grove, and sat on them before she built the fire. Only when the pyre looked favorable, did Jewel dig out her flint. Within seconds the sparks began to smolder, and she breathed life into the kindling. The flames licked over the branches, the heat caressing her cheeks. Jewel stared into the tangerine swirls, watching the tendrils engulf the kindling.

Life sure had a funny way of turning upside down. Days out from Bryce being reunited with his brother, Lucky Chuck steals his life away. Just when Marcus reappears, Calvin turns up. Well it didn't matter what cards she had been dealt, Jewel had to play them. She would get her dissolution of this ridiculous marriage in Dodge. Jewel chewed her cheek between her teeth, did she tell Marcus? Jewel wasn't good enough for Marcus or his family when she was his Ranch Hands' bastard, she sure as hell wouldn't be good enough as a Delano Divorcee. Jewel dusted her hands on her thighs. She was done with men controlling her fate. Well, expect for Garrett Tanner. She would listen to his proposition and make her mind up then. Jewel twitched as Marcus suddenly crouched beside her and unfolded his tiny metal tripod and placed it over the fire.

"Entertainment?"

"It's not what you think Kearby," Jewel mumbled.

Marcus handed her a pan.

Jewel refused to take it, "I don't cook."

Marcus lips twisted into a slight grin.

"Nope she doesn't," Calvin added, digging for another peach.

Marcus cheeks fell flat, "I remember, I'm asking you to hold it."

Calvin snorted as he drunk the juice from the jar, "She doesn't-

"Calvin!" Jewel said as she snatched the small iron pan and balanced it over the small tripod.

The Texas Ranger opened a can of beans and poured them in. Pulling out a knife Marcus carved up slices of dried beef and then tossed them into the pan along with the beans. Marcus brought out a small jar of molasses and added it as well before topping the mix with a lid. Jewel licked her lips unsure if she salivated at the food or the man preparing it.

Calvin threw his head back and covered his face with his crumpled hat, "Let me know when it's ready."

Jewel watched the man's chest rise and fall steadily, her knuckles itched to throw a punch right on his nose.

"So you got married?" Marcus asked.

The dark Stetson sat low over Marcus's brow, the sunset threw dappled shadows across the leaf littered ground, his boots kicked up the scent of earth, and closer to the man, she smelt leather, horses and something darker, mahogany and Mexican Winter orange. It stirred familiar memories that licked at her temper. Bruised lips from urgent kisses and wandering hands that trembled across her skin. The darkened hours of that afternoon bled into this, and Jewel shivered.

"Who'd a thought it? Jewel Daniels married." Marcus baited her.

Well she had shed enough tears in the past, her cheeks heated with more than enough times with embarrassment and rejection. Here Marcus sat on his haunches, that same mocking tone in his throat.

Jewel wouldn't let him have it, "Times change, people change."

Marcus nodded, "That they do. It must be some business deal."

"It must be something real honorable to have you running back to Dew Springs."

Marcus jaw seemed to crack on his back teeth. He picked up a twig and rolled it between his thumb and forefinger, "You know I've only done the right thing by you Jewel."

Jewels fought the temptation to roll her head onto his shoulder as she exhaled long and slow, "I know Marcus."

She wanted to add that was half the problem. Jewel faced him only to see he was already watching her. The reflection of the campfire turned his hazel eyes into a hearth at the twilight of fall. On instinct, her gaze targeted his lips, the gravel across his chin thickened under his straight bottom lip. As if Marcus was the light, and she was adrift in the darkness, Jewel's mouth sought his. For a moment, Jewel hung suspended, inches from familiar delight.

Marcus retreated, "Married in 1874, what's that, six months after leaving Dew?"

Jewel recoiled, her cheeks heated at yet another rebuke, "There's no point waiting for snow in June."

Marcus tossed a twig into the fire, "Does he treat you fair?"

"He does," Jewel sighed.

After that first night Calvin had left her alone, much to her confusion. Her exasperation later turned into anger and finally acceptance when she had caught Calvin out that second night with Delilah the Chorus girl. He had married her as an achievement, a conquest. Calvin loved the chase, the magician in his past allowed him to build an illusion of flattery, promising girls their every desire held secret to their heart, believing that they had found him, the one man that loved them back for all and sundry. Only that man's love had a deficit, he loved the challenge and not the trophy.

Jewel rose as she tossed her own twig into the fire, "He treats me fair Marcus."

Marcus stood beside her, "By making you entertain his crowds?"

Jewel's gut clenched, what the devil was Marcus insinuating? She balled her fingers into a fist and aimed low. His grip closed over her wrist. Jewel over balanced and came up short against him.

Jewel pushed back, "It's not what you think Kearby!"

He let go of her wrist and placed both hands on her shoulders, "I don't care what you did in Delano, Jewel." Marcus expression softened, "Would you tell me if you were in danger?"

Jewel's skin seared where his palms connected, her fingertips pushed meekly back against his solid bulk, until she created enough willpower to step away.

"Not from Calvin that's for sure," Jewel laughed and resumed her seat.

Marcus readjusted his hat and picked up another twig, he snapped it before throwing it into the flames as he remained standing.

"I didn't think any man could slow down Jewel Daniels, and then to find out that one did and it's him," Marcus gestured to Calvin.

His snores ripped out from under the hat, his slight pot belly raised with each labored breath, the flashy clothing at odds with Jewel's denim and checkers.

Jewel laughed again, "He didn't slow me down."

She wanted to add, that Calvin's hooks would only last until they fronted the Judge in Dodge. If only Jewel had thought about it before leaving Wichita. It didn't matter now. Four days left with Marcus, four days left as a married woman.

Chapter 4

Marcus woke to the sounds of Calvin Hadley's snoring. He rolled onto his side and watched the grey dawn as it receded over the tree line. The sun's weak light pierced through the emerald leaves as a soft breeze rolled slowly up from the river, bringing the buttered popcorn scents of Prairie Drop seed.

They had spent last night's supper in relative civility, Marcus's collar heating at the thought of this man, a showman Calvin Hadley married to Jewel. Marcus had to make peace with it. Jewel had left Dew Springs and him with it, decided instead to eke out her future in Delano of all places. His sleep had been disturbed with memories of their last night together.

Jewel had stumbled into the cutting season dance wearing a frilly pink dress that tripped her heels and tugged low on her neckline. Ginger curls piled on top of Jewels head had revealed the creamy skin at the nape of her neck. His offer to dance had been interrupted by Cade Hamerton slogging Rick the Tick. Only after Marcus had wrestled Hamerton free, did he have a chance to get Jewel alone, but by then the dance had ended.

Marcus remembered the slow methodical plod of his father's horses, dragging his family cart back home. Each ground strike another moment lost with Jewel. The cool Texas air sent her intoxicating berry perfume into his skin, stirring his desire and encouraging his flirtations. Marcus had walked her to his porch, each step bringing them closer into the light that undid his bold ruse. The darkness shrunk and in the light, Marcus had thought better of his salacious plans. Instead they rested together on the swing-seat, her hip pressed against his, his arm around her neck. Their conversation had drifted from Cade's fight to the future and then rapidly turned south. Somehow Jewel managed to twist his words into insult.

Her heels kicked up the dust as she ran into night, back to her Pa's tiny house at the back of his barn. The following day at Church, he half expected Jewel to admonish him or ignore him, instead she had arrived in another dress, that colored his neck and heated his groin.

Back then Jewel's slender physique had always gained his attention, and it continued to haunt his dreams until days ago. Now, the maturity to her form had added more fuel to his already torturous visions, now he had new imagery that would disturb his sleep. Jewel's curves had fewer edges, her hips a little more sway, and even her smile had an endearing smirk instead of a petulant pout.

A splash of water made Marcus sit up. He scanned the fire, Jewel was missing. He heard another disturbance at the river front and decided not to investigate. At the possibility of those sounds coming from Jewel his body hardened. Marcus schooled his thoughts to calm, and turned to his side. Imagery of Jewel's partially clothed body infiltrated his defenses. Marcus concentrated on Hadley's snores until the discomfort subsided. After all Jewel was a married woman. Marcus wouldn't bring her reputation into question; he wouldn't tempt her soul to adultery. Marcus's arousal stirred.

A western meadowlark called across the plains, a male searching for his mate. The sharp yet melodic trill spurred Marcus into action. The fire was well in hand by the time Jewel returned from the riverbank. Ginger tendrils clung wet to the side of her neck, the sun rise turning her ringlets into a crown of gold and ruby. Water droplets still decorated her skin at the hollow below her throat, and her cream colored shirt dampened in all the wrong places. Marcus rested on his haunches and concentrated on the flames.

"Mornin," Jewel said, her brow set, her cheeks flushed. She had last night's pot in hand filled with water, "Figured you'd want a coffee."

"Mornin'. That's right thoughtful of you Jewel," Marcus said as he took the pot and placed it on the tripod over the flames.

Jewel rolled her eyes but smiled all the same, "I may not have all those airs and graces you and your Mama were always on about, but nobody said I wasn't hospitable."

Marcus retrieved his coffee stash and pulled out two cups, "You were always welcoming." Marcus laughed until he heard his own words, "In your own way, and I never went on as much as my Ma, I just thought the way you spoke to people sometimes-"

"What straight and to the point?" Jewel said her cheeks flat.

Marcus laughed and this time Jewel joined in.

Jewel set about repacking her change of clothes. Marcus watched as she methodically removed each item, folded it so seams aligned, creases were sharp, and fabric flat. Jewel had pulled out a silver case, engraved with roses on the top that she opened and checked; the contents hidden from Marcus before she slotted it back into her bags.

"How is your Mama and Pa, any news from home?"

Marcus's gut churned. He should tell her about his summons to home. No it would do no good but sour the next few days, "Ma writes from time to time."

"So nothing's changed then." Jewel said.

Marcus snorted, "Yeah, that's right. He's too busy running the Ranch. Besides he has Robert and Reid to help him. Although, Robert and April just had another one."

"So that makes it three bubs then!" Jewel took the boiling pot off the flames.

Marcus handed over his coffee tin and Jewel measured out the required amount before setting it back on the boil.

"Yeah, Reid married that girl from Houston."

Jewel leaned over the pot and watched until bubbles burst, "And what about Whit?"

Marcus cleared his throat, "Ah Whit's been... well you know Whit."

Jewel smiled, "Yeah I know Whit. Now he was always too

um… hospitable for his own good."

Marcus didn't laugh along with Jewel this time. She had come close to the duty that bound him to return. Damn Whit being every girls dream and every father's nightmare. He'd left a string of disaster behind him and Marcus's parents had asked him, the youngest of his four brothers to clean up the mess. It was his duty as their son, as Whit's brother to protect the Kearby family name.

"Well no doubt all the Kearby Brothers are given your Mama something to worry about. And I know Cade and Evie had little Lock. What about those others, Shelton Murphy and Taylor Stone, don't tell me they're still playing cards at the Nine Lives Saloon."

Marcus shook his head, as he watched Jewel patiently wait for the coffee grounds to settle.

"No they're not. Old Man Murphy up and passed away. Shelton's been too busy with the Ranch for much else. And Taylor, he took off to North-west chasing gold amongst other things."

Marcus smiled. For a long time, in the absence of his father's attention, it had just been the four of them. Cade, Marcus, Shelton and Taylor running amok in Dew Springs. Picking fights with Rick the Tick and others, and letting Cade finish them, letting Taylor experiment with fireworks at every opportunity, following Shelton's *sage* advice on women, only to have dire consequences. Marcus chuckled.

"Sorry to hear about Shelly's dad."

"I thought your Pa would have told you."

Jewel hung her head, "He would have, if I told him where to write to."

Marcus's ribs tightened; he knew that feeling, the belief that no news is good news. For all her bravado, Jewel hadn't the heart to tell her father that she hadn't achieved what she set out to. As far as Jedidiah Daniels knew, his daughter was headlining a sharp shooter festival somewhere.

"What about you, Delano can't be all?" Marcus asked.

Jewel retrieved a red checked bandana; unfolding and re-folding it across the tops of both cups and gently titled the pot to the side, not satisfied with the ground settling she let it sit longer.

"No Delano was the last stop. I went up to Kansas City, then Omaha and even Indianapolis. I shot well, too well. They said it wasn't believable that a girl, a woman, could shoot so well. The crowds would think it was trickery or an illusion. They'd feel cheated. There had to be danger that maybe I'd miss."

"And Jewel Daniels doesn't miss."

"Nope. Hadley agreed to take me on, but he already had a sharp shooter; one with a drinking and gambling problem that dropped his shots too often."

Marcus hung his head, "He put you in the back."

Jewel laughed, "Way in the back, behind the curtain. It's my shots that landed on those targets, just not my face on the poster."

"I'm sorry Jewel."

"Ah don't be. I got to play a small part, the damsel in distress, it was fun. It was an adventure."

"Why Delano then?"

"The crowds were too good to pass up. When the cattle trade shifted to Wichita, Delano came alive. It swelled like a ripe plum. You could cross the river and find your sweetest desires. But too much time in the sun and it began to rot." Jewel reached for the pot.

Marcus put his hand on her forearm, "It's a waiting game, Jewel. Be patient."

Jewel's lips curled, "Oh is it now. Well I figured I've done my waiting."

Calvin rolled onto his side, his arms stretching above his head. Marcus held his tongue and he heard Calvin's lips smack against each other before he yawned. Slowly, the man rose from his slumber, "That coffee smells good."

Jewel regarded the two cups and laughed, "Well you'll have to wait."

Marcus stood and brushed down his denims, "He can have mine."

Marcus strode down the riverbank, an anger boiled in his veins that he had missed his opportunity. That in his search for Jewel it had brought him further away, and now his family dragged him back to Dew Springs, to lasso him with another burden. He wouldn't be surprised if Whit's jilted fiancé would refuse to marry Marcus, even if she had a Kearby grandson in her belly. After all the woman loved Whit, why would she agree to marry his younger brother? Marcus needed to shelve his anger. He would part company with Jewel at Dodge. He couldn't hold her from her fortune whatever the business deal in Dodge, not back then and sure as hell not now. Marcus would savor these last few moments, the final glimpses of what their life could have been. He found a spot secluded by a box elder and kicked off his boots.

"Bad timing for you love?" Calvin said.

Jewel blew across her coffee, "You know it is, but that's life. When we get to Dodge, the first thing, and I mean it, the first thing we'll be doing is fronting that Judge and dissolving this. I ain't after any of your money and you know I don't have any of my own."

"You have Selina and Josephine."

"Pfft," Jewel slurped the bitter liquid, the granules feathered her tongue. She spat it out and reset the bandana to filter the next measure.

"What will you do?" Calvin asked.

"I don't know."

"You're not going to go back to that dust bowl you call home, Dew Drop –"

"Dew Springs? No I'll see what this Garrett fellow has to say before I push off to Kansas City. Do you reckon he'd put me on a poster?"

Calvin stood and turned around, sighing and huffing as he pushed his hands onto his hips and sent his pelvis forward, "I dare say he will. So has he told you what stopped him coming for you sooner?"

Jewel regarded the coffee, "Probably something honorable no doubt." This time she scooped the coffee from the top until she filled too mugs. She handed one to Calvin and took the other one down towards the river bank.

She followed Marcus's boot prints through the muddy bank until they petered out. A thicket of box elder prevented her pushing forward. Jewel turned away only to hear swish of water. She froze, coffee stinging her palm. Her eyes tracked over the ground until she saw a pair of boots and then an empty pair of denims. Jewel retraced her steps until she reached the tree line. She heard Calvin burp somewhere nearby. The last thing she wanted was to stumble across Calvin during his morning constitution.

Jewel stepped further into the underbrush away from the camp, only stopping when a cottontail bounded out ahead of her. She almost dropped the coffee over a bunny! Jewel giggled and tried to gather her bearings. Somehow she had managed to track closer to the river bend and it's only occupant. Jewel clutched the coffee and sat down as Marcus came into sight.

The river tumbled down several plateau shaped rock formations, which is where Jewel had taken her own riverside bath. Marcus stood below one and let the water fall over him. Jewel wanted to avert her eyes, but the way the liquid cascaded over his muscular frame trapped her gaze. He reached up to sluice back his hair, his muscular arms, as strong as she remembered, his chest covered in a little more dark fuzz than she recalled. His ribs were lean, the strands of muscles taunt across his stomach.

Jewel's throat constricted as Marcus moved closer towards her position, the tide of the river receding to indecent proportions. His skin painted with hours in the Southern sun. His arms tanned a delicious caramel, his back a lighter cream. The box elder blocked most of her view as Marcus reached his clothes. What was hidden by the waterfall now screamed at

Jewel and her breath caught.

As Marcus turned, the morning light reflected off silvery strands that adorned his left shoulder. After he shucked on his denims he came back into sight. Another jagged line, still pink from healing ran across his hip and another on his back. She spied what looked like a burn across the left of his chest that ran into the spider-web of scars. Bruises yellowed on his right upper arm. Jewel stole several measured breaths before she felt enough strength in her legs to wander back. She should have taken a lot longer, as she reached the divergence, Marcus stood on the bank, tugging one boot on then the next.

"Jewel?"

"I brought you coffee, since –" She looked at her empty cup, "I mean, I meant to bring you back the mug for your coffee –" Jewel dragged her eyes up from his boots past his belt buckle and up to his chest where he now buttoned his shirt. She spied another scar, this one slightly puckered low on his right ribs. Had he been shot?

"Did you wait long enough then?" He smiled.

She licked her lips, "I think just long enough."

Marcus smiled, broad and white and Jewel couldn't resist she smiled back. He had been doing something honorable indeed. He was a Texas Ranger and judging by the scars that marked the last two years, he had barely made it out alive. Perhaps that's why he was being sent home to Dew Springs. A ribbon of guilt spiraled through Jewel's blood and she let it tangle, she hadn't driven him to the Rangers. He chose that. He had chosen the Rangers over her. Then why did the tangle turn into a knot and then a tumble-weed the size of Texas.

Jewel marched through the red cedar and sycamore trees to find the smoldering fire, and Calvin standing over her saddle bags.

"Mounting up are we?"

Jewel regarded Calvin's upright frame as he wrung his hands together. What was he up to?

"Sure." Marcus said as he wandered up the slope tucking

his green shirt into his belt line, "If we keep up the pace we'll reach Ellsworth by sundown."

"E-Ellsworth?" Calvin's chin twitched, "That town's got a reputation just as bad as me!" He let out a slow chuckle, "We'd be wise to keep to our own trails."

Marcus stepped in front of Jewel, droplets trickled down his sable strands and onto his collar, "Is that so?"

Calvin stopped twisting his hands and shoved them into his satin lined pockets, "I was just saying."

Marcus put one boot forward, his shoulders back, "What were you saying?"

"It's just, ah it being cattle season and all, I figured it'd be safer to stay away from crowds -"

"It was cattle season when you left Wichita."

"What about the Indians?"

Marcus's voice took on an acidity that made Jewel wince, "Where were you at the *Palo Duro*? Did you know where the *Quahadi Comanche* are now?" Marcus cleared his throat, and the heat was gone, "By your own admission you haven't been out of Delano for about a year?"

Calvin nodded, "Then well -"

Marcus ran his hand over his damp hair and replaced his chestnut Stetson, "I gave my word to Jewel that I'd see her safely to Dodge, by all means, you're free to take another route."

"Ah, well yes of course, I have no doubt you being a Texas Ranger would be far wiser than me on the Plains, so lead on." Calvin spread his arms wide, his palms outwards.

Jewel had seen him do it a thousand times to the crowds, the showman at the top of his game. She wouldn't be surprised if he bowed next.

Chapter 5

Calvin sat sore in the saddle, his rump tired and aching putting his forearm to his brow wiped away the sweat, the Kansas sun seemed suspended in perpetual umbra, five fingers above the horizon, like a bad debt that wouldn't clear.

He watched Jewel chitter chatter with her cowboy, the stocky man casting his hazel eyes over Calvin a little more frequently and with longer delay. Calvin had to be careful, would this Kearby fellow hand Jewel over, too honorable for his own good? Or did his desire for Jewel run as long and as deep as her own, that long enduring burn that had eluded Calvin for all his thirty five years?

So far, on this long and arduous trek to Ellsworth, he got small measure of the man. It took Calvin seconds if that, to judge a man and his desire, twist it to his own gain. He watched their eyes, their lips, the way their hands twitched to their holster, their coin purse or their belt buckle. Did they rub their nose, tug their ear, or pull their beard? Did their eyes follow the men, the women or the money? Yet what he heard from Jewel about this man, over a bottle of tequila didn't match what Calvin saw. Maybe Jewel still saw the golden glow of her youthful crush, but something was twisted inside Marcus Kearby.

Then again, there was something twisted in Garrett Tanner, and that's who Calvin had to worry about now. Travelling with a Ranger seemed a good compromise. At least until he could get Jewel to Dodge and to Tanner's table. All Jewel had to do was prove her aim and speed to Garrett and that reward would be Calvin's. He would be doing her a favor helping Jewel clear her name. Better Calvin brought her to Garrett than Donnie or Sampson. Then he could take the $1000 reward and ply his trade down the Mississippi. Perhaps he didn't need

Jewel. Selina and Josephine would fetch a mighty price. If he could find the pistols, he might not have to drag Jewel to Tanner. It would be less effort, that's for sure. Maybe Calvin would hear news of Lucky Chuck when they reached Ellsworth.

Jewel let the cadence of *Rocio* blend in with Marcus's deep tones, the rhythm wearing down what little walls she had left. A soft breeze blew across the ripening wheat fields, the fluffy tops shifting in the warm air until it caressed her cheek.

"And then what happened?"

"Well, they retreated into a valley, the river ended into a canyon. We surrounded them. After a while, they eventually surrendered."

"And what happened to them?"

Marcus frowned, "Well the two that shot Nelson, went out firing. The third swung. The others are sitting in Huntsville."

Jewel nodded. Cattle rustling was a serious business, but if they were taking shots at Texas Rangers, it was never going to end well. Marcus hands relaxed on the pommel of his saddle, his forearms turned deep caramel in sunlight.

"And then where did you go?"

"Kept a few Governors safe, went chasing a few fugitives."

"Fugitives like the Turner Gang?"

Marcus smile twisted just as the sun dipped behind a cloud, "Yeah. We got close at few times. What was left of them they retreated, we gave chase, but they disappeared. We found their camp, souvenirs from the train and other trinkets. After that the trail split again and again. We lost them."

"What happened with the Sioux?"

Marcus eyes stared at the hard packed road in front of him. A long while passed before he answered, "That's one reason why I stayed north so long."

Jewel let it drop as riders appeared on the horizon.

Calvin rode up between Jewel and Marcus, "Should we step off the trail?"

Marcus squinted, "No need." Even as he said the words,

Marcus's elbow touched his holster. As the group neared, their heads kept down, their youthful cheeks barely a whisker to be seen between them.

"Greenhorns," Jewel snorted, "Run off from the cattle run."

"Pockets full of coins, and a head full of fame," Marcus winked to Jewel.

Jewel rolled her lips inwards, "Relax Calvin, we're nearing Ellsworth, there's likely to be more than just us on the road."

"Oh I know I know," Calvin said. He tied his hair into a short pony tail just above his collar, and Jewel couldn't help but cringe at the sight.

Relief from the heat came as the cusp of the sun finally touched the horizon. They made Ellsworth just before final night. Marcus headed over to the post office, a telegram itching to be sent to his two other Rangers. Calvin climbed down from his ride, rubbing his rump and groaning.

Jewel eyed the Drovers Cottage, the white washed exterior dark slate compared to the amber light that spilled from the first two stories onto the dusty street. Jewel hefted her saddle bags from the back of *Rocio* and left the horses in the stable boys' capable hands. Calvin stumbled over to her side but Jewel shied away and hefted her bags over one shoulder. As Jewel stepped inside the hotel, the scent of dust and lint, tickled her nose almost until she sneezed. Organ music trickled out from the near empty dining rooms, the tables covered in a patchwork of varnishes the dark rings of many ale mugs still visible. Jewel reached the front counter, a vase of dried flowers loitered, the petals tumbling down onto the cracked paint of the unattended desk. Stepping into the dining hall, the odor of whiskey soaked carpet and ancient cigar blended with the salty beef stew and fresh biscuits smell that wafted from the kitchen. Some of the chairs were empty, their upholstery torn, two glass panes shot out of one window, the board nailed onto the frame suggested the glass was still absent. Marcus thumbed the bell and Jewel jumped.

"That was quick."

"Caught the Post Master just as he was leaving, sent off to Abe at Junction City where I'm headed."

"They're keeping tabs on you?" Jewel asked with one hand on her hip.

"No."

That meant someone was, Jewel mused.

A mature woman, as spread out as a cold supper, appeared behind the counter, "Are you wanting two rooms, or three? We got plenty of vacancies."

"Three," Marcus handed over his money, "I expected you'd be busier,"

"No doubt 'em did too," she raised her chin to the bar that ran along one side of the long dining room, where two soiled Doves sat, their corsets tight, their expressions long.

"They look like they need a little company is all," Calvin's hand jostled his belt buckle.

Jewel refused to look at Marcus and snatched a key off the desk, "Bath?"

"You'll find what ya need upstairs love, we'd be busier, but 'em railroads closed their pens on us. Cattlemen don't come if they can't move 'em cattle."

Jewel turned and ran into the chest of Marcus his hands caught her elbows, "Always in the wrong place at the wrong time."

"That's the tale of my life, Mrs Hadley." Marcus's grip released.

Jewel stormed upstairs, her muscles ached from the effort and yet relieved to be moving all the same. Her hand ghosted along the banister the paint flaking in her hands, the stair tread worn down in the middle. She found her room, surprised as she opened the door and found a large bed with cherry coverlet, a rich cedar dressing table with mirror and a wide corner window that overlooked the street. She let the curtains flounder against the dusk breeze, bringing with it the slightest cool from the scorching day. She tossed her saddle bags onto the bed, a second glance told a new tale. The coverlet was threadbare, the curtains faded by the Kansas sun, the window sill chipped and flaking. Two bullet holes remained unfixed in the plaster. She didn't mind, she'd stayed in far worse. Jewel shoved her hands into her possessions and felt the outline of Bryce's pistols. She retrieved her toiletries case, the rose adorned silver carry-all that held her brushes, soap, oils, and perfumes.

Jewel collected her clothes and marched down to the end of the hall where a sign hung crooked on one peg, *Washroom*. She ran herself a bath amazed at the plumbing and slowly immersed herself in the warm water.

She heard Marcus's boots traipse down the corridor, followed by a few curt words from Calvin. Jewel closed her eyes against the noise, her thoughts drifting back to that afternoon.

Long shadows had drawn across the front of the barn, as Jewel wandered into the darkened interior. She had a bet to settle with Marcus and so far he'd curtailed it into hiding. She rested her long-arm on the nearest bale of hay and called out his name. She heard his boots shuffle in the stall at the far end of the barn. He had a fork in one hand, and a smile on his face.

"I beat you Marcus Kearby," Jewel said as she marched down the alley until she stood at the front of his work area.

Marcus spiked another bale and pulled it apart, the straw spilling across the ground. His horse watched from the next stall, his usual blanket slung over the barrier between them.

"I know, I'm not shirking it." His cheeks were smooth, his eyes ablaze. He rested the fork against the timber wall and closed the distance, "What's your prize then?"

Jewel's stomach fluttered, her throat became dry, "Well" as she stepped into the stall.

Marcus rested against the barrier, one boot against the timber, his knee raised. His horse snuffled at his shoulder. He crossed his ropey arms across his chest, his shirt sweat stained and puckered around his physic.

Jewel considered her words carefully. He was nineteen. She was sixteen what could go wrong? Did she ask for a kiss, or something more? Would his kiss lead to what she really wanted?

"I want –" Jewel said.

Marcus's fingers bunched the front of her cotton shirt, he pulled her onto him. Her body landed against his frame as his lips sunk down to hers. She stood frozen, awkward, her hands unsure of where to rest, only that they wanted to explore. Her palms found his shoulders as his tongue drove past her lips. Her flutters turned to a tornado, her knees losing all strength. His ferocity stunned her, his hot breath scalding her throat, his kiss deepening as Jewel leaned against him. He turned her against the stall barrier, her hands splayed out to catch herself from falling. It didn't matter, she thought as she took her hands from the horses blanket and found Marcus's shirt, pulling and tugging until it came free of his belt buckle. Her fingers dove under the fabric, every ridge trembling under her caress. She could feel Marcus' body stiffen against her hip, his hand slithered into the rear pocket of her denims while his arm curled around her back. Her world titled as Marcus shifted again, the horse's blanket softening their fall. The scratchy noise of the hay startled her, just the same as how eager her thigh curled around his hip. His arousal swelled against her pelvis and she writhed to meet him. His kiss plundered her mouth, igniting her veins and awakening her hunger. She dragged his shirt upwards, revealing his sculptured frame. Her fingers dove through the tiny dark patch at the center of his chest as he worked away her shirt buttons.

"Marcus" she whimpered as he gave her respite.

He didn't respond as his lips rapidly suckled down her neck, his hand roughly cupping her breast.

Jewel let out a little giggle, as Marcus's fingers undid her belt, "Marcus!"

Jewel sat upright in the bath, the washroom now almost totally dark, her single lamp reflected off the chipped tiles as goose pimples rose across her skin. She grabbed her towel, and clambered out, striking her knee on the edge. She howled at her stupidity and stumbled to her feet. She turned up the lamp and dressed, packing her things as neatly as she could.

Only when everything was clean and reset did Jewel finally open the door. She exhaled long and slow, trying to calm her racing thoughts. Despite the comforts, her body was wrought with energy, the same cravings to remain unfulfilled. She almost made it to her room when a door opened beside her.

"There you are, I thought you might have needed rescuing," Marcus joked.

"Not likely and not by you." Jewel snapped.

"Hey!" Marcus snagged Jewel's elbow and turned her to face him, "I know Calvin's gotten you all worked up, so I had a word to him."

Jewel rested her shoulder against the corridor wall, "Damn honorable thing of you to do, Marcus."

"What?" Marcus said as his eyebrows raised, his expression genuinely shocked. "I've only ever done," Marcus shook his head and lowered his voice, "I was thinking of your -"

The ball of energy inside Jewel's stomach slowly settled and Jewel laughed, "Not that it matters Marcus, but I don't care whose bed Calvin warms." Her eyes met his and she studied the dark circles that ringed his almost golden eyes.

"Well," Marcus cleared his throat, his hand crept up to her collar and he wound a wet curl of her hair through his fingers and tugged. The result sent shivers straight down Jewel's spine and into her abdomen, "It matters to me."

Jewel licked her lips.

Suddenly Marcus retreated. His palm grazed her shoulder, "What's this?"

"Present from a dead friend." Jewel stammered.

"Right," Marcus created even more distance, "Now since I cooked last night, you're buying me supper."

Jewel smiled, "Deal."

Marcus left Jewel in the corridor, pondering her wildfire reactions to Calvin. The man was despicable, and yet Jewel claimed she didn't mind. She had loved him at some point, she married the man! Marcus had done what he thought was right. And then he saw her, and every fiber of his body screamed to do what was wrong. Fresh as the first summer blooms, those ginger curls tied back neatly on the damp ones that wanted to rebel. Those few moments in the corridor had taxed him, in Jewels presence Marcus felt intoxicated, almost baited into recklessness. It had frightened him. It still frightened him. Even now, his body seemed to become aware of Jewels', the flush of her cheeks, the rise of her chest against the fabric of her shirt. Marcus tried to distract himself by counting the freckles that splashed across her nose. It didn't work. His hand seemed to move of its own accord trapping her curl, his skin absorbing her perfumed soaps. He hoped the washroom had enough cold water to get him through supper.

Calvin removed his ear from the door, as he heard the floor-boards creak. Lord only knew what the Ranger sent in his telegram. As they neared civilization the risk of someone picking *Ruby Drawers* from the wanted posters would increase. What happened if they never made it to Dodge? Calvin didn't care. Surely, the Ranger would look after Jewel, right now Calvin had to look after Calvin. First he needed those guns. His stomach growled almost as loud as he knee caps as he rose to his feet. But first he needed a full belly.

Marcus made it down for supper, of beef stew with hot biscuits, sitting across from Jewel and Calvin. The Entertainer slurped down every mouthful, a splash of gravy trickled onto his shirt and he dipped his finger in his glass of whiskey and tried to wipe it clean. Jewel had finished and pushed the plate to one side as she watched Calvin run his biscuit through the gravy.

Marcus took a slow sip of his beer, "Thank you for a fine

supper Jewel."

A smile warmed her narrow cheeks, "Mighty fine effort I'd say."

"The best you've ever cooked, my love." Calvin said and patted her hand on the table top.

Jewel snatched it free and rose, "I'm going to see about dessert."

Considering the wait staff consisted of the same madam who issued their rooms and the barman entertained a pair of old faithful customers who would rather drink the establishment dry than visit their wives, Jewel had to wander into the kitchen to find someone.

In Jewel's absence, both Doves sauntered to their table, a canister of whiskey in one hand, four glasses carried by the other. Marcus scanned their features running them through his memory of all the wanted posters, even the most recent.

He pulled out a chair for the buxom blonde while Calvin offered his lap to the brunette. He frowned at Calvin's blatant disregard for his marriage vows. Marcus accepted the finger of whiskey the woman poured, and took the tiniest sip, "What's your name?"

"For you," She ran her fan along the edge of his jaw, "Whatever you desire."

"Don't mind Belle, she's got fancy manners and fancier dreams,"

"I don't mind fancy manners." Marcus smiled politely, "And where did you come from Belle?"

"Just a small town, nowhere you would have heard of." Belle took a swig of whiskey from Marcus's glass.

"Not Delano by any chance?" Marcus asked. He thought of the bill folded in his pocket. He regarded her big blonde curls and the impossible luster it radiated.

"I wish, next season we'll be heading over, ain't that right Darcy."

Darcy didn't answer. She had her arm around Calvin's collar and her other hand no doubt lifting his wallet.

"Do you want to play a game?" Belle pulled out a deck of cards and began to shuffle.

The blonde leaned closer, her corset barely holding all her assets. Marcus gently ran his finger down the side of her cheek, comparing her image to the one that burned a hole in his denims. She was too old, her face too round.

Marcus heard the kitchen doors slam before he managed to pull his hand away. Jewel's gaze darkened. Marcus looked over to Calvin, his lips pressed against the woman on his lap. Marcus stood as Jewel crossed the dining room and dashed up the stairs. Marcus had had a word with Calvin and yet he let him disrespect Jewel again. Blatantly! Marcus clenched his fingers into a fist and sat back down.

"So Belle, you haven't been to Delano, but have you been to Three Bird Creek, over in Franklin County by any chance."

Belle's cheeks fell, her top lip twitched, she tried to stand.

Marcus grabbed her wrist, "Miss Belle Lincoln, you're a wanted woman and tonight you're coming with me."

Belle stoically stood and knocked back the remainder of Marcus's whiskey before slamming the glass onto the table, "The bastard deserved it; him and his brother."

Chapter 6

By the time Marcus woke up the deputy and after the grizzled man cleared the sleep from his eyes, he processed the fugitive Belle Lincoln. Marcus was paid a share of her bounty the rest would be wired to the details he gave. It would take a while but the extra income would help soften the blow with his wife-to-be that Marcus was financially able to take care of her, unlike his scamp of a brother Whit.

Marcus actually yawned as he crossed the road to the Cottage. He would explain to Jewel in the morning, and then he would see the Post Master and check if there was any news from Abe. He climbed the stairs with the single lamp that had been left on the countertop. He threw himself down on the coverlet, and rolled over onto the pillow, he needed sleep yet something nagged at the back of his mind.

Jewel. Her face had worn a mask of anger and something else, even though she claimed not to care what Calvin did with his spare time. Marcus punched the pillow until the lumps evened out and bunched it under his ear. Had Jewel married Calvin for money? His tailored clothes seemed slick just like his thinning hair, even if it did look like it had seen better days. The whole man seemed like he had seen better days. Calvin still chased the ghost of greatness, his own endless pursuit of fame and glory for his name and his life to have meant something. How could he begrudge the man a legacy? Marcus had followed the same pursuit. To make a name for himself other than the Ranchers spare son. His father demanded he make something of himself, and Marcus wouldn't make himself in his image.

If only Jewel had seen it his way. Between what she wanted, what he wanted and what his family would allow, Marcus had nowhere to run. He tried to explain, but his words tumbled over one another. He couldn't tame Jewel, and even if she reckoned she would be content, he knew she would grow to resent him. She called him a bore more times that he could remember. Every time he heard *honorable* from her lips it stung. He sighed and rolled onto his back, staring up into the darkness. And he had been right to be mild.

"I beat you Marcus Kearby," Jewel marched down the barn, her cheeks flushed with having chased him up from the river.

He had sped ahead hoping the time and distance would cool the afternoon's rising heat. At least she'd put the rifle down.

Marcus noticed the recent change in Jewel's demeanor, the extra-long glances, the ones where she tilted her head, and bit her lip, or the way she changed wearing her ginger curls from two plaits to one gregarious tail swept up from her neck.

He rested the fork against the barn wall; his palms itched to skim her hips. He heard the bells tolling in his head, felt the constriction around his chest and groin. Time and distance cooled nothing.

"I know, I'm not shirking it," He took another step closer. His father had warned him about Jewel. Any other pursuit was noble, but this one was folly. His words slithered from somewhere sinister, "What's your prize then?"

Jewel stepped into the stall, her scent of orchids and green apple permeated the hay infused air, "Well."

Marcus stalled his advance and leaned against the barrier, he raised his knee to ease his discomfort. She was so close he could see the tiny flicker of her pulse under the creamy skin of her neck. She tucked a strand behind her ear and licked her lips, "I want—"

Marcus's resolve evaporated and he reached for Jewel. She landed against his chest, as his lips found hers. Wildfire coursed through his body, igniting a thousand infernos where her body connected with his. He felt the press of her breasts tight against his chest. His tongue sort hers, her naivety both tempered and fueled his desire. The wet corners of her mouth teased at the suppleness that awaited him. Her hands found his shoulders and he spun her until he felt the stall barrier tremble.

Jewel was his.

Her fingers pulled his shirt up, his heart thundered in his ears, as she grew bolder, seeking out her prize. He advanced, his arousal pressed against her hip. His palm cupped her buttock from inside her denim pocket, bringing Jewel hard onto him. He felt the blanket against the railing. Her soft kisses were no match for his desire. Her caress on his ribs drove thorns under his skin, piercing through his morals. He needed her now. Jewel was his and she would be his from sundown to sun-up.

He dragged the blanket with them, his only gentleman thought as he crushed Jewel downwards. He deepened his kiss, as the lightening of ardor pumped through his veins. He fumbled with her buttons, one popped from the fabric. He nibbled at her neck, as he felt her nipple harden under his grip. He heard something, a squeak, was it a word?

Jewel called out.

Marcus sought air, he leaned back and his eyes adjusted to the devastation created from his own recklessness. Jewel's lips were bruised red, her hair amess, and her shirt askew. He had almost taken her in the straw like some common Dove. Jewel. His Jewel and he almost rushed it. Her fingers reached for him, but he was already on his feet. He pulled his shirt over his head and tucked it into his belt. He put out his hand to help her up, but she batted it aside.

He could feel his body trembling, the air slowly returning to his lungs and bringing with it eternal shame at his lecherous actions. He needed to say something.

"I won't do this. Not here, not you." He turned on his heel to hide his despair. His father was right, he was weak and foolish; a dullard.

"Some prize!" She snapped.

"Nothing good can come of this Jewel." His throat hurt, "Nothing."

She tore past him into the late afternoon sun. Marcus picked up the fork. He raised it high above his shoulder and drove it hard into the timber.

Marcus eyes snapped open as the Ellsworth dawn rolled across the stained carpet in his room. *Nothing good can come of this,* the same words he repeated to Jewel after the cutting season dance. He tried to make her see it his way, after all her mother had travelled the same path. He was glad Jewel had left Dew Springs, to chase a better life. Calvin's snore's ripped through the thin walls. Better?

Marcus rose and dressed, feeling as if he had one wheel down and the axle dragging. He grabbed a slab of bacon and scrambled eggs as he sat down in the empty dining hall. He would explain it to Jewel again. He managed to finish breakfast without catching a glimpse of her and by the time he decided to visit the Post Master, he felt nervous enough to check that *Rocio* was still in the stables in case Jewel had given him the slip in the middle of the night. Her blue roan was just where she left him.

Jewel marched out of the trading post with another jar of peaches, and a fresh bandana, one that didn't stink of coffee. She replaced her fawn Stetson on her forehead and stepped off the sidewalk to cross the road. She spied a dark chestnut hat crossing the street at the same time, his trajectory clear, his stride casual but determined. Marcus intercepted her on the steps of the Cottage.

"So I hear another woman has been safely escorted to her destination," Jewel smirked.

"Where'd you hear that?"

"Betsy's daughter is married to the Deputy's cousin."

Marcus snorted, "Of course."

Jewel climbed the stairs slowly, Marcus by her elbow. She wanted to pretend her relief wasn't this profound. She needed to bury what she felt for Marcus, cut it out like the deep splinter that it was, so her heart could cure.

"I was only doing, what's right."

"Always Marcus? Doesn't it get boring?" She paused at the

top step, Marcus one below her. His eyes darkened as she stood to face him.

"Nothing boring about the Rangers, Jewel." Marcus stopped at the main stair case, "I'll saddle *Rocio*." Marcus turned and strode down the stairs.

Jewel sighed as she watched him walk out the front entrance. Why did this particular splinter have to be so damn gorgeous and so damn stuck?

Marcus stuck true to his word and had *Rocio* saddled and waiting at the hitching post. Calvin scrambled up his mount, as Marcus sat high in the saddle of *Scout*. She saw his rifle resting on the right side of his saddle. Marcus lips thin, as he cast his gaze around Ellsworth's scant population. He flicked his reins just as Jewel's heel hit the stirrups. She knew the dark clouds under his brim were her doing and an itch in her throat told her to fix it.

As they passed Holyrood, Jewel pushed *Rocio* to close the distance.

"Did you hear back from Abe?" Jewel asked.

Calvin almost leapt from his saddle.

"I did." Marcus said.

Calvin's brown bay neighed, the larger man wiped his forehead with a grey handkerchief, "And was it enlightening?"

"It was" Marcus replied.

"No Indian trouble, I hope, nothing in the Territory." Calvin said, his eyes flicked to the rifle now pride of place at Marcus's right thigh.

Marcus shook his head.

Jewel pushed her boot toe into Calvin's shin, she knew when to quit. When Marcus was set, Calvin had no more chance than a June bug in the chicken coop trying to get him to shift. Calvin's bottom lip jutted out, before he let his horse drop back.

Jewel let *Rocio* fall into step, his hooves thumping the hard packed trail in time with Marcus's horse. She inhaled slowly, taking in the rolling fields of crops. The colors blended into one another swirls of caramel, coffee, lime and toffee. Spurts of emerald lined the distance where pockets of hackberry competed with the golden glow of Honey Locust along the many tributaries that crisscrossed the Plains. Sunflowers bowed to the slightest breeze, their black pitted sundials drinking all they could of the midday Kansas sun.

"What did Miss Belle Lincoln do?"

Marcus revere broke, "Shot her husband and his brother."

Jewel felt the leather reins crackle under her fingers. An ache worked through her forearms and she twisted her wrists to release the tension, "They probably deserved it."

Marcus snorted, "Miss Belle shares your sentiments."

"Did he treat her kind?"

Marcus brought his canteen up from his belt, and offered it to Jewel first, she shook her head, "He didn't treat her kind, no."

Jewel tapped the pommel of her saddle, "Now there you go, Miss Belle Lincoln was doing the right thing, freeing herself from an abusive husband, sending him to be judged by his maker, and now she's likely to hang for it."

Marcus raised his eyebrows, "She won't hang for killing her husband. But she might for riding his horse over to the next County and shooting his brother in front of his family."

Jewel almost dropped her reins, "Well -"

"She thought she'd end up with the house but her husband had a massive gambling debt and mortgaged the property to his brother."

Jewel bit her lip.

"Doing what's right isn't always easy," Marcus turned to look at Jewel, the hint of a smile lurked under his thickening whiskers.

Jewel clicked her tongue, "Sometimes."

"Like you leaving Dew Springs, would have been for you."

Here it came, Jewel told herself. She had to be quick, pull the splinter out and staunch the bleeding, "Yes -"

"Your mother -"

Jewel squinted underneath her brim, "What?"

"You know what I mean Jewel, your Ma and Pa."

She waved a fly away from her face, her eyes began to water, "My Ma and Pa loved each other so much, Kearby," she heard her voice heighten, "That they didn't let a little thing like rules get in their way."

"Coat it how you like it Jewel, she left and she hasn't been back."

Jewel reached for her own canteen, her throat coarse, "She followed the music," she let the warm water pour down her throat, she wet her new bandana and tied it around her neck, "She'll be back when the music stops."

Marcus shook his head, "You made the right choice Jewel." He squeezed his thighs, and *Scout* pranced forward.

Jewel waited until Marcus was a full horse length in front before she splashed the water on her face. Some splinter! Jewel let her breaths even out, concentrating on the canter of her horse and the tumble of the wildflowers. Her mother had been a chorus girl, she followed the music, the only thing that slowed her down was having a daughter with an infatuated Ranch Hand. Jewel knew her mother couldn't take her on the trail or the river. Jewel had never sought her out. Her Pa raised her, certain that one day Miss Georgia Jade McIntyre would return to claim her daughter and his heart. If she hadn't made the time for Jewel, then Jewel didn't have the time for her.

Jewel scrubbed the back of her hand across her eyes. Damn Marcus for bringing her up! The man was as stubborn as a mule! She hoped her wound would heal quickly now he had been so harsh. But as she watched Marcus's shoulders roll with the stroll of *Scout*, she realized his curt words did nothing. The shard was still wedged firmly in her chest. Only now the ache was double.

Marcus led them off the trail under a grove to rest. Marcus sat quietly under the thick sycamore branches, waiting for Calvin and Jewel to reach him. He kept his head down until she neared, for a moment he opened his lips, before closing them. He dismounted and came to her side, again his mouth twitched. This time he sighed. Jewel clambered onto the grass, her thighs burned as she stretched. She rubbed her buttocks to loosen the ache, only to find Marcus's hazel gaze targeting her movements.

As if the sun had been peeled back from the clouds, an idea dawned on Jewel. If Marcus was her splinter, then perhaps she was a burr in his side. Her laugh caught her by surprise and she clamped her hand over her mouth.

"So those other Rangers going to tell your Superior you've up and left?" Jewel asked.

Marcus handed Jewel some dried beef, while Calvin tipped his canteen over his head.

"Nope, they're heading south west now."

"Got the trail of the Turner Gang?" Jewel mocked only to gasp at no answer from Marcus. "Serious! What a guess!"

Marcus scratched his nose, "I never said that."

"You don't have to Kearby, you're a bad liar. I wonder what they're going to rob now, a train, a bank, maybe a stagecoach."

"It'd be hard to do with only half of them. Jessie Harkin, Cooper Brady and Benny Bolt are the ones they think they're tailing. Miles Garcia and his brother Nate hung in '74."

Calvin slicked back his hair and undid his top button, "What's them names you just said?"

Marcus repeated them and Jewel liked the way Calvin shifted under his stare.

"Which way are they headed did you say?" Calvin asked, tugging at his shirt collar.

"It's only rumors, south by south-west. And there's enough gold from their last robberies for them all to give it up. They don't need to hit another Train."

"There's n-no accounting for greed, Ranger Kearby." Calvin said flatly, "And you said so yourself, not a single gold bar has been spent."

"That we know of," Marcus put his hand out to Jewel and she handed over her canteen.

"Maybe they hid it? Loot like that would be hard to move when the whole country is looking for it." Jewel said.

Marcus snorted, "Possibly."

Marcus took his long-arm and wandered down to the nearby stream leaving Calvin and Jewel to rest in the shade. Jewel's lids felt heavy as the sun reached the zenith. She heard Calvin wander off to relieve himself.

She sat upright as she heard boots approaching, "I reckon we'll reach Cheyenne Bottom by nightfall. Then only two days till Dodge." Marcus said.

Jewel caught her sigh before it escaped. She chewed her bottom lip and nodded, "Sounds about right."

Hours passed on the trail until the sun slunk low into the fields, a mirage of shimmering silver appeared on the horizon. A thousand birds descended for the night, their squeaks and noises echoing into the cool dusk air. Marcus kept to the tiny strip of foliage that edged one side. Jewel staked out the horses, while Marcus started a fire. Her rump ached, her back tight and hands dry. She enjoyed the trail, the sights and sounds of nature at its rawest. What she didn't enjoy was the dust in her hair, the dirt under her fingernails and the constant feeling of sweat between her breasts. Odors of beans and beef with a hint of sweetness captivated her and she decided a bath could wait for now.

Marcus dished out their dinners, while Calvin moaned at every movement.

"Shhh!" Marcus said.

Across the darkening sky the sounds of wagon wheels and horses whispered to them. Marcus stood upright, straining to sight the travelers, to no avail. His fingers tightened around his long-arm.

"You wanna take the first w-watch?" Calvin whispered.

Marcus tilted his head, what had spooked the Carnival man now? He seemed full of bravado and now he jumped at every chirp. The sounds of children chatting and a dog baying cut through the air. From a distance, Jewel might look like another rancher, likely the family would keep their distance.

"I'll take a look after supper."

Jewel stretched out with a full belly, her saddle bags too comfortable under her weary head. She closed her eyes for a moment, the flames of the fire licking over her lashes.

Marcus watched Jewel's eyes close. He'd been harsh, too harsh. Yet it was the right thing. Why did he feel like he chewed coal? Marcus waited until the sounds of the night had consumed the sounds of the camp before he stole away into the darkness. He left Calvin with a pistol, as he crept through the river reeds trying to keep his rifle dry.

He neared the far side of the wagon without concern. He peered into the sleepy campsite. One hound snoozed on its owner's leg as the man sat upright at the fire, his rifle in one hand, the other propping up his lolling head. One youth slept on the other side, his cheeks bare, his limbs lanky. Another youth, this one a little older came wandering into the light of the fire. He rubbed at his prickling cheeks and sat down by his father. The interior of the wagon was dark, no doubt any woman-folk and the younger children inside. Marcus spent another few minutes confirming his initial assessment before slinking back to their camp.

"So?" Calvin whispered.

"A family wagon, nothing of interest."

"Good."

"The Turner Gang got you thinking?" Marcus joked.

Calvin gestured to his slumbering wife, her petite frame curled up in her swag, "Ain't you?"

Marcus nodded, "Always. They aren't the only ones running around tearing up the country-side."

"Oh yeah, some wear badges do they?"

Marcus cinched his jaw, but nodded all the same, "Besides, Jesse, Cooper, and Benny are nothing without the Turners themselves."

Calvin's gaze snapped to the fire, "There is no accounting for greed Marcus Kearby."

"That there's the truth, Hadley. I'll take the first watch, just in case."

Calvin yawned, "Sounds like a good'un." Calvin slumped down on his own saddle bags, his chin to the stars. Within seconds his snores ripped across the camp fire.

Marcus yawned himself. The Turners were heading south. After Dodge, he would be heading south. He would wire Abe when he got to Dodge and meet them near Dallas perhaps. Marcus ignored the redheaded temptress across the fire. If he got called into chasing the Turners maybe Marcus wouldn't have to return to Dew Springs. He picked up a twig and dug it under his fingernails just to feel something other than the slice in his chest. It was pointless, he had to return, just like he knew he had to leave Jewel.

Chapter 7

Marcus woke to the sounds of crickets and geese honking off in the distance and the rush of the breeze in the soft reeds. And of course Calvin's nasal orchestra. Marcus stretched his arms overhead and rolled over. A wave of ash coated his throat and his coughed his way upright, wiping his face and blinking through the debris. Calvin snuffled in his sleep. Marcus coughed again. He rose to his feet, squinting he saw Jewel's lumpy blankets and stumbled his way down to the river. Damn Calvin! He wiped at his eyes the tears struggled to remove the grit from his lids. His boots squished, his ankles suddenly cool and Marcus filled his cupped hands. The sweet water turned the ash to sludge, eventually soothing his eyes. Marcus tugged his shirt up and wiped and then sat back on his haunches to survey his surroundings.

He sat in a sandy gully that trickled further into the marshland, eventually colliding with the primary lake. The glassy surface rippled as a flock of geese took flight in the middle of the giant pond. Waterfowl rushed into the reeds and disappeared as the clouds paled slowly across the sky like a wolf retreating to its den. He thought of the Wagoneer's hound and how sooner or later it would be racing down to chase the birds.

A humming noise sent Marcus flat to his belly, his ears straining to place the sound. Lilting tones in rich soprano drifted down to Marcus's position, the lyrics came measured yet wandering; the unknown source distracted.

"Don't listen to the enticing words, Of the men who own droves and herds, For if you do, you'll rue the day, That you left your homes for the lone prairie."

Marcus crawled on elbows and knees further down his sheltered gully, the reeds thinning out as he neared the shoreline. Slowly rising until the singer fell into his crosshairs.

Jewel knelt along the shoreline, her curls all bunched to one side, as she brushed her locks in the sunlight. Jewel could sing? Why had he never heard her before?

Memories of his brothers teasing her, especially Whit, about every little thing that Jewel did flooded his mind. From how she tied a hitch, to how she raked a stall, even right down to how she carried a pale. Marcus was the only one she said, that had held his tongue. And he did, most of the time. He admonished his brothers only to have them change target and throw their barbs at him. The Spare Heir, with a soft spot for a cow-poke's bastard, had erupted into more fist fights than he could count. No wonder he chose to kick around with Cade, Shelly and Taylor instead of his brothers.

Marcus watched Jewel as she bunched her hair behind her neck, revealing her red gingham shirt was unbuttoned, and her dampened linen shift puckered at the front. Marcus buried his face into his hands, as his body betrayed him. He wished for the strength to resist but found his gaze returning to her position. With one hand in her hair, Jewel carefully replaced the brush into her silver case that sat beside her and selected a ribbon. In efficient movements, she tamed her unruly hair. Next she selected a glass vial and removed the stopper; gently she brought it to her finger and tipped it upside down. As she dabbed it along her neck, Marcus's throat constricted. He licked his lips and swallowed hard. Tenderly she dipped it between her breasts. Marcus's hands began to tremble. He should return to the fire, to Calvin; but what about the Wagoneer's and their hounds? It was a weak reason, but Marcus couldn't move. Jewel grabbed a cloth from the lid of her case and leaned forward to the water's edge.

A groan escaped Marcus's throat as her shirt rose, revealing her bare thighs. Marcus surveyed the greenery, her denims and boots rested a little way off.

Suddenly her, voice rang out,

"We buried him there on the lone prairie, Where the buzzards

fly and the wind blows free, Where rattlesnakes rattle, and the tumbleweeds, Blow across his grave on the lone prairie."

As Jewel brought the wet cloth between her thighs, Marcus pressed himself down into the cool water, closing his eyes against this visual onslaught, the pleasure wrangled every ounce of self-control he possessed.

Jewels lyrics carried on and Marcus slowly retreated. Would his dreams never be free of Jewel! He made it back to their camp without notice. He sat on his saddle bags, his elbows on top of his knees concentrating on Hadley's snores and not the thousand thoughts that raced through his mind.

Jewel marched up from the riverbank carrying her silver carryall and Marcus's pot she had washed and filled with water. When she saw Marcus Jewel halted. His eyes were alight as if he had just ran half a mile through Indian Territory, his face covered in ash and dust, his shirt front black and damp. His gaze met hers and for a moment she felt bare, exposed to the elements and somehow it was her fault. Did Marcus suffer from nightmares, memories of the some skirmish, or was it losing *Cutter* at Lost Valley? The scars on his body told more tales that Jewel was sure she wanted to hear.

"Are you alright Marcus, you look – out of sorts."

"Fine," he rasped.

"You should wash up at the lake, it'll make you feel better."

Marcus's body stiffened, "I might just do that," his words sounded like gravel sliding down a scree.

"I'll make you a coffee," She said but he was already gone.

Calvin threw his arms behind his head and propped himself upright, "What you got there?"

"Nothing that need concern you Calvin."

Calvin put a finger to the side of his nose and tapped it twice, "I understand."

She rolled her eyes and stuffed it into her saddle bags. Then she set about making a fresh pot of coffee.

The coffee had settled nicely by the time Marcus returned, his features had calmed. He stood behind his horse and shucked his shirt. Marcus caught Jewel's unashamed appreciation of his muscular frame. Well if she had to deal with the Marcus-splinter, she might as well enjoy the scenery. She frowned as his scars came into view. Jewel took them in one by one, the burn, judging by the size and location, and the spiderweb that joined it, the injury had been substantial to need stitches and cauterizing. She surmised the smaller ones were more likely knife slashes and possibly the one at his hip was a bullet wound. *Scout* shifted and blocked any further assessment.

Jewel held his gaze, his hazel eyes more like a red maple at sunset, "You got some decorations there," Jewel managed.

"Just a few," Marcus wandered back to the campfire, buttoning up his olive grey shirt and tucking it into his denims. Their fingertips connected as he took the coffee mug from Jewel. She froze.

Calvin stretched as he rose to his feet and let out more of a howl than a yawn as he stumbled down to the river.

Judging by the state she saw him in this morning, she thought better of asking Marcus about his scars.

"Do you miss Texas?" Jewel said surprised at the softness in her tone.

Marcus slowly sipped his coffee, "The sky is just as blue in Kansas, but –"

"It's just not the same."

Marcus hummed, "Yeah, maybe it's not Texas itself but more so the time. Things have changed from when we were - when I was running amok with Cade or taking Shelly home drunk, it's that time that I'll never get back."

"The time before everything got serious," Jewel smiled.

"I thought decisions would get easier the wiser I became," Marcus smirked.

Jewel wondered about her decisions, leaving Dew Springs was a personal challenge, Marcus would come for her and she would accept nothing less. When he didn't she joined Calvin's troupe to concentrate on her name and her future. The days were exciting, well at least at the start, but the nights were lonely. It hadn't taken long for Jewel to realize she couldn't live with an empty heart, even if Marcus didn't want to give her his. She fell for Calvin quickly, but it didn't take as long to realize her mistake.

She could have left then, could have filed for divorce. She decided that being Calvin Hadley's wife was 'safe'. She didn't have to put up with a drunkard or a cruel man, in fact she didn't have to put up with a husband at all. But it kept her and her heart safe from other men. Leaving Calvin had felt good, a decision all on her own, and yet here she sat on her way to meet his business partner, someone who she would again be relying on again to change her fate.

"I suppose not, but knowing more about you should help." Jewel sipped her coffee.

"Is that so?"

Jewel looked at Marcus, his lips were half curved up at the sides, "If you know what you're willing to sacrifice, what you're willing to compromise and what you're not, then the decision makes itself." She had compromised enough. She would use Bryce's brother in Dodge to get what she wanted, to hell with waiting around. Then she could farewell Marcus in Dodge once and for all.

"Wise words," Marcus hung his head and stared at the fire, his eyes unfocused, his brows dipped. Suddenly he stood upright, "If we ride hard today, we should make Garfield by nightfall."

Jewel tossed the remainder of her coffee, spurred on by Marcus's activity. He scooped up Calvin's saddle bags and slung them over his weary mount.

Rocio and *Scout* had held up fine on the trail, but Calvin's pony looked like it would appreciate a long quiet rest.

"If we do, it'll be only one more night you'll have to suffer my tedious company."

"I never said that," Jewel mumbled as she busied her own

belongings.

They travelled hard over the distance, stopping first at Great Bend and then at Pawnee Rock where Marcus checked the Post Office, before they continued to parallel the Arkansas River south-west.

Strands of clouds whispered across the pale blue sky, each brush stroke feather light, to dust the horizon in beautiful delicate strands. The heat simmered on Jewel's skin, beads of sweat pooled in all the wrong places and more than enough times she considered telling Marcus to halt so she could take a dip in the river that lay just across the fields. It would do no good, the Texas Ranger's magnificent jaw was set. His stubbornness would see them into Petersburg even if they arrived like a half sucked prune.

At Garfield, they got another chance to rest as Marcus surprised the Post Master with a telegram to Abe and Theo.

It was sunset when Jewel finally called it, "No more Marcus, I'm done in for the day. We're stopping here, before I shoot you in the back."

The sun had sent her mind to wander in all different directions. She led them off the trail, and *Rocio* quickened his pace as he sensed the river. Even Jewel thought she could taste the cool water on her throat. She stumbled off her horse as if swimming through mud. She dropped *Rocio*'s reins and scrambled down the river bank on her hands and feet. The water rushed down her face and dripped past her collar, closing her eyes she repeated the gesture until her body simmered instead of boiled. Beside her Calvin moaned, his knees creaked as he lowered himself to the water. She sat there for a while letting her temperature cool down. The clouds revolved from peach to lilac, the sun retreating across the fields, to slumber the night away.

By the time Jewel rallied herself up the slope, Marcus had set out a fire behind a gully, shielding them from the trail and she wandered over as she smelt the beef warming in the stew.

"One more mile and I would have shot you, twice." Jewel

said.

Marcus laughed, "You did good, it was a hard day today."

In more ways than one, Jewel thought. Tonight would be her last night under the stars with Marcus Kearby.

"Must be mighty keen to see the back end of me," Jewel said without thinking.

Marcus frowned as his neck heated, his avoided her gaze.

"That's not what I meant," she said, "Soon you won't have to worry about me."

Marcus lips parted as if to say something, but he must have thought better of it.

She picked up the spoon and stirred the stew.

"See you can cook," he grinned.

Jewel narrowed her eyes and pursed her lips, without saying a word, she dropped the spoon.

Marcus snorted, his grin split wide across his thick jaw and he shook his head, "Never change Jewel."

Calvin stumbled back up from the river, his shirt front wet, "Did you hear any news in Garfield from your friends? Any more bounties caught?"

Jewel leaned back on her elbows and crossed her ankles, the roses peeking out from underneath her dusty denims. She knew Calvin was angling for news of Lucky Chuck.

"They left a message that they reached Cottonwood Falls, they're sure it's Harkin, Brady and Bolt, they're tailing."

"Whacha think they d-doin'," Calvin said as he straightened his shirt collar.

"Hopefully leading Abe and Theo straight to the Turners."

Calvin rested his elbows on his knees, "Y-you reckon! I read the papers, they're just youngen's with guns."

Marcus nodded, "They are malicious, callous murderers. The Turners may have gone into hiding, but the other three still made a name for themselves carving through innocent people."

"Why haven't they been caught?"

"No-one can point a finger to them. If they do they end up

–" Marcus ran his finger underneath his whiskers.

"I heard they hang them from the -"

Marcus's gaze caught Calvin's and then Jewels. She knew Marcus would try to protect her from the worst of the world, but it was a wasted sentiment.

"Well not to worry about them, it ain't like they are headed this way." Jewel could taste the beef at the back of her throat, when would dinner be ready? Her stomach growled as if in protest of Marcus's delay.

Marcus gave the pot another stir while he pulled out a serve of dried biscuits. Jewel set out the bowls faster than she anticipated. Marcus grinned again.

"I'm hungry is all," She said.

"Well I'm just a tad bit thirsty," Calvin rustled into his saddlebags and slowly revealed a flask he undid the lid and grabbed one of Marcus's mugs. "I thought I'd thank the good Ranger here for seen us safely to Dodge City, and since it's our last night we could do with an after dinner favor."

The dark liquid splashed into the mug and Jewel's nose twitched with the scent of whiskey.

"I don't think -"

"Alright, alright, alright," Calvin hushed him, "If you take first watch, one won't hurt. And I'll have slept off mine by the time you wake me."

He poured another one for Jewel and she took the cup with aching fingers.

Calvin pushed his flask into Jewels outstretched mug and then clinked it with Marcus's, "To new futures and old friends."

Jewel watched the amber liquid glow with the light of the fire. She reached forward and Marcus slowly tapped her mug.

"New futures," Marcus said and knocked it back.

Jewel let the alcohol sizzle her tongue and scorch her throat. The warmth exploded in her chest and she held back her cough. She let Calvin pour her another, but didn't get to finish it, as the weight of her full belly pulled sleep down upon her.

Calvin wiped his hand down his face, the heat of the day had long past, yet his fingers coated in sweat. Gently, inch by inch, he pushed his hand into the soft wrappings, listening and watching in the thin crescent moon if the redhead sentry moved. He had made his decision before they left Cheyenne Bottoms that his time was limited. Hearing the Ranger's information had spurred Calvin into action. He spent the last few nights with Tanners chasing Turners around in his mind. Garrett Tanner wasn't who he said he was, he admitted that on the first day he'd met Calvin. Offered him gold. A fair amount if he hid his kid brother as 'Bryce' in his sharp shooter show. The boy couldn't shoot no more than Calvin could hold his pennies. Not to mention, Donnie, big and brutish Donnie had the unfortunate luck of Brady as his surname. The minute the Ranger hit Dodge City with Jewel the game was up. Either the Ranger killed him, or Gabriel Turner did.

It spurred Calvin into action. Marcus Kearby wouldn't turn Jewel in. Calvin wouldn't wait around to see Dodge, knowing all too well he would be dead as soon as he walked down Central Ave. No he would take his chances and head north and find his way to Colorado Springs. First, he needed money to build his new future without old friends. Besides, if Jewel handed over those guns in Dodge, Sheriff Bassett would lock her up without question. Surely it would be safer for Jewel, especially safer for Jewel, if Calvin alleviated her of her burden. She could slip right through Dodge and out the other side without raising suspicion.

His fingers struck silver. The cowgirl stirred and began to roll. Gently Calvin shifted her arm over to the Ranger who lay motionless beside her. Her head lolled onto his shoulder and Calvin seized his moment.

He retrieved the heavy silver box, the ornate roses emblazoned on the top. He thought better about opening it and instead, scrambled to the horse lines. He didn't dare touch the

Ranger's gelding or Jewel's. Both horses appeared indignant at the midnight disturbance, if he dared lay a hand on them he bet they would kick his teeth out. Instead he led his own dun a short distance away and then swung himself into the saddle. He stifled a wince as his sore rump lowered into the leather so soon. Calvin marked the road by the stars. He had spent enough nights on the river boats to navigate at night. Calvin sniffed the air. For the briefest moment, he thought he smelt cigar smoke. He put his head down and kicked the horse into a trot. Calvin Hadley always knew when to cut and run.

Donald Gary Brady the 3rd cracked his neck from side to side, as the moonlight splashed down on his shoulders. He had spent enough days trailing the damn Carnival Man and his lame pony that he needed a good bed and a better whore to feel all right with the world again. The lame pony had a right hind shoe with a crooked nail and had been easy enough to track up until Abilene. Then the man joined another party of three. Two horses with riders of their own.

He was a day behind them in Ellsworth and he didn't dally with the details. Hadley was one, silk trousers and slick hair. Another rider was a woman with flaming hair and a narrow waist. The last, a lawman from a piss-hole somewhere down in Texas. The chattering little bird Betsy couldn't keep her mouth shut and he didn't even have to put an iron to her.

He felt only hours behind them at Cheyenne. And then today, they must have flogged their horses to chase the devil. He sat back in his saddle and opened his tinder box. He struck his flint and let it burn. Carefully he pushed his cigar into the embers and drew deep. He snuffed the tinder box and inhaled slowly on the rich tobacco. Normally he would save his cigars for the end, especially when he had them on their knees begging. Then he felt a job well done and he could treat himself. Today had been especially hard and he decided to smoke it anyone. If he arrived in Dodge empty handed he would likely be the one with the circle burns etched on his own skin.

Donnie tapped his pocket. The Ranger's telegram replies might just save his skin. If he could get them to Gabriel and if they could crack the cryptic messages! He was sure two other Rangers were trailing his cousin and the others. Donnie's ears pricked as a horse neighed. Soundlessly he took himself off the saddle and ran a hand down the flank of his horse. A lone rider crouched low as his weary mount entered the trail. Donnie would bet his last dime it was the Carnival Man taking another dash for his life. Donnie didn't care. Gabriel needed Bryce's guns. If he had the right measure of this man, Calvin wouldn't leave loot like that behind, not in the hands of a woman and a Ranger. Donnie stubbed the end of his cigar on his boot heel. If Calvin had those guns, there might be time for celebration after all.

Chapter 8

"Jewel, Jewel honey wake up."

"No," Jewel mumbled against the warmth of solid muscle. She felt the urge to stretch her limbs and wrap them all the way around this slab of man, but it was no use. Marcus gently grabbed her elbow and brought her up, "I'm not making you breakfast." She felt Marcus chest rumble under her palm.

"No, come on."

Jewel groaned until she sat upright as Marcus rose to his feet and stoked the fire. She heard him stretch as he kicked something with his boot.

"Hadley?" he called.

Jewel slowly stretched her arms above her head. The sky was a deep sapphire blushing with tufts of dandelion as dawn had escaped them. The sun beamed down on her skin and she squinted, a bite already in its early morning rays. She regarded her dusty appearance, today would be hot and thanks to last night's whiskey, sweat beads already formed on her skin. She heard Marcus stride back, this time with speed. She turned to face him, his Stetson already back on his head.

"Hadley's gone."

"Who?"

Marcus cursed and Jewel rushed to her feet. She rubbed at her weary eyes until she counted only three horses. Calvin's tired dun was gone. As Marcus stormed over to the horses, an ache sliced through the middle of Jewels forehead and forced her to sit on her bags. Damn whiskey. What the devil was Calvin up to? Chasing her all the way out here and then taken off just before Dodge?

"What is it?"

"There goes my divorce." She said as she rubbed the temples on either side of her curls.

Marcus rubbed a hand down his face, "Pardon?"

"Not that it's any consequence to you, Marcus but soon as we got to Dodge, I was gonna march that man up to a Judge and have it sorted. He agreed and all, so why then did he -"

Jewel turned onto her knees and dug through her saddle bags. Past the linen, and her socks, past the frills of her underclothes, she felt Bryce's pistols. She pulled out the bundle and rested it on top. She shoved her hand into her belongings again coming up short.

Marcus's shadow fell over her form, "What is it?"

"Damn that man!" Jewel said as she turned to sit on her buttocks again, "Well I guess the jokes on him."

Marcus knelt down in front and grabbed her shoulders, "What's going on Jewel?"

Jewel gave him half a smile, "He stole my silver case, my hair brush and oils."

Marcus looked down into her lap where she curled her fingers around the real treasure, "What does Hadley want with that?"

Jewel undid the linen coverings and revealed the two silver pistols, "He was looking for these."

Marcus inhaled sharply. A vein at the side of his jaw twitched. With one hand he picked up the first pistol and read the inscription, "Josephine." His nostrils flared as his brows dipped. His lips rolled inwards as he spoke again, "Let me guess this is Selina."

Jewel gasped, her breath stolen from her lungs, "How did you -"

Marcus rose with Josephine still in his palm. He pulled a piece of paper from his pocket and threw it down in Jewels lap, "Because they are worth $1000 dollars, together with Miss Ruby Drawers."

Jewel unraveled the poster that landed in her lap, a caricature of her alias now revealed, the lines hastily scribbled and the edges rough and unflattering. The description just as bad, she was never blonde or busty and Bryce wasn't her lover. Her curls were there as was her narrow face. They got her cargo accurate as well, ...carrying two .38 Colt Navy Revolvers, 2 ½ inch barrels, Nickel plated, with mother of pearl grips inlaid with silver. One engraved with Josephine, the other engraved with Selina. Her reward an easy $1000.

"Is this some joke!" She marched over to Marcus who had stopped halfway to the horses. His back was to her, his shoulders broad, the veins on his neck twitched as she spoke, "Where did you get this?"

Marcus head turned half an inch, his eyes like pits of coal, his lips thin, "Abe and Theo gave it to me in Abilene."

"No," Jewel's tongue cleaved to the roof of her mouth, the whiskey fizzled through her head the liquor dissolving the wake of the fire that brewed in her belly. She overheard them talk about some whore who shot her lover. "We were never lovers," she said as the bile rise up her throat.

Marcus eyes focused on the horizon.

A wave of fury stirred with the whiskey in Jewel's gut, within seconds it evolved into a tornado of rage, "Its horseshit Marcus! Damn Calvin! I don't know what game he's playing at. I won those guns fair and square!"

Marcus pivoted, his eyes livid, his jaw cinched tight, "I asked if you were in trouble and you lied to me!" Again he turned his back on her.

Jewel reached out to touch his tensed shoulders, she regarded the olive fabric that puckered between his shoulder blades half wanting to punch him into believing her, the other half wanting to rest her spinning forehead against his bulk. She turned away as her words came out in a rush.

"I won those guns! I didn't shoot anybody. You have to believe me Marcus. Trust me, Calvin told me that Lucky Chuck killed Bryce, just before his brother came to town. Lucky Chuck's a mad bad gambler with an evil streak!" Jewel felt her words tumbled over one another, her voice strained in her throat, "Someone saw Lucky Chuck digging through his pockets! Calvin told me! Bryce's brother is in Dodge, there must be some mistake…..” Jewel took a few short sharp breaths, “Calvin…..” She cocked her head to one side, “Calvin….then why’d he come rushing out here?” She trailed off. The heat rushed up her abdomen and she swallowed hard. She stepped away from Marcus in case she ruined his boots. “He wanted to hand me in to Dodge…”

“Calvin set this up?”

Jewel nodded weakly, “You have to believe me,” she said as she scrambled through her belongings, eventually finding her canteen. She splashed her face with the water and took a long sip. “I swear Marcus Kearby on the grave of anyone you name, I’ll swear to it. I won those guns from Bryce. When I left he was alive. He had just cheated Lucky Chuck for the last time. When Calvin met us out here… oh that man!” Jewel’s veins heated and she swallowed again, “I’ll make him pay!” Jewel hiccupped and scrubbed her face. “He’s got what half a-nights distance on me? I’m going to find him and sort this out.”

Marcus shoulders squared, “Jewel!” he cut her off at the fire, his hands clasped onto her shoulders, “You’re not going anywhere….”

She shrugged off his grip, “You going to hand me in Ranger Kearby.”

He blocked her path, “Jewel.”

“I didn’t shoot anyone Marcus! Someone saw Lucky Chuck in Bryce’s pockets! You have to believe me!” She could hear her voice heightened and swallowed instead of continuing. Slowly she wound her fingers through his collar bone, “Marcus you have to believe me, I didn’t kill anyone.”

Marcus’s tone softened as did his gaze, where there had been pits of coal, now his eyes raked over her like torchlights in the distance, “I believe you Jewel. You’re hot headed and naïve.”

“Naïve!”

Marcus ignored her outrage, “But you’re not a murderer. You need to get to safety, to a Marshall or a Sheriff before someone else tries to claim that bounty and then we’ll sort this out."

"And what spend a month or more in a jailhouse while you sort paperwork!" Jewel rammed her elbow into his bulk; Marcus didn't flinch but instead stepped aside. "Don't try and do the right thing now. You go your way and I'll go mine, there's no need to say you even saw me, it's not your worry..."

Marcus grabbed her wrist, which brought her up short and within inches of his chest, "You are always ...." He inhaled slowly, "I'll take you to the Rangers myself and we'll get it sorted."

She snatched her wrist from his grip with ease, and put her hands on her hips, "What are you going to do arrest me?" Jewel snorted.

"I will if I have to." Marcus's measured words made her pause.

Jewel met his gaze, the sunlight highlighted the hard line of his cheeks. His unflinching glare and the way his hands hovered over his belt line drove a worm of doubt into Jewel's chest and serpent of fire into her blood stream.

She wanted to dare him and thought better of it, Marcus was stubborn, but unwaveringly honest, he would hand her in quicker than she could spell Mississippi. She wasn't going to hang for conspiracy to murder!

"I'm going after the one person who can fix this, Calvin Hadley and if you can find a loophole, Lawman you're welcome to follow along, if not I'll say my farewell and wish you peace Marcus Kearby. Either way I'm going."

Jewel looked to *Rocio* and then her empty hands. She would need her guns and her saddle bags before she went anywhere. She turned to find Marcus already stuffing her belongings into her saddle bags. She reached for the silver pistols only to have Marcus pull them out of reach.

"I'll hold these for now."

Jewel exhaled and stomped her foot, "Like Hell Marcus Kearby!"

"There'll be no argument Jewel." Marcus said.

Jewel cleared her throat ready with another string of curses.

Marcus smirked, "What it's not like your unarmed." He raised his chin to her ordinary gun belt.

Jewel puckered her lips. She picked it up and tightened it around her waist.

"We'll find Hadley, but I want your word Jewel, that if it goes to the dogs I'm taking you to the Rangers."

Jewel picked up his canteen as well as her own, "If you think you're handing me in for that reward."

"I didn't say handing you in, I said we'll find the Rangers and get it fixed."

Jewel considered her options. She should be thankful she had Marcus and wasn't still following Abe or Theo. She was lucky she never made it to Dodge City. She would have been forced to hand over those guns to the Marshall and Calvin would be counting his reward.

Jewel nodded, "Alright, but Calvin first."

Jewel dashed down to the water's edge, and splashed another wave over her face to smooth out her awry curls. She watched Marcus ready the horses, how much disgrace would she have brought on him if they'd been caught together? Fancy that a Texas Ranger aiding and abetting a murderer. He said they could go to the Rangers but knowing Marcus he would do the right thing no matter how difficult it was. Could she really trust him? Jewel straightened her red gingham shirt wishing she had time to bathe. They would find Calvin and wrangle it out of him, the reward and the divorce. As she neared the remnants of the fire, she picked up her poster. She always wanted her name to be a headline just not this way. Jewel dropped the poster into the fire and watched it heat and curl until the ashes disintegrated in the dirt.

Marcus kept his eyes on the dusty tracks with the bent nail, his anger subsiding at each mile they covered. Sometimes the trail dissipated in a paddock of wheat, the recent bent stems like a wake through the grasses, easily guiding Marcus to his quarry. Jewel naivety irritated him, she married Calvin who promised the world and delivered nothing. Then she managed to get mixed up in another lovers' poker quarrel that landed her in hot water. Well specifically *Ruby Drawers*. What a stage name! Marcus audibly groaned. Jewel shot him a disgusted look.

Calvin had a lot to answer for and by the time Marcus found him, it would take a good measure of his restraint to be professional and not pummel Calvin into dust. That's if Marcus found him soon. He picked up Calvin's tracks quick enough, so that didn't worry him. It was the sign of another follower that crisscrossed Calvin's path shortly after he left the trail that gave Marcus concern. A lone rider, who rode heavy in the saddle and stalked with experience. Marcus tapped the stock of the rifle at his thigh. If he put it across his lap, he might worry Jewel, so he left it.

"So it was Calvin's idea to call you Ruby Drawers?"

Jewel sighed, "He thought it was amusing. He already had his sharp shooter up front and I was supposed to be the damsel in distress. Pity his sharp shooter was always drunk. Winning those guns was easier than beating Bethany at the Cutting Festival."

"And this Bryce fellow -"

"He was Calvin's sharp shooter who was also a sore loser at poker. He would turn the table if the cards weren't in his favor. I guess, Lucky Chuck ran out of patience."

"And he -"

"We were never lovers Marcus." Jewel snapped. Her cheeks colored.

"Yet your husband chases you down to hand you in for killing a man who's not your lover?"

Jewel clicked her tongue, "I told you Lucky Chuck did the killing and then took off. And I don't know what Calvin was playing at, yet. He always worried more about his bank balance than he did anything else."

"He's obviously the jealous type."

Jewel let out a cold chuckle that made Marcus flinch, "Calvin jealous?"

Marcus wiped his forehead and reset his Stetson. The midday sun had peaked and now it bore down on them as they closed the distance. Calvin shouldn't be too far ahead of them, his bulk and his skill would see him being overridden easily. Marcus spied a divot ahead, lined by several trees, one larger than the other. For the untrained eye, the wheat field continued unbroken, but the way the tips altered from a sandy ocean to a dusty caramel told him a gully or irrigation channel was up ahead. *Rocio* and *Scout* both needed a break. Marcus felt his skin prickle as they neared, the day's heat had only intensified, the humidity sticking his shirt to his skin with not a cloud in sight. He slowed his mount as the small grove came closer into sight. The shadowy outline of something not natural caught his eye.

"Whoa Jewel." Marcus hissed.

"Huh?" Jewel mumbled as she reined in her blue roan.

"Up ahead," Marcus said, "Do you see that?"

The minute the words left his mouth Marcus wished them back. A slight breeze curled its way across the wheat fields until it struck the emerald leaves of the grove. The shadowed mass swung awkwardly outward, Calvin's bulk trussed up in an all too familiar sight.

"Calvin!" Jewel called and spurred into action.

"Jewel no!" Marcus hollered as he kicked his heels and *Scout* dove forward, his mount stretching to catch up to the deep grey horse as it rushed through the field. The air now still, the black swarm of flies had returned to their feast.

Jewel crossed the culvert before Marcus could stop her and dismounted in a single move as he pulled *Scout* to a standstill.

Jewel reached for a knife at her belt. Ignoring the scent of caking blood and spilled innards. She put the blade to the rope that hung above Calvin's neck. Their horses shifted uneasy, and the pack horse dun had drifted into the field, the stench filling their nostrils. Calvin's horse was nowhere to be seen.

A shiver of ice slid down Marcus's spine as he recognized the style of ligature and method of execution. He took Jewel's knife from her hand; her jerky movements sliced his palm. He gently pushed her aside and hacked at the ankle rope until Calvin's corpse splashed in the dirt.

Jewel froze her hands covered her mouth, her blue eyes filled to the brim with liquid, unblinking from the scene before her. The rope had been curled around Calvin's boots up over the branch and down around his neck, before the man had been gutted. Marcus had only seen it twice before. The infamous method had spread fear amongst those who knew and witnesses who refused to talk.

Slowly Marcus approached Jewel, "Jewel honey, its okay,"

Marcus pulled her into his embrace. She shuddered against his chest as he flicked the flies away from their faces. He pivoted on his heel to turn her eyes aside. He scanned the horizon for the briefest moment, his boots kicking the spilled contents of her personals case, the hair brush coated in blood, the oils cracked.

"Why?"

Marcus hackles on his neck rose and he turned back to the field of wheat. Along the culvert, the sound of a single hoof reached his ears.

"Mount up, now!"

Marcus whistled which brought all three horses to him. He scooped Jewel up into her saddle and smacked the gelding's rump before he leapt onto *Scout* and grabbed the pack horse's reins.

A single rider emerged through the wheat fields. His trail dusty jacket opened, a pistol fired.

A sting bit Marcus shoulder as he kicked *Scout's* flanks, his rifle twitched in his hands. Releasing the pack horse Marcus brought the rifle sights up just as the rider clambered up the bank and onto their side of the field. Marcus watched the blue roan gallop away with Jewel and calculated the strangers' trajectory. The rider didn't have to cross Marcus's path to reach her. Marcus fired a single shot. The rider ducked over his pommel and sped after Jewel.

All moisture evaporated from Marcus's lips as he dug into *Scout*. Abandoning the horses reins as the animals' training kicked in. Hooves thundered across the paddock as the sky rumbled above. The horizon darkened as the killer closed the distance. The field took another divot this time more trees sprouted along the river bank. A line of dark green beckoned from across the field as Jewel leaned low over her saddle. He hoped she saw it too and would head for cover. Marcus took a wider line hoping to intercept the rider as the culvert curled to the right. Suddenly the girl turned and fired, the man's bulk crouched again. Marcus heard her shouts to her mount as *Rocio* changed direction again.

Marcus spurred *Scout* forward, willing every tendon and every muscle to move faster and harder to reach Jewel. The rider slowed. His horse flagging and Marcus fired. The rider banked towards Marcus instead of Jewel. Marcus's sigh of relief was cut short as the rider stood in his stirrups. A shot rang out. The horse screeched and Jewel screamed as *Rocio* stumbled into the culvert. A roar erupted from Marcus's throat as *Scout* tore forward. The rider turned towards Marcus still standing in his stirrups.

Marcus licked his lips as he took his left heel out of his stirrup. He let out a sharp shrill chirp as he rose in his saddle. *Scout's* momentum kept him turning and Marcus barricaded himself on the horses' right flank. Standing in one stirrup, with his rifle high, Marcus fired.

The bullet landed. The Rider grunted and clutched at his pommel. His horse turned on a dime and sped across the field. Marcus resumed his seat and scooped up the reins. A crack split the air, another shot rang out. Jewel! Marcus yanked the reins as the rider drew further away.

Chapter 9

A sickening feeling swirled through Marcus as he rushed through the wheat. He dismounted when he found her. Jewel stood over *Rocio*, pistol in hand, the horse unmoving, the geldings front legs askew. Rivers of tears streamed through the dust that coated her face. Her hat was gone, her curls frizzled. *Scout* pawed at the dirt as Marcus clambered through the irrigation trench. He pulled her into his embrace, his own memories compounding her grief. He kissed her hair as lightening cracked overhead. Slowly Marcus took the pistol from Jewel's trembling hand and slid it back into her holster. Marcus raked his hands down her back and arms searching for any break. Relief flooded Marcus, thankful Jewel was all right. Well not entirely. She trembled against his chest and he pushed the curls back from her face. He dropped another kiss on her temple. Jewel still didn't move. The air prickled his skin as lightening again split the sky. Marcus couldn't ignore the darkening emerald clouds as the wind whipped through the fields. Marcus put two fingers passed his teeth and whistled.

"Jewel we need to find shelter."

Scout awkwardly strode down the edges of the culvert to his masters side. Marcus leaned Jewel back, her normal cornflower blue eyes were ringed in red and failed to focus. He cupped her cheek and a smear of his blood tainted her dusty skin. He pressed his lips gingerly to hers.

"Jewel honey, we've got to move."

Her fingers curled into his shirt only for a moment and then released. Marcus lifted her onto *Scout* and returned for her saddle bags before he swung himself up behind her. As they topped the culvert he spied the pack horse nervously prancing a little off to the side.

The clouds churned their ominous olive tint, sending

lightening through his veins as the wind picked up. Marcus surveyed the land and kicked *Scout* into action. It took him a moment longer to regather the pack horse before they could head north. The fields belonged to a farmer somewhere; hopefully they could find shelter before any funnels appeared.

Jewel's skin felt ice cold under his touch and Marcus hoped his warmth might dilute some of her shock. Marcus would work out later what Jewel and Calvin's connection was in all of this and why a part of Marcus, was glad their connection had severed. As they crossed another irrigation ditch, the gusts increased, buffering them to the side, a fork of lightening speared across the sky and seemed to awaken Jewel. She sat upright, her spine against his chest.

"There!" She pointed at the tiny white triangular that broke the horizon.

Marcus willed *Scout* forward as he felt the beasts energy lag. A two story house stuck up amongst the wheat like a sore tooth, the tiny yard fenced away from the barn, where a dark skinned woman stood with a bundle in her arm, her clothes plastered against her slender frame as she held open a hatch to a storm cellar several yards away. Marcus called out and the woman turned her head in his direction. Her arm shot out to a barn where the two stable doors jostled against their holdings.

Marcus glanced over his shoulder at the looming blackness, as a roar rolled through the air. The sound intensified, the raging winds howling through Marcus's ears, the lightening making the hair of his forearms stand on end. A low wall of dust seemed to spread across the horizon.

Jewel twisted around, her eyes wild, her lips thin, "Marcus!"

"Hold on," Marcus threw his arm around Jewels waist as *Scout* leapt over the boundary fence. He pulled the horse up short and Jewel scrambled down, falling onto her buttocks.

Marcus dismounted as Jewel snatched *Scout*'s reins. She snatched her saddle bags as Marcus grabbed a length of rope. His Stetson tumbled from his head and flapped into Jewel's chest, she tucked it under her arm.

"Get inside" he shouted as he tore across the distance. He glanced back to the cellar and watched Jewel dash inside. The farmer's wife's stricken face still visible from the stairs.

The gusts clawed at his clothes, as Marcus ran to the barn. The double stable doors battered against one another, the cross bar still in place. Marcus looped the rope around one end and stood well back. As he tugged the blasts of air did the rest. Timber cracked as hooves thundered the ground; four broncs pushed clear of the doors and leapt to safety. Marcus headed inside fumbling through the tumbled hay bales until he struck a boot.

The farmer was on his back, one arm across his head, Marcus put his palms on his chest, thankful to hear a groan.

"Come on," Marcus heaved the man to a sitting position, his eyes opened. "Up you get," He howled in the man's ear.

The farmer wiped his hand across his bleeding brow, "The shelter."

"Soon as you're ready," Marcus chuckled as he dragged the man clear of the shed.

His legs filled with lead, leaves whipped through the air stinging his face and neck. Marcus threw the farmers arm around his neck and stumbled forward. Each step strummed an ache through his bones and into his left shoulder. Marcus gritted his teeth.

Twenty yards. Fifteen. Ten.

The man was wiry yet solid, his weight bore down as the gusts pushed them sideways. Jewel's face appeared at the edge of the shutters, and Marcus inhaled deep. The last yards fell away as they closed the distance.

The musky odor of hard packed dirt and vegetables reached Marcus's nose and he sighed.

"Ira!" The woman shouted.

Jewel rushed forward and helped the couple down the stairs. Marcus watched Jewel make it past the second barrier door and then Marcus leaned outside and brought up the main shutter bringing the timber up to meet its mate. Marcus halted at the scenery.

The olive thunderheads had given way to violet ebony. The blustering howl dimmed, the monster voice fell silent. Suddenly a tendril shot out and touched the ground. Marcus let the timber slam. He pushed the heavy slat through the handles and rushed down the short dug down stairs to the secondary barrier. The farmer slammed the timber hatch behind him.

Darkness enveloped Marcus and for a moment he enjoyed the release. The roar had been muted only slightly. Jewel struck a match and lit a tiny lamp as the wife pulled a pale from under a shelf; Marcus took the woman's apron and wet it pushing it into the cut on the farmers head. He winced but smiled, his white teeth gleaming from his black beard.

"Thank you for letting us shelter with you," Marcus said, glad to see his Stetson on a dug in shelf loaded with root vegetables, "I'm Marcus."

The man took his palm and shook it, "Names Ira," he said as he slapped Marcus on the shoulder, "Thank you."

"What kinda man would I be if I left you out there?"

Ira smiled, "Besides, you gonna help me keep these closed."

Marcus nodded as he looked at the occupants of the shelter. Ira was probably five years older than himself with a thick crop of short hair on his head and a healthy beard on his cheeks. The woman who must be Ira's wife wore a simple farm dress, the hem frayed, the faded apron outline on her skirts. She stepped back and picked up a small bundle, holding it to her chest as she paced up and down the narrow aisle with a tiny infant in her arms. Two more children, both boys huddled at the other end, their backs against the dugout shelves, their tiny dark faces peering out at Jewel and Marcus.

"Slick as a whistle, but we'll do alright to keep the hinges on," Marcus shouted over the din. The shutters buffeted as if in agreeance. The main barricade would take the most of the damage; this second barrier had been cut further into the earth to protect the occupants if the gusts breached their defenses. Marcus sat with his back against the barricade, and saw his rifle out of reach. Jewel must have taken it from *Scout*.

Jewel crawled further into the shelter and took a seat on the floor beside the two whimpering boys. A squawk made Jewel jump and she laughed as a flock of ruffled chickens voiced their concern. One boy took the rooster into his lap and cuddled it. Jewel ran her hands down the back of the indignant bird as it put his head on the boys shoulder.

"He's a beauty," She said.

"He's not Billy." The boy said as he scrubbed the back of his hand against his eyes.

"Amos!" The wife hushed.

Jewel threw her arm around him. "Well I'm not Billy either, I'm Jewel, and thanks for your hospitality."

"Winnie" The woman nodded, and pointed to the smaller of the two boys, "Ezra," and then the baby, "Myra."

It took another moment for Ezra to sidle up to Jewel's ribs as Amos did and Jewel slung her arm around him as well. The reverberation thickened the air, as the shutters fluttered. Marcus threaded his forearm through the leather strap then through to the other. A bellow grew around them seemingly filling all the corners of the cellar, the baby's wail barely audible over the crash of thunder.

Marcus strained at a scratch against the exterior shutters. Debris, possibly a fence, hopefully not the farmers house had scraped the heavy boards. Marcus exhaled, the dust infiltrated his lungs as an ache throbbed in his left shoulder. He readjusted his grip as scratches now peppered the trembling timbers. Suddenly a yelp cut through the howl and Marcus stood up.

"You gotta dog?"

"Billy!" Both boys hollered, the rooster slumped in the dirt.

"Boys!" Ira farmer snapped.

Marcus lost the rest as he opened the secondary hatch,

"Shut them!"

The farmer grabbed his forearm to stop him but it was too late. Marcus dug into the dirt as he fumbled around in the pitchy half-light at the main shutter. He closed his eyes against the dust that gusted between the timber gaps, the darkness almost total. The scratches intensified and another yelp squealed against the roar. Marcus found the thick cross-bar. He wedged himself against one wall and heaved. The wood groaned as inch by inch it shifted. He pressed his back to the timber slats. The wind tore around his frame like tendrils of the devil pulling him to certain damnation. He slipped his arm through the gap, his fingers finding fur and he yanked. The animal scrambled down the stairs.

The shutters slapped against the frame, the hinges squealed in protest. Marcus replaced the cross bar and stumbled downwards, his bulk struck the second barricade. It creaked open and he stepped inside.

The hound rushed to his tiny masters, the chickens erupted into the air, the mother wailed, as the puppy leapt onto the arms of both boys. Jewel's laugh brought Marcus's gaze up as the dog found his way onto her lap, the three chickens and the rooster still berating the newcomer. A grin split Jewel's cheeks, her eyes suddenly heavy; her laughter desperate as the pain slowly surfaced through her façade. Jewel buried her face into the animals caramel neck.

Marcus sought air as his ribs ratcheted tighter, a spear of heat dug deep inside as he watched Jewel's tortured release. Within seconds her head was back up, her tears blended into her already messy cheeks. She exhaled slowly, her eyes catching Marcus's for the briefest moment. A smile, hesitated across her features, until she opened her mouth.

"When the storm breaks in its fury and the lightning's vivid flash, Makes you thank the Lord for shelter and for bed, Then it is he mounts his pony and away you see him dash, No protection but the hat upon his head."

Jewel's bold soprano voice seemed to slice through the

darkness, infecting every corner of their tiny shelter, the two boys sat upright and watched as Jewel sung away, her boots tapping in the dust.

Winnie's hum added to the chorus, as Jewel sung the trail ditty. The hound, more legs and ears than any muscle eventually settled, every now and then his snout would search for his feathered friends that clucked and bristled in the far corner. Ira's forehead stemmed and his eyes stayed focused.

Marcus reclined against the timber barrier, letting Jewel's voice wash over him. The energy that pumped through his system began to dissipate and a shadow of weariness lowered itself over his shoulders. His palm trembled, the skin rough and raw, his left shoulder ached, unable to lift it without wincing so he pulled it across his lap. The lantern light flickered as the monster loomed closer. Ira pulled a canteen from one shelf and handed it to Winnie who passed it to her boys, Jewel took a swig and handed it back until it found Marcus's hands. He took a quick sip, hoping *Scout* was safe.

"Do you know the Yellow Rose?" Winnie asked.

Jewel nodded and Marcus listened to the exterior shutters staccato compete with Jewel's next ballad. The dog howled until Amos shushed it, and Jewel let out another laugh, this time without dark tones. Marcus found himself unable to take his eyes off her. Jewel huddled with the others, her exquisite features smeared in dirt, her blue eyes sparkling and yet filled with sorrow. She was clever, brave and sweet with more than a little bit wild. She was supposed to be his. His Jewel.

The wind abated and Marcus didn't need to say anything as Ira held his hand up to his boys, "We wait."

The soft glow of the lantern made Marcus's lids heavy and he yawned. He could feel grit irritate his skin, the throb in his shoulder now replaced with icy shivers. He sat up and winced.

"You hurt?" Ira leaned into his shirt, the fabric tearing at the open wound.

"Leave it." Marcus hushed, listening as Jewel's song continued, "I think it's passed."

Ira cocked his head to one side. Marcus leaned forward and let Ira open the second shutter. The farmer clambered out the narrow gap. Timber groaned, Ira huffed but the darkness remained.

Slowly Marcus rose to his feet. He slipped sideways through one shutter until he reached the main hatch. Marcus pushed his back against the barrier and stretched his legs. Ira shoved his hands across the beams and dug his heels in. The wood cracked, something scraped across the front and the hatch flew open. Marcus stumbled and caught himself on one knee. Ira dragged him to his feet. Together they stood and surveyed the damage.

Trees and fencing pushed against one side of the barn, the earth flattened, crops torn from their trenches. Marcus patted Ira on the shoulder as they regarded the house, still standing, the porch coated in soil and leaves, the windows on the second floor shattered.

The Kansas sun slunk low sending shafts of violet and tangerine behind smoky thunderheads, their silken edges, now lined with gold as they drifted across the sky. "Everything worth saving was with me." Ira smiled as Winnie stumbled into the late afternoon light.

Marcus put two fingers between his lips and whistled a long sharp howl, "I'll help you find your horses."

The time listening to Jewel made Marcus even more certain of his decision. Calvin's body loomed on the edge of Ira's property, a killer on the loose. Marcus would check the trail to see how far the thug made it before dropping from his horse. Hopefully the twister got him.

"You need to rest," Ira said.

"You more than me," Marcus said, his eyes scanning the horizon for a lone pony. He let another whistle out.

"Nonsense it's the least we can do for saving ma life. Winnie?"

"Yes please stay, I'll fix you something to eat, once I find ma plates," Winnie wandered into the house pulling Jewel along with her and the two boys.

"Rest man, I appreciate all you done but you don't need to go running outta of here."

Marcus leaned closer to Ira's ear, "I left a dead man at the edge of your wheat field."

Ira ran his hand up to his head and winced, "Anyone ever tell you not to be so honest?"

Marcus dug into his pocket and pulled out his silver star, "I know this ain't Texas, but I'm not leaving him on your land or near your family."

Ira stumbled over to the barn and dug around until he pulled out a shovel, "While the grounds still soft. What about the girl?"

Marcus took the shovel, as *Scout* whinnied in the distance. Marcus watched the horse trot up to him. He threw a glance back towards the farm house.

"I'm coming back for the girl."

Jewel watched Marcus mount *Scout* from where she sat inside the living room of the farmhouse. Her chest compressed till it seemed not a single breath remained. *Rocio* was gone. Calvin too. For those dire moments in the shelter, before Marcus entered the barn, Jewel hadn't taken breath or even blinked. She knew Marcus was strong, dependable, loyal and honest. It was his inability to see his own danger that worried her. She saw Marcus chase down the lone rider, watched him open a stable filled with terrified horses, Marcus even opened their shelter for the lanky pup that now yipped at their heels.

Jewel picked up a broom and swept the shattered glass away from inside the lounge room which Winnie swept back and forth along the short porch, humming the Yellow Rose again, her hips swinging from side to side as she worked. And now Marcus rode off, in the aftermath of a twister to bury her conniving husband. Regardless of the hatchet man on the loose and his savagery inflicted, Marcus rode out to do what was right.

Jewel blinked away her tears. She couldn't close her eyes. The scene would replay in her head, the lulling swing of his body, the pungent odors and the flies. Jewel swallowed the flash of bile that climbed her throat and swept the broken glass along the bare timber floor.

And then *Rocio*. Jewel's hands trembled. Her ears filled with blood at the gunshot that tore open her heart. It seemed that lead sunk in her belly at the treacherous feelings that brewed. Marcus. *Rocio*. Calvin. What the devil was she going to do now? She had given her word to Marcus to go to the Rangers. Would Marcus hand her in? Jewel didn't want to think about it, she just wanted to see Marcus ride back over the horizon.

"You alright honey?" Winnie's palm came to rest on Jewel's back. She hadn't even heard the screen door open.

"I will be."

The woman was a few years older than Jewel, a head full of tight dark curls, and bright brown eyes ringed in thick lashes, "Your man will be back soon," She cooed.

"He ain't my man."

Winnie stepped back at Jewel's tone.

Jewel scrunched up her face and softened her words, "I'm sorry it's just been a long day."

"Nobody arguing with that," Winne sighed, "Well with that fire in your belly, it's only a matter a time 'till he is."

Jewel laughed and ran her fingertips across her lids, wiping them on her denims.

"We'll get this done and dinner fixed. Way to a man's heart is with a belly full o' chili beef." Winnie winked and walked back out to the porch.

"Thank you but I can't cook." Jewel could feel the tears well again.

Winnie sighed, "I see some of your trouble already." The woman swept another pile onto the grass, "I'lla do the cooking you finish sweeping, do your laundry if you need, and then go on back and get fixed up, ain't no man turn you down then."

Jewel laughed, "Thank you."

Jewel had missed her routine cleanse this morning, she hoped to feel right as rain after a bath and a change of clothes. The image of the strewn contents of her silver case spattered with blood popped into her mind. Marcus would definitely hand her in to the Rangers now. Whoever killed Calvin was most definitely after Jewel as well. Marcus being by her side was putting him in danger. She remember his reaction, she had seen his scars. Marcus would throw himself into wildfire if he thought it was the right thing to do. To hell with wanting the adventure Marcus owed her, she had brought this on him. If Marcus hadn't agreed to accompany her to Dodge, he would be on his way home to Dew Springs by now. If she got rid of those guns, then Marcus wouldn't have to hand her in. He would be free. Free from danger, free from her.

The two boys, Amos and Ezra, chased the dog into the house.

"Boys!" Winnie hollered and broke Jewel's revere.

"They are delightful."

"Only when they're sleeping" Winnie smirked.

Jewel listened to the boys' footsteps thunder overhead. The farm house wasn't large but larger than her father's shack back home. The front sitting room contained a small settee and two worn chairs, a basket of yarn and needles on the chair nearest the fireplace. The kitchen to the side had a long timber table and miss-matched chairs, children's scribblings marked the adjoining wall. The warmth of the house and the occupants tumbled through Jewel like a loose wheel on a cart, at odds with her somber mood. Marcus had a home to go to. He had his Mama and his Pa waiting for him. By the time the last glass shard was collected Jewel had made up her mind.

Chapter 10

Jewel pulled on Winnie's clean dress, the woman was tall and slender, so the dress fell tight around Jewel's hips and long around her ankles. It was a delightful dress, cream with tiny blue flowers across the sleeves, thin enough to stay cool and no fluffy skirts to trip over her boots. Winnie had pointed her to the tub and rack and Jewel retrieved Marcus saddle bags from the cellar.

Once Jewel was back on the porch she opened the contents, not surprised to see Bryce's guns still wrapped in their package. Her fingers caught on an old cigar box. Peeling back the lid Jewel found a stack of papers and letters from home. She recognized Mrs Kearby's hand writing and shut the lid.

Jewel spent the next few hours grinding the trail dust out of her clothes and had done a better than average attempt at washing Marcus's as well all the while, the scents of the man who should have been hers, infiltrated her senses. Winnie was certain their clothes would be dry by morning in this heat.

The sun had turned the remaining clouds into cherry coated swirls, when Jewel saw a rider on the horizon. His boots and denims coated in mud halfway up his knees, his shoulders slumped, sweat and blood staining his shirt. Marcus towed a string of two horses behind him which Ira grabbed by the reins and led away to the barn. Marcus stumbled down from *Scout* and Jewel took the reins.

"Are you alright?"

Marcus took a moment to stand upright and nodded, "I'll be fine in a minute."

Jewel ducked under the horses' neck to take a look for herself. Marcus's eyes were etched with lines, his lips thin and his cheeks hollow. His olive shirt splotched with dried blood.

"Nice dress," he squinted his eyes towards the line, "Are

those my clothes?"

"You can thank me later, right now Winnie has a bowl of chill beef waiting for you." Jewel led *Scout* by the reins only to see Marcus stumble, "No you're not alright."

Ira returned and threw Marcus's arm around his neck, "He was hurt before I can't see he'd be gettin' any better outta there."

Marcus protested as Ira dragged him to the porch and inside to the lonely settee now free of glass. Marcus landed with a harrumph. Jewel put her hand on his shoulder only to have the stained fabric dampen, and her fingers slick with blood.

"Marcus, your shoulder!"

"I'm fine!"

"Don't you mess this dress!" Jewel snapped as she unbuttoned his shirt and pushed the cotton back revealing a piece as wide as her finger missing from his skin.

"It's a graze, but you've bled out a fair bit." Jewel said.

"Scar tissue, it'll be fine." Marcus growled.

"Nonsense! Hold this" Winnie had appeared from the kitchen and handed Jewel a clean cloth. "I'lla fill the tub, Ira get his boots."

"Serious?"

"Nothing kills quicker than infection Mister!" Winnie huffed.

Within seconds Ira had snatched Marcus's boots and had him up and walking towards the bathroom. Marcus stepped away from Ira and used his other shoulder to support his weight.

"You scrub that wound good 'n clean Mister or I'll send Jewel in there with a washer 'n pair o' tweezers!"

Marcus just groaned and shut the door.

Winnie took Jewel to the kitchen and passed her a bottle of rubbing alcohol and more clean cloths. She found a bandage and laid it out on a tray with a needle and thread. Jewel's eyes flew wide.

"I didn't see much, hopefully it don't need stitching. You

make sure it's good 'n clean and pat it dry, then wrap it."

Jewel followed Winnie out the main room as she set the tray on the settee. The older woman opened her mouth but Ira had already returned with a set of his own clean clothes.

Jewel paced nervously in the main room, her fingers trembling, she could barely stop the bloody images of Calvin swinging in the breeze than she could face a wounded Marcus. Damn the man for being so honorable. And brave. And compassionate. He could have left Calvin for the coyotes.

Winnie set both boys at the table and served out two bowls of steaming chill beef and bread. Jewel could smell the flavors wafting through the house, stirring her hunger. She looked down at the tray of bandages. Maybe it was good she hadn't eaten yet. Jewel straightened her shoulders, the dress revealing more of her chest that she cared to. Who was she kidding? Jewel had spent the last few years in Delano fixing glassings and shootings and stabbings and broken noses. A shoulder graze was nothing. Ira banged on the door and Marcus grumbled in reply. Winnie lit the lamps and put two on the tiny table near the settee.

Marcus staggered out in the lounge room, a pair of fresh denims long around his ankles but tight around his thighs, and nothing else. Jewel tried to control her gaze, as it lingered from his grizzled jaw down his throat, cross crossing the scars that decorated his sculpted form. Jewel resisted the urge to lick her lips at the indents of muscles that lined his rib cage and the sinister curves that ran inwards from his hip down into his unbuttoned denims. Marcus carried a spare shirt in his left hand, his right holding the bandage to his left shoulder.

"Sit down."

"So it's cowgirl to gunslinger and now nurse."

"Sit down or it'll be back to gunslinger Marcus Kearby." Jewel felt the color return to her cheeks.

Marcus sat with his back not resting against the settee, the cloth at his shoulder now more pink than lemon. Ira came in with a knife and a bottle of whiskey.

Marcus snorted as Jewel took a seat beside him, "I thought you never miss."

"I fired from horseback running down a gully I'd like to have seen you do better."

Those last few moments of *Rocio*'s life replayed in her head. Wait Marcus had shot from horseback and struck the killer, "You had a rifle."

Marcus snorted, "I taught you to be better."

"*Scout* wasn't moving."

Marcus threw his hands up in surrender, "I'd have liked to seen you shoot in a show -" Marcus stopped short as Jewel pealed back the cloth. He didn't wince as she doused a wad in alcohol and wiped. She looked up at him, his eyes ringed in gold in the lamp light.

Calvin. He didn't want to mention Calvin she thought.

"Well it's a little too late for that," Jewel managed, thumbing the rough edges, the flesh underneath raw, yet shallow.

"Are you alright?"

"Me?" Jewel smiled, "I've cleaned up my fair share of bar room brawls." She threaded the needle and bit her bottom lip. Loops. It was all just one big loop if she remembered correctly.

"I mean -"

"Shhh!" Jewel hushed as she dug the needle into his skin.

Marcus inhaled sharply and she pushed her thumb downwards to ease the tiny instruments passing. Marcus exhaled, his breath heating down her neck. She moved the lamp closer and pulled her leg up under her knee, fluffing her skirt into her lap as she did so. She leaned forward and pushed the point through again. Within moments she reached the end and tied a knot. Jewel picked up the knife and severed the end.

"I'll be fine Marcus" Jewel said. She picked up a fresh wad of fabric and applied it to the wound. Then she wound the bandage around his thick bicep and tucked the edges in. "Thank you for burying him."

"I took him to the road side and placed a marker. I never wanted any harm to come to Calvin."

"I suppose you mean I don't have to front a Judge in Dodge," Jewel moved on to bandaging his hand.

Marcus clicked his tongue and sighed, "I mean, what he got you mixed up in..." Marcus shook his head.

Jewel sniffed, she could feel the tears welling. When she thought of Calvin, she thought of *Rocio*. "I know what you mean Marcus."

"He was your husband."

"For a day and a night," Jewel groaned. She spied the whiskey bottle and decided to wipe her hands and have a swig rather than explain. She offered the bottle to Marcus who declined, "It's just that..." Her bottom lip trembled. She held her breath hoping to stem the liquid. She dipped her head.

Marcus threw his wounded arm around her shoulders, "I should just say I'm sorry, Jewel. I'm sorry for your loss."

Jewel let her forehead rest on his bare chest; her fingers instinctively caressed his solid form, his sparse patch of hair tickling her palm. Jewel's stomach clenched at the raw pain she felt, the treacherous emotions that confused her grief. Jewel looked up, his eyes blazed, like sunset through the bottle of whisky.

"I'm more upset about the horse."

Marcus slowly stroked his knuckles down her forearm to her elbow and back to her wrist, sending ripples to dance through her veins. Marcus brought her closer; his thumb traced the line of her spine under the thin fabric spreading more ripples, this time between her thighs.

"I know that feeling."

"You do? I feel so wretched about it," Jewel rested her cheek against his collar bone.

"I lost two men, when *Cutter* was taken down. I can't remember their faces, or how they fell, only the sound he made."

Jewel sat up and put her fingers to his lips, "Don't."

Marcus eyes targeted her lips. Her fingers tumbled down to his chin and slid along his jaw. Gently he brought her hand down, "Jewel tomorrow -"

"Don't you say the Rangers!" she sat back.

"You gave me your word."

Jewel stood upright and stepped to move past him, his arms curled around her waist and brought her downwards, they tangled in her hemline as Jewel squirmed across his lap. All manner of hard ridges scored flames across her body and she gasped. Marcus winced and Jewel surrendered. She scrambled backwards, her shoulder blades on the settee, his hands on her wrists. With his elbow he trapped her legs together across his lap, her skirt aiding in his defense, "Listen."

"You're going to hand me in! You'll only do that one way Marcus Kearby!"

Marcus leaned forward, his weight restricted any further movement, "I drag you, kicking and screaming?"

Jewel gathered her breathes, "Yes, that's right!"

"You're already in my custody Jewel it's just whether I put you in cuffs."

Again this overwhelming sense to dare Marcus to try and do exactly that sprung into her mind. Damn Calvin for dying!

"Listen Jewel, Calvin is dead."

"I'll sell those guns and be done with all of this!"

Marcus released her hands, "Selling those guns ain't gonna end this. Do you know who killed Calvin? Because I do."

Jewel sat up and smoothed her curls back from her forehead. She left her knees across Marcus's lap and pretended to straighten her skirts, savoring the heat his arm brought to her calves, "Who?"

Marcus reclined, his hand came to rest below her knee as his other hand ran down his weary face, "The Turner Gang."

"Gang? I saw one rider."

"Yes, and no-one kills like the Turners. The hangman's over his neck, the Bourchier knot at his hands, the double constrictor on his ankles and the taut-line hitch over the lot. You saw when I cut that one rope how it unraveled the series of knots. But whilst alive, the more Calvin struggled the more it tightened."

"Stop!"

"There's been a few mimics, copycats, easy to spot if the knots aren't in the right sequence or the right amount. I checked the ropes Jewel. A member of the Turner Gang killed Calvin."

Jewel took another swig of the whiskey.

"Question is why?"

"I don't understand."

"Who were you supposed to meet in Dodge?" His voice was clinical, probing and efficient.

"Garrett Tanner, Bryce's older brother, he said," She wiped the back of her hand across her trembling lips, "Bryce said, that he had a job, that our talents were wasted on Cowtown crowds" She hiccupped.

Marcus slowly rose and stumbled his way to his saddle bags heaped in the corner. She had emptied them of their dirty clothes earlier. He pulled out a small cigar box and she was suddenly glad she hadn't disturbed the contents. Marcus opened the lid to a stash of aging papers, until he found the one he wanted. Marcus shoved it into Jewel's hands.

She pulled her legs back and allowed Marcus to regain his seat on the settee. She spread the paper between her fingers, until two sketches became clear, she read aloud, "Gabriel Turner and his brother Francis 'Baby-face' Turner." She let the paper re-scroll and snatched the whiskey bottle. She put it to her lips, only to have it taken away.

"You can't be sure."

"I am, you know I am. Look again. You heard Calvin getting twitchy when I mentioned the Turners, he knew they were closing in. He up and left." Marcus exhaled, "You gave me your word Jewel, the Rangers."

She pushed a palm onto his chest and stood upright, her thighs now between his thighs, "Fine, Ranger Kearby, but I choose the Rangers."

"You can't -"

"This is my mess Marcus, I'm glad for your help, but if we're going to the Rangers it's got to people you trust."

"Fine."

Jewel wandered out to the porch and down across the fields, until she reached the raised side of the storm shelter. The sun had finally disappeared and now eerie post storm clarity descended across the fields. Calvin was dead. *Rocio* as well. And now if she didn't accept Marcus's offer he might be too. The stars slowly rose from their daytime slumber, shy at first and then glistening beyond belief across the ebony. Fearless in numbers perhaps, she mused. Marcus was fearless and alone. He would choose the law over her and she should best remember that. That is if the Turners didn't catch them first.

She chuckled a little, Bryce's name was Francis! Well no respectable gunslinger would quake in the face of a 'Francis'. She wondered if he had a proper burial, probably didn't deserve it, judging by Marcus's tales. And Calvin? Did he know Bryce was part of the Turner Gang? Something about the way he deferred to Bryce's drunken decisions, gave in to his wild whims suggested he knew something. Calvin had probably taken a healthy buck to hide Bryce for his brother. It hadn't brought Calvin any peace. His death was not her doing. She needed to remember that.

But now Marcus was in the firing line. Jewel wouldn't have it. She would see Marcus back to his Rangers and find a way to make it right. She took another sip. Calvin said Lucky Chuck was heading to Indian Territory. Could Jewel cross the border and hunt for Chuck on her own? Jewel was good at running. She might have to do just that. Sell those guns and pay a gunslinger to join her. She wandered back inside.

The scents of beef rolled over Jewel as she made it through the screen door. She straightened her dress, well Winnie's dress and sat down at the table. Marcus sat to one side, wafts of steam rising off his bowl, his spoon already soiled. Marcus watched Jewel as she accepted a fresh bowl from Winnie. Marcus dug in again when she did. The stew scalded her tongue as the chili seared her throat.

"Good chili," Jewel nodded, her nostrils widening, her eyes watering.

"And you Marcus?" Ira asked.

"Marcus loves chili," Jewel said.

"I do," He took another spoonful, "Despite what some people say, I don't mind a little bit of flavor to my otherwise tedious days."

Ira laughed, "That's the secret of it," he winked.

Winnie rolled her eyes.

"We'll be heading off tomorrow, where's the closest post office?"

"Petersburg be ta one," he pointed to the south, "I'll ride out with you and see if I can't find those other two nags."

"Sorry Ira, I didn't find more."

"Nonsense, two is better than none," Ira lowered his voice, "You've done enough already."

Jewel persevered through Winnie's chili, until her bowl was clean. Jewel did the dishes enjoying the time chatting with Winnie about their exit from Kentucky, their new start in Kansas and her relatives in Graham County. Jewel listened to the boys plead with their Pa for a later bedtime, to let the pup Billy sleep inside and whether or not Marcus was a real Texas Ranger.

Winnie moved the boys into her bed for the night despite Jewel's protests. The older woman was even so bold as to offer the bottom bunk to Marcus. Jewel tried not to look so disappointed when he declined, instead chucking a pillow on the settee, mumbling something about keeping watch.

It took a single moment for Jewel's head to hit the linen before her eyes closed.

The rooster crowed a glorious song as Jewel sat bolt upright in the bunk. She spun to the side to the see the rooster sitting on the window sill, his chest gleaming in ebony and gold. He clucked as Jewel's pillow forced him from the ledge, a spray of feathers the only evidence of her crime. Billy bayed a long low bark and the rooster clucked again.

After bacon and eggs, Jewel wriggled into her clean clothes, enjoying the comfort of fresh denim and her navy gingham shirt. Marcus stood at the end of the porch, coffee in hand, hat on head, inspecting his clothes. This morning he had his caramel colored shirt on, highlighting the tint of his eyes.

"Is it up to your standards Kearby?" She asked.

Marcus nodded, "From nurse to washer woman, I like it, soon you'll be cooking up a storm."

Jewel snorted and stood by his side, "I never said that."

Marcus offered her his coffee cup and she took a tentative sip, "So that's what it's supposed to taste like."

Marcus laughed and lines around his eyes appeared; his teeth bright white in a beard of black, "It really is something without the grit."

Jewel handed him back his cup, "Don't get used to it." With her thumb she gently grabbed his dimpled chin, "You need a shave Kearby. You're looking way too notorious."

"That's what you get for running around with Delano outlaws." Marcus winked.

A chord strummed in Jewel's chest at his cheeky expression. It seemed too easy, too relaxed, they could have been standing on the Crooked K ranch, any minute his Mama would raise an eyebrow and make some excuse or his Pa would blatantly shout some warning about "pursuits of folly", anything to turn Marcus aside, to save their youngest son from the Ranch Hand's Bastard, because that girl was trouble. Now look what she had gotten him mixed up in.

Marcus's brows dipped, "I didn't mean to make light of it, we'll get it fixed you have my word."

Jewel sighed. She didn't want to think of the alternative, "Yes and what an adventure to write home about." She added her own wink and stepped into the early morning sunlight.

Chapter 11

Jewel sat high atop the dun pack horse, as they rode into Petersburg. A street sign had been erected on the street, "Midway" and the distance of 1561 miles either side to New York and San Francisco. As they dismounted, Jewel pointed to the post office and the lettering over the door stating "Kinsley".

"You sure you know where you are Ranger Kearby," Jewel joked.

Marcus greeted the postmaster who cleared up the confusion, "Renamed in January in '74",

Marcus nodded, "Seems there's been a lot of name changes in January '74."

Jewel narrowed her eyes, "I'll head over to the store."

Marcus caught her by the waist, "No you don't, you stay right here."

The thin man behind the counter raised his brows, his glasses slid down his hooked nose a bit but he held his tongue.

"Howdy, I need a telegram, please." Marcus continued.

Jewel harrumphed and sat down on the tiny stool against the wall. She listened as he sent off a coded message to Theo and Abe, hoping to catch them somewhere outside Cottonwood Falls. Jewel's ears pricked up when she heard him mention the Sheriff.

"Thomas Wiley, he'll be over at his office."

"Thank you," Marcus bid the man farewell and it wasn't until they strode across the street, that Marcus answered her raised eyebrows, "I don't think it's wise to let you out of my sight Jewel."

"And the Sheriff?"

"If the Turners are heading this way, I have a right to warn them." Marcus sidestepped into the General Store and surveyed it briefly, "Stay here."

112

Jewel watched him march into the office next door, his words trickled down the boardwalk and into the open windows of the trading post.

"Texas Ranger Kearby,"

Jewel couldn't hear the Sheriff's words but Marcus laughed at his response.

"Business. A member of the Turner Gang killed a fellow from Delano just outside the Anderson Farm. I've buried him near the road and set a marker."

Jewel held her breath. The woman behind the store counter peered at Jewel through the shelves. Her hair was in a bun and her lips lined with age. Jewel smiled as if to appease the woman she wasn't thieving. The woman raised a dark eyebrow and continued tying a package with twine.

"I'm afraid so." Marcus said.

She heard a scrape of chairs and decided to walk around the shelves and take a look. The store smelt of spices and oils and leather. All manner of things lined the walls, a cabinet of sweets caught her eye. She rummaged in her pockets for some coins and decided to buy two of the wax paper treats.

"Will there be anything else, dear?"

Jewel regarded the perfumes and oils behind the counter, she spied a hair brush and comb set, even tooth powder and a bone brush. She calculated the rest of her coins and decided the tooth powder and bone brush were more important.

Jewel counted out the quarters and grabbed her purchases, "What time is the next train?"

"Ten dear," the woman said.

"Thanks, ah any boarding houses or the like in town?"

The woman behind the counter dropped the coins, "Ah the Roses Hook" she stammered as she pointed to the left.

"Thanks," Jewel turned on her heel, convinced it was an omen. She followed the boardwalk as directed until the two story dwelling came into town. Jewel counted her coins hoping someone inside might lend her a hand.

Marcus stood at the counter of the General Store, his palms splayed across the bench, "And after she bought them?"

"She asked about the train, and then, um and then the Boarding House." The woman quivered.

"And which way would that be?"

The woman nodded and pointed out the door. Marcus sighed, he had left Jewel for no more than five minutes and she had run again. Marcus made it to the front door of the white washed two story building before a Dove greeted him. The front picket fence leaned heavily forward, held up with the scrawniest rose bush Marcus had ever seen. The Dove stood in the arched doorway, hands on hips.

"She said you'd be around quick as sticks"

Marcus tipped his head and leaned one boot on the bottom step, "What else did she say?"

"She'll be finished soon."

Marcus tucked his hands into his belt and climbed the stairs until he stood over Jewels messenger. A Dove with a mess of blonde curls on her head smelt of lilies and ginger, kinked her hips and sent her breasts forward, "You sure you don't wanna stay down here, we'll keep you company?"

"Where?"

"Out back in the laundry."

Marcus cleared his throat. When he got a hold of Jewel he would shake the nonsense out of her! What the Hell was she doing in a Boarding House laundry? Marcus had meant to compliment her on doing his washing and now he knew why. The woman washed like she was cleaning Solomon's sins and then some. Jewel always looked impeccable and fresh despite the trail dust, memories of her intricate and intimate bath routine at Cheyenne Bottoms popped into his mind. Marcus steeled himself with irritation at her flippant attitude, which drove away his wicked thoughts. Marcus thought of his thickening beard and how its unruliness would irk Jewel. He smiled.

Marcus wandered down the narrow hallway until he reached the screen door at the back, he peeled it back and stepped in the alley behind the boarding house. At the near end, the street opened up to the plain grass fields that rolled towards the outskirts of town. A line of linen flapped in the breeze, Chinese fabric, mixed with bright purple silks spliced between the calico. To one side clung a steel tub, with Jewels head dipped in it.

"Lend us a hand will ya?"

He walked over to the sink only to have Jewel lift her head and flick water from his belt line up to his collar. Her whole hair was black.

"What the Devil are you doing?"

"Language Marcus!" Jewel joked. Someone unseen giggled. "What's it look like Kearby, I'm dying my hair."

Marcus picked up the bottle and read the ingredients. Surprised that Jewel might be onto something. "Is this permanent?" He would hate to see the end of her ginger curls.

Jewel rubbed her fingers through her blackened ringlets, "Sheena reckons it'll fade after a few washes, but I can keep the bottle. Have I got it all?"

Marcus replaced the bottle on the tar coated sink and stepped closer to Jewel. He put his hands up to her hair and ran his finger and thumb through her thick strands. As he massaged the water through the oily coal mixture, more color ran down his hands to his elbow.

"Dip your head again."

She obeyed and he slowly poured more water over her now ebony curls. The wanted poster said strawberry blonde and her alias was Ruby, who knew what Calvin had actually told Gabriel Turner. He had harbored Francis Turner so Calvin was already as crooked as a dog's hind leg to Marcus.

Jewel's hip came to rest against his and Marcus worked the dye through her hair, the murky water running down the sinkhole and splashing onto the dirt. His fingers caressed her neck and Marcus heard Jewel moan. The fire that Marcus had only just tempered started to reignite. He stepped back and Jewel straightened up. Streaks of grey wound from her forehead past her ears, down on to her throat quickly disappearing into her collar. Marcus grabbed a towel and dabbed at the trickles, soaking them up with the soft fabric. Jewel leaned against the sink, her eyes closed as Marcus gently wiped. His forearm brushed against her breasts.

His breath quickened as the energy ran into his finger-tips. Jewel's eyes opened, a bright cornflower blue with damp lashes.

Jewel's lips pursed as her palm ran up to his jaw, "Maybe you should keep this Marcus, it makes you look wilder than an acre of snakes."

Marcus cleared his throat and gently pushed her hand away. Why did doing the right thing suddenly hurt? Marcus wanted to kiss Jewel then and there, take her lips and anything else she would offer. He wanted to wrap her legs around his hips and lose himself in this woman. His Jewel, his girl. But nothing good would come of it.

"Come on, I've got to get *Scout* and the brown ready for the rail."

The sinister realization that Marcus was the leach preying on her grief worked its way under his skin. By her own admission Jewel was grieving about *Rocio*. Marcus should hand her in, just to keep her safe. Sort the paperwork of getting Bryce Tanner recognized as Francis Turner and Jewel might even end up with a reward. Marcus shouldn't involve Abe and Theo but if he could protect Jewel without locking her up, he would. Marcus couldn't imagine the sunflower that was Jewel locked away in one of those places. She was all light and noise and energy. It would ruin her.

Marcus grabbed the bottle of charcoal tint while Jewel rubbed the rest of her hair as dry as she could, a frown creasing the freckles across her petite face.

Jewel sighed, "You as exciting as a mashed potato sandwich sometimes."

"I like mashed potato," Marcus replied with a twist of his lips.

Jewel groaned. She rung the towel to the end of its life through her hands and hung it on the line. She marched back through the boarding house thanking Sheena on the way.

The Doves said farewell to Marcus in as much cooing and giggles as if he was a fox who had run through the hen house.

Marcus led them to the Depot, and pulled a wad of cash from his pocket. He bought their tickets to Emporia. He had hoped to catch Theo and Abe at the junction. Hopefully they didn't think with their wallets and try to hand Jewel in. Jewel stood to one side, her eyes tracing the line of the rail upwards, her head cocked to one side, her bottom lip rolled inwards. She turned to face him and smiled.

Marcus smiled back, he knew the tale too well, if a Texas's girl smiling she's about to do something crazy.

When the train arrived Marcus loaded both horses in the livestock section before finding Jewel in the passenger carriage. He had paid for a booth with a sliding door and blinds. The trip would take six hours given the station stoppages and Marcus wouldn't risk discovery in the main carriage.

Jewel had already put her bags up in the overhead shelf. She sat with her back against the brown leather bench, and her rose embroidered boots resting on the opposite one. Her hands were under her chin as she peered out the double hung window. Her dark curls more than a little startling, now braided down her back.

Marcus ran his gaze over her profile, her peach lips and sun-kissed cheeks. As if the sun had delivered the perfect Texas rose after a storm, Marcus recognized what he missed. Jewel was beautiful, more than beautiful than Marcus had acknowledged, now that her coloring had altered. It was if the lamp had been snuffed and Marcus longed for the sunlight. He mourned her brightness as Jewel had been; a sudden need to preserve the naïve but rowdy woman that could outshoot any man.

Jewel faced Marcus and the shadows that haunted her features vanished. She smiled again reminding Marcus that it would be prudent to search her belongings. After all Jewel had been through his washing. Those guns might prove too much of a temptation, especially since Marcus had just caught her counting stations. Besides Marcus had his own ideas for those guns, and no doubt Jewel wouldn't like it.

Marcus took off his Stetson as the train billowed puffs of steam. Marcus pulled the thin timber doors closed, rattling in the tracks and lowered the coal soiled blinds. Jewel rummaged in her pocket. As he sat down she tossed him the small object. Marcus opened his palm to reveal a tiny taffy wrapped in wax.

"Thanks," He popped it in his mouth.

"How'd you afford this cabin?"

"Care of Miss Belle Lincoln."

"Oh" Jewel replied. She turned her gaze to the window, as the whistle let out. A waft of coal smoke gusted down the side, "I guess Ruby's reward might come in handy. Calvin owes me two years of wages" She brought her knees up to her chest.

"I suppose that as his widow you inherit the Hadley Sharp Shooter Carnival."

Jewel shrugged her shoulders, "If I'm the only one."

"Huh?"

Jewel shook her head.

It wouldn't surprise Marcus if Hadley had more than one widow though. Marcus didn't ask again as he chewed his sweet.

"What do you think Theo and Abe are going to say?" She asked.

"I dunno, question is what am I going to tell them?"

"They've seen the Ruby Drawers reward, it's hard to tell them anything else." Jewel said.

Marcus nodded and scratched his nose. He watched Jewel stifle a laugh.

"The Turner Gang are doing something. Three of them

heading South West, another one was following Calvin. And as Calvin said Garrett, I mean Gabriel was waiting for me in Dodge."

"Mmm" Marcus said still chewing his taffy. Better that than giving her too much information.

Jewel's gaze suddenly unfocused, her lips pressed inwards. The station platform drew her attention but Marcus knew it wasn't the images that replayed in her mind. Calvin's body, *Rocio*'s death whine.

Marcus didn't want to disturb her mourning and yet couldn't watch Jewel twist herself into knots over a man like Calvin Hadley. Calvin had no doubt given the Ruby Drawers description to the Turners, he had considered handing her in at Dodge and then tried to rob Jewel of the one thing that might clear her name.

"Hey," Marcus said softly.

Jewel faced him, "I'm alright Kearby"

"I know you are."

Marcus rose to the parcel rack. He opened his back and lifted the cream Stetson and the primitive vanity case he bought from the Petersburg general store. He plonked the hat on her head and handed her the little leather pouch before he sat down.

Jewel took the Stetson off her head and ran her finger around the brim, her eyes glassy. She rested it carefully on the seat beside her before she unrolled the kit. A tiny gasp escaped from her lips.

"And all I bought you was a damn sweat." Jewel carefully rolled it back up, "Thank you Marcus. I am grateful for your .... company Ranger Kearby."

"You mean my help?" Marcus joked.

"I never said that." Jewel smiled, "So long as you're not going to get all Lawman on me when we meet the Rangers." She gave her new Stetson another careful caress, picking a tuft of dirt from its pristine brim.

"I give you my word, I'll never let you see the inside of a cell

Ms Jewel Hadley."

Jewel rose from her seat just as the second whistle blew. "He never gave me anything but his name, so I'm not keeping it now he's gone."

She tucked the vanity case into her bag as the carriages jolted. She stumbled her arms cartwheeling until she landed in Marcus's lap.

Marcus grunted as her buttocks collided with his groin, his hands on her ribs, his fingertips pressed against the plush edges of her breasts. Thorns of desire wove deep into his flesh, his nerves alive. His throat rumbled before he could stop it. With his breath, a dark curl moved across Jewel's porcelain cheek and the thorns began to throb.

"Thank you," Jewel regained her footing and sat down in her own seat. Her cheeks a little more pink, her hands fidgeting with her shirt. She kept her gaze out the window, unable to hide the kink of her lips. When would his body ever quit wanting her?

"Your welcome" Marcus mumbled as he lay himself flat against the bench seat. He put his hat across his eyes waiting for his thoughts to cool down.

"Your stitches might need a new bandage soon so don't get too comfortable."

"I'm alright Nurse Daniels" Marcus pretended to yawn.

Jewels thumb went to her lips and she bit down softly. If she was to make it out of Emporia she would need money. More than the few dollars she had left. Being Calvin's widow was unlikely to be any wealthier than being Calvin's wife. She would pay Marcus back for all his expenses, even his latest gesture of kindness. Her throat had tightened at his kind thoughts. She sighed. Even more so now, Jewel couldn't involve Marcus any deeper into her problems. And despite all of her wishing on every star that she could, she knew it was too dangerous. She needed to cut ties with Marcus, send him safely home to Dew Springs.

When Jewel had placed Marcus's gift in her bag she spied Winnie's dress. The woman must have packed it for her, God Bless her. She would wait until Marcus was snoring and find her way to the bar carriage. Surely some cowpoke had a drives worth of pay to gamble with. Hopefully she had enough time to fill her pockets before Marcus woke.

Donald Gary Brady the 3rd clung one handed to the pommel of his saddle, his other palm slicked in his own blood. He licked his numb lips, thirsty and yet unable to swallow. The Reaper was coming for him and he'd be damned if he'd go peacefully. First he needed to find Turner. The deputies at the town gates halted his progress. Dodge City had gotten all civilized thanks to Sheriff Bassett. He tumbled off his mount, one deputy caught him. The wound gaped as he tumbled and Donnie cursed in English and Spanish. He sucked in two deep breaths, sitting there in the dust while the deputies shouted for a Quack.

"Get Gab – get Garrett Tanner." Donnie said and clamped his jaw shut. Gabriel had made a fair living out of his second identity. A business man with an eye for detail and a trigger finger faster than most. A few times Turner could have gone legitimate, but he had been blooded with the scent of power and greed. Why bother wrangle deals and approvals, applications and governments when you could snatch it out from under them. Gabriel Turner had deals with the rail before the Panic. His boys lost work, he lost money. The rail owed him and so did the rest of the country.

The deputy tried to carry him, and Donnie batted him away with bloodied fingers. He could feel the color drain from his cheeks, his skin suddenly cold. The deputy dragged him backwards until his back found a joist. At least the sun was out of his eyes. With trembling fingers he fumbled in his jacket for his cigar.

A boy sprinted into the growing crowd, his cheeks coated in grime. "I fetched him for you Mister."

Donnie gave a nod in appreciation and tried to find his flint, "Got a light?"

"Here," Sampson Clements, voice was soft.

Damn, if Sampson was talking low, then it really was bad. Donnie inhaled sharply, the cheroot glowed ruby.

Sampson remained crouched as he slowly pulled back Donnie's other hand, "Sun's setting soon."

Donnie looked at the mid-morning heat, for a moment he closed his eyes, "Ain't it just." Donnie groaned. He inhaled again, the tart tobacco flavor calming his breaths and the nicotine invaded his blood stream.

Turner appeared as the majority of the crowd had dissipated. Another cowboy shot, no-one famous or noteworthy. Soon the deputies would be asking questions.

Turner knelt down, "The guns?"

Donnie shook his head.

Turner leaned closer, "Hadley?"

"Gone. Proper job too."

Turner nodded. At least Donnie had done something right. "And this?" Turner pointed to the gaping wound.

"A Ranger with the girl."

Turner leaned back on his haunches, his steel grey eyes narrowed, his hair lip twitched, "What sort of Ranger?"

Donnie inhaled his cigar again, the flavors muted, his lips failing to hold the cheroot so he bit down with his teeth, "Texas." He shivered. The mid-morning sun had turned blue, the shadows of those around him grew long and pale, white against a backdrop of violet. He managed to get a few droplets of information from Calvin, before he gutted him. Donnie tapped his coat pocket, maybe Turner could decipher the Ranger's telegrams, "From Dew Springs."

Gabriel put his hand in Donnie's pocket and pulled out tiny scraps of paper. He patted Donnie on the shoulder only to have the man slump to the side, his cigar smoldering in the dirt. Gabriel gently extinguished it and slid it back into Donnie's top pocket. Gabriel rose to his feet, knowing too well Donnie's death would raise more than questions with the deputies. Gabriel cleared his throat. He ran his hand down his cheeks. Even if he failed to kill the girl and retrieve the guns Gabriel could turn Donnie's death to his benefit.

"Well Deputies, you may have to up the reward. That hell-cat Ruby Drawers has killed again."

Chapter 12

Jewel sighed and tossed her cards into the center, "All I've got is a few aces."

The table audibly groaned as two aces faced up next to three queens on the emerald green felt. Two cowpokes sat opposite Jewel one named Matt with a bad attitude the other one named Tim and soaked in gin. They both threw their cards in. The drunk burped into his hand and stood up to the adjacent bar to order another glass. The sully one sat back with arms crossed and his blue eyes watching Jewels every move.

"That's a full house!" A businessman from Dallas said as he turned over his two kings. He ran a tired hand over his balding palate, his piggy eyes rimmed red with whiskey.

"That's another goodun'" said the woman to her right. Her numerous curls lumped onto of her round face, her navy skirts in as many ruffles. Her husband was a politician somewhere and she had been forced to spend the summer visiting his constituents. "You have a knack for this girl!" She cheered as her husband snorted and tossed in his hand. He pulled out a cigar and chopped the tail.

"So it would seem, although it's mainly just luck right!" Jewel said as she scooped up the winnings. Her buttocks had grown sore on the worn velvet seat trying to hold on as the train rattled down the tracks.

"I ain't seen someone as lucky as you!" The Dallas businessman picked up what was left of his pot and put his bowler hat back on his head, his shirt was already undone at the collar, his pockets now empty. He folded an ornate leather satchel under one arm, "I'll take my leave, my dear" he kissed Jewel on the back of her hand as he rose. He sat next to the drunken cowboy at the bar and together they drowned their sorrows.

The door between carriages opened, a gush of air jostling

of the tumbled cards until Jewel slapped her hands to stop them flying away. Everyone turned to regard the newcomer.

The politician's wife began to fan her sweaty jowls,

"Deal me in," Marcus said.

Jewel clicked her tongue, "Are you sure?"

"Sure as a -"

"I dunno if that's wise, Mister, for a woman who has only just learnt the game she's doing well." The Dallas businessman hollered.

"Well ain't that good luck for me then." Marcus replied without a smile.

Jewel could tell Marcus was fuming like a pot still on the boil.

"For you and nobody else!" The drunk at the bar howled. He slapped a hand on the table top, his eyes focused at Marcus's deliberate lengthy assessment.

"You're a terrible liar," Jewel smirked.

"You know each other?" The politician's wife asked.

"He's my ah...." My what? Ranger? Father's boss? Unrequited love?

"Chaperone...." Marcus said.

Jewel took a stack of her cash and flicked it across the table to Marcus, "That's for the train ticket and the.... supplies"

Marcus nodded as he pulled out the chair next to the sully cowpoke only to have the timber stall.

"Seats taken," the sober cowpoke snapped.

"It is now," Marcus replied and dragged the chair back and sat down.

The businessman choked on his whiskey, as the politicians wife's eyebrows climbed her high forehead, "Oh my!" She exclaimed and rapidly fanned her blushing cheeks. She even gave Jewel a wink.

The cowboy took another moment to size up Kearby and didn't bother arguing any further.

Jewel sighed and purposely misdealt, "Oops I guess I don't have the hang of this still."

Marcus scooped up the cards before Jewel could and started shuffling, "Never mind I've got it."

Jewel sat back in her chair and tried her best 'damsel' voice, resisting the urge to cross her arms. She never deliberately cheated at cards just a small advantage from time to time. She had watched Calvin and his illusionist tricks enough to pick up a few tips. Those tricks would be futile now that Marcus was here. Didn't he know Jewel was doing it for his best interests? She would be lucky if Marcus didn't expose her and make her hand it all back.

"What's the wager?"

"I might sit this one out" the politician's wife smiled, "Watch from the sidelines" she gave Jewel another wink.

"I'm in! The cowpoke pushed his pot to the Centre, "Ya can't win it if ya not in it"

"That's the way Matt!" The drunk at the bar cheered.

Jewel laughed softly, what would Marcus do? His eyes raked over her exposed collarbones briefly touching the hem at her breasts before moving away. Jewel felt the shiver caress her body as if a shadow had dashed across the sun. Marcus was furious alright, yet his open appraisal hinted at something else.

"Deal," Jewel tempered her voice, the sweet and naive country girl facade was slipping. She sighed, "If you wouldn't mind Sir." She barely managed the word but it made Marcus smirk. Sir? She would never call him that ever again!

"Certainly" Marcus said. The politicians wife's gaze lashed over Marcus grizzled cheeks, his hazel eyes burned across the table. The older woman ran her tongue under the inside of her lips as if Marcus was her next meal.

With considerable caution Marcus dealt the cards. The Businessman and the drunk cowboy returned to watch the game unfold. The businessman still clutched his leather satchel, the name McGauff stamped one side.

Jewel picked up her hand and held her reaction as tight as she did the cards. How could she play her tricks with Marcus across from her? She resigned herself to lose a few until she could deal again.

The next two hands went to the cowpoke until businessman McGauff and the politicians' wife joined in again.

Jewel seized the upturned cards and began shuffling, her fingers gliding over the higher cards and directing them to the bottom. She watched Marcus watching her hands intently. Jewel rolled her lips inwards. How could she wrangle this?

She let out a little laugh which brought Marcus's eyes up for a moment, then she leaned out of her chair and then forward to deal to the cowpoke and Marcus. She inhaled increasing the gap between fabric and skin and what little cleavage she had swelled against her linen shift.

Matt, the sober cowpoke, rolled his tooth pick between his teeth and winked. Marcus cheeks heated, his eyes unable to avoid the view she offered him. His burnished copper gaze met hers and Jewel froze. There was so much heat Jewel didn't know if she should stand and fight or run and cower. An urge to discover the source and surrender flourished in her abdomen. She cleared her throat and winked, dealing two cards to Marcus from the bottom.

She finished the round and sat down, the politicians' wife beamed from ear to ear.

The first round of antes came and went and Marcus folded.

Jewel tried to hide her scowl. What was he doing? She had dealt him two aces and had two kings ready for him.

Marcus smiled as the cowpoke took the win and Jewel sighed. Marcus let Jewel deal the next hand, this time Marcus held her gaze despite how low she let her neckline drop. Jewel had both aces and kings ready, but again Marcus folded.

Jewel shook her head. If Marcus was watching her hand like a hawk and he refused to take what she dealt him the game was pointless.

Jewel yawned, "I'm feeling a little weary with all this movement, I think I'll leave you to it." She scooped up what was left of her winnings expecting Marcus to stop her at any moment.

"I'll be more than happy to walk you back to your cabin," Matt said.

Marcus clamped his hand on the cowboys shoulder and prevented his rise, "No need."

Jewel walked around the table and said her farewell as Marcus shadowed her. His palm gripped her elbow as Marcus opened the door between the carriages. Jewel reefed her elbow back just as the door closed. The wind whipped her hair into frenzy and her dress tight against her legs. The rattling of the train as it sped down the tracks forced Marcus to shout.

"What were you thinking?"

Jewel held onto the rail but refused to move, "I was trying to win you back some of your expenses and -"

"Anyone of them could have recognized you?"

"No I was having some fun that's all and -"

"Do you think this is a joke?

"I was just -"

"What cheating at cards?"

"That fellow from Dallas was as crooked as a dog's hind leg!"

"You were taking an honest days' pay from a couple of cowboys. Not so long ago that would have been you."

Jewel huffed, "I was trying to do the right thing by paying you back," And getting enough money to leave him behind at Emporia but she didn't dare say it.

"I don't want your money Jewel," Marcus said.

The jostling of the train closed the distance between them. Marcus's face tilted down, his hat shading her eyes from the noon sun. Lashes of golden yearning heated his gaze and Jewel couldn't resist any longer. She pressed her lips against his, a lick of desire uncurled in her veins.

Marcus kissed her back, his lips pressed hard as if to punish her and she relished in the delight. His scent invaded her senses, a tang of citrus engulfed in mahogany. The whiskers tickled her chin as she drove her fingers through his shirt front, sending an echo of shivers through her abdomen.

Marcus relented only slightly and Jewel's instinct took over. Tentatively she ran her tongue gently across his closed lips. His mouth slanted, his lips parted. Jewel clung to him as his tongue penetrated the soft corners of her mouth; his intensity demanding, dominating, and coveting her as his own. She gasped at his furious ardor and his hands that wandered. The world that was Marcus engulfed her and Jewel arched her back, his arm curled around her back until she was brought hard against him. Jewel melted in his embrace. As if Marcus was the current and she had been swept away, Jewel surrendered under his unrelenting strength.

The movement of the train rocked their bodies together, pulsating liquid lightening at each connection. Marcus's thirst unleashed, stinging her lips, as his tongue streaked across hers. The liquid lightening dove deep between her thighs. Her own unfulfilled hunger dared her onwards; her nights would be forever tortured by this man. Marcus's lips dragged across Jewel's, his teeth tugged at her bottom lip and her moan was silenced by his tongue.

Jewel needed air, needed respite from the tornado of passion that Marcus wrought across her body. The slickness between her thighs ached, her skin begging for his rugged caress. Jewel wound her arms around Marcus's neck and pressed her breasts and their taunt centers into his muscular chest. There was only Marcus, this man, who she would dare share her heart with. His calloused palms scorched her hips as Marcus bunched the thin dress at her thighs. Marcus trembled against her swollen breasts. Suddenly, he withdrew, and Jewel shivered like it had been the first breeze after sunset. Slowly Marcus brought his hands up and unwound her from his neck. Jewel blinked at the midday sun as if she had been doused in a snowdrift.

"I want you safe, Jewel." His chest heaved his eyes down cast, "From everyone."

Jewel winced as the splinter in her chest that was Marcus

turned to ice, "Where's the fun in that?" She mumbled.

Jewel couldn't raise her eyes and instead stepped past him into the next carriage, rushing as she found their cabin. How had she found herself red-faced in Marcus's rejection again? Marcus followed right behind and she slammed the door on his boot toe.

"I need to change."

Marcus retreated and Jewel slammed it twice as hard. Jewel pulled down the blinds and waited until she heard his bulk rest against the door. Jewel ran her hands down her cheeks, the thoughts colliding with each other until she squeezed her eyes shut to find peace.

Jewel slapped her thighs. She had very little time before Marcus realized. Quickly she buried her poker winnings in her saddle bags and then retrieved Bryce's guns from Marcus's before she undressed.

Marcus knocked on the door as Jewel was finally pulling her boots on again.

"Come in, if you dare." She laughed at his shadow that hesitated beyond the frosted panel doors. A little bit of torture was only fair. How many times had he rejected her?

Jewel admonished herself only once more, after all Marcus more than attractive. Eyes like polished amber, his grizzled cheeks added a splash of wildness about him on that jaw of his, the size of Texas. His heart was twice as big, and so damn decent he made her teeth ache. Soon Jewel would be free of him and hopefully her dreams would be too. She needed him gone, for his safety and her pride.

The misted door panels slid open and Marcus sheepishly entered.

"We'll be approaching Emporia soon, hopefully Abe and Theo have received my telegrams."

Jewel inhaled slowly. A tiny part of her hoped they hadn't. She needed Marcus safe, perhaps with two other Rangers he would be. Could she trust Marcus not to turn her in? Could Marcus trust the others? With Calvin dead, Lucky Chuck was the only key left to clearing her name, with the Turners and the law. Lucky Chuck and Bryce's guns. She would find him in Indian Territory and drag his sorry ass to Waco. Gabriel Turner could take him from there if he wanted revenge. She would have to shake Marcus lose, once and for all. Both their lives depended on it.

"Don't forget which side of the law you're on, Marcus." Jewel said.

Marcus ran his fingers down his bearded throat, "I like the outlaw look." He joked.

"I don't."

"Then I like it even more." Marcus added.

Jewel ignored him as the train pulled into the depot. The billows of steam retreated to reveal platforms lined with future passengers and those that waved farewell and others awaiting the train. Handkerchiefs waved from trussed up women; Jewel felt their heat in sympathy at their hooped skirts and corseted waist lines. Children raced the train to its finish. Businessman sweltered in their three piece suits as their porters carried luggage down the depot platforms.

Marcus pointed Jewel to a timber bench at the far end of the station, "You stay there, while I sort the horses."

Jewel nodded, it gave her plenty of time to study the timetables, ticket prices and route maps. She would jump the train to Humboldt and get as far south to Parker as she could. There she could buy some supplies and cross over into Indian Territory. If she didn't find Lucky Chuck Jewel could disappear from all this mess, Marcus included.

Jewel watched the Dallas businessman, McGauff, greet a party of three suited men. One of the suits clicked his fingers and two porters dashed to obey carrying the man's luggage as he tucked his satchel firmly under his arm, his bowler hat stoic on his head. She gave him a short wave, which he nodded as they moved off the platform.

In no time Marcus returned and practically dragged her to the horses, the brown as fidgety as *Scout* to stretch their legs and be away from the iron horse. They rode down 6th Avenue, as the heat dispersed from the afternoon sun. They stopped at the Post Office for Marcus to check for news. He exited stuffing a piece of paper into his denims pocket. He led the horses by the reins across the bustling street to the Emporia House Hotel. Jewel regarded the two story red brick building, the lower level with ceiling high glass windows boarded in white timber, the second level had two bay windows facing the street and a row of simple white arched windows down the other side.

"I expressly asked for a balcony overlooking the street." A thin man wearing dark brown three piece suit barked at a man who Jewel assumed was the manager. He ran the brim of a black Stetson between his fingers as he huffed as much as his thin moustache would allow.

Marcus waited patiently behind, while Jewel listened in on the exchange examining the foyer. The wooden floor had been covered in large paisley rug that softened the footsteps of patrons crossing the foyer. A bunch of small tables cloistered in a narrow restaurant down the far side, the red buffalo check cloths covering each circle, and a dainty vase with wildflowers sat on top.

A high oak bench rounded out the other side, with rows of keys and pigeon holes on the wall. With his fingers splayed on the counter top, the manager, dipped his head, "I don't know what to tell you that you don't already know Mr Smith."

"I don't like our chances," Marcus mumbled as he moved to the front reception desk.

Jewel didn't reply instead she regarded the scuffed shoes at odds with the man's pressed suit.

"I want to be notified immediately as one becomes available."

"Of course."

The man named Smith turned on his worn heel, throwing one glance over Jewel and Marcus before storming up the stairs.

"We got one room left. It's a single room, top of the stairs, far left." The thin woman behind the counter snapped. Her greying bun wound as tight as her pale cheeks, even the wrinkles that lined her forehead seemed starched. She ran her gaze over Jewel's feminine form in denims and navy gingham.

"And the stable?"

"Full too I'm afraid, horse room only. The muster's been quite large this year, after the locusts last year."

Marcus cheek twitched as he considered their predicament.

"You know I don't snore Kearby." Jewel said, disappointed that she failed to raise an eyebrow on the woman's plain face.

"I'll sleep on the floor," Marcus muttered as they climbed the stairs.

"Whatever floats your boat," Jewel said.

She listened to the organ music playing from the restaurant, the sounds of clinking glass and dinner plates, cutlery being re-set on timber tables. A string of girls, all about seventeen or eighteen, wandered down the double wide stairs, their booted heels barely raising a whisper on the plush carpets. Every single girl fell silent as they descended past Marcus, their youthful eyes on his gun belt, some regarded his caramel shirt tight across his shoulders, two smiled and one almost stopped. Jewel cleared her throat, "I guess the outlaw look does suit you. Might land yourself a respectful woman one of these days."

Marcus only grunted and moved past, the curious girls giggled as they dashed down the stairs.

Marcus gut sank at Jewel's words. Little did she know, he had a wife waiting for him back in Dew Springs. Whit's fiancé to be precise. His moment of weakness on the train had only fueled his hunger instead of satiated it. Stealing a kiss from Jewel had been the last thing on his mind until she pressed her lips to his. In one instant, Jewel had demolished all the barriers Marcus had built, and he preyed on her like the lecherous rogue he never wanted to be. Her tongue had dared him to advance, seizing Jewel in his embrace, his body unwilling to let her go until he drank his fill. And Marcus wanted more. He wanted all of her; to take her as his woman from dusk till dawn.

Marcus cleared his throat and cursed himself. No good would come of it. In fact only the opposite. Marcus was to marry Whit's jilted fiancé, ensure another Kearby grandson would be born. Destined to live out his days on the Crooked K Ranch wishing a good horse underneath him in the day and Jewel underneath him at night.

"Maybe it's you they're giggling at, maybe wearing a dress would make you less conspicuous." Marcus threw back at her.

"Ya think so?" Jewel rolled her hips in front of him, her rose embroidered boots clung to her calves, her denims tight around her hips, her navy gingham shirt bunched around her breasts. No, definitely not Jewel in a dress. "Inconspicuous doesn't suit me, Marcus."

"Ain't that a pity." Marcus opened the door to the room, trying not to remember the delectable view she had offered him at the poker table of her creamy curves and the barely there freckles. When Marcus kissed her, he expected rigidity, not the infinite suppleness that curled in his arms. Jewel might throw barbs at him during the day but during that kiss, she was all womanly soft. Except her breasts, the dimpled centers that had compressed against his chest. Marcus felt himself hardened and cleared his throat, inhaling the dusty air of the tiny room wondering how he could sleep when Jewel's intoxicating berry scent invaded his pores.

He surveyed the room, a single wire cot squished flat against the narrow window. A pair of beige curtains, their lace ends now frayed, billowed inwards as horse hooves and heated conversations drifted up from the busy street below. Marcus dumped their saddle bags beside the single dresser that balanced a pitcher of water and a basin.

A knock at the door tore Jewel's eyes away from the patina stained mirror where her now darkened reflection stared back. A young maid handed Marcus a blanket and a pillow which he thanked her while Jewel took the linen and tossed it on the bed. She dug into her saddle bags, "I guess Mr Smith wouldn't settle for just a window?"

"Huh?" Marcus replied. He was too busy working out just where to lay his blankets.

"Nothing… did you get any news?"

"Theo and Abe will be here tonight if not tomorrow. I will meet them while you stay here."

Jewel undid the top button of her navy shirt as Marcus backed into the corner, "I need a bath Marcus and this will not do." She pointed to the pitcher and basin. "And I'm hungry."

"I'll send something up," Marcus found the door knob and twisted. "But you stay here. Emporia is only a hundred miles from Wichita, and bad news travels fast."

Jewel rolled her eyes, "Fine. Where are you going?"

"Out."

Marcus closed the door behind him and exhaled in the hallway. He could almost taste her honeyed lips again, the way she curled into him, the hot breath of her kisses that drove lightening into his groin. Tonight would test his resolve like no other. First Marcus would do his rounds.

Chapter 13

Jewel's eyes flickered open as soon as the door opened, "Bath's occupied!"

"I know, darl," the woman's harsh drawl thundered through the wash room, "He sent me up to check on you."

Jewel clicked her tongue, "Well next time tell him to check himself."

"Can't Miss, he's over at the boarding house."

Jewel sat upright in the now tepid water. Marcus had taken the afternoon to visit a Brothel! Well wouldn't she let him have it! The honorable Marcus Kearby consorting with soiled Doves. No wonder he was eager to leave. A spear of anger coiled through her chest. Even Doves were good enough for Kearby when the Bastard Jewel Daniels wasn't!

"I bet you see all sorts through here." Jewel sat up trying to think of anything else to cool her temper. The quicker she left the quicker her wounds would heal. Her eyes wandered around the darkened room, the walls were paneled in red cherry right down to where they met the emerald green floor tiles. Jewel sat in one large porcelain bath while the woman busied over the other, an oriental folding partition separating the tubs.

"I do." The woman laid out a towel and began refilling the soap stacks.

"Even those you don't want." What Jewel needed was a gun for hire to take her into Indian Territory, maybe Lucky Chuck had come through Emporia. "Like Mr Smith downstairs."

"He's been like a lion with a thorn ever since he came to stay. Only paying one day at a time."

Jewel nodded, "And I guess you get ones that would steal the nickels off a dead man's eyes."

"Them we get every now and then too." The woman

stopped her fussing and wiped her hands on her apron. "But you and your man got yourselves a room, so you don't have to worry about the likes of them."

Jewel's ear's pricked. The stable would be her next stop.

"He ain't my man."

"They never are until they are." The woman said, without even a hint of a smile.

"I guess that's the truth." Jewel replied.

Jewel stood up from her bath and snatched the towel. Marcus could visit a bordello if he wanted, she would find what she needed in the stables. The maid excused herself and left Jewel to dress alone.

As soon as she tucked in her fresh green shirt and rolled the sleeves up to her elbows did Jewel decide she was presentable enough to leave the bathroom. She strode into the carpeted hallway only to run chest on into a slender frame, his bundle dropped to the floor, the man squeaked as if stood on.

"I'm sorry Sir," Jewel stammered as she came face to face with the thin Mr Smith from downstairs, his moustache twitching faster than Jewel could blink. She looked down to the scattered satchel of papers and rushed to sweep up her mess. Jewel snatched at the inked paper as Smith bent down to assist.

"Enough, there is no need!" He huffed, his voice nasal and tense.

Jewel could feel her cheeks heating and shoved the rest of the papers into the brown satchel before shoving it against his chest, "I said sorry Sir."

Smith harrumphed as he clutched the leather to his chest. Jewel's eye caught the ornate decorations, "That's the second like that I've seen today."

Smith stammered into his whiskers, "The second my dear?"

Jewel paused at the sudden soften in the thin man's tone, "Yeah you and McGauff have the same expensive taste. You some sort of special leather worker?"

The man's lips curled slightly, "Oh this, no I'm not the artist, a woman in New York makes them and you're right she is quite expensive. You have a keen eye."

Jewel shrugged her shoulders, "Well like I said Mister, I'm sorry for running into you like that."

"No need to apologise, I suppose your tired from the train?"

Jewel nodded and moved passed the man, "Yeah something like that." Not as tired as she liked to have been. Marcus's rejection still stung. "I best have a lay down." Jewel finished in her best 'damsel' tones.

Smith scuttled down the hallway and Jewel waited until he closed his door before she ventured down the stairs. She watched the bath maid open a side cupboard and pull out a mop. When her back was turned, Jewel dashed across the foyer and out the door. She skirted along the alley until she found the stables. She spied *Scout* shuffling indignantly away from a youth, his pale cheeks coated in muck, his fingernails stained with dirt.

"Hey lady," He shouted as Marcus's buckskin snorted his disgust.

Jewel laughed, "Don't call me that!"

The boy stumbled back, "Sorry Miss, I mean."

"It's okay," Jewel wandered around the stall barrier to pat *Scout's* rump. She hummed slowly as she walked and the fussy gelding started to calm.

"Is he yours ma'am."

Jewel tried another laugh but couldn't, "No I just lost mine. One just as thorny as this one."

The boy picked up a brush and started grooming again, "Sorry to hear."

Jewel picked up another brush, "What's your name?"

"Davie."

"I'm Jewel. Do you mind if I stay, Davie?"

"Oh Rodney says there ain't supposed to be no guests back here, well not the good ones anyway." Davie smiled, one crooked tooth marred the gleam, his blue eyes squinting against the afternoon sun.

"I'll keep him settled and give you a hand, and you can tell me all about the guest that aren't so good." Jewel began brushing out *Scouts* coat as she regarded the other horses in the stables. She saw a painted gelding, the saddle and tack hanging over the barrier looked hard worn and she guessed the rider would be just as tough. Jewel listened as the boy, recounted the guests, confirming the painted gelding owner had ridden in under a thundercloud. Barely spoke and had a pair of six shooters he carried around his waist. Perfect, Jewel thought.

"What's his name?"

"Didn't give a name."

"I suppose names are not important some times." Jewel mumbled. She asked a few more questions until Davie moved onto the next stall. Was it possible Lucky Chuck was here? If she caught him, she could clear her name. "I'll help you with this one." Jewel said as she moved into the painted gelding's stall.

Working her way around the horse, Jewel stopped when she was safely out of sight, quickly she dug through the saddle and tack, hoping to find some clue whether Lucky Chuck was the horses owner.

"Mister?" The boy shouted.

Footsteps marched Jewel's direction. Jewel ducked down below the stall barrier, the horse unmoved by her presence.

"Wilson?"

Jewel froze. She couldn't mistake the nasally tones of Smith. "Wilson?" Jewel held her breath.

She heard the hay shuffle as he moved away. Slowly Jewel raised herself up, her eyes watching Smith wander down the alleys until he stood over the stable boy. His fingers curled through Davies sweat stained shirt.

"He's over at the boarding house Mister!" the boy answered.

Smith released him and stepped out onto the street.

Jewel followed his rushed footsteps until she reached the end of the stable. If she could find Wilson she might have a way in with Smith. Maybe Jewel could wrangle a gunslinger today? She could even leave town tonight, while Marcus dallied with his soiled Doves.

"Which boarding house is he in?"

"The Jolly Widow" the boy answered, "But Ma'am -"

"Don't worry about me," Jewel winked as she stepped onto the street.

She lost Smiths crumpled Stetson hat amongst the late afternoon crowds. The sun had yet to set as the legitimate businesses closed for the afternoon and the saloons and dance halls began their trade. Jewel pushed through the citizens careful not to draw attention to herself, her hair plaited and wound underneath her new cream Stetson that she dipped low over her brow.

She edged closer to the double story brick building that's patrons spilled onto the street. The walls were red brick, the windows tall and narrow. The interior was well lit with girls wearing all manner of colors swaying between the tables serving mugs of beer and offering their wiles. Jewel paused as she passed the corner, where the silhouette of a crumpled Stetson leaned into a taller much broader man. Jewel would bet all her cards, the other silhouette was Wilson. Now all she had to do was introduce herself and ask his terms.

Jewel started to cross the street as Wilson stepped into the fading light. His narrow jaw was grizzled, his dark brow hidden in shadow. He swaggered towards the main entrance with hips that rolled with the casual weight of firearms. He threw a few measured glances either direction before he ducked into the bar.

Jewel loitered on the opposite side of the street, wondering how many patrons might recognize her. Would Marcus chase her down when she finally gave him the slip? His honor would make him. For his sake, Jewel would leave a note. Send word when she was safe. Jewel cocked her head to one side as she watched Smith adjust his starched suit and enter the Jolly Widow.

Smith was certainly as crooked as a barrel of fish hooks, was this Wilson going to honor any bargain she made? Jewel crossed the street, following a lady and her gentleman to conceal her approach. She rested on the corner of the boarding house, closest to the darkened alley that Wilson and Smith just vacated. Jewel watched the interior theatre with a mix of amusement and boredom, until she spied a familiar face. The Dallas businessman McGauff sat surrounded by three more suited companions as they entertained a bevy of Doves. Jewel groaned. A whirlpool in her chest heated as the biggest jaw this side of the Red River strode into the dining hall.

Marcus greeted the Dallas businessman with a knowing nod, before a pair of shoulders blocked the view. Jewel cursed under her breath and rolled her back against the brickwork. The darkness of the alley hid her welling tears. A shout snapped her head up. Glass smashed, a flock of Dove's squealed. Jewel dashed forward, her hand hovering over her right hip. She had dressed in her gun belt without thinking. Her palm coiled around her barrel, just as a window splintered in front of her. Jewel ducked, her heels jarring her buttocks as two bodies flew over her head.

She countered her breaths. If living in Delano had taught her anything it was to stay cool, stay out of reach and think on your feet. Jewel pressed her back against the brick work. She glanced behind her as the crowds rushed outside to watch the melee. Marcus? Where the Devil was Marcus! A thin shadow, sidled up to the distracted McGauff. Jewel watched Smith drop his own satchel and collect McGauffs with the Dallas Businessman none the wiser.

Jewel turned to tell someone, but the crowd had intensified. Suddenly the two men wrestling in the street, stood up. Wilson's grizzled cheeks caught Marcus's fist. Jewel heard the knife before she saw it and bit her tongue. If Jewel called out, Marcus would turn to her sound. Instead Jewel stepped around, her gun useless as McGauff's strong-arms came from either side. Marcus ducked, his shirt snagged in the blade and he pivoted. His forearm struck upwards, his other hand followed through. With a boot behind Wilson's heels, the taller man went down. Marcus stood on his wrist. The knife scuttled out of reach. His knee dropped into Wilson's chest, something cracked as McGauff's heavies launched.

Jewel exhaled as she watched Marcus stand upright. She withdrew into the surrounding crush, just as Smiths crumpled Stetson bobbed along the far edge of the crowd. Jewel slipped between the cheering audience, her boots almost tripped over one another until she reached the darkened alley. She reclined in the shadows and Smith dashed past. Jewel kinked her boot toe, and caught his shin. The thin man sprawled in the dust, his moustache coated in dirt.

Jewel cocked her pistol, "Going somewhere Smith?"

The man reached for the satchel, coming briefly to his knees. Jewel fired one shot. He snatched his fingers backed and cowered on his haunches, "Please I have a daughter. She's just like you please,"

"Whatcha doin' anyway Smith?" Jewel bent down and opened the satchel. She felt a wad of paper, without the light to identify what it was.

"Stop right now!" A female voice hollered behind Jewel.

The cock of two pistols made Jewel let her gun swing on her index finger, "I'm just helping a friend." Slowly Jewel turned to see her captor.

A woman, only a few years older than herself stood at the entrance to the alley way. Her black satin skirts had been slashed with emerald and purple, a riding jacket tight against her slender shoulders. She had brunette curls framing her proud forehead.

"I see that. I thank you for your assistance, however Julius Smith is my case."

Jewel slowly holstered her pistol, "I ain't interested in bounties, what did you say your name was?"

"Helena Ash, Pinkerton National Detective Agency." The woman whistled and McGauff's heavies entered the alley.

Jewel held her breath and her tongue as McGauff's men lifted Smith to his feet, they snatched the satchel and handed it to McGauff. Jewel wanted to run. Instinct told her that this Helena had a bag full of suspicious already and Rudy Drawers was still wanted. Her poster might be plastered somewhere around Emporia right now.

Helena wandered into the light and beckoned Jewel to follow. She schooled her nerves to calm and followed. The crowd from the fight hadn't dispersed and now they watched as the woman accepted the Smiths satchel from inside the boarding house. She spilled the contents onto the porch, "Railway Bond Specimens."

"Specimens?" Jewel asked.

"Yes, completed samples of bonds, the finished product without stamping. They use them to prevent counterfeits, but it appears Smiths is somewhat of an artist and has been using these as inspiration."

Marcus pushed through the crowd, a smear of blood on his shoulder told her his stitches had opened. He came to stand beside her, his whisper barely audible, "Why is it, where you are trouble ain't far behind?"

Helena marched up to Marcus, "And who are you?"

"Marcus Kearby, Texas Ranger."

Helena nodded, her rouged lips pursed, "Well Ranger Kearby you and your," Helena eyed Jewel's rage, "...wife did an excellent job collaring Smith for me, he's been slippery as an eel since him and Wilson left Chicago."

"I dare say, I should have saved some money and hired you!" McGauff stumbled down the brick stairs and stood beside Helena, he shook Marcus's hand and then Jewels.

Marcus ran his hand through his damp hair, "It's no trouble."

Jewel seethed as his arm curled around her waist, "And if you don't mind, we'd rather be getting back to our evening. If you need anything further we can drop by tomorrow. Where are you staying?"

Marcus must have been referring to paperwork of some degree, because Helena looked satisfied with his response, "Thank you. I have rooms at the Continental."

Jewel paused, "He mentioned a daughter."

"Ha!" Helena laughed, "He tried to sell her." Helena started.

"Wed her!" Smith hissed.

"To a miner in the West." Helena pulled out a tiny photograph and showed Jewel a slender mousey haired girl maybe 20 years of age, "Cassidy Smith took off and hasn't been seen since. If you see her," Helena pulled out another item and handed it to Jewel. She turned over the card to find the details of the Pinkerton Detective Agency. "Send her our way."

Jewel pocketed the card and stepped off the porch. She didn't register that Marcus hadn't spoken to her until they were halfway up the stairs of their hotel. Jewel didn't feel like talking either, knowing Marcus would only shout her down for running about, yet he had been consorting in a brothel all afternoon.

"What were you doing at the Bordello?"

"Looking for my chaperone," Jewel cut back.

Marcus inhaled slowly as he opened the door. Jewel stormed straight to the single cot and undid her gun belt, she tossed it onto the covers with such speed that Marcus almost ducked. How could he explain in a way that she wouldn't twist his words? He rolled his shoulders hoping to shake out some of the adrenaline he still felt from his fist fight. The stitches pinched. A wry thought entered his mind and wouldn't shift.

It was deplorable, pathetic and sly but Marcus would enjoy every moment of it. Marcus stretched slowly and winced. Within seconds Jewel was by his side.

"You've probably popped a stitch." Jewel rushed down his buttons pealing the fabric away to reveal the bloodied bandage.

"I'm sure I'm okay," Marcus lamented. His gut twisted at his sickly tone.

"Let me see," Jewel uncurled the dressings, her eyes focused, more sapphire in the lamp light than before. Marcus's palm itched to cup her narrow chin. Her lips still pouted and every fiber in his body wanted to turn her lips to his.

Jewel's gaze met his, her brows dipped, her iris's glowered. She retrieved Winnie's needle and thread from her saddle bags. Marcus registered the care Jewel took to slide her hand down the side of her bag and not empty the contents onto the bed. He would bet all her poker winnings the Turners pistols had ended up in her rucksack. Jewel returned to his side and dug the needle into his skin.

Marcus flinched but remained silent. It wasn't until Jewel began wrapping a fresh bandage around her repaired handiwork that Marcus couldn't hold it any longer.

"I was there for information only." He said.

Jewel let out a sharp hum.

"I swear it," Marcus dipped his head lower to force her eyes upwards. Jewel turned away. "When the Turner Gang gets close to these big towns, they can't help themselves."

"Just the Turner Gang hey?" Jewel snapped.

A smirk developed on his cheeks and it wouldn't shift. She returned with a fresh shirt for him. Marcus couldn't stand her this close with the rush of fresh blood pumping through his veins. She faced him, the freckles across the bridge of her nose twitched as the rise and fall of her chest drew his attention. Scents of berries and honey and all-woman tempted his thirst. If Jewel reached for him, all would be lost.

Marcus snorted, "You know me Jewel, too proper and too boring for that."

Jewel ran her eyes down his physique, Marcus felt his muscles tense, his lungs starved for Jewel-free air, his desire ached to be buried deep within her supple heat. Something dark twisted across Jewels features, her hand reached for the large puckering scar near his collarbone. She retracted her fingers, the shadow now passed. Jewel stepped back.

She snorted, "You threw a man out a window."

"He started it."

Jewel laughed.

As if a lever had been released, tension bled from Marcus's limbs. Jewels pout evolved into a smile and to Marcus it was as if the lamps had been turned up to full. The curtains billowed against the sill as a cool breeze shifted through the tiny room.

"I'm going to see about dinner."

Marcus entered the hallway, his bones a little lighter, his head definitely clearer. How did both trouble and sunshine seem to follow Jewel? He wandered down to the kitchen and arranged for dinner to be brought to the room. The hotel manager stopped to congratulate Marcus and his "wife" on the events of the afternoon and Marcus didn't correct him. Theo and Abe would be here tomorrow. He would have to address how and why Calvin died at the hands of the Turner Gang. He would have to persuade them of Jewel's innocence, of the need to have Bryce Tanner recognized as Francis 'Baby-face' Turner. Marcus would have to send word to his family of his delayed return, his delay to take up with his real wife. But for now, on this sweltering Kansas evening, as the street bustled with color and intrigue, he had Jewel Daniels as his wife.

Chapter 14

Boom! A shot rang through the air. Jewel sat bolt upright. Her hands searched for her holster, her eyes blinking rapidly in the dark.

"Jewel," Marcus hushed. His whisper rose up from his sleeping mat on the floor.

"Did you hear that?"

A weight dipped the bed, his sleepy warmth leeched into her shivering skin.

Marcus pealed back the curtains to survey what he could of the street. Empty. Marcus scrubbed a hand down his face as he resumed his seat. His hand lazily stroked her back.

"It's probably some cowboy loosing at poker."

Jewel skins rushed in goose bumps, her cheeks suddenly cold. She nodded and leaned forward to the window. Another shot rang out followed by a 'yahoo' and then another.

"The Sheriff will have him soon enough." Marcus yawned.

"Okay." Jewel nodded in the darkness. The mattress sprung upwards as Marcus made to move back to the floor.

Another 'yahoo' echoed off the brick buildings, this time further away. Marcus sat on the edge, his shirtless form barely visible in the shadows. Jewel slunk down into the blankets, her body shivered into the thin linen.

"You alright?" Marcus patted his hand on her ankle, his voice still coated in sleep.

"I will be soon." She whispered. Jewel craned her neck up again as if watching the empty street would keep the shadows in her mind away.

Marcus sighed and rested his back against the wall, his eyes on the street, "I'll keep watch for a bit, you sleep."

Jewel turned away from the window, her eyes wide open as Marcus yawned again. The warmth of his body oozed into the mattress, driving away the images of Calvin trussed and gutted from her mind.

"Anything ever haunt you Marcus?" Jewel asked.

Marcus scoffed, "D'ya know why I'm in Kansas and not down south?"

"No."

"The Sioux. That first raid..." Marcus words strained. He exhaled slowly, "I kept seeing Cade's sister Pearl in every one of them, you know. They're just people. Just like us. What's done is done, but it ain't the right thing."

Jewel rolled over, his silhouette remained still, "No, not always. I'm sorry Marcus."

"So am I. Nothing I can do can change what happened."

Jewel swallowed hard, the pain in his voice tore through her, "Only what you choose to do now."

Marcus inhaled sharply, "Something like that."

Jewel laid there silently for a long time, she heard Marcus's breathing, his casual surveillance of the street below. "How come you remained in the Rangers? I can't imagine they'd keep you around if you refused to follow orders."

"McNelly tried, but Johnny Quinn wouldn't allow it. I've never met a better Ranger than Quinn. He saved my life a few times."

"If he is the best then –"

"He ain't the closest. He's down south with McNelly. Abe and Theo are our best shot for now." Marcus folded his arms, and stifled another yawn. Jewel could feel sleep waiting for her.

"You're the best Ranger I've met Marcus."

She heard his snort just as the darkness thickened, his weight comforting.

Marcus furrowed his brow at the soft tapping; slowly he tightened his grip on the soft curves that warmed his bare chest. Marcus inhaled the sweet berry scent as he opened his eyes to a waterfall of faded black curls. Jewel? A fleeting notion that she would need to redo the color facade soon was chased away by the memories of people referencing Jewel as his wife. Marcus's body stirred, desire licked deep within his chest, tightening his throat and his groin. He enjoyed that thought, Jewel, all to himself, all of her for all of him. The soft rapping still demanded his attention. Carefully he unwound himself from her slumbering form and met the stable boy at the door.

"Sorry Mister, two riders came to see you, they gave me this."

He handed over a slip of paper. Marcus unwound it and read the hotel name. The Green Horn, a disreputable shack on the city limits.

"What did they look like?"

"Like they rode from Hell and ain't done yet."

He rephrased his question, "What horses were they riding?"

"A real sweet bay and one testy pie bold."

Marcus looked back to where Jewel slept.

"Don't worry Mister, she helped me with your horses yesterday I'll keep her busy today,"

Marcus smiled as he donned his red shirt and grabbed his gun belt, "Good man."

By the time Marcus landed in the saddle the sun tipped the horizon. He decided to take the back alleys to the edge of town, the sound of hooves rang off the white brick walls, their narrow window arches colored a rusted ruby in the earlier morning light.

Marcus rolled his shoulders as he rode through the alleys, his bandage tight but neat across his shoulder. He hoped Jewel stayed put this time. The Pinkerton Agent, Helena Ash wouldn't take long to work out who Jewel was once they didn't appear at the Continental. What the Devil had she been doing chasing Smith? Marcus stewed over the nights' events, slowly piecing them together. Jewel hadn't found Smith, she had found Wilson. Did she know him? Was he another thug from Delano? Marcus wished his head would clear from the lingering berry scents so he could think straight.

He reached The Green Horn and rested *Scout*'s reins across the hitch. Marcus could smell the tempting flavors of fresh coffee and sizzling bacon. He hoped his plate would be clean. The interior was deserted except for the two weary men at the far table, a low bench to each of them instead of proper seats and no cloth across the wonky table.

Abe and Theo sat hunched over their coffee mugs, several days' growth on both men's cheeks. Abe the taller of the two brushed back his beige strands, his brown eyes ringed in red. He smacked Theo, the older of the two on the shoulder. The dark haired man put down his mug and turned, his brown eyes raking over Marcus, smirking under his bushy moustache. Marcus, having done his reconnaissance the day before, nodded to the cook.

"Ain't you supposed to be at a wedding?" Theo said as he greeted him. Marcus shook his hand.

"Told you he'd be bored!"

"Yeah something like that," Marcus replied as he sat down.

The waiter brought over a menu and Marcus ordered coffee with a side of bacon and eggs.

"So tell us about this pickle you've gotten into."

As Marcus relayed the events of Calvin's death, the Dodge City connection and Jewels identification of Baby-face Turner, he watched the Rangers expressions turn.

"Ok, so what's your plan?" Abe asked.

"You've been tailing the others right?"

"As far as we could, the trail went cold two days ago."

"My estimate is they are meeting Gabriel Turner somewhere."

"For another heist or a payout on the last?" Abe scratched his bearded chin.

"Either or," Marcus added. He took his plate from the bleary eyed hostess and waited till she was out of ear shot. Soon all manner of patrons would be filling the tables.

"And they want the girl you reckon?"

Marcus nodded. A chill ran down the edge of his neck and ended between his shoulder blades. Theo threw Abe a dark look.

Theo cleared his throat.

"No!" Marcus hissed.

"Hear him out Kearby." Abe snapped.

The hefty cook raised his head over the counter top.

Abe lowered his voice. "We're supposed to be on task in Kansas City not chasing some phantoms just 'cause your girl got mixed up in some Delano dust up. You've dragged our names into the mud, any day now Callaghan is going to be hauling our asses in asking what we've been doing traipsing over the countryside."

"You can turn around right now, tell him you never seen me."

"Or we could report you to McNelly," Abe threatened, "He'd love that."

"Do it then," Marcus went to rise, but Theo grabbed his forearm.

"Now don't be rash Kearby, you always go off half-cocked and hot headed."

Marcus shook him off.

Theo sat back and adjusted his collar, "Always cursing about what's right and where does that get you? Shot up or worse. Now so far we're with you. Ain't nobody gonna pass up an opportunity to hang the Turner Gang. No one rides alone. So hear me out."

Kearby exhaled slowly. He owes them that much. Captain Callaghan might be looking for disciplinary action if they deliberately went against his orders. And he couldn't keep Jewel safe and clear her name at the same time.

"Go on."

Theo took a sip of his coffee and cleared his throat, "They want the girl, whether its Turners boys or not we dunno. Say you hand her in, locked her up nice and secure. We set an ambush, and we all get a piece of hauling in the biggest outlaws on both sides of the Red River."

"No," Marcus crossed his arms. The danger of using Jewel as bait was too much, not only that, but he'd given his word she'd never see the inside of a cell. If it all went to Hell in a hand basket, no-one would be able to declare her innocent. She would hang.

"Come on the girl's perfect!" Abe hissed.

"And if it goes wrong?"

"You said she's a sharp shooter I reckon she can look after herself. Besides, if she spent her nights with Baby-face Turner, she can handle herself."

Marcus ground his jaw. Jewel had said they were never lovers. Why was she chasing a thug last night?

"Well what's your plan then?" Theo asked, "You got something else to dangle in front of them?"

Marcus leaned back, "Yeah I think I do." His hands went to his gun belt. The pearl and silver inlaid handles were snug in his holsters. Abe and Theo leaned forward. Marcus lifted them up slightly so the other Rangers could see his prize. "We can get this Bryce Tanner sharp shooter declared dead as Francis Baby-face Turner. The working girls up there must have some idea. Hadley's dead but he had posters of the show drawn up. There is another fellow, a Lucky Chuck or Lucky Charles who is the one who actually pulled the trigger."

"And what about the Turners," Abe picked up his knife, the knife point pirouetting on the scratched table top, "You just gonna let them go?"

Marcus balled his hand into a fist. Abe was always searching for an angle. "A minute ago you weren't even sure it was them?"

"This Garrett fellow sounds about right. I'm willing to take a risk, if you are?"

Theo snorted, "When is Kearby not risking his hide for something grandiose?"

Marcus smiled, at least Theo kept his sense of humor,

"Having Francis Turner declared dead will put the heat back on them. If we can't prove Gabriel Turner is this Garrett fellow yet, mention of the Turner Gang will put the attention back on him."

"It might drive them underground." Theo mused. "So long as this stays quiet. The moment that girl gets recognized you're done for. You'll have a Devil of a time convincing anyone she's innocent and then the Turners will be coming for her regardless. McNelly, Callaghan, Quinn won't believe you didn't know about her as you crossed the countryside. You'll go down for aiding and abetting."

"And if we're in Delano what are you doing?" Abe paused the spinning of cutlery.

"I'm going to get the girl safe and then -"

"You're not planning on walking up to Gabriel Turner." Theo crossed his arms over his chest.

Marcus didn't answer. If Theo and Abe got Francis Turner identified, then Jewel might be clean and clear, she might get the reward for his death. Then no-one had to prove her innocence or find this Lucky Chuck. It seemed the quickest and easiest option to clear her name. She had been seen arguing with Baby-face only minutes before his death and she rode off with his guns. Once Tanner was Turner, and Jewel no longer the target. Marcus would walk those silver inlaid pearl handled colts, right up to Gabriel Turner and fire both hammers.

"Well I'll say my farewell now if that's what you're planning." Abe joked.

"See what comes of Delano first." Theo rose and placed his Stetson back on his hat.

Abe rose as well, "You go round up that girl and we'll head on out."

Marcus paused, "That's not part of the deal."

Abe drove the point of the knife down into the timber, "Don't think we're going to Delano alone. Get the girl and we'll meet you on the trail."

"I don't think it's wise all three of us being seen with the girl." Theo said.

Abe let the knife stand upright, "I'm not talking about being seen. We'll meet you half a click out, by the oak groves. I'm not risking my neck for nothin', the girl comes to Delano to clear her own name or I'm out."

A chill speared through Marcus's abdomen, "I said no cells."

"Nothing like that Kearby," Abe said. His eyes scattered around the room, flicking only briefly at Marcus's face before dashing away to regard the cook. Abe jabbed Theo with his elbow, "We'll do it your way, no noise, no cells."

"It would make things easier," Theo said as he replaced his own hat.

Marcus stood with them. Marcus didn't doubt Theo, "Your word then?" Marcus put his hand forward.

"Of course Marcus," Theo said and shook his hand.

Marcus turned to Abe. The taller man met his gaze for a second before diverting again, "I said so didn't I."

"By half ten." Marcus said and put his own Stetson back on his head. He tossed a coin on the table for a tip, "Oh and stay clear of the Continental, there's a Pinkerton Agent there by the name of Helena Ash. She busted some counterfeiter from Chicago named Smith. "

"Yeah we heard. Callaghan wanted us to chase his cold, very cold, almost ice cold trail up in Kansas City. They had nothing on him or the stolen specimen bonds for the construction of the rail through Texas. Lucky for you I guess we've got time on our hands now." Theo huffed.

"And time's wasting Kearby," Abe said.

Marcus wandered to the front entrance, and paused on the top step. A youth walked briskly down the empty streets, a satchel over his shoulder bulging with his burden. He strolled past Marcus and dipped his faded hat.

"What's the news today?" Marcus asked a coin in one hand.

"Straight off the press!" The boy pulled out a newspaper.

The banner across the top screamed in bold black letters,

The Kanzas News. Marcus scanned the front page for news of Smiths arrest not to be disappointed. A sketch of the man's likeness and a list of his exploits filled a column and a half. Marcus folded the newspaper in half until a familiar face and name caught his eye. Halfway down the page, the headline stole his breath, *"Ruby razes Kansas, page 2."*

Marcus almost tore the paper, as a large sketch of a voluptuous girl with endless curls splashed across the page. Marcus skimmed the words, Hadley's killer had made it to Dodge, his last breath uttered his killer's name, Ruby Drawers from Delano. Her bounty now stood at $2000.

Marcus exhaled slowly as his thoughts raced. He caught the boy's shoulder, "Where have you delivered so far?"

"Only to the Western, the Heritage and the Cowboys Dream."

Marcus cursed.

The boy sniggered.

Marcus pulled out a paper note, "You can have this if you wait till noon to deliver the rest."

The boy whistled through the gap in his front teeth, "For two I'll back track my steps if you want Mister."

Marcus tucked the paper into his pocket and handed over his cash, "You'll be your own boss in no time. And maybe skip the Continental altogether."

"Consider it done." The boy winked and skirted down the empty street.

Marcus leapt onto *Scout* and hurried back to the hotel, praying that Jewel had finally stayed put. A sinking feeling rolled around his abdomen, Marcus knew he had crossed the line. If he was honest with himself, Marcus had crossed it long ago. Marcus sighed. He would cross it every second of every damn day if it kept Jewel safe, but the Turners were still out there. Justice needed to be done, before they created more havoc and took more lives. Yet Jewel was now between a rock and that hard place.

Marcus let *Scout*s reins drop at the hitching post and tried his best not to dash up the stairs. He found the room empty; Jewel's possessions gone. Marcus sprinted down the hallway, until he reached the stairs. With every inch of restraint Marcus took them one at a time. He entered the stables. Both *Scout* and the dun lifted their heads in greeting. The dun's saddle bags were Jewels.

"Where're you going?"

Jewel shrugged her shoulders and turned away from him, "I thought about that Pinkerton Agent, coming back, it was only -"

"Good, get up." Marcus came behind Jewel. His hands on her waist, he lifted her upwards. She scrambled onto the saddle.

"Where are we going?"

"Anywhere but here."

Jewel didn't object and waved farewell to the stable hand.

Marcus led them out the stable, an itch stirred between his collar and he couldn't shake it. Jewel had been chasing that Wilson thug for another reason, and now when he took off to meet the Rangers, she had been saddled and ready to go. Marcus teeth ground down on her jaw. Wasn't he risking enough for her? Here she was trying to run again! Marcus thought of Abe and Theo. He couldn't meet them now. Not only would he putting Jewel's life at risk, he would be risking their lives and ruining their reputations. Ruby's new $2000 reward would be too much of a temptation for Abe.

Marcus turned *Scout* to the west wondering where they could run. Quinn was south. McNelly wanted his hide and when Abe and Theo read the paper, they would have no choice but to chase them down. A soft chug cut through Marcus's thoughts.

"The train?"

"Sure there's the one to Humboldt at -" Jewel stopped mid-sentence.

Marcus felt his cheeks pinch, his gut sinking into his boots, "Fine we'll ride to Hartford and meet it there." Marcus kicked

Scout in the flanks and the horse leapt into long strides, their hooves echoing off the empty streets.

Jewel held onto the dun as it galloped out of Emporia, the dawn air rustling through her hair, she tucked her chin to keep her Stetson on her brow. Hard lines set Marcus's face, a vein pulsed at his jaw, his brows furrowed. Marcus held onto his reins tighter than necessary, his hazel eyes scanning the horizon as his mind churned over. What had happened with Abe and Theo to spur him into action?

Jewel had saddled the dun thinking she might get a chance to slip out of sight, only to have Marcus tear back into the stable and catch her in the act. Jewel let her thoughts wander. What was Marcus risking for her now? She pulled alongside him as they crossed the Cottonwood River; the narrow slip of water barely deep enough to splash the toes of her boots.

"What happened with the Rangers?"

Marcus exhaled, "They can't help us now."

Jewel cocked her head to one side, "Now?"

"They had agreed to go to Delano, to help clear your name. Get Francis identified as the dead sharp shooter."

"That's good then right?"

"Yeah," Marcus pulled *Scout* into a trot.

Jewel rolled her bottom lips inwards at the corner, "Until?"

"It seems Calvin's murderer made it back to Dodge."

He dug into his pocket and handed Jewel a piece of newspaper. She unfolded it against her saddle and read the lines.

The moisture evaporated from Jewels mouth, "But -"

"I know." Marcus said. He scanned the brush. A set of train tracks slithered through the hard packed earth, a constant guide to Hartford.

"Two thousand dollars!" Jewel rushed. What did this mean for Marcus? A Ranger, escorting a double murderer across the Kansas countryside? Marcus was aiding a fugitive. No wonder Abe and Theo refused. "Will the Rangers be hunting us too?"

Marcus slowly nodded, "Likely. Abe and Theo wanted to meet us out of town, escort you to Delano."

The way Marcus hissed the word sent shivers up her spine. How likely would the Rangers double-cross Marcus for $2000?

Jewel tucked the newspaper into her pocket as she watched Marcus pull ahead. He was risking his life and his name for the mess she had dragged him into. With the strangers death now pinned on Ruby it was only a matter of time that Calvin's would be too. Then what would Marcus do with a "triple murderer". Ruby Drawers, the murdering whore of the Kansas Plains. Jewel ran her gaze over his broad shoulders remembering each and every scar that was etched in his flesh. Marcus Kearby would do the right thing. Always. With Ruby Drawers by his side, Jewel knew that would lead to his death.

Chapter 15

Jewel tried to relax in the train seats but the midday Kansas sun gave her nowhere to run. Marcus had paid for two side by side in the general car. No cabin to hide in this time. Jewel tried to remember the stops from Hartford to the south. Humboldt was the next big exchange depot where she could slip off and switch trains. The more Jewel thought about it the more certain she felt. Marcus would always do what was honorable and the guilt of his life and reputation at stake for her was too much to bear. Jewel needed to reach Indian Territory, if for nothing else but to run away.

"Where are we going?" Jewel whispered.

"Dew."

Jewel almost rose that instant. Marcus's hand clamped onto her leg, just above her knee. She flinched.

"I need you safe before I can get to the bottom of this."

"There's no way I'm going back to Dew Springs."

"Unless I drag you kicking and screaming, what do you think I'm doing?" Marcus leaned closer, his eyes golden in the early morning sunlight.

The train rattled down the tracks, the scenery speeding by faster than their horses could carry them.

"How is me being in Dew going to help?"

"I'm going south to Quinn, he's the only one I can trust."

Jewel winced at those words. Clearly harboring a criminal gave Theo and Abe no choice. Jewel crossed her arms. "What about -"

"Don't bother mentioning 'Lucky' whatever. If his neck is on the line would he save yours? I'll take you back to your Pa and then head south."

Jewel leaned back into her chair, an internal heat stirring in her gut. Worms of panic doubled and tripled. She had to ditch Marcus to save his life. And there was only one way to get rid of Marcus Kearby and it started with his horse.

At the trains slow approach, Jewel eyed the gable depot building at Humboldt, the small timber dwelling greeting passengers on both sides as the tracks converged. They waited until the passengers disembarked before Marcus bought tickets on The KATY. The Missouri Kansas Texas Railway would take them to Chetopan before crossing the border and down to Vinita.

Jewel took her time scanning the timetable and the surrounding rolling stock. The KATY was due to arrive shortly and so Jewel spent her time wisely. She wandered down the lines, watching the rolling stock and listening to the station masters conversation to others. A Leavenworth, Lawrence & Galveston Freight Train would be departing to Coffeyville soon. Jewel surmised the tiny outpost on the edge of Indian Territory, a perfect destination as any.

The station clock ticked the minutes and hours by waiting for the freight train to move. She heard a shout and turned to see the KATY pulling into the station. Jewels window of opportunity was shrinking. The Leavenworth train was still being packed with all manner of parcels, mail and animals. Jewel might have to share a seat with the horses, but she didn't mind. Marcus marched down the platform and gave directions to a porter on transferring the horses. Jewel tapped her heels on the platform and rubbed her sweaty palms down her thighs. Marcus raised his hat and looked at Jewel, his eyes squinting in the afternoon sun. Jewel cracked her knuckles and then sat still. A long puff of steam billowed from the freight train engines. She scanned the KATY carriages, as the passengers stood ready to disembark. If Jewel got on this train with Marcus there may never be another opportunity. Jewel regarded the distance to the Leavenworth carriages. The KATY Passengers suddenly flooded the depot, porters rushing up and down the platform to greet passengers. The Depot master blew his whistle.

Jewel spied *Scout* in the end stalls. She stood up and casually followed the crowd. A woman with a tall feathered hat veiled Jewel's movements as she crept closer. She knew the horse was trained by Cade Hamerton and he trained them well.

Jewel edged closer to the double bars and let out a low sharp whistle. *Scout* suddenly baulked in his stall, as the handler grabbed his bridle. Jewel ducked and ran as the raucous horse whinnied in protest.

"Damn it!" Marcus put two fingers in his mouth and whistled just as the freight train blew its departing whistle. Marcus dashed down to the stock carriage and whistled again.

Jewel lumbered across the tracks, her saddle bags hampering her speed and scurried to the far side of the depot yard. She slipped through the gap between carriages. Someone called out but Jewel disappeared in the rolling stock. Keeping her body low, Jewel tossed her saddle bags onto the deck of the rear carriage and climbed the stairs. Jewel brushed herself off and entered the mail cart. Confidently she had slipped her captor Jewel slid her back down the wall and waited.

Jewel exhaled slowly as the second whistle blew. She felt the carriage jolt as it slowly chugged forward. The wheels screeched along the steel lines. She imagined women cooling themselves with oriental fans and gentleman wiping their sweaty faces.

Jewel patted her saddle bags and then turned on her heels, she glanced between the narrow slats that allowed air to pass through the car as the Humboldt platform slipped away. She would get to Coffeyville and sell the guns.

A caramel Stetson stood to one side on the rail lines. The wearer with his hands squarely on his hips, his red gingham shirt ruffled. His eyes regarded the unhurried passage of the carriages with amusement. Slowly Marcus Kearby raised his hands upwards a flash of silver caught Jewel's eye.

The damn pistols! Lead sunk through Jewels guts and tumbled down into her boots. She rose from her position and dragged her saddle bags with her. As Jewel opened the door she watched the ground speed by faster and faster. Soon she would run out of courage. Jewel took a single step and landed awkwardly, her ankle twisting in her boot. By the time Jewel stood upright Marcus held onto her elbow.

"When will you stop running?"

Jewel didn't answer. When did Marcus have time to take the Colts? And why? Jewel eyed his waist line as it ran down into his denims, trying to ignore the images it brought up. Both silver handled Colts rested neatly in his holsters. Marcus held onto her upper arm tighter as they neared the crowds. If she made a scene she would bring more attention to herself. Jewel huffed.

"With your new bounty every man and his dog is looking for you, what good could you do taking off now?"

"I was trying to help you Kearby," Jewel spat.

"You got yourself into this mess Jewel and I said I'd help you, I gave you my word Jewel."

That's the problem! Jewel seethed. She had to save Kearby from himself. Once they crossed back to the depot house, Marcus paused at the edge of a timber bench. At the glower in his eyes, Jewel retreated. She heard a loud click before she felt the cool steel against her wrist.

"Marcus!"

Marcus gently added pressure to her shoulder until her knees relented and Jewel landed on the hard timber. She heard the other clink around the slats between the seats.

"I'll be damned if I let you get yourself into worse trouble."

Marcus plopped her saddle bag across her legs and Jewel caught it with her free hand. She shuffled it quickly to conceal the shackles holding her in position.

"Don't say I didn't warn you," Marcus said as he looked down the platform, satisfied that no-one knew any different and walked off.

Jewel sat quietly for five minutes before she tried to find

a pin in her saddle bags. Rummaging around she came across the toiletry kit Marcus had bought. Jewel opened up the tiny mirror and regarded her complexion. Her dark strands were fading, her freckles all the more evident as slivers of red began to peak through her curls. Damn Marcus for being so... Jewel scrubbed the back of her hand across her moist lashes. Why did he have to be such a gentleman? She shifted awkwardly and the cuff clanked across the wood. Marcus would end up dead because of her folly.

Agreeing for Marcus to accompany her was a mistake, marrying Calvin, leaving Dew. All selfish mistakes, made without proper consideration. She didn't even care about Lucky Chuck, she just wanted to run. Now because of Jewel, Marcus would hold his word to his last breath. She needed to run far enough away that Marcus would forget about her. She had done it before she could do it again.

Jewel dug further into her rucksack, maybe her belt hitch would help unhinge the cuffs. She laughed. What kind of a woman was she? She couldn't cook, had no manners and didn't even own a hair pin!

Jewel rested and watched the passers-by. Passengers had finished disembarking from the KATY and now the porters ran up and down the train cleaning off rubbish and checking tickets. Maybe Marcus wouldn't make it back in time. Jewel looked down either side of the depot platform. Where the Hell was Marcus? She spied a pair of black coated shoulders and spurs step onto the platform.

The stranger rested his elbow on the edge of his gun belt as his head turned casually down one side to the next. He spat a wad of tobacco onto the ground before readjusting his black Stetson. He turned to one side and Jewel caught the glint of a silver star across his chest. Jewel cursed under her breath.

The Sheriff slowly wandered to the far end of the depot building, his gaze checking passengers as they filtered past him and into his town. What if Marcus ran into the Sheriff, or worse, what if Theo and Abe had chased them down? Jewel swallowed hard. She casually smiled to the exiting passengers as she dug into her bag. Marcus had left himself unprotected. Jewel found the needle from Winnie's sewing kit. She slid her hand beside her thigh and got to work.

One spike slipped as Jewel wiggled the needle through the edges.

"Time to go," Marcus hushed.

Jewel jumped, the cuff cut into her skin as it tumbled off her wrist.

Marcus groaned and pulled both her hands upwards, the slender needle still clutched between thumb and forefinger.

"I was worried Abe and Theo or even the Sheriff," Jewel didn't get to finish her sentence as Marcus dragged her to the train.

He pushed her ahead of him, one hand on the small of her back, the other carrying her saddle bags over his shoulder. The seats pushed past, Jewel watching the Sheriff on the platform.

"Slow down Kearby." She whispered.

The idea of what would happen if the Sheriff had to intervene, suddenly planted in her mind. Could Jewel escape in the confusion? Could she be sure Marcus wouldn't suffer in the outcome?

"Keep moving." Marcus growled in her ear.

Jewel thought about his handcuffs left swinging below the platform seat.

The livestock carriages were at the rear followed by the freight cars, and then a single passenger cart. A shabby galley had been constructed at the rear, the rail staff washing glasses and refilling liquor bottles, while a dark-skinned cook clattered with pots and pans. Marcus pushed Jewel forward as the carriage gave way to rows of seats, two on each side leading up to strange curtains at the far end of the car. The noise of the engines had been separated by the mail cart. The Sheriff on the platform turned around and wandered past the windows.

Marcus's hand left her back and she slowed her steps. Jewel put her hand on straps of red velvet curtains to steady herself and almost fell face first onto a four poster bed. An elderly woman sat up from her reclined position, a dime novel tumbled from her fingers.

"Excuse me!"

"Excuse us," Marcus redrew the curtains. "No cabins on this one honey," Marcus said loudly through gritted teeth.

Marcus pushed past Jewel to another set of drapes, a number scrawled on the floor. He opened them wide to reveal a set of chairs with a partition in the middle that could be lowered to make a bed. The cushions were covered in a vibrant Damask swirl now faded with the summer sun. Above a similar eye watering fabric covered a double bunk that hung from the carriage ceiling.

Marcus threw the saddle bags on the lower chairs and pushed Jewel to the narrow metal ladder that folded down from the bunk. He put two hands firmly on her rump and lifted. Jewel thumped onto the upper bed, the cover expelling tiny particles of dust. Marcus drew the curtains behind him closing both bunks off from the rest of the train.

Jewel groaned.

"You know how to pick handcuffs."

"Calvin taught me a few things."

"I bet." Marcus snapped back.

Jewel rained her fists down onto the lumpy pillow and growled into the linen. The scent of sour lemons and dusty lace clogged her throat. She rolled over and faced the curved ceiling.

"Wouldn't you like to know Marcus."

There let him stew on that for a while. The handcuffs were rude but Jewel had earned his distrust. His insults were totally unnecessary.

Marcus didn't retort and Jewel lay still waiting for the inevitable chug as the car responded to the tug of the engine. Billows of steam washed past as Jewel open window, the stoic Sheriff stood on the platform, his gaze running down the length of the train. Jewel sighed and leaned back into her straw stuffed mattress.

"Is *Scout* okay?"

"He's fine. You try that hogwash again and you'll be walking to Dew Springs." Marcus replied.

"Soon you'll be telling me I ain't too big to spank." Jewel rolled onto her side, instantly regretting her words.

Again Marcus fell silent.

Jewel watched the black coated Sheriff suddenly shake hands with three armed men. Their fingers hooked in their belt buckles, all with a rifle slung over a shoulder.

"Marcus?" Jewel whispered.

She saw the bottom edge of the curtains flick, "Rail police. To protect the train. Maybe you'd better start listening to me."

Jewel exhaled loudly and shut the curtains.

The rattling of the cars down the steel tracks diluted the anger through Jewel's limbs until it faded away. The depots raced passed as time ticked by and Jewel let her mind cool as the sun began to set.

The man below didn't make a sound until a food cart clanged down the aisle. The curtains parted briefly and Jewel dared leaned over to see Marcus shuffling coins and polite manners. Jewel watched the curtains remain open, glad for the break of the stuffy air. She heard Marcus loudly sipping on something. Slowly the distinct scent of sarsaparilla wafted up to her bunk.

Jewel should apologize? Her heart had been in the right place. She had set off for an adventure and ended up wanted for two murders, none of which she was responsible for. Somehow Marcus's misguided loyalty and chivalry would get him killed. If she handed herself in, would she find a fair trial. The bastard daughter of a farmhand turned Delano strumpet, now the widow of a dubious showman?

The tempting flavors of beef and gravy soaked into her skin. Jewel thought about her apology as she licked her lips. Jewel craned her neck over the edge of the bunk, to see Marcus in the fading light as he took another bite out of bun slathered in beef and gravy.

Marcus took another gulp of his bottle of Sars, tilting his head back until the last drop was gone. She had missed a decent breakfast since Emporia. Jewel spied another bottle of Sarsaparilla and another roll of beef and gravy sitting beside Marcus's thick thigh. She really did need to apologize.

Jewel cleared her throat, "How's your stitches?"

"Fine," Marcus loudly burped.

Jewel put a hand over her grumbling stomach, "I'm sorry about stirring *Scout* up."

Marcus took a loud bite, the sound of the bread tearing as he slurped the gravy from his fingers.

Jewel swallowed, her mouth salivating at the salted flavors, "I'm sorry about Emporia."

She heard the crispy paper unwrapping from the second roll, "I'm sorry about running and tailing Wilson and trying to ditch you in Humboldt and everything else," This time Jewel leaned over the edge.

Marcus raised an eyebrow, his dark beard coated in crumbs. His grip paused around her lunch. Marcus raised his arm upwards. Jewel reached down as the train hit a bend and Jewel overbalanced. She wrapped her hand around the curtains and hooked a boot heel in the chains. Marcus was already on his feet. Her fingers clutched at his shoulders, his muscles tensed under her grip as she unwound herself. For a moment, as Marcus brought her down to the floor with his arms around her waist, Jewel was reminded of another sort of hunger. Jewel cleared her throat and gently ran her hand down his unruly whiskers.

"Half your lunch is lost amongst this mess."

"I thought you were apologizing." Marcus said.

Jewel sat down on the far side of the chairs, the partition slid down creating a safe distance between them. A porter slipped down the aisle quietly lighting lamps.

"I am sorry, Marcus. I know you're helping me, and by

doing so you're putting yourself in danger."

"I'm a Ranger."

"And you're risking your name and your reputation." Jewel lowered her voice. "Honestly you'd be better off leaving me behind."

Marcus handed the sandwich over to Jewel, "How's that working out for you so far?"

"What about Theo and Abe, are they going to be chasing you down?"

Marcus ran his finger down the bridge of his nose and stopped. Jewel put her heels up on Marcus's seat.

She ran her thumb nail along her bottom teeth, "Any news of the T... the others?"

"No good news."

Jewel took a sip of her Sarsaparilla and regretted it. She rose and Marcus suddenly stood upright. He placed his hand on her forearm, his bulk preventing her exit. The top button of his gingham shirt had come undone. A patch of soft dark hair was visible and Jewel's fingertips tingled at the thought of running her hands over his sculptured chest. Marcus's mahogany citrus scent coated her throat.

"Where are you going?"

Jewel narrowed her eyes, "To find the utilities, Marcus." She rustled through her rucksack and pulled out her vanity set. "Are you going to follow me in there?"

His lips barely moved, his voice like thick caramel, "Don't tempt me."

A rush of energy coursed through Jewel's veins, sending goose bumps to flush her skin. Her cheeks heated, the nerves got the better of her and she laughed. Jewel slipped into the aisle, glancing casually as Jewel could manage at the rail guards, two sat scoffing their beef and gravy while another stood sentry outside the cabin, on the platform between carriages.

Jewel followed the porter down to the narrow wash closet. Once inside, she refreshed herself as best the tiny sink allowed, the water spiraling down the plug hole to disappear into the night. Opening the door she spied Marcus's figure reclining, his head on his chin, his eyes unyielding from his surveillance.

A flutter of invisible wings stirred within her chest. Why couldn't Marcus look at her that way two years ago? She would never had left Dew Springs if he had. No that wasn't true, Marcus had looked at her like that. Looked and nothing else. All number of excuses why she couldn't expect more from him. In his gun belt, the silver guns were gone, replaced with his regular Colts. Against Jewel's best intentions she rolled her hips as she walked back to the bunks.

Marcus watched Jewel saunter down the train aisle. Even in the lamp light he caught every undulation as she advanced. He hated himself for the thoughts that infiltrated his mind. She had run from him again, despite all his efforts to keep her safe, she still thought him less than enough. Too official, too honorable, and too boring. Jewel would always see Marcus Kearby the dull small town cattleman that she left. Well perhaps it was time she saw him for what he was, the Texas Ranger, who had lived and lost and learned a thing or two.

The Turners were hunting Jewel while she was wanted for two murders, and now when Theo and Abe worked it out, they would be chasing both of them. Not to mention three rail guards and their rifles. And Jewel still wanted to run off under some hair-brained notion of an adventure. Perhaps it was time Marcus Kearby put Jewel Daniels in her place.

Chapter 16

Sampson Clements clasped his hand on Cooper Brady's shoulder, "You're Cousin Donnie wouldda shot craps with the Devil himself, you know that son."

Cooper Brady twisted the rope around his fist, the tighter it got the less pain he felt in his ribs. He starred through the flames of the fire, the hunger in his belly retreated as anger brewed in his guts.

"He hanged that Hadley bootlicker well and good I'm told." Sampson added.

"And the whore?" Benny Bolt asked as he pointed a flask of whiskey Coopers direction. He shook his head.

"She'll get what's coming to her, her and her bastard Texas Ranger." Cooper hissed.

Sampson rolled a cigar between his teeth, "You had any other trouble?"

"None, we shook off those other two. They never got close enough." Cooper said. He released the twisted rope and focused, "We thought about teaching them a lesson but -"

"Thought better of it, that's why Gabriel's proud of ya'll." Sampson patted Cooper stoically.

Cooper watched his fingers turn from white to purple and then pink again as the blood returned to his skin. "Why are you here?" Slowly he rewound the rope. "Are we getting what's owed to us?"

Jessie Harkin stumbled to his feet, and took a few steps into the darkness the sound of him relieving himself interrupted Coopers mood.

Jessie wandered back into the light, "Yeah, Gabriel said, once he sorted out that mess in Kansas City we'd be paid. I'm all for loyalty but a man's gotta eat." Jessie Harkins went back to squatting around the fire.

Cooper looked up to the bright Kansas stars that loomed overhead. His last family member had left this mortal life. Cooper smirked to himself, why was he looking at the heavens? He refocused on the fire. Donnie was a savage bastard, he would be dicing with the Devil like Sampson said.

"The Kansas City mess isn't sorted. Some Pinkerton Agent caught …" Sampson cleared his throat, "Some Pinkerton Agent ruined our Chicago connection in Emporia."

"We can't take on Pinkerton Agents with just the three of us. Not since Baby-face is gone, now Donnie too."

"Shut it!" Sampson spat, "They both went out fighting, brave and loyal to the end, you're pissing and moaning in the desert, you've got your freedom you're still breathing!"

"What's Gabriel want?" Cooper asked.

"Forget the rail bonds. For now, he wants the bitch dead and her property brought to Gabriel in Shreveport."

"Why?" Benny whined.

"T's got nothing to do with you, Bolt! Finish the job and get to Shreveport."

"Shreveport?" Jesse moaned, "We gotta traipse all through Indian Territory."

"Word is they're headed south, and the KATY rattles through there faster than a sneeze through a screen door." Sampson said.

"We'll be doing it wading through girls and whiskey," Benny took a swig of the liquor.

Cooper looked down at his purple fingers, the lines around his palm white and tight. Gabriel wanted his brother's guns. It was the only property listed on the wanted poster. Gabriel Turner had been laying low for years taking no interest in his brother, claiming to wait for the heat to blow over before he divided up their treasure. Cooper had worked with Francis on several heists. He was a drunk and a loud mouth, a risky business partner from any direction. That's why Gabriel had dumped him in Delano. He couldn't kill family but it didn't mean he had to keep him either.

Gabriel had hidden when Nate and Miles had swung. Loyalty hadn't saved them. They died broke and hungry, not a dime between them. Yet Gabriel cavorted around cities playing the businessman while his Gang starved in squalor. Now with Francis dead, Gabriel had been on his plight for revenge. Cooper wasn't buying it. This new information gave credit to his theory.

"Give us a name."

Sampson nodded, "I knew you'd see light. Dew Springs some Cowtown in Texas."

Cooper released the rope, "I'll kill this Ruby bitch and gut her cowpoke. But Gabriel can come get Francis's guns from me." He stood to meet Sampson nose to nose, "I ain't his lackey no more. Benny's right, my cousin followed Gabriel into his own grave. The Garcia brother's too. If he wants those guns he can get them from me."

Sampson leaned his face closer to Cooper but he refused to retreat, "I'll pass on your comments to Mr Turner."

"You do that." Cooper heard Sampson's horse take off into the night.

Benny crawled closer to Cooper, "Nobody said nothin' about his guns?"

"Ain't you worked it out yet?" Cooper looked at Benny's wide brown eyes, the hollowness of his cheeks emphasized in the flickering campfire, "Gabriel ain't splitting the loot with us. He reckons he's been waiting for the heat to die down before he retrieves it. It's us Benny. We're the heat. He's waiting for us to die. Wherever that loot is, Francis guns lead him to it."

Jessie cursed into the whiskey, Benny turned back to the fire.

"I ain't going out broke or hungry. I'll kill them, kill them all, but those guns are ours." Cooper rewound the rope.

Jewel awoke to momentum slowing down. She heard the unmistakable rattle of elevated train tracks, the rat-ta-tat-

tat of metal trembling through a steel bridge. Jewel rubbed her eyes and tried to make sense of the scenery as the half-moon splashed silver light across the plains. A mountain range appeared in the distance and Jewel judged the time to be late in the night. They must have crossed into Indian Territory, perhaps Creek or Cherokee. Jewel wondered how long it would take her to find Lucky Chuck in this vast wilderness or if she would even make it out alive. If they arrived at Denison, perhaps Jewel could convince Marcus to hunt for the fugitive instead of drag her down to Dew Springs.

If the Turners and the Rangers were chasing them, perhaps they could catch Lucky Chuck like a wedge between them. As Jewel rolled the thought over in her mind, it began to blossom. She didn't need a thug like Wilson, when she had Marcus by her side. If Marcus was intent on risking his neck, then Jewel would be better off making it work. If they brought the Turners and the Rangers together, surely Marcus would be cleared. Gabriel or Garrett or whatever his name was would be arrested and hung, Bryce's murder would be rewarded.

Lucky Chuck could even cash in the bounty. Surely Marcus would see the benefits of setting a trap for the Turners? Marcus had taught her to shoot, despite his cattleman traits he was a trained Texas Ranger! What would it take to convince Marcus that Jewel was onto something? Right now she had no leverage, none that Marcus was interested in anyway.

Jewel hung her head over the edge of the bunk catching a glimpse of a sprawled Marcus as the moon flicked past the train windows. Jewel put her toes on the edge of the ladder, her stockinged feet silent as she clambered down to the floor. The trains rocking made it difficult, the intermittent light even more so but tenderly Jewel knelt across the slumbering Ranger. Like her, Marcus had slept in his clothes, prepared for whatever might occur during this night. He had hung up his gun belt, and his saddle bags lumped against the window.

Jewel listened to his regular breaths, the constant shallow movements spurring her on. Her knee pressed into the mattress, her fingers found the buckle on the leather. She felt a weight curl around her left hip and suddenly her back slapped onto the mattress, her feet tangled in the curtains until Marcus's forearm wrapped her legs and brought them up to her chest.

"Jewel?" His groggy voice slithered into her ears, his breath hot against her cheek. The moonlight danced across Marcus's expression, his features dark and foreboding. His skin was warm with sleep. Marcus frowned and relaxed his grip. Jewel brought her legs down but didn't move. "No more games."

Marcus speared his knee between Jewel's thighs, his palm splayed against her hip. Jewel curled into his chest as his hand ran slowly up her waist. She trembled as his fingers massaged up her rib cage dragging part of her shirt up to reveal the skin underneath. Marcus tenderly traced her arms up over her head as he leaned more of his weight trapping Jewel beneath.

Jewel tilted her chin hoping to reach his lips but Marcus pulled away. His fingers caressed the soft skin at the back of her upper arm as he rocked his thigh between hers. Jewel gasped at the pressure and the spike of pleasure it sent through her abdomen. Marcus wound his grip around her wrist as his other hand plied his saddle bags from her hands.

"I said enough." He growled. His knee withdrew as Marcus rolled onto his back.

Jewel lay frozen, the iciness of his rejection blasted the heat that had ignited. She rolled onto her side and surveyed her surroundings. Jewel threw a leg over his groin and raised herself upright. The bunk above prevented anything more ladylike and she didn't care for it anyway.

Jewel hovered over Marcus's groin, her hands on his abdomen, "I will get those guns back Marcus one way or another."

Jewel could feel his ribbed stomach beneath her trembling fingers. Marcus tensed, his breathing now uneven. She met his gaze, the moonlight added a sinister shadow of black to his hazel eyes. Marcus hovered his palms near her upper thighs. Jewel didn't know if he would toss her sideways or pull her down onto him. For a second she considered lowering herself, only to realize the rejection would sting twice as bad, "Did you hear me Marcus?" Jewel snapped.

Marcus raised himself up on his elbows, "Remember who you're talking to Jewel."

Jewel's legs began to quiver, an ache flourished between her thighs, "I do, do you?" Jewel's fingertips traced upwards, tripping over his buttons.

"Haven't I always done right by you Jewel?" Marcus said through gritted teeth.

Jewel relented. Slowly and without an inch of decorum she rolled herself off his bunk. "You have," She whispered. She clambered up to the top bunk and lay down. "And just for your information Marcus that's half your problem."

The linen ruffled, "That ain't a bad thing."

Jewel snorted, she couldn't handle the peaks of wildfire and the icy troughs of his behavior, "Suit yourself, but remember I've never said no, never said stop and I ain't ever tell you I've had enough."

The linen tousled again, the sound of Marcus thumping his pillow drove giggles into Jewel's chest. She squeezed her eyes closed, hoping that her dreams were filled with the wide open Plains and not the man beneath her.

"And then end up like you Ma?" Marcus voice drifted upwards.

Jewel grit her teeth, "My Ma and Pa never let a boring thing like rules get in their way."

"Well I see it differently."

Her throat constricted, her ribs ached, how he could turn her emotions on a dime, "Congratulations Marcus you've turned out just like your father." Jewels cheeks scratched as she wiped the moisture on the dusty linen.

Marcus sighed into his lumpy pillow. He cursed his callous words. Confusion chased fatigue through his veins. Again Jewel had managed to twist his intentions into insults. Marcus wasn't sure Jewel would ever bend to his will. He was an idiot to think it was possible. Her words slashed through his chest like a razor, cutting deep within, yet his body shuddered at the desire her taunts stirred.

What did she mean? Surely not that day in the barn?

Marcus shook his head at the images that popped up. He needed to get her to Dew Springs and fast. No doubt her latest venture for the Turner's pistols was brought on by another scheme. Marcus would have to keep his wits about him when they arrived in Denison. Marcus exhaled wishing that sleep would arrive. He tossed and turned into the linen. He had a wife waiting for him in Dew Springs. Dragging Jewel all the way home would certainly douse any lingering amorous feelings. Maybe he should tell her now? No, once Jewel found out about Whit's fiancé all Hell would break loose. There would be no way Marcus would be able to stop Jewel running if the secret was out. Marcus could feel sleep haunting him as the bunk creaked above.

"Marcus."

"Please Jewel, at least one of us needs to get some sleep."

"No Marcus there's horses out there."

Marcus rolled onto his stomach and peeled back the curtains, shadowed figures thundered past the carriage.

"Shit!"

"Everything alright?" A thick voice called from the aisle.

Marcus tugged open the barrier to greet the groggy rail guard, "Riders!"

A screech echoed down the cart, the windows rattling at the sudden change in speed, "Tell the driver not to stop."

"Who are you?"

Marcus dug out his badge.

"Ranger! Tell him yourself," The guard slapped Marcus on the shoulder causing his stitches to twinge.

The guard sprinted down the aisle, snuffing the few lanterns that glowered along the edges, his rifle swinging by his side. The other guard woke, his head swiveled side to side before he was on his feet, rifle tucked under his arm as he opened the door between passenger carriage and the freight car, stepping out into the night.

Marcus wondered if he should bring his long-arm. If he delayed any longer there would be no room for handguns only fists in close quarters. Marcus dashed to the front of the passenger cart. He could see over the coal tender to the engine. Ahead on the tracks a red signal glowed in the distance.

Marcus pushed the door and it snapped backwards, the air sucked around his torso and down to his ankles. Marcus snatched the rail of the tender's ladder. A weight collided with his ribs, the floor pitched sideways as Marcus tumbled.

His arms cartwheeled as the darkness clawed at his flailing form. He sucked inwards to no avail. Like a brick had landed on his chest, his lungs screamed for air. His fingers snagged a rail, his right forearm slammed into the side of the passenger car. His throat tight, the words of warning trapped inside. Heels struck the gravel alongside the track, and Marcus's thighs pumped to keep up.

Marcus strained his left arm until the socket felt sure to pop. With both hands grasping the rail he pulled his feet upwards. Another screech ricocheted through his ears as Marcus surveyed his predicament. The darkness shielded the menacing wheels that loitered under the carriage. He could lose both feet with his next move. Marcus curled upwards until he could hook a boot on the same rail. With one hand he checked his ribs, nothing damp.

Marcus took a moment to inhale, his ribs expanding only slightly. A jolt of pain strummed through his bones. He took a shallow breath through the compression around his chest.

The speed of the train diminished as Marcus rested. Movement caught his eye. He watched in horror as a shadow stalked down the interior of the carriage. Marcus opened his mouth to call out. Instead he slid himself forwards over the rail. Hand over hand Marcus dragged himself along to the gap between carriages, the red lantern increasing in diameter every passing second.

The platform neared, his fingertips stretched and missed the edge. As Marcus swung downwards his chest collided with the external flashing. Marcus retracted his right shoulder as far back as he could; resisting the urge to use his hand to steady his fall. The scent of coal and oil billowed across his face. The brakes engaged again sending heat to dance across his cheeks; the discs glowed like the eyes of the devil. Marcus stretched his right arm above. His fingers finally found purchase. Slowly, inch by inch he reached the platform.

Marcus rolled onto his back, a moment's reprieve before he scrambled to his feet. Jewel! Marcus drew his pistols and marched forward.

Jewel tugged on her boots as the wheels screeched again. Marcus had left but the train kept slowing. Her heart thundered against her ribs, the moisture gone from her lips. With trembling fingers she inched back the curtain. A hunter had entered the carriage.

"Rubies are red and corpses are blue, it's only a matter of time, before I catch you."

The man's voice was low and measured with a final twist of infliction that sent chills rocketing down her spine. Jewel retracted as far as she could into the bunk only to have her shoulders cramp against the window. Gently she rolled onto her side and dug into the hinges of the window, tugging until it opened. She brought the linen with her, as she slid her arms out. Her fingertips found a ridge barely deep enough for two knuckles, but it was all she had.

The night air whipped her shirt against her chest. Quickly Jewel kicked until her hips were free. The steel cooled her abdomen and her thoughts. Jewel heard the man call again and dug in until she stood on the edge of the window. With three quick breaths Jewel lurched upwards, her hands sliding over the slippery surface until her nails snagged something solid. Her palms sweaty squeaked along the metal.

Jewel clambered upwards until she lay flat. The half-moon scattered shadows across her path. Below noises and shouts echoed with a rifle that clattered. Someone grunted. A shot fired. The silence forced Jewel to move. She slithered down the steel. The gap between carriages abruptly ended her journey. Jewel steadied herself. She took two backwards steps and launched. Her boots skidded across the freight cart's roof, tumbling, her knees struck hard.

Jewel glanced behind as the carriage door squealed open. The view of inside was obscured by the hunter and his comrade.

"Coops, I don't think she's here."

Jewel slithered face down on her steel.

"She has to be,"

"Well we better be, Benny's gonna be pissed."

"Bolt and me both,"

Jewel heard grunting and someone whistled, suddenly a thump struck the gravel. She pushed her hair away from her forehead as she wriggled down the carriage roof until she was out of sight, standing she dashed down the carriage. Suddenly the carriages jolted. The pistol shot must have reached the engineers ears as the ebony landscape whipped past at increased speed. The shunting brought Jewel to her buttocks.

"Hey!" A shout rang out.

Jewel's thighs quaked as she ran. Marcus! She wiped her cheeks realizing it was her own tears that fell. What had happened to Marcus! Another void approached and Jewel leapt. Her palms slapped the steel. The scent of manure piqued her nostrils.

The sound of hooves strumming along the edge of the train made Jewel cower, the rider brought his mounts closer to the train. Any minute now all three would be on the train and she would be trapped in the stock cart. The guards if not already dead would be slung up like Calvin. And Marcus! Jewel swallowed hard. She surveyed the livestock carriage. Quickly. She knew she only had one chance.

Chapter 17

Marcus stumbled down the aisle, the door at the far end of the carriage slammed in the wind. The bunk was empty. Jewel was gone. Marcus kicked something with his toe. He bent down to lift the rail guard upright. His hands came away slick, but the man groaned.

The old woman from the other curtained bunk peeked her head out. Marcus guided her hand over the man's shoulder, "Keep pressure on it."

"My rifle," the man groaned.

Marcus picked it up and handed it to the guard. What good it would do him he didn't know.

Marcus steadied his path as the red signal flashed past the windows. Marcus halted as the sensation of the train increasing in speed trembled through his boots. At least the driver had enough sense to recognize a gunshot and the risk of stopping in Indian Territory. Marcus needed to find Jewel.

Marcus found the second guard unconscious and breathing slumped into the back row of seats.

A coarse voice catcalled ahead, "Rubies are red and my balls are blue, my knife's rusty but I'm saving it for you."

Marcus tore through the end door, only to have his ankles slingshot from underneath him. Marcus caught the end gates in his stomach and grunted. He ran his fingers along the frayed rope. A weight strummed the fibers; whatever dragged along the ground still had life in it.

Marcus wrapped the rope around his forearms and leaned back. Length by length Marcus reined in the mass until it reached the stairs. In the half-light Marcus recognized the trussed up form of the rail guard. Marcus dug into the man's belt loops and dragged him onto the platform. The man was coated in dust and blood, his face puffy. Marcus ran his hands over the ropes bound around his hands to his neck that tightened to obscene proportions.

Marcus dug the tip of his knife dug into the man's flesh, hacking and cutting as strands severed. The guard gasped for breath. Marcus rotated the man to the side. The guard coughed without reprieve. Marcus grabbed him by the ankles and dragged him into the passenger cart.

Something banged beyond the freight cart, the jolt sending lead into Marcus's gut. Next came a shout. It was loud, raucous and feminine. Marcus dashed into the freight cart only to hear Jewel's "Yeehaw!" echo in the distance.

Marcus leaned against the narrow siding slats, the soft moonbeams highlighting the silhouette slumped over a saddle. The horse galloped into the night leaving a trail of dust barely visible. Marcus slammed his fist on the paneling and rested his head against the rattling walls. Jewel had abandoned him again! Marcus rolled onto his back the musty scent of grain and goods thickening the liquid at his lids. The sound of boot steps and curses followed Jewel's escape.

"Bolt! The horses, come on!"

"Coops!" Another called.

Marcus gritted his teeth. The Turners!

Heavy hooves thundered alongside the carriage and Cooper Brady and the other one Marcus surmised to be Jesse Harkins leapt into their saddles.

Marcus dashed down the freight train watching helplessly as they pursued their prey. He needed *Scout* if that wasn't the mount Jewel had stolen. It made sense she would take the stronger faster horse.

Marcus reached the end of the carriage, the open air hissing around his ears. He jumped across the gap to the stock carriage. Scrapings along the roof halted his advance. Marcus checked both pistols and retreated into the shadows. An embroidered boot swung over the gap, struggling to find the ladder rung. Marcus holstered both pistols, his arms ached as he wrapped them around Jewel's alluring curves.

She rained down blows on his shoulders until Marcus dropped her. Jewel brought her knee up, driving all the air from his lungs.

"Jewel," Marcus coughed.

"Oh Marcus!" Jewel raked her hands from his head down his chest and arms, "I'm sorry!" Jewel gasped when she felt the moisture on his hands.

"Not mine. Guards. Come on."

Marcus clutched his stomach and dragged Jewel back through the freight cart, stopping only to scavenge cloth and alcohol. Marcus leaned over the roped guard, relieved to see him upright and breathing. The man held a cloth to one side of his face.

Jewel moved past him to the guard with the wound in his shoulder. She dashed to her saddle bags and pulled out Winnie's medical supplies.

"You might need to dig it out."

Marcus nodded surprised at how calm Jewel was this time with a bullet wound. The older female passenger sat huddled in her bed, her linen slowly soaking into pink. A porter stumbled down the aisle relighting lamps.

An engineer, wearing grey overalls and coated in coal dust opened the passenger door, a pistol in his hand. "Alright down here Thomas?"

The injured guard raised his good hand, "We will be soon. Thanks."

Marcus knelt in front of Thomas, "At least the driver's not slowing down."

"Company orders. Lost too many good men and too much coin to slow down again."

Jewel returned and gently helped Thomas to lie on the older woman's bunk.

"Excuse me Ma'am," Marcus smiled.

"Dolly, call me Dolly and this looks like it needs a finger of whiskey, or maybe two."

"Yes Ma'am," The porter stammered.

"And two glasses!" Dolly called as she scrambled to the edge of her bunk in her nightgown. She picked up a lantern that hung on the side and held it above the guard's bloodied form.

Jewel smirked, "I brought this."

She handed it to Dolly who took a swig and then pressed it to the lips of Thomas.

"I ain't about to fuss so make it quick." Thomas said as he took a swig.

Marcus knelt on Thomas's hip, with one hand on his shoulder. He handed the knife to Jewel. She took a swig from the bottle and then splashed it over the blade. He watched the focus on Jewel's face, her freckles paling twice while she slid her fingers into the wound. Gently she dug the knife point in to increase the width of the wound and Thomas grunted, his body tensing under Marcus's weight.

Dolly snatched the knife and held the blade in the lantern flame, the steel glowing cherry red. The train shifted to the right and Jewel paused. Marcus felt the carriage swing back and Jewel dug her fingers in, pulling back with a sucking tear. A deformed lump of metal rolled into her palm. She hiccupped and snatched the whiskey bottle. Marcus took the knife from Dolly and pressed it into Thomas's skin.

The guard howled and shuddered, gritting his teeth as sweat broke out across his forehead. The porter returned with two glasses and a bottle. He poured one for Thomas and another for Dolly. Jewel padded the wound and Marcus leaned Thomas up to wrap the bandages. Dolly sat down on the mattress and plumped up Thomas with her pillows.

"Here," Dolly offered Marcus the next pour.

"No thank you."

Dolly shrugged her shoulders, "Suit yourself"

"Someone better keep watch." Marcus added.

"I doubt their coming back tonight." Jewel said, her blue eyes glowing violet in the tangerine light, "If their horses weren't already blown from catching the KATY, dashing off to catch your brown will do them for the night."

"Very clever," Thomas raised his glass to Jewel.

"She can be sometimes," Marcus added with a smirk.

The second guard came to stand beside the bed, "Wyatt took a blow behind his ear, I reckon he'll be out for the night, but he's still breathing."

"We all are Jeffrey."

Jewel stood in front of Jeffrey and directed him to sit down on the bunk. Slowly she pulled down the bloodied and dusty cloth. One side of his cheek had been grazed from his chin to his dark hair line and a ligature mark ringed his throat in purple. Jewel dampened the cloth and slowly began to wipe away the muck and blood. He winced only once until she narrowed her eyes at him. He sucked in his gut and straightened his shoulders allowing Jewel to clean the wound without another sound.

Thomas shot his hand out to Marcus who shook it, "You saved my life."

"Don't mention it, I'm sure you'd do the same."

"Who were they?" Thomas asked.

"The Turner Gang or what's left of them. It was Cooper Brady that got me at the tender and Jesse Harkins back here. Benny Bolt had the horses." Marcus strolled down to the back of the carriage and picked up the slashed rope from the floor. He thumbed the knots as he returned back to Thomas.

"The T-T-Turners!" Jeffrey stammered, "I thought they were dead."

Marcus handed him the knots, "Soon."

Thomas chuckled and then winced, "I thought there were supposed to be more of them."

"Miles and Nate Garcia hung in 1874, and Baby-face was shot dead in Delano last month." Marcus said.

Dolly burped and clicked her fingers. The porter refilled her glass.

"What the Hell do they want with the KATY, they took nothing." Jeffrey asked.

"They were after revenge for who shot Baby-face Turner."

"And they thought he was on our train?" Dolly burped and clicked her fingers. The porter refilled her glass.

Marcus nodded, "Jeff can you hold a rifle?"

The man rolled his shoulder, "I can. I'll take the freight end, keep an eye on Wyatt."

"I need another bed." Dolly hiccupped.

"Take mine," Marcus stepped back.

Dolly held her arm out and the porter helped her across the aisle.

"The Turners! It's all very exciting!" Dolly prattled as she wandered to her new dwellings.

Jewel stood to move and Thomas caught her wrist. Marcus pivoted, his hand slammed down on the guard's wrist.

"I have no truck with either of you." Thomas whispered, "But I'm no dullard either. It was your horse that led them away. I know who else is on the run from Delano." Thomas released his grip.

Jewel inhaled. She threw a glance to Marcus who watched Jeff taking his position at the rear. The lamps flickered in the midnight air.

"What are you going to do?" Marcus hissed.

"You saved my men, you saved this train."

"I didn't kill him." Jewel said.

Marcus sucked in air through his teeth.

"Lucky Chuck did, after a crooked hand of Poker. But they killed my husband. Hung him and gutted him like an animal. I had to shoot my own horse." Jewel's voice quavered. She closed her eyes for a second. When Jewel opened them, Thomas was running his fingers down his thin moustache.

"And you?"

"Besides the fact that she's innocent, would you leave her to the Turners?" Marcus said.

Thomas shook his head, "If you're on this train when we arrive at Caddo, I won't have many options."

"Caddo?"

"Floods took out the KATY bridge at the Red River in 1874 Colbert's Ferry is the only way to cross."

"Till Caddo then."

Marcus took his position at the front carriage, dousing the lamps as he went.

Jewel squeezed Thomas's hand gently before wandering up to Marcus. He rested his back against the carriage door, as he sat on the platform. Marcus eyes scanned the inky horizon, ebony shapes pock-marking the slate landscape, with Thomas's rifle on his knee.

"Get some sleep."

"I will soon." Jewel sat down with her thigh touching his.

"He's right you were clever with the decoy horse."

Jewel snorted, "Yeah but now what do I ride?" She thanked the darkness for concealing the blush on her cheeks, "We're a mount down and I'm not about to become a horse thief."

Marcus exhaled, "Well get to Caddo first, it's gotta be about a full day's ride from there to the Red River. I can sell my rifle."

"We could sell Bryce's, I mean Francis's guns."

"Nah ah." Marcus slowly shook his head. His grizzled cheeks looked all the more sinister in the shadows. "Those guns stay with me. If the Turners catch up and we don't have them it'll be worse."

"And yet every lawman in the west is looking for them."

"That's right. You try and sell them and it'd be like waving a red flag at a bull."

Jewel smiled, a thought curled around her mind and wouldn't let go. She laughed.

"What? Come on out with it."

"Find me an alehouse and I can win us a horse."

Marcus started to shake his head and paused. He patted Jewel on the knee, "Get some sleep."

As Jewel rose a yawn escaped her lips, leading to Marcus's own yawn.

"Wake me up so I can take over."

Marcus didn't answer.

Jewel returned inside her limbs suddenly as heavy as lead as she climbed over the slumbering Dolly. The steady rocking of the train brought sleep to her overwrought body.

Dawns subtle heat caressed Jewels' cheek, a thundering rattle disturbed her thoughts and she sat upright only to thump her head on the carriage ceiling. She bit down a curse as she rubbed her hair line. Marcus! Jewel scrambled down the bunk as fast as she could, only to find Marcus chatting to the porter slowly sipping on a coffee.

The horizon was a smear of ash and steel, fingers of the sun piercing the ruffled clouds ready to embrace the landscape. Jewel savored the rockier outcrops, Texas was close. She could almost smell it. Her stomach growled as she approached.

Marcus thanked the porter and handed a bundle of food to Jewel, "Time to go."

Jewel frowned but followed Marcus down the carriage passed, Thomas's sleeping form. At least the guard had given them a head start, but how far could they get in a day? On one horse at that! Marcus shouldered their saddle bags as they walked through the freight cart. Jewel grabbed her saddle bags and unloaded half her belongings. She kept Winnie's dress, a pair of denims and two shirts. The rest was shoved behind the boxes that lined the carriage. Marcus did the same.

Jewel waited until his back was turned before she stuffed a bottle of whiskey into her saddle bag. Who knew when they might need it? When they reached the stock car, *Scout* was more than amicable to stretching his legs. Marcus unhinged the rear panels, the tracks rushed underneath.

"It seemed a lot slower in the dark." Jewel mumbled.

"Well wait till they hit the brakes." Marcus unwrapped a bacon roll and handed it to Jewel. She scoffed it down in four large bites.

She didn't have to, as the sun rose, the train still sped along the tracks, *Scout* shuffling in his bay. With the scent of freedom just beyond his nose, the horse was just as ready to be free as

Jewel. A whistle blew and Jewel twitched.

"Stay close." Marcus pulled his Stetson low over his forehead as he climbed into the saddle.

"Wait!"

"*Scout*'s good, but he'll break a leg with both of us on his back." Marcus edged the horse closer, the tracks reduced from a blur to single slats, the train whistle shrilled again.

Marcus kicked *Scout* in the flanks and the horse skittered to the edge. With one flick of the reins and quick whistle, the man and horse were gone. Jewel shielded her eyes against the dawn as Marcus brought the animal alongside the train. Jewel felt the color drain from her face as she measured the distance.

"Come on," Marcus shouted.

Jewel pulled her own hat down, stuffing her hair into the lining to hold it safely on her head. She took a deep breath and then climbed out onto the siding. It had seemed less daunting when she couldn't see the ground! Jewel concentrated on Marcus as he brought *Scout* closer. She leaned out with one arm and one leg. Marcus brought the horse closer, his fingers hooked in her belt loops. Jewel felt her fingers snag, the air between train and horse sped beneath her. The dust clogged her arid throat, she closed her eyes.

Solid leather landed under her buttocks and Jewel opened her eyes. She clutched the pommel and threw her leg over the other side of the saddle. Marcus's bulk buffeted her back, his arm wrapped around her waist, his palm splayed across her stomach. Jewel gasped as *Scout*s momentum rocked Marcus against her. Fear evaporated as his thighs trapped hers.

"I've got you." His whisper sent a flurry of tingles down her spine.

Words evaded Jewel. The wind tried to lift her hat and she slapped her hand on her hat to stop it. Marcus's whiskered cheeks gently caressed her neck as his desire hardened. Marcus let *Scout* pace out alongside the train. The decreasing rhythm only brought more torture to the betrayal her body delivered. Jewel's breasts swelled as molten heat blossomed. Slowly

Jewel rolled her spine back until it melded to Marcus's muscular chest.

Marcus's breaths became ragged, the heated air licking the back of her ear. His hand descended, traversing below her belt buckle and halting at her buttons. She rotated her pelvis back, a moan escaped as Marcus pulled her tight against his arousal. For the briefest moment, she thought she felt his lips press down on her shoulder before both his hand and his mouth were gone.

Ahead the township of Cobbo loomed on the horizon, the town about to awake to the news of the Turner gang shooting in the middle of Indian Territory. If Jewel hadn't been in the mix herself, she would agree it was a good yarn. But they had three injured guards to prove it, and a sighting of the infamous Ruby Drawers. If she had a shovel, she would dig till she couldn't see sky.

"How long till Colbert?" Jewel finally managed.

Marcus grunted and exhaled slowly, "Sit behind me."

Jewel nodded as he slowed *Scout* down to a walk. Marcus met her gaze and instead of climbing down, Jewel rotated in the saddle, rolling around his waist. Jewel reached his hip only to have Marcus shove her into place.

"You don't have to be rude, Marcus" Jewel squealed as *Scout* leapt forward. Her arms coiled around Marcus's waist, her cheek pressed against his back. She felt Marcus chuckle as they sped across the Plains. Jewel hoped her smile didn't trickle through his back.

Chapter 18

"You should rest" Jewel lamented. It wasn't just the unending momentum of *Scout*, the twitching of Marcus's muscles under her hands, or that the midday sun had reached maximum temperature. They had alternated walking beside *Scout* to give the horse some rest and now Marcus slumped in the saddle the reins dropped from his grip. "Come on, you'll be useless to me if the Turners or anyone else for a matter of fact catches up to us."

"Fine," Marcus grunted.

Jewel took the reins and directed *Scout* to a grove of elms that lined a narrow bayou.

"I reckon we're just outside of Carriage Point." Jewel said.

She missed what Marcus mumbled as he slowly climbed down from the saddle.

"That's probably a good thing. I know the Overland Stage ain't running anymore but Carriage Point might still be a busy station." Jewel unloaded the saddle bags and let *Scout* range free, heading first to the tiny tributary for a drink.

Marcus stumbled over to one of the thick trees.

Using one of the bags as a pillow Marcus lay down and dragged his Stetson over his face, "Wake me in an hour."

Jewel nodded. The man needed more than an hour. Jewel set about making camp, gathering wood for a fire and unpacking Marcus's coffee tripod. She took time to wash what she could of herself in the cool water and changed into her cream shirt. By the time that Marcus actually woke she had a pot of beef and beans over the heat and the Kansas sun was a full hand span above the horizon. The elms glittered emerald and gold as a breeze swept along the bayou. Jewel swished the flies away from her dinner as Marcus stirred. He stretched, his joints cracking as he rolled his shoulders. His eyes adjusted to the afternoon light, his hazel gaze, like a sunset across the wheat fields.

He stood up abruptly and scanned their surroundings, "That was longer than an hour."

"I know." Jewel stirred the pot of beans, blowing across the hot liquid before she tasted it, "Not bad."

"We shouldn't have stayed so long. We need to move."

"You needed your sleep," Jewel said.

Marcus wandered down to the water's edge and disappeared out of sight. He returned with his face moist. He scrubbed his hand down his beard, squeezing the water droplets onto his already sodden shirt.

Jewel scooped up another helping of beef and beans on the spoon, gently cooling it with her breath, as she strolled over to Marcus. She raised it to his lips and he obliged, sucking it tenderly off the spoon. Polished amber gemstones trapped her eyes, as he began to unbutton his shirt.

"Could use a bit of spice, it's a bit bland, a bit boring." Marcus said as he turned his back to her.

Jewel frowned and moved back to the fire, "Feel free to spice it yourself."

Marcus shucked on another shirt this one green, blue blemishes climbed his ribs and shoulders.

"Eat up. We'll move out as soon as we can. I wouldn't be surprised if a posse is forming already."

"They'd go after the Turners first wouldn't they?"

Marcus shrugged into his fresh shirt, "Hurry up."

Jewel clicked her tongue at his tone, and dug into her meal. Marcus allowed her the briefest moment to scrub the pot before he mounted *Scout*. Marcus put his hand down to Jewel who refused it, clambering onto the rear without assistance.

"I figured you'd want to cross Colbert's as close to dark as possible." Jewel said.

"As long as the Turners don't beat us to it, or you don't try and run off again."

Jewel rolled her forehead against his shoulders, "I'm not

running. I'm not even arguing with you any more Marcus."

It was true. The Turners catcalls echoed in her mind. If things had been different it could have easily been Marcus or herself hanging from a tree like Calvin or worse hanging from a podium in the town square. Jewel wanted to trust in Marcus's plan that the Rangers would somehow be able to help. But what if they betrayed Marcus? They had no reason to believe her innocence.

"I'm grateful for your help Marcus. I'm not sure I could do this alone." She felt a wave of tension coil through her muscles. Her lids became moist and she tried to blink it away, "Thank you."

Marcus gently squeezed Jewels leg above her knee, "I gave you my word."

Jewel couldn't answer for the tightness in her throat. She nodded and wrapped her arms around his waist. He nudged *Scout* onwards breaking the horse into a trot.

Jewel watched the scenery wander by listening to Marcus's steady breathing, the easy silence between them comforting to her mind. Slowly Jewel began to hum, the hum spiraling into another Cowtown ditty and she felt Marcus's shoulders relax even further. His plans would see her safely back to Dew Springs but then what? Marcus would ride onwards with Baby-face's guns to either his own arrest or the Turner's noose. Her thoughts seemed to drag through a quagmire, each tendril of an idea sucked down into the mud at the thought of Marcus putting himself at risk. Could Jewel face knowing that Marcus was riding off to fix her problem? His father would have a fit, knowing Jewel was the reason for his son's absence. But, she blinked her eyes clear, if she got Marcus to Dew Springs there would be no way his father would let him leave.

Marcus took the first turn at walking from *Scout* and now it was his time again. He lost count of the miles they crossed in between. Marcus pulled his sore muscles from the saddle, glad to stretch them out over the Plains.

"When we get to Dew Springs, you might see about getting another horse."

"Only one of Hamerton's."

"Of course," Marcus added.

Time was slipping through his fingers like sand. When they arrived at Dew it was only a matter of time before the arrangement of Whit's fiancé became known. Jewel still seemed intent of getting under his skin, although she now seemed to take their predicament more seriously. Marcus scanned the horizon as it thickened into a swampy forest. An array of buildings could be seen, with an open galley between several houses and smoke rising from an outbuilding in the rear. Marcus tasted the air, salted meats and smoked pork made his mouth water.

Marcus eyed the clearing through the dark emerald trees that revealed the river bank. He could feel the pull in his chest. Texas, his home was calling him. He glanced at Jewel as she sat higher in the saddle, with one hand shading her gaze, her sapphire eyes ignored Colbert's lodgings focusing instead on the sunset tinted mud now coated in swathes of copper and gold. Her lips were pulled tight, her eyes wide.

"Almost there." Jewel whispered.

"I know." Marcus smiled back, he pointed to the log corduroy road, "You head down to the river. I'll pay the guide."

It was two dollars and a quarter all up to cross the river. Every cent was worth it as the workers dragged the timber barge across the guide ropes to the Texas bank of the Red River. Even *Scout* seemed to sense the change, pawing the wooden boards as the drawbridge lowered. Marcus climbed into the rear and pulled Jewel behind him. They didn't even spare a word for the ferryman as the horse leapt onto the bank. *Scout*'s hooves slid up the steep embankment until the darkened leaves enveloped them.

Marcus pulled the horse back to a consistent pace, trying to put as many miles between themselves and the river as possible until making camp.

The moon rose to its peak, the silvery sentry lit the path as the hours wandered by. Jewel remained pressed against Marcus for the last hour as she slumbered. Her warmth leeching into his soul as the night's temperature cooled. His mind wandered with *Scout*s regular plodding.

The Turners had been close. Striking their train as it crossed Indian Territory. Were they raiding every train? What had Calvin told Gabriel Turner? Marcus thought back to the stranger outside Petersburg. The killer made it back to Dodge, so what else could he have told Turner? It was a possibility Marcus couldn't ignore. Without Abe and Theo's support he needed to reach Quinn. But first, Marcus needed to get Jewel to safety.

Then he would be free from the restless energy that multiplied in his veins when she touched him. Under the luminous crescent, his thoughts twisted to hazy afternoons, and wicked nights. As Jewel slumped around his waist it sent a jolt into his system. He felt his desire stir and Marcus cursed himself. He steered *Scout* into uneven ground, until he reached a thatch of cedar elms.

Jewel squeaked as she came awake and Marcus gently pulled her out of the saddle. She meandered around *Scout* and yawned as she helped drag the saddle bags onto the ground. Jewel wandered off out of sight, leaving Marcus to stake the horse out in the darkness. He set about making a quick scrub fire and had a mediocre effort by the time Jewel returned yawning into her fist. He had laid out their sleeping mats either side of the fire but he needn't bother.

Jewel brought hers over to him where he lay and curled up beside him. She flung her arm across his chest and her lips nuzzled into his neck. A northern mockingbird let out a sweet song, as if to challenge Marcus's thoughts. He ran his fingers down her plait, the ginger shining through the black more than ever. What Marcus wouldn't give to take a step back in time, before the Turners, before Calvin and before the Rangers. It could be just him and Jewel on the Plains, the moon the only witness if he was to satiate his deepest cravings.

"Is this how you imagined it?" Marcus said.

Jewel had to think hard for an answer as somewhere she had envisioned exactly this, "I'm sure this is not how you thought you'd be returning."

Marcus sniffed. His profile proud and distinct in the moonlight, "Tell me about Delano?"

"It was fun, wild, free," Jewel said, her breath warming her nose against his grizzly neck. She resisted the urge to press a kiss against the vein that throbbed under the skin.

"You ever shoot anyone?"

Jewel leaned back and looked him in the eye, "Only in the hand," She laid back down, "and like Belles' husband he deserved it."

Marcus scoffed and dug a finger into his collar, "Calvin didn't seem to have any bullet holes in him."

Jewel's arm retracted resting between her breasts and Marcus. The night's air seemed to drop another degree, "He'd have to have ...."

Marcus shuffled across the sleeping mat and rolled onto his side. His eyes had been shielded by the shadows, now the gentle flicker of the camp fire curled tendrils of gold through his irises, "More than once, you've started to say something about Calvin and you."

Jewel rolled onto her back as if facing Marcus rejection time and time again hadn't been hard enough, "He never raised a hand to me, he fed me, kept me clothed, promised adventure."

"But?"

Marcus shoulders were raised, sending a shadow across her form. Tendrils of his hair coiled downwards, the strands like fingers clawing at her face and Jewel shivered.

"Calvin loved the chase. His bed was always warmed with the latest girl, until another one came along," She said.

"You must have loved him?"

"Only that one night."

Marcus coughed, "I meant in order to marry him."

Jewel ignored the rising warmth in her cheeks, she had married Calvin. Why? Deep down she knew. Calvin promised what she chased, "He said he loved me."

Jewel listened as the mockingbird increased his shrill call, no response from his aloof mate somewhere out on the Plains. Jewel's chest ached. Running away from Dew didn't solve her heartache over Marcus, just like running now hadn't solved her latest problems. Because deep down Jewel loved the chase too, only she wanted to be caught. You have to stand still to be caught, Jewel mused.

Marcus rolled onto his back, so they lay flat side by side, "Why didn't you divorce him earlier?"

"I was someone's wife. I mean if I had a husband I didn't have to -"

"Worry about any others."

Jewel nodded, "Something like that."

They lay there silently listening to each other's breaths, disturbed only so often with the hiss and crackle of the camp fire. Jewel watched the embers float upwards, endlessly chasing one another until they finally ran out of spark. The ash floated away on the wind, the constellations overhead none the wiser to their futile chase.

Marcus threw his arms behind his head, "How did you win Bryce's guns?"

"Six cans. Six bullets. Six seconds."

Marcus laughed, "That's my girl!"

Jewel laughed and listened to the crickets finally at ease with Marcus and her presence that they resumed their nightly choir, "Why did you leave Dew Springs?"

Marcus turned on his side, his breath heated her cheek, his voice somber, "To find something."

Jewel rolled to meet him, a little hummingbird inside her soul tried its wings, the door to the cage firmly shut. She had been down this road many times before. Perhaps Marcus and

Jewel were destined to chase each other until they fizzled out like the embers of the fire. "And did you?"

"Sorta," His answer slithered under her skin as Marcus cupped his palm over her hip.

Jewel rose up on one elbow, her fingers traced down his elbow and onto his ribs, "You found a lot of trouble by the looks of you scars."

"I did."

Jewel worked her hands around to the concealed scar on his hip, "What's this one from?"

"Stagecoach robbery. Three of them stole the coach leaving the passengers in the desert. We crept up on them at dawn, caught one with his pants down literally."

Jewel laughed.

"The other two put up a bit of a fight."

"And this one," She felt the purple scar on his back through the fabric of his shirt.

"Knife. Bar fight in Louisiana."

"And this one?" Jewel ran her hand up to his shoulder the biggest scar of them all, the silvery spider webs joined with a burn.

"That was when I lost *Cutter*. Indian spear. They had to cauterize it after they got it out."

"Are you always in the wrong spot at the wrong time?"

"On the contrary, Quinn said I'd die putting myself in the right place."

Jewel couldn't meet his gaze, "So it would seem."

Marcus stroked a curl beside her ear, sending a raft of tremors down her spine, his voice was low and thick, "Enough excitement for a dull cowpoke."

"I never said that," Jewel mumbled. Jewel traced her fingertips along his neck and up to his rough jaw, "It's been more than enough these days."

Jewel arched her back bringing her breasts in contact with Marcus's chest. The hummingbird inside its cage beat its wings into frenzy. Marcus rolled forward, his knee driving between her thighs as his mouth clamped down on hers. His tongue rushed over her lips and Jewel shuddered in his arms. The soft mahogany scent of Marcus overwhelmed her senses as his frame trapped hers. Every muscle in his body seemed to tense and writhe under her caress.

The fire creaked and sizzled, the heat on her cheek was nothing compared to the wildfire of the man in her arms. Her body slickened, as Marcus rocked his thigh slowly between hers. She drove her fingers under his shirt, savoring every contact that ignited a blaze in her blood. Her body ached for his touch to linger.

Jewel slanted her mouth across his, as his breathing deepened. The pressure of his body increased, his hand trailing lightening down her ribs to the small of her back. His grip curled around her buttock and squeezed. Jewel moaned into his feverish kisses, the man was all power and heat.

The air vanished from her lungs as Marcus knee drove her thighs further apart, his desire hardened, barely restrained in his tight denims. Jewel couldn't resist and rocked her pelvis to his rhythm as his arousal ground down on her molten center. Jewel trembled, her breath stolen, surrendering to his hunger. She fumbled with his buttons, tracing over the feathery hair that crossed his chest. His heart beats strummed under her palm. Jewel pushed his shirt further backwards, a snarl rumbled in Marcus's throat. His muscles clenched under her caress, rolling as he bucked against her. Marcus suckled along her jaw line, and Jewel's eyes closed, exposing her throat. Marcus thrust forward as his teeth sunk into her tender skin. Jewel whimpered at his blistering touch. She focused on her own buttons, "If only I'd never left," Jewel laughed.

Marcus suddenly leaned backward, his eyes ablaze, "Why did you leave Dew?"

The buttons were too small, her fingers too shaky, she would have to shuck the shirt over her head, "Cause you wouldn't give me what I wanted," Jewel laughed.

Marcus didn't move.

Jewel curled her arm around his neck to pull him down but Marcus resisted.

The tendrils of gold and ruby through his gaze suddenly cooled, the ardor now replaced with something else. Was it disgust?

Marcus retreated to his knees, "I still can't." With that he stood upright.

Jewels gut clenched, the fire that had burned for Marcus now fizzled, replaced with the ash of fury. Jewel rose to her feet and picked up her sleeping mat. She dragged it across the other side of the fire.

"Jewel you are -"

"Don't bother explaining Marcus." Jewel tried to keep the sound of tears from her voice. When would she realize that Marcus would never find her good enough? The hummingbird would never fly, "I got it. There's a fine line between fun and trouble."

Marcus growled, "I know you were always on the side of trouble Jewel."

Jewel threw herself down to the mat, "And you were never on the side of fun." Jewel rolled over, her shoulders blades warmed by the wave of heat, "And for you and your Mama, and your Pa's benefit, you should know I was married like a proper lady, so if you start thinking I'm like Bethany Sampson, ashes on the wind, you can eat your hat!"

"I never said that."

"You ain't ever said otherwise either Marcus."

Marcus stormed into the moonlight, his body shuddering, his chest aching. How did she turn his words against him? What Jewel teased wasn't what was right. He had given his word to his father and to Whit's fiancé. Damned if Jewel would crucify him for keeping his word! He never said she was a loose woman just a wild spirit.

Marcus replayed the conversation back through his mind. Maybe he had insinuated it, judged Jewel too quickly. Marcus assumed that Jewel would find a lover, a high stakes, wild man that would satisfy her.

Why? Because it made Marcus feel safe. Like Jewel married to Calvin she never had to marry another. With his perception of Jewel chasing wild men, Marcus had kept his heart safe. Marcus would never have to live up to what Jewel wanted or needed. Had he even tried?

Marcus sat down on a dirt mound and picked up a handful of stones. Every scar on his body should mark as a testament that he had tried. His mind flashed through a dozen women whose bed he had warmed in the last few years. Marcus didn't want to admit the striking familiar ginger curls they all had.

Jewel. Marcus hadn't tried to forget her and he hadn't stepped up to be what she needed either. Marcus looked to the glittering skies above; he had less control over his destiny than he had the day he rode away from Dew Springs. He couldn't compromise his promise to Jewel, or to his father. As Jewel drew him in, every step he took closer, he would only break her more. He needed to get her to Dew Springs as fast as he could. For both their sakes.

Chapter 19

Jewel didn't talk to Marcus all the following day and for half of the next as well. He asked her when to break and when to swap riders, he offered her food and drink with no response. Jewel took her leave when they rested walking just out of sight until he moved them on again. At the night, the crackle of the small fire Marcus built was the only warmth he felt. The intermittent squeaks and hisses, hoots and scurries of their woodland surrounds were the only sounds that offered Marcus comfort. And he deserved it too. Jewel's silence gave him time to think through the fog that plagued his mind.

As they crossed the landscape, the caramel rolling plains became crisscrossed here and there with wide slashes of emerald and yellow. He had kept them from the main thoroughfare as the Cowtown crowds thickened. Texas blue bells dotted the edges of the wheat, corn and cotton fields as they travelled further south. Marcus kept a vigil on the horizon and their back tracks, while keeping a wide berth of the caravans, wagons, and cowboys that billowed dust as high as the clouds as they moved down the Chisolm Trail.

It wasn't until Marcus and Jewel reached the outskirts of Fort Worth the following day that Jewel finally spoke to him. The afternoon sun began to slide down the cornflower blue sky. The ivory tufts of cloud blushed orange.

"We need another horse." Jewel said from *Scout*'s saddle.

Marcus almost lost his step alongside her, regaining his footing without trouble, "You going to cheat at cards?"

"You gonna walk to Dew Springs?"

Marcus cinched his jaw. He didn't like it but Jewel had point. It put them in danger in more ways that he could counter-act. They could be recognized and they would hang or they could be called out in the game of cards and be shot.

His elbow tentatively touched his pistol on his hip. Marcus was fast, and Jewel was faster. But travelling with just *Scout* had them hamstrung on speed. He had heard that Fort Worth had suffered greatly after the Panic of 1873, perhaps in such a sleepy Cowtown, they could slip in and out unnoticed. Marcus watched Jewel's ashen curls spark with glints of garnet and amber as the sun reclined. Jewel couldn't go anywhere unnoticed.

"You do exactly as I say."

"Marcus only one of us has spent the last two years in dance halls and saloons, maybe you should follow my lead."

Marcus hummed his annoyance. Her tone definitely had more acid in it, part of him still found it alluring, she was like a kitten hissing at the wind.

"No running."

"No running Marcus."

"I want -"

"You have my word. No running."

Marcus waited until darkness fell before he climbed into the saddle and lead *Scout* and Jewel into the city limits of Fort Worth. He kept their pace sedate as they crossed the Trinity River and made their way through the wide streets. They trotted past the railway construction yards, piles of steel and timber piled in an area. Soon Fort Worth would have a railway connection from the south to the north. The railways triggered something in Marcus's mind. He could feel the cogs turning in his head trying to connect the thought to a memory or an idea. Marcus let it go.

Music from the saloons spilled through the open windows as patrons tumbled through the main doors to end up in a heap beside the hitching posts. Marcus threw Jewel a dark look over his shoulder. She raised one eyebrow and pouted.

He took them further into the town and the streets bustled with cowboys, buffalo traders, and railroad workers. Marcus surveyed the jam-packed gambling parlors as the cigar smoke hovered above patrons, the men clutched their wallets close and their women even closer. They passed numerous bordellos that hollered their wares, groups of cowboys some young and other young at heart, sure to be parted from their money.

Marcus clambered down from *Scout* outside The Lucky Gelding a gambling parlor whose interior was reasonably well lit by a large chandelier that dangled over the crowd. Men and women wandered from bar to table while an organist kept time with a fiddler in one corner.

Marcus put his hand out to help Jewel down but she dismounted without a word. Marcus hitched *Scout* up next to a fine black bay gelding with four white socks. Marcus managed two steps up the timber treads only to have Jewel pull his elbow. He gritted his teeth as Jewel led down the alley between parlor and dancing hall to the street at the rear. The gambling dens here had significantly more shadows between their windows, the stench of manure and body odor thicker in the air.

Marcus regarded the grizzled jaws and heavy hips that wandered these narrow streets. A window smashed behind them. He turned to greet the threat, only to see two men jump on a third and pummel him into the sawdust. The barman came with thick clubs and rained blows down on the others until they broke it up. A woman came to the victim's aide and lifted him to his feet, together they scurried away into the night, leaving a trail of blood to be trampled by the crowds.

"This is -"

"Shhh!" Jewel snapped, "They've got proper dealers, see! And my hands would be seen in all that light." Jewel whispered.

Jewel grabbed Marcus by his shirt front and dragged him up the boardwalk. Jewel released him as she stepped into a dingy gambling den. Marcus paused to read the rotten wooden sign that swung above the entrance way, A Kings Ransom.

Marcus watched Jewel meander to one of the tables, and take a seat. The men around her didn't object and suddenly she had been dealt into the round. Marcus took a stool at the bar and ordered a beer. He sipped it slowly just to cool his ire and calm his mind and he scanned the crowd, finding at least three walking wanted posters in the narrow room. Maybe handing in a bounty would fill their pockets quicker than poker. Marcus resumed his count of pistols and furrowed brows. Having this many thugs in one area wasn't a coincidence, the law had no reach here.

"What brings you to Hells Half Acre?" the barman started, "Chasing luck or chasing tail."

Marcus took his beer and paid the man, "A bit of both." He grimaced.

Jewel won the first hand. Unlike her 'damsel' portrayal on the train, this time Jewel didn't clap her hands enthusiastically instead she scooped her winnings in front of her without so much as a smile. Slowly Jewel began to stack her pot as the cards were dealt again. Marcus shoulders itched and he tried to ignore the clench in his gut as he watched the corruption. He justified it in his mind that they all cheated and it became a contest of who cheated the best.

Working girls came to loiter between the tables, as men leaned back to sample the wares. A voluptuous blonde came to proposition Marcus, and he moved her own. At the den's entrance, a man loitered on the threshold stroking his greying beard with stunted fingers. Marcus watched as the man considered the crowd. He must have thought better of it, and stepped back to the street.

Jewel took the second hand, and lost the third. She had a considerable pot in front of her when Marcus ordered his second beer. He took one sip and left it to warm on the bar. He had bought *Scout* for a bargain from Cade at a hundred dollars. Normally, he'd have to pay two hundred for the quality that came from Hamerton's breeding and training. With this crowd in Fort Worth, a decent horse with tack and saddle might cost one hundred and fifty, less if the cowboy had lost his pot. Jewel won again and Marcus sensed the mood alter around her table. Of the four men that she opposed, two put their heads together and whispered. Jewel bought a round of drinks for the table and the mood shifted again. She lost the next round when the blonde working girl came back to Marcus. The Dove had drawn a mole on her cheek just below her left eye. Her personality seemed as genuine as the beauty spot and her bleached hair.

"Can I getcha anything love?" She chirped, a gap between her rear teeth evident when she smiled.

"No thanks."

"It's unlike a man like you to be without company?" She ran her hand down his forearm and pressed his bicep between her breasts.

"I'm taking a rest tonight, I hope to be pissing straight by Tuesday." Marcus sniffed.

The woman tried a laugh, her bosom trembling as she did so. She put her hand on his upper thigh and ran it down to his knee and upwards again.

"You look as clean as a whistle to me," She licked her painted lips.

"Yeah but I ain't got a pot to piss in." Marcus tried.

"You got money for beer," The woman tugged on his arm until he turned to face her, she ran her other hand up his collar to his cheek, "Besides a looker like you, I'll give you a quick one on the house." The hand that had been on his forearm ran down to cup his groin, "Oh" her eyes widened and she smirked, "In fact, I might take my time with this hun,"

With as much manners as Marcus could muster, he increased pressure on her wrist until the woman let go, her brows raised as the pressure became too much and she stepped back.

She rubbed her wrist rapidly, "If I don't take your fancy, I can find another. Whatcha like? Petite, big, oriental?"

"None that take my fancy," Marcus turned back to find Jewels eyes on her cards, but something about the set of her jaw told him she'd witnessed the exchange.

Jewel had control of the deal this time and Marcus moved to take his seat.

Marcus heard tobacco spittle land on the floor beside him and ignored it. Another patron didn't.

"Watchdya say?"

The spitter stood in his spot and tossed his cards, "Someting wrong wit ya ears!"

The accuser shouted back and Marcus lost his reply in the sounds of glass smashing. He saw Jewels cheeks pale, her lips moved and he had just enough time to turn and duck as a beer bottle flew overhead and smashed another gamblers mug from between his fingers.

The crowd erupted, tables overturned, a weight collided with his back and Marcus splayed across the next table. He spun and threw punches, catching a blow in the ribs and another glanced off his shoulder. The piano man kept thumbing the keys, the music adding to the bedlam.

The publicans bully men pressed through the crowd. Their clubs raised as they struck indiscriminately at heads. Marcus popped his head up and glimpsed the chair where Jewel had sat was now upturned. His fist connected to jaw and gut as Marcus worked his way to the other side of the saloon. Chairs became projectiles and even the pianist gave safety his priority and dashed upstairs. Suddenly buck shot ran out as the owner stood on the bar, his shotgun smoking, the timber ceiling charred with pellets.

"Take a seat or get out!"

The hired ruffians grabbed a few by the collar and tossed them out the doors.

Marcus surveyed the crowd that spilled out into the streets. The longer he looked the heavier his chest became as Jewel was nowhere to be seen.

Jewel felt the arm curl around her waist and the chair fly from underneath her as the melee began. She kicked and punched at the attacker behind her, her screams lost in the riot. She tumbled into the alley, a kick of sawdust obscured her vision. A dark shadow loomed over her and she lashed out with both heels. One kick collected the an ankle. Like lightening the man's fist drove downwards. Jewel twisted her head. The right side of her face exploded in pain as the shadows grew longer. The scene doubled and Jewel choked on Marcus's name.

Jewel awoke with aching shoulders, and something scratched at her wrists. She tried to move but the images shimmered and nausea spiked. Jewel squeezed her eyes tight until the pain return to her cheek bone. What the Hell had happened? Momentum bounced her in odd directions as the sound of merriment faded through darkened alleys. She could smell leather, as when she opened her eyes, she focused on four white hooves strolling along the pavement. Was she upside down? No. She was strung across the back of a horse, the rump of the black gelding from beside *Scout* at the main street. Jewel listened to the man's gravelly voice and tried to place it in her memory.

"You thought I'd forget didn't ya. You and all your yapping. Texas this and Texas that. Glad I never had to wait for you all the way down in that piss-hole of a town you grew up in."

Jewel tried to form his name but it eluded her, she twisted slowly to see his face. His silhouette with long grey beard drove needles into her chest.

"Lucky Chuck! You bastard!"

"Shh now I was just telling ya how lucky can I be! *Ace* here, had delayed me with a loose shoe just outside Dallas, then I hear a train gets almost robbed. The Turner Gang looking for their lost partner, Ruby 'the whore' Drawers! Imagine you walking in and seeing me at the poker table first, instead of the other way round." Chuck laughed.

"You shot Bryce! It's you who should be on that wanted poster! Not me!"

"Well ain't that a bitch. Ruby Drawers is worth $2000, I ain't worth a dime" he spat a wad of tobacco to the side.

Jewel twisted her head but a part of it caught her hair all the same and she dry retched.

Jewel unloaded a string of curses until Chuck turned in his saddle. This time she couldn't avoid the blow. The dimly light shadows warped until they became whole and she sunk below the surface.

Marcus returned inside the den and scanned the crowd as he moved through it. Jewel's ashy braid and gingham shirt was gone. He spun back around but the blonde woman was working her angle on another man. Marcus dashed into the street. He ran to *Scout* to find the horse still there, but the black bay gone. Had Jewel ran off? Had she played him by getting him to a gambling parlor and then running with the winnings? She had given him her word! He ran his hand down *Scouts* rump. No, if Jewel was to run, she would take his horse. Jewel wasn't a horse thief and she knew Marcus wasn't one either.

Marcus skirted the gambling den, dashing down the alleys either side trying not to panic, and not to be noticed. He returned to the parlor and found the blonde working girl still having no success.

He stepped up behind her and pulled her to one side, "Out with it."

"I thought you weren't interested? Your friend's already paid me, hun so I'll take you upstairs."

"Friend? Who?" Marcus's thumb and forefinger squeezed her elbow. If Jewel had paid a Dove to distract him it was an all-time low. The woman winced and Marcus let go.

"Your friend, the tall one with the grey beard. Said you needed a woman like he needed a pay day."

"I don't know any friend like that."

"Well I can't help you hun. He paid me, but the way his temper is, and yours I ain't inclined to follow through unless you double it."

"Sorry," Marcus cleared his throat, "Tell me more about my friend. He had a grey beard, what else?"

"He was missing some parts of his fingers," She held up her hand and gestured to the top knuckles, "Reckons it's what made him lucky."

Who the hell was she talking about? Whoever it was had taken Jewel. For a payday, he was going to cash her in, "Where's the jail."

"Follow Rusk almost to the river and take a right, corner of Jones and Belknap."

Marcus sprinted from the gambling den to *Scout,* leaping into the saddle. If Marcus raced down the street he would only draw more attention; especially when he reached the more civilized parts of town. Marcus needed to think, to plan.

Marcus regarded the single story timber building that was the county jail, the black bay with white socks was hitched at the front.

Marcus hung back in the shadows and tried to think logically. Suddenly his silver star on his chest didn't seem powerful enough. Marcus wanted to walk in there and demand Jewel be handed over. This small town dullard of a cowboy needed to march into the Fort Worth jail with a plan to save his Jewel!

What options did he have? Marcus had his pistols, the Turner's guns, and not much else. Whoever this man was, he knew Marcus enough to organize a distraction so he could snatch Jewel.

Damn it! Marcus had given Jewel his word and despite it, she was sitting in a cell! A man wandered outside and spat a wad of something onto the ground. Slowly he pulled a cigar out of his pocket and with a clutched fist, lit it from the lantern on the jailhouse porch. Marcus couldn't see his stubby fingers but his movements confirmed he had some difficult with his hands. The flame briefly ignited his profile and Marcus didn't recognize him.

The man mounted his horse and put him into a trot. He tipped his hat to the passers-by commenting something cheerful. A few people wandered around the near side of the jailhouse and shouted obscenities through the window. Marcus didn't need to hear the words to register the sentiment.

Was the man part of the Turners Gang? Would he lead Marcus back to Gabriel or the others? Why would he hand Jewel into the deputies if he was part of the Turner Gang?

Marcus retracted into the shadows as the rider turned east along the river. The anger inside Marcus was unable to be contained. He had experienced this level of intensity every time he faced a foe but this time it was compounded triple time. Marcus squeezed his knees into *Scout* who moved silently through the streets. Marcus wandered down the adjacent alley keeping the man in his sights. He couldn't let the man recognize him from the bar. He would follow him to be sure the Turners weren't hiding in Hells Half Acre. The hairs on Marcus's neck stood to attention, so long as it wasn't an ambush.

Chapter 20

As the stranger rode his black and white pony down past the rail construction yards, Marcus booted *Scout* into a gallop. Marcus should return to the jail, although if the Turners were in Fort Worth, Jewel was safe in her cell. The idea of her fear and panic tightened Marcus's already raw nerves. He needed to keep himself calm. Quinn always chipped him about diving head first.

Marcus pulled ahead and cut down the street. This far out of the main thoroughfare, the moon remained the only light. The warehouses and butchers, saddlery, storehouses and fabric merchants were all closed for the night. The longer Marcus tailed the stranger, the more his motive became clear, the man wasn't scurrying off to find the Turners, he strolled his pony down the street, celebrating his victory. The more Marcus let him wander the longer Jewel suffered. A plan formed in Marcus mind. He still had his star. He was a Ranger and it was Texas after all. But first he needed someone to arrest.

Marcus waited until the man slowly came towards him before he pushed himself into the street.

As the man came in hailing distance he tipped his hat, "All the men of Fort Worth are safe tonight! Tell the town that Ruby Drawers has been caught."

The last string that held Marcus's heart together snapped. He leapt across to the other man's saddle and bore him to the ground. Marcus wrapped his hands around the bearded throat as a handful of dirt was thrown in his face. Marcus wiped his hands across his stinging eyes as a fist landed in his gut. Marcus retracted his shoulder and blindly connected with the man's face. He coiled his hand around the stranger's throat again and as the man tried to stand up. Marcus coughed as the shirt fabric tore through his fingers. A river of anger coursed through his veins and tore at his lungs. The rage had built inside Marcus so suddenly he feared he might kill the man. Marcus inhaled sharply bouncing on his back knee he tried to calm his furor.

"You!" The man hissed.

"Yeah me!" Marcus spat back, blinking wildly through a sheet of muddy tears.

"Ain't no Ranger gonna collar me!" The man barked.

Marcus heard a scuff of feet and twisted his hip. He caught a knee on his inner thigh instead of his groin. Marcus snatched the stranger's leg and held on. Within this distance, and off balance, the man couldn't reach his pistols. Marcus pushed forward and the man slipped. He tried to kick out with his boot, but Marcus trapped it under his arm and dug his fingers into the man's belt. His guns were useless but so were Marcus's.

The stranger retracted his knee and stumbled backwards. His boot came free, the distance between them increased. Marcus rushed forward as he wiped his face again. He heard a knife unsheathe. Marcus put his arm up and caught the man's wrist on his forearm. The stranger spun and the knife bit fabric and caught flesh. Marcus jumped back. His brain registered the location across his stomach but the pain didn't reach his mind.

Marcus threw an uppercut and another, catching the man's chest. He held onto the man's shirt and tried to drag it over his head. If only he hadn't left his cuffs at Hartford! Marcus mind started to cool, the immediate rush had passed and now his attention focused on the situation. If the man couldn't lead Marcus to the Turners, he would lead Marcus to a free Jewel.

Marcus trapped the knife wrist between both of his hands and drove the stranger backwards. Together they landed in the dirt. The older man wriggled for top position grunting as he wrestled with Marcus's strength. He released one hand from the knife just as Marcus felt his gun belt snag. The stranger wasn't going for his own guns! He was going to shoot Marcus with his own!

Instinctively Marcus clutched his pistols only to have the

stranger slash with the knife. Marcus focused on the point of the blade rushing to his eye. He ducked and caught the blade across his eyebrow. A sheet of red ran into his eye. Marcus winced, but increased his weight on the taller opponent. With both hands on the hilt of the dagger, Marcus drove it down. He felt it slide into flesh. The man called out. Marcus drove it deeper. The blade jarred in his fingers as it connected with bone. Marcus plunged it further.

The stranger gasped, his jaw went slack. Marcus retracted the knife and sat back. He gasped for his own breath as the man gurgled, the blood bubbling across his whiskered lips. Marcus cursed. The wide eyed start of a dead man me Marcus as he knelt regathering his breath. Marcus tugged his shirt up and wiped his brow. It stung only slightly, his body felt numb. It always felt numb after a fight. That was his problem. The pain was never strong enough to override his instincts. Quinn knew it. He had seen it too many times. Marcus would throw himself forward, when everyone else was holding back. Idiotic. Stupid. Reckless. And now Marcus had killed his arrest. Marcus inhaled deeply. The black and white horse has wandered off to the side and now pawed the ground at the scent of blood. *Scout* stood stoic, his reins dragging on the ground as the horse surveyed either end of the street.

"Yeah I know, before someone comes along." Marcus answered.

The man had long stopped gasping as the blood pooled in his chest and Marcus dragged him from the street and into the rail construction yards.

There Marcus turned him over and riffled through pockets. A pair of dice, too heavy on one side, a flask of whiskey, that Marcus washed his cuts with. A wad of tobacco, a few coins, Ruby's wanted poster, a handful of bullets, something that looked like a tooth, and a rabbits paw tied to a ribbon.

"Who the Devil are you?"

Marcus didn't care. His body started to tremble as the adrenalin rushed out of his system, his legs became heavy.

Marcus returned to the street and gathered the man's horse, tying him up between the stacks of lumber ready for the rail line. What the Hell was Marcus going to do now! Marcus left the man in the dirt and surveyed his surroundings.

The rail yards comprised of stockpiles of timber and steel for the future expansion. The stacks of lumber lined along one side were high enough to hide Marcus, two horses and a dead man. Across the yard Marcus could see several shacks with the Texas and Pacific Railway logo visible. He couldn't kick the feeling of regret at his own stupidity. Marcus ran his shirt up to his eye and wiped away the blood. The stranger was going to kill him but Marcus had picked the fight. Marcus's fingers trembled as the rush ebbed from his system. Which side of the law had Marcus landed on?

The loaded dice had Marcus in a spin. The stranger was some bounty hunter out for an easy payday but he was also a gambler and a cheat at that. Wait, the man had identified Marcus as a Ranger. Marcus let the dice tumble in the dirt. Jewel needed him. He couldn't waste any more time on his conscience.

Marcus dashed from pile to pile staying out of sight of the street, until he reached the storehouses. Perhaps the rail line had tools he could use to break Jewel free. From his earlier recognizance, it was a single story timber building with the jailer stationed at the front. The windows were high with bars and who knew how many cells inside. Jewel would have to be kept separate from any others surely.

Marcus intended on making his arrest and getting a better look at the inside, but now the man was dead he had to think on his feet. Marcus found a storehouse and slammed his hand on the metal caged doorway, the lock jangle in its place. He took a few minutes to empty a bullet of its gunpowder. With a flash of his flint the lock blew open.

Marcus scavenged inside the storehouse for bolt cutter or an axe, maybe a large chain to wrap around the jailhouse bars. Then, with the strangers horse and *Scout* Marcus could pull the bars from their joists.

A familiar and sickly almond scent coated the back of his throat as Marcus regarded the darkened interior. He flipped open the lid of a nearby box and picked up a parcel of cylinders. Unraveling the waxy paper, Marcus walked back into the moonlight and studied the object. As the silvery light cascaded down to splash over Marcus, he froze as he recognized his prize.

Jewel rolled her head from side to side as someone spoke to her, the words not making any sense as she blinked her eyes, "Huh?"

"I said, did ya really shoot two of your lovers in Delano?" A spotty faced youth stood outside of her cell, he must be no older than nineteen.

Jewel mumbled her words, "Francis Turner was never my lover."

"Horseshit! You killed Francis Turner?" An older and thicker jailer said from somewhere behind.

"I never said I shot him. Or the other one, but he killed my husband."

Jewel used the cell bars to pull herself upright and tentatively ran her fingers over her swollen cheek trying not to wince. The thin youth with spotty cheeks leaned on the other side of the bars.

"Well, you got till morning to think about what story ya telling the judge. Two murders and a train robbery! You better have a good yarn ready!" The older man sat behind a desk, his balding head visible between the bars, his boots on the table top.

"I never robbed a train."

"Well, how do you explain three guards injured one of them shot? What's your excuse Miss Drawers?" The younger jailer spoke softly, his eyes wide. Was he impressed or disgusted or both?

Jewel ran her eyes around the jail. She sat in one of two

cells that lined the back wall and a tiny window had been cut into the timber above each cell. Five bars in each. Jewel rested on the floor despite a cot with a thin straw mattress occupying the only other wall. The other cell thankfully was empty. Jewel's mind went back to the gambling dens in Hell's Half Acre. There was not enough law officials and not enough concern to fill this jail. The bordellos, ale houses and gambling dens brought much needed money to the struggling town after the Panic.

"The Turners are coming for me. You better call in the Sheriff, or the Marshall or whoever you need to because as soon as the Turners know I'm here, they'll be here."

"Ahh," The older jailer sneered, "That's what they all say. 'You better watch out, my crooks and cronies are coming for you, you better run, you better hide.' Yep we've heard it all, right up until they swing. No-ones coming for you honey." He turned the page of his newspaper and leaned further back in his chair.

"I doubt that very much," Jewel mumbled.

"Come away Samuel."

"I'm only talking Porter."

The younger deputy obeyed anyway and sat on the edge of the desk watching her. Jewel hoped Marcus would beat the Turners. That he had given his word and despite her being arrested, he would somehow come to help her. Although, he was a lawman...This one time, Jewel prayed for Marcus to keep his word, do the honorable action instead of the lawful action. It wasn't fair to hope Marcus compromised his morals. Jewel had gotten herself into this mess and dragged Marcus down with her. Perhaps getting caught would solidify his route of action, making it easier for Marcus to decide to save himself and move on.

Boot steps thumped along the floorboards, dragging something heavy with it.

"Howdy," Marcus voice sliced through the fog in Jewel's mind.

She froze in relief and self-hatred.

"Howdy, what can I do for you? If you're here for a look-sey, you can turn around right now." The older jailer, Porter, didn't put down his paper.

Samuel stood up, "Whatcha got there, Ranger?"

Jewel's gaze targeted Marcus's brow where a rush of blood had dried down one cheek. At his feet was a lump, for some reason wearing Marcus's navy checked shirt. At the word Ranger, Porter flicked the edge of his paper down to look at Marcus and the shining star on his chest.

"I caught this fellow sneaking around the Texas and Pacific railyards."

"Hey?" Porter folded his newspaper and rose from his seat to inspect the prisoner, just as an explosion ruptured the air. "What the Devil!"

Samuel ran outside only to return a second later, "The railyards have exploded!"

Porter dashed out to the boardwalk as if to verify Samuel's description. He returned only to scoop up his gun belt and loop it around his belt. "Damn dynamite! You stay here Samuel and lock him up." Porter paused for a moment, "What's wrong with him?"

"I knocked him out, but only after he took a swipe at me." Marcus pointed to his brow and lifted up his shirt to reveal another slash on his ripped abdomen.

"Righteo, but I ain't doing any paperwork."

"Or course," Marcus nodded as Porter dashed out into the night.

Jewel sat as quiet as a church mouse, what the hell had Marcus done. And he had done it for her!

"What's his name?" Samuel bent down and turned the man onto his side, where Jewel recognized the grey beard. Her breath caught in her throat, as tears welled in her eyes.

"Hey he was just in here, cashing her in."

"You sure?" Marcus wandered closer to the record book, his eyes skimmed over the keys that hung on the jailers hips.

"Yeah he just signed for the infamous Ruby Drawers. Samuel said as he pointed at the page, "Charles Rogers Senior, but he gave us his autograph in the name of Lucky Chuck.""

Marcus groaned and closed his eyes, "Lucky Chuck."

"You alright?" Samuel asked.

"Yeah the sooner we get this done, the sooner I go find the Doc."

The sound of the town rousing to douse the fire increased in pitch and ferocity. A series of smaller explosions ripped through the melee. Laughter and howls echoed through the streets. Jewel watched Marcus size up Samuel as he opened the cell.

"He looks dead."

"Dead drunk." Marcus tried to laugh, "He stinks of whiskey. I caught him skulking around the railyards looked like he was mixing his own fireworks." Marcus dragged Lucky Chuck into the adjacent cell and tossed him onto the mattress.

Jewel tried to ignore the pink liquid that smeared across the floor.

"He did me more damage than I did him."

Jewel watched as Marcus looked at the bars and back. With the flick of his hand, he pointed to the keys. Suddenly his eyes paused on her swollen cheekbone, his lips thinned. "He'll be right by morning I guess."

"Come on make it quick." Sam flicked his hand back and forth.

Marcus moved slowly from the cells, wandering behind the youthful jailer back to the desk. Jewel saw his fists clench and unclench. What was Marcus going to do? She bit down on her bottom lip. She didn't want to stay here a minute more but she didn't want to be the reason Marcus struck down another lawman.

"Name," Samuel pulled a thick book out from under the desk.

"Lucky Chuck–"

"No I need your name."

Marcus looked at the page, slowly he picked up the pen. He put the nib to the paper just as Porter dashed back into the jailhouse.

"Come on, we need all the men we can get on this." Porter rushed Samuel out the door, "You too Ranger, come on."

Marcus threw Jewel a dark look as Porter pushed him over the threshold before barring the door behind.

Jewel listened as she heard the mobs rushing past the window. She stood on the top of her tip-toes and saw a large orange glow emanating from a few streets away. Jewel could imagine the row of townspeople throwing bucket after bucket of water onto the blaze, and Marcus knowing that he set the fire would be front and center.

Jewel scooted closer to the barrier between her cell and Lucky Chuck. She could smell whiskey for certain but his stillness was eerie. She watched his torso. It didn't move. Not one inch. She slunk down to the floor. Any hope of clearing her name with the Turners dissipated like morning mist.

Jewel hugged her knees into her chest and rested her cheek on her elbow until the ache became too much and she lay down on the bare floor, the cool stone heating her cheeks.

Tonight of all nights, Marcus felt cursed. He was no good as a crook as all of his plans were destined for failure. He stood at the head of the line tossing bucket after bucket to the blaze. He had set a small fire in a stack of old lumber and a few black powder tricks when the flames got high enough. Except despite his care, the embers had reached the dynamite store and started a new wave of destruction. Jewel needed to find Porter!

Citizens of all kinds poured onto the streets, some to aid in the salvation, others to loot and a few just watching and cheering, their hatred for the railways and their poor treatment of the workers burning brighter than the flames. Marcus became lost in the rhythm of the work and yet Jewel sat in her cell. He tossed his last bucket, the dynamite store extinguished, the looters brave enough to clamber over the ashes to pick amongst the treasures. Marcus spied his moment.

A whisper crept through the window. Jewel strained her ears. The whisper hissed again. She sat up wiping her face. Judging by how low the lamps were she must have slept some. The jailhouse door still closed. She stood up as the next noise, a sharp whistle, echoed around the room.

Marcus stood below the window, his hand squeezed between the bars to hand her a set of keys. His face and arms were coated in soot, his whole body drenched in sweat.

"Here!"

Jewel froze. Everything that Marcus was he was compromising for her. The honest Lawman was breaking her out of jail.

"Marcus."

"Jewel don't argue, hurry. There's no time."

Her voice trembled, the sounds of the town drowned out her words so she had to shout, "No Marcus, leave me here and go."

His hazel eyes bore through the metal bars, his dark brows furrowed. A string of gunshots erupted from somewhere out of sight.

She couldn't see his mouth but she heard his deep voice growl all the same, he dropped the keys through the bars, "Damn it Jewel run!"

Jewel watched Marcus sprint off to answer the gunfire and Jewel stared at the keys. If she ran, Marcus would be implicated yet if she stayed she might be hung. That's if the Turners didn't reach her first. The seconds ticked by, hollers and hoots echoed through the night, another burst of gunfire and Jewel snapped. She picked up the keys.

The first lock was easy, the heavy lumber that blocked the front door, not so. Jewel levered it upright and it tumbled to the floor just as boot steps scuffled up the boardwalk.

Jewel scanned the room; Porters desk her only option. Jewel tossed the keys across the table top and scurried underneath, pulling the chair tight to block her in. Jewel's heart boomed in her eardrums, her lungs screamed for air. A string of curses came to mind as she listened to the scraping of something across the timber.

"Jewel?" Marcus whispered.

Jewel peeked from under the backboard of the desk and recognized Marcus's dusty boots, only to see him dragging another behind him. The man wriggled in Marcus's strong grip,

"I wasn't looting, I was looking for my lost dog!" the man squeaked.

"Shut it!" Marcus barked as he dragged the man further in.

"Hurry up Ranger! We've got another two coming." Porter growled, "Never a dull moment in Fort – Hey!" Porter snapped.

Jewel curled inwards biting her thumb nail until is snapped.

"Where the Hell is the girl!" Samuel whined.

"My keys?" Porter spat.

Jewel heard more scrapes and bangs as the looters were manhandled into the cell, the metal clanging as the cage slammed shut.

"Right here," Marcus said. The keys clinking as he picked them up from the desk.

A litany of prayers ran through Jewel's mind as Porter cursed. The footfalls encroached on her hiding place. A pair of soot coated denims came into view blocking the chair in place cutting off Jewel's exit.

"Porter..."

"Shut it Samuel, you did this..."

Jewel put her hands on the worn leather chair. She couldn't let Marcus take the blame. The wheels stalled as the back landed hard against Marcus's thighs. He grunted.

"You did this with all your jabbering to her Samuel! You'll never hear the end of this Samuel, mark my words, I'm not going down as the one who let Ruby Drawers escape!"

"But I -" Samuel started.

Marcus interrupted, "Samuel go get the Doc for these fellows, Porter you round up a few more men to secure the rail-yard and I'll take care of this lot for now."

Porter harrumphed, "Damn the looters, we have to form a posse, she can't have got far!"

"You do that," Marcus snapped. The keys jangled as it exchanged hands.

"Samuel fetch the Doc," Porter ordered. "You get their names down in the books, while I'm gone. I know this one is Billy Maddox."

"Right," Marcus shuffled something across the desk as the timber creaked under foot.

It took another few moments before Marcus pulled the chair away. He whispered, "*Scout* and the bay are out the back."

His boots carried him towards the cells as she heard him address the captives, "Surname first."

Jewel scurried out the front door as someone shouted. Her heels slipped in the sawdust as she dashed around the side of the jail house, their faces peeping through the cell bars as she mounted Lucky Chucks horse he had called *Ace*. Jewel booted the horse into a gallop as the hollers and hoots ebbed. The streets of Forth Worth sped past, the bordellos and gambling dens had already emptied into the streets thanks to the earlier explosion, now the people raised their beer mugs and cheered at the new spectacle. Ruby Drawers hurtled down the main thoroughfare.

As Jewel reached the city limits, a rider closed the distance, she twisted *Ace* to the left, hoping to lose him between the darkened buildings only to hear a shout. Jewel blinked back her welling tears as she recognized *Scout*. Marcus should turn and run, he had rescued her from jail and now a posse would chase them down. Jewel pulled *Ace* up short only to have Marcus slap the horse on the rump.

"Run Jewel run!" He hollered.

Damn the man, if he didn't look like he was having fun!

Marcus pushed the horses hard and thankfully Lucky Chuck's black bay could keep up. The moon sat high in the glittering Texas sky splashing enough light on the terrain for the horses to safely cross at speed. The hours passed by as the moon slid lower on the horizon, until it disappeared completely. The array of sparkling stars faded with the warm light of the dawn. Just as Jewel expected Marcus to stop he didn't. He handed her a flask and she drunk as shallow as she could before handing it back.

"How are you feeling?"

"I'm fine. I'm truly sorry Marcus, I didn't -"

He brought *Scout* closer to the black bay, both horses flanks were coated in sweat and salt.

"Don't be. You're safe, that's all. Couple more miles I think." Marcus said as he pushed his knees into *Scout* who begrudgingly obeyed.

Jewel had no choice but to follow. Marcus had come for her, he kept his word, but at what cost? She hated the whirlwind that brewed in her stomach, his not only compromised his morals Marcus had decimated them to keep her safe. Jewel let her tears fall, glad Marcus was ahead and not beside her.

Chapter 21

Jewel brought her mount beside Marcus and squinted into the sun. She slowly ran her hand down the salt-caked flank of *Ace*, as she stared at the white washed building, a single spire rested on top.

"A Church?"

"Oh now you have morals." Marcus smiled through gritted teeth, his eyes rimmed in red.

"I never said that." Jewel offered a weak laugh. What had she done to him?

The journey had clearly melted Marcus's mind as well because he laughed back, "Time to rest for sure."

They stood in a patch of elm trees that had encroached on the building in front of them. The greenery bordered a narrow stream, which Jewel could imagine might have had, in years gone by, children playing in its cool waters after a long Sunday morning. The horses had drunk their fill and Jewel managed to wash Lucky Chuck's, tobacco taint from her hair just as Marcus washed the majority of the soot and blood from his face. She wanted to check his cuts but he pushed her away and now they stood watching for the presence of others. The horse shuddered under her palm. They were blown, hopefully they had put enough miles between themselves and Fort Worth.

"Where do you think we are?"

"Hills County, I hope." Marcus twisted his head from side to side. "Come on," He put his hand in hers and dragged her into the sunlight.

They crept bent over to the rear door possibly the rectory. In the last few years she hadn't spent enough time in Church to know the difference. They rested at the door and Jewel noticed, now that they were up close, how the paint had pealed beyond simple neglect, the spire at the top was leaning more to one side. Marcus popped the lock and a rush of birds stirred in the rafters.

"Abandoned."

"Here's hoping." Marcus whispered.

He let Jewel rest in the back room. She peered around the corner as Marcus put his pistols back in his holsters and stood upright. He checked the main chapel area, the doors were boarded up just like the empty windows.

"It'll have to do."

Jewel nodded and found the cleanest spot she could. As Marcus returned with a single sleeping mat and their saddle bags, she didn't wait, curling up in the space between his arm and chest before Marcus could argue.

Jewel woke to the late afternoon warming her cheek and Marcus sculptured frame slumbering underneath her. She carefully climbed to her feet and entered the rectory. There she found a sink pump-fed from the nearby stream and began to wash.

Lucky Chuck was done. Marcus had blown up the Texas and Pacific rail stock and yet Gabriel Turner and his hounds were still out there. Jewel silently riffled through her saddle bags until she found her supplies. She changed into the freshest clothes she could manage being a new pair of denims and a pale blue shirt.

Jewel filled the sink and dunked her head into the soapy water. There was no point being the black haired Ruby Drawers now. Porter and the youthful Sam would have her latest description out to the press. With a botched train robbery to add to her tally, how high would her reward climb?

Jewel stood upright the tub was now stained with ash and soot, the water churned into grey as she rubbed her hands through her fingers. She heard Marcus stir and squeezed out her strands satisfied they were the closest to her regular ginger she could manage.

Marcus rubbed his grizzled cheeks as he stumbled into the rectory. Jewel squeezed out of his way. If he hadn't resented her before surely he would now.

"I'm sorry about Fort Worth." She said

"I walked us into it," Marcus said.

"But I led us straight to trouble."

Marcus laughed, "That's not what I meant, I said trouble finds you Jewel". It took him another moment to realize she'd washed out the dye. He smiled, "Smart. They're looking for a brunette. Maybe a redheaded Ruby, will give us a few days."

The tiny room seemed too small for Marcus as Jewel leaned her shoulder against the joist.

Jewel managed a weak laugh, "Marcus we're in Texas now, you could probably head south and I'll head east, by the time -"

Marcus sighed as he faced Jewel. Even though she stood in the hallway, his arm reached her hip and pulled her closer.

"I'm truly sorry about Lucky Chuck if I'd know it was him-" Marcus hand cupped her cheek as he slid his thumb over her swollen cheek, "Actually I'm not sorry."

Jewels chest quivered, exhaustion seemed to weigh down her limbs and she wanted to curl up in his arms and have him tell her everything was going to be okay. She ran her hand up to his eyebrow.

"You need to clean this properly."

Jewel released the plug and watched the black stains blend with the rusted ones. She ducked past Marcus to the pump and gave it a few presses while Marcus washed his wounds. He undone his shirt and stood back regarding the shallow slice on his ribbed abdomen. Jewel admired the view as the afternoon sun sifted through the high narrow window, the sunlight breaking through the overgrown branches to send swirls of shadow over Marcus bare form. Caramel tones cascaded into satin, a smattering of dark hair across his chest, running in a faint line to his belt buckle. Her fingers twitched at the thought of caressing the taunt ridges and shallow valleys.

Instead Jewel returned to the chapel area and found Marcus a fresh shirt and pulled out the last of Winnie's bandages.

When she returned to the tub Jewel resisted pressing the fabric onto him, and left it on the narrow bench beside the sink.

His hazel gaze ran over her form, the drips from her hair had coursed down her chest, the fabric clung to her breasts, the damp shift underneath felt almost transparent.

Jewel tugged the edge of his beard, "You're taking this outlaw look a bit too far, time to take it off."

Marcus nodded holding his breath against the clean fresh scent of Jewel. She had managed to rinse almost every last drop of dye from her hair, the afternoon sun found garnets and rubies, refracting amber curls into his sights. He had missed the champagne mix of ginger and gold.

Marcus realized his thoughts on Jewel still hadn't reconciled. He couldn't cope knowing she was locked away and he could handle her roaming free. If Marcus managed to end this, to clear her name, what would he do then? Return to Dew Springs to his brothers' wife and the boring life of a Rancher? Could he watch Jewel Daniels ride off into the Texan sunset again?

Jewel had challenged him with her last words. He had never fought for her. Not for her name, her honor or her reputation. He had let his parents think the worst of her, his brothers sneered and whispered lewd comments. Marcus knew what the other townsfolk had said behind her back. Marcus prided himself on being honorable yet he had never defended Jewel or tried to set the record straight. And worst of all, he knew why. It kept her safe from others. It kept Jewel safe from any reasonable man who would make an honest woman out of her. It was the same reason Jewel had stayed married to Calvin. It was the same reason Marcus had chosen the Rangers.

Jewel handed him his razor and he put blade to work.

Jewel returned with a small portion salted beef and a mug of water, "That's all there is."

"It'll have to do then."

"I filled the canisters too."

"Good." Marcus mumbled.

He tried to avoid looking directly at Jewel. Her damp hair had thinned her pale blue shirt considerably. The ginger hair darkened the freckles across her nose highlighting her eyes that seemed to shine like the first bluebells of spring. Even the bruise on her cheek couldn't diminish her beauty. Damn, exhaustion twisted his mind into a hundred sordid places.

He inspected his work in the cracked patina mirror.

Jewel frowned.

"What?"

"You're not going to leave it that way?"

A vein in Marcus throat twitched and he felt his nerve endings leap to conclusions. He handed Jewel his razor, "Be my guest."

Jewel squeezed forward an inch, "There's not enough room."

Marcus felt his hands on her hips before he realized what he was doing, carefully he lowered Jewel down on the narrow bench beside the sink.

Jewel smirked as she lathered up her hands. Tenderly she covered his cheeks and set to work.

Heat coiled through his veins one by one as Jewel slowly and with gentle precision slanted the razor across his skin. Talking would distil the wicked thoughts that ran through his mind, "I've been thinking."

"Don't hurt yourself," Jewel teased.

"Hey," Marcus tugged her red curls.

"Oh I wouldn't do that!" Jewels voice seemed to reach a notch higher and her fingers trembled around his throat.

Marcus laughed, was she making him more reckless or was he making her panic?

"Go on."

"Francis Turner what did he say to you?"

"Bryce? I mean Francis."

"Mm-hhh" Marcus leaned his neck backwards.

"He said his brother had big plans something our shooting

skills would come in handy. Why?"

"I'm not sure it's just a thought, but Abe and Theo were tracking that counterfeiter Smith in Kansas City. He had those specimen rail bonds."

"So?" Jewels voice seemed intrigued.

"Gabriel Turner lost a lot of money investing in the railroads in the Panic of 1873. The Turner Gang hit a stage coach in '74, but that was the only one, they robbed nothing but trains."

"You think the Turners could defraud the railways or even the government with fake bonds?"

"I don't know if that is their plan, but the gold train, the last one before they went silent never had a complete manifest."

"You think it had something worth reprinting on it?"

"Possibly. I just think it's a bit coincidental that I follow whispers of the Turners from Kansas City. Abe and Theo were supposed to chase Smith in Kansas City. And yet Smith ends up in Emporia, and Brady and the others are just outside. Gabriel's been hiding low for a while, why now?"

"You think Turner and Smith were working together?"

"Nobody works with Gabriel Turner. He might have needed Smith to make the counterfeits. Why? So he could steal the real ones. Why did Smith try to steal the real ones?"

"Greed." Jewel replied, she ran her fingers down the line of his jaw checking her work. "Why is he still interested in me then?"

Marcus closed his eyes as the sensation of Jewels ministrations pulsated through his muscles. His desire swelled as her breath caressed his wet throat.

"Not you, Ruby Drawers."

It felt like Marcus was grasping smoke with his bare hands. He needed to make inquiries, send some telegrams but that would reveal their position. Blindly he placed his hands down, expecting the hard surface of the bench, pleased when his fingers curled around Jewels knees. Marcus opened his eyes focusing on Jewels slightly parted lips. Her lids were heavy, her chin tilted upwards.

She raked the blade across his right cheek and he swirled his thumb in slowly intricate circles up her inner thigh.

Jewel inhaled shallowly as Marcus ascended his grip. She arched her back, begging for the connection of her swollen breasts against his bare chest. Marcus massaged her thigh until he reached her hip. Jewel concentrated on his jaw line, the blade trembling in her fingers. She held his shoulder with her left hand as if to steady herself, to no avail. Marcus dragged her closer so he stood between her knees, her buttocks on the edge of the bench. He couldn't stop, knowing he should. Marcus pulled one of her legs behind his back and hooked it over his hip as he continued his deliberately slow ascension to the apex between her thighs. Jewel gasped as his thumb manipulated the peak of her arousal.

Marcus cursed the thickness of her denim; his desire to relish the silken delights within surpassed his common sense. His left palm cupped the nape of her neck as he tilted her soft lips to his. Sparks of desire pulsated through his body, he felt himself diving head first again, only the fight was within. Jewels eyes closed, as pleasure colored her cheeks. Marcus paused savoring the slight edge of power he had over her, her rapture dependent on his touch.

Jewel gasped as the razor bit into her skin, the metal clattered into the sink. Marcus took her thumb into his lips and sucked the tiny cut. The purring sound from Jewel's throat spurred Marcus on. He dragged Jewel closer, until she enveloped his arousal. He watched the hollow of her throat flutter to the thunderous beat of his heart. Jewel's arms coiled around his neck as she claimed his mouth; her kiss reckless, fevered and eager. Marcus's desire throbbed, to consume Jewel his only thought. Marcus needed to take her now, his wanton feverish woman, all soft velvet and scorching passion, his demand outweighing common sense.

Somewhere a horse whinnied. Jewel ignored it as Marcus's tongue slaked across hers, his mouth possessive, his thirst for her unrestrained; laid bare for Jewel to relish in. The lethargic circles of his thumb between her thighs not enough. She needed all of him, right now on the floor of this church. No more running away, this time Jewel wanted to be caught, naked and writhing under this wonderful man and his wildfire caresses.

Voices suddenly breached the thunderstorm of rapture. Marcus withdrew as the voices became louder. He frowned as he registered the noises for what they were. Quickly Marcus shrugged into his shirt. With a finger to his lips, he pushed Jewel into the chapel. Her mind raced to catch up with her body, as Marcus tossed items at Jewel. The fiery moment stolen and replaced with ice cold fear. Jewel rolled the sleeping mat and Marcus loaded his rifle. He crept to the door, his eyes regarding their surroundings as Jewel heard the tread of hooves over hard packed dirt.

Glimpses of riders rushed over the horizon, their eyes to the ground, their leader wearing a wide brimmed hat over a leather vest. Jewel's heart clogged her throat. Marcus pulled his coffee colored Stetson onto his head and shoved Jewel into the afternoon sunlight. Hunched over, they rushed to the thicket where *Scout* and *Ace* waited. As silently and as fast as they could, they tied their belongings. Marcus crouched low and led the horses further down the stream.

A tornado of hooves thundered the ground as the posse of riders neared the abandoned church. Jewel counted at least eight riders, four with rifles. Her fingers trembled as she clutched the leather reins of Lucky Chuck's horse. Jewel tried to steady her breathing, scanning the area for routes of escape. Marcus was already ahead of her. Jewel mounted and flattened herself against the saddle. She followed Marcus out of the thicket, putting the horses to a gallop as soon as they reached flat ground.

Marcus kept them to the river as far as possible, using the edge of the trees to break up their horizon. He crisscrossed the stream several times, and circled back behind Jewel to cover their tracks. Jewel kept *Ace* to a healthy pace, only slowing for Marcus to catch up. The next hour sped by, dashing from thicket to thicket; resting the horses when they could as they raced south, the threat of the hunt consuming their thoughts.

The sounds of horses ahead made Marcus halt. He stood in his saddle and regarded the lay of the land. A caravan of riders moved slowly ahead. Behind, the posse dust cloud rose on the horizon as the hunters closed in. Marcus booted *Scout* in the flanks, the horse was flagging, they hadn't rested enough. He tried to skirt the side of the caravan, taking it wide to avoid being seen.

Suddenly a shrill whistle cut through the air and *Scout* missed a step. Marcus flicked the reins as the whistle sounded again. The horse, unsure what to do abruptly skidded to a stop.

"Kearby!" A voice hollered.

Marcus turned *Scout* to face the rider, who trotted out from the caravan on an impressive brown stallion. It took him a moment to place the shoulders of the man Marcus had known for most of his life. He pushed *Scout* to greet the cowboy and Jewel followed.

"Cade Hamerton!" Marcus called as they neared.

The tall Rancher sat high in his saddle, his skin tanned by the long hours of breaking horses, and trailing cattle. He dipped his beige Stetson in greeting, revealing his brown curls had lengthened. His twice broken nose retained his hard edged scowl. Marcus had been there when Cade had broken it on another man's fist. The first time was defending Shelton Murphy and the other when Cade had nearly killed a man. Cade's temper had been cooled by Old Man Lock, and his daughter Evelyn had somehow tamed him; although, the pushy blonde from New Orleans had seemed just as wild as

Cade sometimes.

"What the Hell are you doing out -" Cade started until he saw Jewel, "Miss Daniels?"

"Howdy Cade and it's just Jewel." Jewel greeted him.

"We don't have time," Marcus twisted in his saddle to the approaching dust storm behind them.

Cade didn't hesitate, "Come on," he turned his brown stallion Maverick on the spot.

Marcus and Jewel fell in behind. They reached the caravan of cattlemen and immediately Marcus recognized an assortment of vaqueros from Hamerton's Double E Ranch.

"Settle in." Cade instructed, and the Mexican cowboys shuffled around to accommodate Jewel and Marcus. A young greenhorn led *Scout* and Ace into the horse lines.

"How much trouble you in?" Cade asked.

"Enough." Marcus said.

"And Jewel?"

"Even more so," Marcus rushed.

Cade nodded, "I've picked up a few broncs in Dallas, I could use an extra hand or two."

"Cade I can't ask you to do this," Marcus said.

"You're not asking," Cade shrugged his broad shoulders.

Marcus lowered his voice, "Listen Hamerton this is bigger than you and I."

"How bad can it be?" Hamerton even dared a wink at Jewel, no doubt the biggest trouble-maker in Dew Springs thought he could handle a posse of riders all with his bare hands.

Jewel's lips parted, "Well...,"

"Come on," Cade gestured as the dust cloud encroached.

Marcus followed, trying to think of ways to avoid a confrontation. Could he keep Cade safe? Knowing the man, he wouldn't doubt Cade would throw himself to Marcus's defense. What would Cade do if the posse put a noose around his neck and dragged him back to Fort Worth? Marcus knew what Cade would do and a part of him felt relieved he had another set of knuckles, and pistols by his side. Without Cade's caravan of fresh broncs, vaqueros, cooks and Hands, Jewel and Marcus would be exposed.

The vaqueros came forward and greeted Marcus with handshakes and others bowed when they greeted Jewel, their Spanish warm and comforting.

Jewels mount was led away while Cade muttered instructions in Spanish. A cowboy threw Jewel a hat with embroidery around the wide brim as she shucked on a multi-colored striped poncho. A greenhorn led her to the camp fire, as the others sat close to shield her feminine form.

Chapter 22

Cade raised his hand in greeting, "Howdy."

A man leaned over his pommel the dimple in his chin so deep it looked like the pips of dice, his voice sharp like a prairie dog bark, "We're looking for this woman and any accomplices..." he pulled out Ruby's wanted poster.

Hamerton took the poster and unrolled it. A smile creased his cheeks.

"Accomplices?" Marcus stood facing Hamerton, providing only his profile to the posse leader. Jewel watched as he readjusted his hat to cover his injured eyebrow as he pretended to scan the poster.

"She's been known to be working with the Turner Gang, she's riding a black bay with white socks."

Jewel exhaled slowly, they had her horse pegged, but no mention of Marcus thankfully.

"She looks harmless," Cade laughed.

"Harmless. She's wanted for three murders and a train robbery,"

"Three murders?" Marcus asked. Jewel watched his palm itch, and her chest constricted. How could he stand there so calmly?

"She stabbed a man last night, after the Gang blew up the rail yards and she escaped from Tarrant County jail."

"Jesus," Cade mumbled, a smile cutting his hard cheeks.

"Have you seen her?"

Cade laughed his blue eyes alight, "No but I married one just like her."

The posse leader laughed as well, "I know the type," the man licked his lips. "But she's riding with the Turner Gang,"

"I thought she shot Baby-face Turner?" Marcus added.

"First I've heard of that." The posse leader snapped.

236

"Yeah Baby-face got shot up in Delano last month," Marcus added.

"Says right here -" Cade pointed to the scroll.

The posse leader dismounted and looked at the poster, "Killed her lover.... Well I'll be damned. They should call her the Widower of the West, the cold-blooded bitch!"

Cade must have sensed a change in Marcus.

Suddenly the posse leader walked forward his hand on his holster, "You seem to know a lot about the Turners?"

"Taylor and I heard about them up in Dallas, feel free to have a look around," Cade gestured.

"Taylor?" The man eyed Marcus up and down.

"Yeah Taylor Stone," Marcus shook the man's hand.

"Alfred Goldman," The posse leader stood next to Marcus and again ran his gaze from Marcus's boots up to his hat, satisfied in his Ranch Hand demeanor matched his appearance.

More of the posse dismounted and wandered to the camp fire while two others went to the horse lines.

Jewel inhaled shallowly, keeping her eyes on her red leather boots, the embroidery peeking out underneath her dusty denims. Hamerton was a brazen fellow at the best of times. Although she had seen Hamerton in enough fist fights to know he could more than handle himself, she didn't want to place him in danger.

The posse came closer to where Jewel sat tipping hats and kicking boots of those pretending to be asleep.

"Hey where did you say they were from?"

"Fort Worth, if you reckon you came from Dallas?"

"Oh yeah we came from Dallas, just sold a few horses there to Devine."

"Devine?"

"Yeah Thomas, do you know him?" Cade smiled.

"Do you mean Justice Devine?"

"Yeah that's the one, we're headed to San Antonio to deliver another few, Devine's got plenty of arrows in his quiver ain't he Taylor."

"Yeah he's bright as a new penny," Marcus said.

"Whatdya say your name was?"

"Cade Hamerton, while we're down in San Antonio, we might have a spell at Steele's place."

"Adjutant General Steele?"

"Yeah, some of his Major's ride my horses." Cade smirked, "And some of those uppity Texas Rangers down at the Frontier Battalion." he added.

The posse leader paused and really looked at Hamerton. Jewel felt a tap on her shoulder and she shuffled to the left as a cowpoke took her place. Jewel didn't know if Hamerton spoke the truth or not, but the names had an impact of Goldman. He tipped back one more sombrero, the cowpoke who had taken Jewel's place.

The vaqueros smiled, "You already checked me, Boss."

Goldman grunted, "Alright, if you see Ruby or any of the Turners, don't go taking them on their own, I know you've got a few boys here, and the bounty is up to $5000 but ...."

Cade whistled through his teeth, "Well leave them to the big boys who can handle them," he tapped Goldman on his shoulder and walked him back to his mount. "I'll say howdy to Steele for you when I see him, Goldman."

"Keep your saddle oiled and your gun greased," The man climbed into his saddle and dipped his head in farewell.

Jewel wrapped her shaking hands around her sombrero and pulled it down over her eyes. She sat there for a moment until she felt a warm hand on her shoulder.

"Lo peor ha pasado, bella dama".

Jewel managed to nod her head, her voice caught in her throat.

Only when the posse had cleared the horizon did Cade order his cowboys up and into the saddle. He gave Jewel a pack horse and cut *Ace* free with a smack on his rump.

"Pity he's a good piece of horse flesh but not good enough to take the risk."

Marcus patted Hamerton on the shoulder, "I'm sorry to

put you in this position."

"It's nothing."

Marcus took his hat off and brushed back his hair before re-setting the brim, "Have you actually met Devine and Steele?"

"Ah yes and it's a long story," Cade smiled and Marcus smiled back.

Jewel marched between them, "Cade I don't want to run your name through the muck as well, and that's without the Turners...."

The big man crossed his arms, "My my Jewel Daniels, you've been busy."

"It's not all true," Jewel said sheepishly.

Marcus wandered away to the vaqueros and assisted in tying saddle bags and kicking over the fire.

Cade barked a laugh, "Not all but a fair bit then?"

"Well,..."

"Explain it to me over supper but right now I figured you want to put more miles between you and Fort Worth. Lucky we've got a few spare mounts."

Jewel stood in his way, "Cade you don't have to, I'll head on my way. We don't owe each other anything."

"That's right, we don't owe each other anything. You know the Kearbys very well, you know Marcus has three brothers. I got Pearl and no brothers. Instead I got Kearby, Taylor and Shelly."

Jewel tilted her head to one side and considered the rough exterior of the Rancher. Marrying Evelyn had certainly mel-lowed Cade.

"And I figure, where you are Marcus will be and I owe him a fair bit."

Jewel nodded. Men.

"Besides Evie would have a pink fit if I left you in some situation. Wait till she hears about this!"

"Oh Cade no."

"She'd be a mix of jealous and proud I reckon...." Cade winked, "Now mount up outlaw."

Cade kept their group to a rapid yet manageable pace. He had a train of fresh broncs with nervous energy that needed to be expelled and a cast of cashed up cowboys eager to see home. None of them complained when he pushed them to cover more ground for an hour after the Texas sun had set.

Marcus sat astride one of Cade's pack horses, while *Scout* ran free of saddle and tack with the herd of wildings. Jewel sat on top of another pack horse, a young gulla filly with mousy brown hair and a dark black dorsal strip down to her rear end. Jewel patted the horse's neck as the skittish filly sniffed the air, eager to keep moving. Cade had a party of eleven cowboys with a mount each and another six horses for pack horses. As Hamerton eventually called a halt, the vaqueros quickly made camp, short instructions in Spanish as to who was setting out the horses and who was taking first watch while Hernandez started supper.

Jewel felt at a loose end as Hamerton's team went about their business. She had taken the reverse journey over two years ago, riding with Hamerton as he drove his angus-long horn mix up to Kansas and leaving Dew Springs and Marcus behind.

Marcus returned from the horse lines and sat around the camp fire, the vaqueros were busy at their tasks, leaving the camp fire almost empty. Cade reclined next to Marcus while Jewel plopped her saddle bags in a heap and sat down. She idly watched Hernandez chop, stir and season his beef stew without paying an ounce of attention to the process.

Marcus spoke first, "I'm taking her back to Dew Springs."

"You think that's wise?"

"That's what I said." Jewel huffed.

Hamerton and Marcus had picked a sheltered spot, bordered by an embankment along the Brazos River. A large southern oak kept watch at the top of the embankment, long gnarled branches stretched out from the knotted trunk, like the tendrils of Medusa. The regular stirrings of the camp settled Jewel's nerves. The sky above blushed with diamonds, the camp fire buffeted and sizzled as the tinder crackled and popped, even the cowboys curses and the scent of the trail soothed her.

Marcus gave Jewel a harsh look as Hernandez spooned out the servings of stew. They ate while Marcus caught Cade up with a shortened version of what had transpired. Calvin. The Turners. Smith at Emporia. The Train. Lucky Chuck. Even the railyards which Marcus claimed was an accident.

Marcus then raised his theory of the Pinkerton Agents and the Rangers, reinforcing his need to head south to the Ranger named Quinn. Jewel watched Marcus wrestle with his unspoken notion; Marcus would ask Hamerton to deliver Jewel to her father so he could ride on.

Hamerton scooped up a handful of dirt and ran it between his fingers, "Well I bought out some of Rick the Ticks' Four Star Ranch and with Windy Hill in Taylor Stone's hands, and your fathers Crooked K on the other side, what do you think about the Double E?"

"I couldn't put your family at risk." Marcus said.

"Neither could I," Jewel added.

"There's a chance they know we're headed exactly there." Marcus finished.

Cade hummed in agreeance and let the dirt sift through to the ground again, "Seems to me you're fighting a war on all sides, posses, Rangers, the Turner Gang, but you ain't got enough soldiers. Between all four ranches, we have enough eyes to keep watch while you head south to this commander, unless that is you've got more Rangers in your pocket?"

Marcus head dipped, "No, I don't."

Cade shrugged his shoulders, "Think about it." Cade stood up, "I'll check the boys and then head off to sleep. Wake me when it's my turn."

Marcus nodded. He lifted his rifle and wandered into the darkness without a word to Jewel. She looked at the dirty bowls beside the fire. Did he expect her to wash them? She sat transfixed by the discarded timber bowls and cutlery until she shivered. Marcus was back with Hamerton, surrounded by others from Dew Springs and Jewel was back to being the bastard's daughter, the hell-rasier, the disreputable woman. It slammed into her gut with full force and Jewel gasped. Surely she was wrong? Her knees trembled as she rose and stumbled into the darkness to find Marcus.

He sat in a distant branch of a southern oak, his rifle across his knee.

"Marcus?"

"You should get some rest Jewel."

Her voice quaked, "If you try to leave me with Hamerton I'll run."

Marcus sighed.

Jewel knew it! Marcus would put himself at risk, running head into the Turners or the Rangers. If Jewel got him back to Dew Springs she could tell his father who would make him stay put. Jewel should push aside her selfish feelings, keeping him safe was the idea, whether Marcus cared for her or not.

"That was the deal Marcus, I'm not going back to Dew unless you drag me there yourself."

Marcus looked around, Hamerton was still roaming around saying a few words here and there to his men, a few vaqueros stirred, somewhere cards were being dealt, and someone laughed.

"I think you should get some rest" Marcus said his eyes on the onlookers.

Jewel lowered her voice, "I'm serious Marcus when they figure out what happened last night, the railyards, the jail, you could end up being just as wanted as Ruby."

Jewel didn't want to know, but a burning desire inside her, had to test it. She had to see if the old Marcus had returned, the one that was too good for Jewel, the one that saw nothing but a bad reputation and ill-manners. Jewel put her arm on his forearm. He looked directly at Hamerton as he pulled his arm away.

"Go back Jewel," Marcus growled.

Jewel cast her gaze over to Hamerton, before returning to glare at Marcus, "Go back? Go back to what, the old Jewel Daniels, the old Marcus Kearby."

"Damn it Jewel," Marcus hushed.

Jewel crossed her arms, "The same Marcus Kearby who thinks he can just pick me up and put me down when he wants."

Marcus dipped his voice, "That's not what I intended, I try to do right by you Jewel, I warned you..."

"No need to warn me Marcus, you said it yourself, nothing good can come of this. Now we're heading back to Dew, can't have righteous Marcus Kearby been seen too close to the town bastard, the reckless ill-mannered strumpet, that's sure as Hell going to drag you into damnation." It came out in a hushed rush, the fact Jewel didn't raise her voice seemed to rattle Marcus.

"You're the one that left me in Dew" Marcus replied.

"Looks to me, like Marcus Kearby, never really left Dew Springs at all."

Jewel strode back to the camp fire, her head held high despite the tears that coursed down her cheeks. She rolled herself into her sleeping mat and let her anger fuel her resolve. The tears dried with the heat of the flames, as she stared upright to the glittering sky. The hours ticked by until she heard Marcus return to wake Cade. They sat around the fire, their reminiscing punctuated with hushed laughter and acclaim at the events that had unfolded since they last saw each other.

Jewel awoke before sunrise, her eyes gritty and her curls coated in smoke. She grabbed what was left of her vanity kit and the freshest shirt she could find and wandered down to the stream. She passed a sentry, the cook Hernandez. He dipped his hat and withdrew as Jewel gingerly climbed down the crumbling bank.

She placed her items down in the long grass just as a snapping twig made her jump. A hare the size of a kitten scooted out of the underbrush. Jewel laughed and undid the top button of her shirt.

"What do you think you're doing?"

Jewel squeaked. Marcus stood at the Brazos riverbank his rifle in one hand his hat dipped low over his brows.

"Freshening up, you don't have to stand guard."

"Yes I do."

"Fine suit yourself!" Jewel snapped as she undid another button. She heard Marcus growl as he rolled his back against a tree. Jewel knelt down and wet her wash cloth.

Marcus let the scratchy bark of the cedar numb his shoulders. Jewel was right. Marcus had left Dew behind but not it's prejudices, he had an opportunity to start a life new when he joined the Rangers and he had, but when it came to Jewel, Marcus was ensnared. She was the wildcat, the hell-raiser and the impious woman. Yet she had married a man who let her trust and passion wither away. Calvin had housed a fugitive and cheated Jewel of her earnings and her heart. What about Marcus himself, he had treated Jewel like a temptation that he fooled himself he had control over, that Marcus could pick Jewel up and let her go at will, when he knew the truth. He was as no more honorable as he was in control.

What to do about Jewel? Marcus knew what he wanted, and it was about time he admitted it. He needed to make his intentions clear, and honorable. Marcus couldn't take advantage of Jewel and she deserved to be treated like a respectable woman.

Marcus listened as the water splashed, imagining the droplets caressing her exposed freckles. He wanted her. When Marcus eventually had Jewel, he would never let her go again. But first the Turners.

Marcus began to whistle hoping to inspire Jewels regular bathing singing ritual. Nothing. He left it. When she was done she climbed up the rock face. Marcus offered his hand but Jewel declined it.

Marcus had his own bath in a short space of time, not trusting Jewel not to run again. He checked his stitches. The skin scabbed over the tiny pieces of thread that had hardened. He thought about luring Jewel in with his injuries? Although if Marcus succeeded in his pursuit; he would be unable to act on it without disgracing Jewel.

Marcus pondered his predicament throughout the day whilst Jewel ignored him. Even when Cade broke to rest the horses Jewel sat by herself, ate by herself and had very little to say to anyone but Cade.

Cade kept the pace fast, eager to be closer to Dew Springs, to Evelyn and to his son Lachlan. Marcus had always counted on the older man to have his back, but now, he wondered how much impact it would have on Cade's family. If the Turners came for Jewel, the Hamerton's would be at risk. Marcus had to reach Quinn and fast.

Jewels' deliberate silence, continued until they reached Waco. Marcus gave Cade the heads up on the woman's previous escapes, despite her reassurances that Marcus would have to drag her himself.

Marcus took no extra time than necessary to send his telegram to Quinn. He loitered at the Post Masters door step, until curiosity got the better of him and Marcus sent another two telegrams, this time both north.

The only change in Jewels' demeanor occurred when Marcus rode back to their cattleman's camp from Waco, her pinched cheeks blushed, her wide eyes narrowed. She nodded to Cade and resumed her dismissive behavior. The only time Marcus spent in her company was when he kept watch over her bathing ritual. Even though Marcus saw her, heard her talk to others, he realized he missed her. Her chatter, her barbs, the scent of her against his clothes, the warmth of her body curled beside his. This was more profound, it was resignation, disappointment and disdain. It clenched his gut and stung under his ribs. Jewel's physical presence wasn't enough, the absence of her closeness, their connection severed and it made him forlorn. Irrational in the whole scheme of their predicament and yet it made perfect sense to Marcus. He damn well loved her.

This time as Jewel cleaned her clothes at the next watering hole, Marcus tried again. Whistling as she soaped and scrubbed her shirts. He wondered what her reaction would be if he asked her about his laundry?

"Not long now," he tried.

"Dew Springs and your father ready to welcome back its favorite son."

Marcus whistled, "That was low." His father's favorite was Whit. Maybe he was his mother's favorite; after all she was the only one that wrote to him.

Jewel just shrugged her shoulders, and walked back to camp, her sodden clothes dripping in her arms.

The closer they got to Dew the harder it got to not make his offer, to make Jewel his woman. After the Turners, Marcus would set things right with his father and Whit's fiancé first. Then he would ask Jedidiah Daniels for Jewel's hand. She was right. He had no intention of returning to the old Marcus, the boring dull cowpoke who did his father's bidding. His scars told the story of another Marcus, one that faced danger head on and refused to cower. And taming Jewel Daniels was the most dangerous of all.

Chapter 23

"It's been eight weeks," Cade sighed as they crossed over the river that marked the boundaries to the Double E Ranch.

Jewel squinted in the distance as the pitched white roof of the homestead sparkled. The fields were a rolling ocean of green, a small herd of heifers lolled in the shade of the cedar elms.

"It looks bigger than I remember," Jewel said.

"We built some extra rooms for Pearl, when she comes and stays."

"I thought she was all set to marry Rick the Ticks cousin, what's his name? Jesse?"

Cades jaw cinched, "She made the right decision and went to New Orleans with Evie's Aunt instead."

Jewel looked sideways at Marcus who hid a wry smile.

"Letting a pretty young lady run off to find her place in the world, what could go wrong?" Jewel asked.

"Everything," Marcus mumbled.

Cade didn't answer.

Jewel let it go, "And more stables?"

"Plus more room for the vaqueros and their families. I bought a few hundred acres from the Four Star, Rick the Tick wasn't happy but Bethany is all but sending him broke."

Jewel felt her limbs leaden. The sun was just past its peak and her throat was dry from the trail dust, but Jewel knew that was not what made her shoulders heavy. She had envisioned returning to Dew Springs under her conditions; as the famed and fastest sharp-shooter of the west or as Marcus Kearby's bride. Not a triple murdering train robber and Kearby's captive.

As they neared the homestead, Jewel could fathom the real size of the Double E. Cade Hamerton the no good thug of Dew

Springs had excelled.

"Jesus it's huge!" Jewel said of the sprawling property.

"Ah," Cade dismissed, "You wait till you see Evie, she was expecting our next little one when I left, I rushed the drive to make sure I'd be home when he or she arrives. Lachlan is so big now he's …."

Cade stood upright in his saddle, he leaned forward, his cheeks paled. Suddenly he booted *Maverick* into action.

Marcus looked ahead to a single female figure on the rear porch of the extended dwelling. A long pony tail the color of corn silk drifted in the breeze. Jewel's gut sunk. It was Evelyn no doubt, but something about her silhouette made Jewel's breath catch in her throat. Suddenly the woman waved and rushed forward to greet her husband.

A large woman, Jewel recognized as Maybelle, stepped down the porch steps carrying a small bundle, behind her, a little blonde boy rushed across the distance towards his father. Evelyn caught Lachlan Hamerton before he got too far just as Cade leapt from the saddle to greet his family.

Jewel's chest ached as Cade peered into the bundle of blankets that Maybelle rocked to greet his latest child. It wasn't until another figure, this one slender and graceful that stepped off the porch that Jewel realized her cheeks were wet. It was Cade's sister Pearl without a doubt, her long ebony locks curling around her shiny blue dress. In her arms she carried a second bundle of blankets. Jewel's heart swelled and she turned away. She was riding her hornets' nest straight into this blossoming family. Jewel couldn't do it. She turned the head of her dainty horse only to have Marcus snatch the reins.

"With fresh horses, it'll take three days to reach Quinn and return, I'm asking for that."

Jewel looked at the expanding Hamerton brood as Cade waved his hat overhead.

Marcus cleared his throat, "Would you prefer the Fox Hole on the Crooked K or to be here surrounded by friends?"

Jewel kinked her head to one side. The Crooked K Ranch

had a shack built into the scrub on the rear boundary, they used for the longer stock drives. Jewel didn't mind the Fox Hole even if it was a derelict shanty built into the side of a hill. The old oak panels had weathered many decades, now held together by the willpower of Marcus's father rather than its rusty nails. It was him, Pendleton Kearby that Jewel was more concerned about. Pendleton would keep. For one night at least.

"Three days and then what?"

"Run. Run as far and as fast as you can, I'll find you." Marcus let the reins drop.

Jewel hands trembled as she decided. Hamerton had put his hat back on his head and this time, Evelyn waved them in. Jewel squeezed her shaking knees and the horse moved forward.

"Three days." Jewel sighed. She couldn't decide what the right thing was to do anymore.

Jewel's filly followed Marcus up to the rear of the homestead. As they dismounted Evie wandered over to greet them.

"Have you come to take back your shooting trophy?"

Jewel kinked her lips at the older woman, "That depends whose taken it?"

Evie swung her lock of blonde hair over her shoulder, she hadn't seemed to age a day, her curves had thickened only slightly, and her green eyes flashed with a hint of mischief.

"You're looking at her two years running."

Jewel hooted and clapped her hands together.

Evie closed the distance and put her arms around Jewel hugging her tight.

"At least it's not that skivvying Bethany Simpson." Jewel laughed.

"Howdy Jewel," Pearl, Cade's half Indian, maybe part Mexican sister edged closer to the other women, her arms free of the baby bundle that Cade now doted over while Maybelle stood at his other shoulder.

"Miss Pearl," Marcus dipped his hat, "I didn't think you

liked all them shiny dresses?"

"I'm glad to see you too, Mr Kearby," She said kindly. Pearl performed a little bow with her head and Jewel was amazed at the change from cowgirl to lady in such a few short years.

"But them dresses sure do like you." Jewel added and they all laughed together.

"Thank you, I honestly didn't expect to be back here um so soon, but when Maybelle said Evie had started laboring two days after Cade had left. Two days" she clicked her tongue at her older brother, "Well I just had to rush out on the very next stage."

"And imagine twins!" Maybelle cackled.

Jewel peered into the bundle of pink and yellow patterned wraps, to see a squishy little face, "Congratulations Evie-lyn."

They walked up the rear stairs together the screen door squeaked allowing them to enter through the quaint kitchen, the interior of the homestead substantially more feminine since Jewel had seen it last. A large well-worn table graced the dining room, the sitting room to the left, bordered by two bay windows. Jewel could see the front door that entered onto the wide porch that ran along the front of the homestead. Just before the front door a narrow set of stairs led upwards to the bedrooms above. It was bigger than her father's cottage, bigger than Winnie's and Ira's farmhouse but nowhere near as sprawling at Marcus's parents Crooked K homestead.

"What's their names?" Jewel asked.

"Edwina after my mother," Evelyn said.

Cade and Marcus entered the kitchen, Cade snatching biscuits from the counter before Evelyn could offer them around.

"And Eleanor."

"Eddie and Ellie," Cade said. "The Double E?"

Evie clicked her tongue and picked up Lachlan, the little boy babbled a dozen words a second and pointed all around the room until his mother handed him a biscuit, the jam centered treat crammed in his mouth.

Marcus slapped Hamerton on the shoulder, "You've done

well Hamerton. Real well."

"I had a lot of help," Cade wistfully said.

"Enough about us," Evie sparked, "Tell me Miss Jewel Daniels, what mischief have you been up to lately? I can't imagine you've got any dull stories to tell about laundry and nappies."

Jewel held her breath and looked at Marcus.

"Or you Marcus, the famous Texas Ranger." Evie added.

Marcus rubbed his nose.

Thankfully Cade interrupted, "Aw let them get cleaned up first," Cade tiptoed across the timber floor, "While you and I put these two down."

Evie beamed, she released Lachlan who ran over to Pearl who handed him another biscuit. Evie took a baby from Maybelle and followed Cade up the rear stairs.

"Come on Jewel, I'll find you something of mine to wear," Pearl said as she scooped up Lachlan.

Jewel almost stumbled over her feet, "Ah…"

"What's your favorite color Lachie?" Pearl sung.

"Purple."

"Oh Lord no!"

Pearl just giggled.

Marcus stood on the front porch, leaning over the railing the timber fresh under his grip as he surveyed the fields of Hamerton's Ranch. The graveled drive led to the narrow stream that ran across the front of the land, a bridge, just wide enough for the wagon signified the end of Hamerton's patch. The front yard contained several meandering chickens while a blue lacy hound reclined in the shade. Just past the house yard, Hamerton's stables expanded on the right hand side, the white poled training arena just visible from the porch. Marcus heard the squeaks of Lach as he chased something through the hedges that lined the porch. Maybelle handed Marcus a bottle of sarsaparilla and he thanked her as she returned inside. The screen door failing to retain the salivating flavors of fried chicken.

He turned back to watch the Hands push the new horses into the stock yards. He would have to ask Hamerton to loan him some spare mounts. He had *Scout* and he would need two or three to reach San Antonio in any kind of condition to return with speed. Marcus was betting it all on Quinn. The Turners were closing in, Abe and Theo might have tracked them from Emporia and now a Fort Worth posse. Marcus hadn't meant to destroy the rail yards, it was just a distraction. He hadn't meant to kill Lucky Chuck either. Then again Lucky Chuck inadvertently murdered a member of the Turner Gang. It all began to blur together and Marcus rolled his shoulders. He would pull his stitches out in the bath, but his other scars reminded him to be cautious.

The screen door creaked and Evelyn wandered out with Cade to sit down at one of the four timber chairs that lined the porch. They were handmade, some from Old Earl and others no doubt from Cade himself.

"So Cade caught me up on some things..." Evelyn started, "I want you to know Jewel will be kept safe here at all costs."

Marcus smiled, "Jewel doesn't like being kept Evelyn, that's half the problem."

It was Evie's turn to smile, her green eyes narrowed, her blonde ponytail bristled in the breeze.

"I have plenty to keep her busy. But I must impress on you to stay one night. Maybelle has made enough fried chicken and hot sauce for the entire town and despite Cade's assurances of his hunger," Evie's looked to her husband, her cheeks flushed with color, "He will simply not be able to finish it all."

Marcus wasn't sure if it was safe to comment, "Only if I can ask your husband for a few horses."

Cade nodded, "Whatever you need Marcus, but rest for one night."

The screen door squeaked again and this time Pearl stepped out followed by Jewel. Marcus couldn't conceal his grin as Jewel strolled out in fresh dark blue denim and a pale blue silk shirt.

"I half expected a dress?"

"It was hard enough getting her to agree to the shirt, let alone a dress." Pearl smirked. "And besides, I suspect there is only one dress that's going to suit Miss Jewel Daniels and I didn't seem to pack one."

Hamerton nodded his head, "I would hope you wouldn't have any dresses of the sort."

"Careful Hamerton," Marcus warned, his eyes unable to shift from Jewel's freshly washed face, her freckles bright and lively.

Evie slapped her husband on the shoulder.

"I meant a white one," Pearl whispered.

"So did I!" Cade barked.

"I've already worn a white one Hamerton and it didn't work out." Jewel replied, her cheeks reddened as she leaned against the railing, careful not to sully the silky material.

For once, Marcus didn't wince at Jewel's sharp answer. He knew she hadn't said to mean harm, her blunt words were just brutally honest. It put her at odds with others more polite, but Marcus preferred her raw honesty than others hackneyed conversations.

"Oh I'm sorry, Jewel." Evelyn said, with pure authenticity, the woman unruffled by Jewel's self-deprecating humor.

"Don't be," Jewel laughed, "It was one hell of a party."

Evelyn laughed, "I bet!"

Although Evelyn had some semblance of a lady, the woman was as wild as her husband. She would have to be to marry Hamerton.

Lachlan thundered up the wide steps with his hands cupped over one another, as he neared Evie he opened his hands only to have a critter leap out and land on her lap. She threw her hands up as she jumped out of her chair, the tiny frog leapt to the floor.

"Lach!"

Everyone laughed, until the frog jumped again and Marcus was forced to put his hat on it to stop it.

"My bunny!" Lachlan squeaked and everyone laughed again.

Marcus scooped up the frog and covered it in his palm. He picked up Lachlan in his other arm, "He sure can jump, but if you want to see him at his best, you've got to let him go. See him swim."

The little boy nodded his head as Marcus walked down the stairs and across the grass, heading to the narrow creek where the drive entered the main road.

Jewel sighed. Was that a message to Jewel? Let her dreams of Marcus go? She didn't need his sly message. She was already done. No more hiding. No more risking others for her mess. She would wait until the dead of night and make her way to the Crooked K. She would tell Pendleton Kearby that his son was home. The Rancher wouldn't let Marcus run off to San Antonio. Not for the sake of a bastard temptress woman such as Jewel. She heard Evie excuse herself with Pearl to help Maybelle with dinner.

"Texas is too small for both of you," Cade said.

"I know."

"I mean it kindly Jewel, when you left he was like an untied knot, he didn't know what to do with himself. You forced him to act on the things he had only dreamt of, and it hasn't changed now."

"He's one stubborn son-of-a-gun."

"I think you mean he's loyal."

"You heard me Cade." Jewel turned to face the taller Rancher. "You keep him safe, have you seen what's he's done to himself over the years."

Cade nodded, and put his leg on the lower rung of his rail. Together they watched Lachlan release the tiny frog. Marcus patted him on the shoulder.

"I heard. But don't think you're going anywhere. Where you are Marcus is too, so if you want him to come back safely, you stay put right here. Marcus may be above tying you up, but

I ain't."

"He didn't tell you about Humboldt? Handcuffed me to a railway bench."

Cade laughed, "No doubt you brought him cause to."

Jewel didn't answer which made Cade laugh even harder.

Jewel watched Marcus come back to the homestead with Lachlan in tow. Jewel was surrounded by all the things she couldn't give Marcus. A good wife, with a brood of offspring, a good name and nights of home cooked dinners. Although the towns other wildcat Bethany came good; trapping Rick the Tick with a baby landed her the Four Star Ranch. Jewel couldn't do it. She didn't want a plot of land to toil over or even a head of cattle to chase. She wanted the stars overhead and a good man beside her. Marcus was definitely a good man, the best, but his dreams lay elsewhere. He needed a stable life.

Marcus strolled back up to the homestead, looking at all that Cade had, a full house of Hamertons, a bustling ranch and acres of land. Marcus had an almost ready made family waiting for him, a wife if not the one he chose, a child that was not his, and a plot of land his father would gift him rather than earn it.

Marcus rolled his shoulders. This life fit Hamerton like a glove. But to Marcus it would feel like a noose. The best parts of his life so far had been since he had left Dew Springs. What good would he do being a Rancher like his Pa. Marcus wanted the endless horizon, the feeling that came with a purpose greater than himself, and of course a good woman beside him. Not any good woman, his woman. Jewel.

Marcus looked at Jewel now standing on the porch, she had chosen a husband full of color and adventure and Calvin had ignored her. What did Marcus have to offer her? Nothing. No children, no money, not even a famous name, nothing but his horse and the shirt off his back. His Ranch would be the summer stars, his hearth a camp fire.

Jewels brow furrowed, her cheeks sunken. Did she doubt

him now? That he would always treat her like a whim, while he settled down with someone else. Only one way to show her, Marcus decided. But first Quinn and the Turners. He was in no better position to ask for her hand as she was to agree to it.

"Dinners almost ready."

"I better wash up then," Marcus handed Lachlan to Jewel. "Miss Jewel here is a famous singer from Kansas, and she knows every cowboy song there is...."

The child's eyes flew wide.

"Thanks Marcus" Jewel grumbled.

Marcus laughed and made his way to the bath listening as Jewels sweet voice broke out into a ditty.

After dinner Cade opened a bottle of whiskey and poured a glass for everyone except himself and Pearl.

Pearl laughed and grabbed the bottle pouring one for herself, "I'm almost old enough and besides Aunt Eustace says it's best to build an resilience as you never know when you might need it."

Jewel smiled thinking Aunt Eustace probably has some wild nights tucked up in her magnificent bouffant.

Cade sighed, "Remind me to send a letter to your Aunt."

Evelyn threw back her glass, "Well she never taught me that," She squinted and shivered as the liquid disappeared.

Jewel knocked hers back and poured another one to sip slowly, "It's been a long couple of weeks." she splashed another dose of the amber liquid into Marcus's glass.

"Ease up."

"Relax Marcus we both could do with a good night sleep."

Marcus chugged back the spicy liquor and put his glass back down to be refilled.

They all reclined to the porch for the night, the summer heat still sticking clothes to their bodies, the sound of crickets and every now and then a bray from a horse or a lament from cattle broke their stories of times gone by.

"I didn't know you set off those fireworks, in the Church.

That explains Fort Worth." Jewel mumbled.

The whiskey must be doing well because Marcus laughed, "It was more Shelly's fault he cut the fuse too short and as I said Fort Worth was an accident."

"He's always been up to mischief, Shelly. I hear he is in some pickle in Colorado with the conditions of the mining lease he bought and how it came with a bride." Hamerton said.

"I can't imagine any woman that would make Shelly settle down."

"She'd have to have a good sense of humor," Jewel said as she topped up Marcus's glass.

"And not take him too seriously," Marcus added over a yawn, "And Taylor has taken over Windy Hill Ranch?"

"Yep, he's run off his feet." Cade sipped slowly on his mug of coffee, "I'll head on over tomorrow and let him know,..." Cade looked at Jewel and then back to Marcus, "... the situation."

Upstairs a baby howled and Evie excused herself as did Pearl. Evie came back and pointed to Jewel, "Come on I'll find you something to sleep in."

Jewel nodded and followed. She didn't really care what she was going to sleep in, so long as one of those babies woke her up when she needed it.

"You can share my room," Pearl smiled as Jewel followed them up the stairs.

Good Jewel thought. She knew where Pearls bedroom was and it suited her just fine, close to the rear door and the stables.

Cade listened as the floorboards creaked overhead, "I heard about Whit too."

Marcus swirled his whiskey around his glass and swallowed it. Marcus winced as he exhaled letting the spicy liquor sting his taste buds and heat his insides.

"Yes, my father called me back, as a solution to Whit's dalliance; it's his revenge I reckon for me taking off."

Cade exhaled and shook his head, "Ain't that something."

Marcus splashed another measure into his glass, "Jewel doesn't know and I'd appreciate keeping her out of it."

Cade snorted, "That'll be like keeping the cat from the cream."

"At least till I get it sorted."

"What do you mean?"

"When all is said and done, and if I get my way with Quinn, I'm going to marry her."

Cade lifted his coffee cup and chimed it to Marcus's whiskey, "Then ride hard and fast my friend and I'll try to hold your bride without ropes and cuffs."

Marcus almost spat out his next gulp, "I never said that."

Chapter 24

Jewel's eyes flew open at the sound of footsteps overhead tip-toeing in a rush to hush a crying baby. Jewel wiped a hand down her face and licked her parched lips. Evelyn's Aunt Eustace was right; there was a benefit to building resilience to whiskey. Jewel crept out of bed, confused at the frills and laces that caressed her skin, until she remembered the night-gown Evie had lent her.

Jewel carried her saddle bags through the darkened rooms to the rear porch where she pulled on her calf high boots. She ran her hands down her damp clothes that hung on the washing line, annoyed that Maybelle had taken the liberty to wash for her. Jewel almost stomped her heel, wondering how her plans could come undone by wet denim. Across the yard she regarded the vaqueros' cabins, single rooms in a line for the single men, separate huts further back for those who stayed with their families.

Jewel watched as a lone figure stumbled from the nearest room in just denims and boots, his scared torso clear to see in the crescent moon light. Marcus almost fell, holding onto the wall for support and took a breather. Whiskey was not his friend. Jewel regarded the distance, could she make it in and out with the silver guns before Marcus returned from reliev-ing himself? Probably not, she would have to wait it out.

Jewel sunk low as Marcus returned to stumble into his room. Jewel sat in the cool grass, listening as the upstairs floor-boards creaked back and forth with someone's rocking. Jewel would take *Scout* if she could saddle him. She was only riding over to the Crooked K, technically she was not stealing, only relocating Marcus's horse.

As the minutes ticked by, Jewel shivered. She crossed the lawn, leaving her saddle bags on the porch. As she neared, the sounds of snoring tore through the cedar planks. With her finger over the latch Jewel slowly turned the handle. The snores intensified. Jewel widened the gap until she could peek through. Marcus lay on his front, his face turned to the wall. His saddle bags lay in a heap at the end of his bed. Jewel pushed forward. The door squeaked and she froze. Within two seconds, Marcus's snores returned to normal.

Exhaling, Jewel opened the door faster, the squeak turning into a hiss and she quickly crawled across the floor. As quiet and as fast as she could, Jewel dug into the leather pouches feeling nothing but fabric. Jewel stood up and scanned the partially open door behind her, and a silhouette of something hung on the back.

Jewel reached it in two steps, her fingers retrieved her prize and she twisted them out of the holster to confirm the flash of silver in the pale moonlight.

The silence made her shiver. Suddenly a weight collided with her back and she tumbled against the door, slamming it shut. Strong hands spun her around, her heels tripping one another. Marcus's bulk compressed her. With her shoulders flat against the door, Marcus's hand trapped both of hers and raised them above her head.

"Jewel?" His voice was thick and groggy. His grip relaxed, "What the hell are you doing?" His fingers found the gun belt in her hand, "Running again?"

Jewel's chest constricted at the betrayal in his voice. It was for his own good! When she reached his Pa, it would be out of Marcus's hands. He would be stuck between choosing his family over her and as much as Jewel didn't want that, she felt she deserved it. Her anger boiled over, irrational, seething, wounded.

"What are you going to do about it lawman?"

Marcus released her arms, his bare torso pressed against the sheer fabric of her nightgown. The thin shift underneath betrayed her body's reaction as her breasts swelled, her nipples puckering the fabric. Marcus breathed warm air down her exposed throat, the soft air caressing between her breasts and Jewels knees wobbled.

Marcus tilted his head to the side, "Something I should have done a long time ago."

In one swift movement Marcus hands cupped Jewel's buttocks and lifted; instinctively her legs wrapped around his hips as his desire cradled between her thighs.

Marcus captured her mouth, his lips pressing hard, his tongue driving deep into the soft corners. Jewel moaned as her veins coursed with heat. She coiled her arms around his neck as Marcus hands rushed under the layers of her nightgown to cup her frilly lined buttock. His fingers stroked the laced hemline of her drawers sending a rush of tremors down Jewels spine. His kiss reached fever pitch, holding her in place as his fingertips breached the lacy barrier. Jewel arched, a noise strangled in her throat. No denim this time to prevent Marcus's ministrations as his thumb rolled at the apex of her velvet folds. Jewel curled around him, bringing him closer, hoping to never let go, she traced down his sculptured bared shoulders as Marcus slid his finger into her slick heat. Jewel's gasp was lost in his kiss, his own moan echoing his shudders and ricocheting through her chest.

Marcus withdrew, snagging Jewels bottom lip between teeth, his voice a husky growl, "But only if you're su-"

"Never been surer Marcus," Jewel rushed before their lips met again. She felt his laugh against her tongue that writhed to match his intensity.

Jewel's world spun and dipped as the mattress met her shoulders, Marcus crouched between her thighs, with his hands on either side, Marcus pulled her nightgown over her head and tossed it on the floor. He lowered himself beside her, pulling her thigh over his waistline.

Marcus watched the anticipation blend with apprehension on Jewel's freckled cheeks. Was she worried? He kissed her again, this time slower, his tongue delving, caressing and savoring all that he could of the woman he loved. Jewel responded in kind, with her hips rolling in his grip. Marcus stroked upwards, raising her thin chemise to her ribs. He watched her arousal peak, and his patience gone. He cupped her swollen breast, her hardened center between his thumb and forefinger. With the gentlest of pressure he rolled the hard nub, catching Jewel's gasps with his mouth. Marcus released her, the sensation of the fabric not enough as his hand drove under the material to caress her, flesh on flesh. Jewel moved closer, as he trailed a string of kisses down her jawline, tenderly nipping as he descended. Marcus used his knee to part her thighs, the heat from her arousal increasing his own. His flesh strained against his denim, his chest hot with her frantic touch.

Jewel fingers tore through Marcus's hair, as flashes of lightening sparked across her skin. She ached to feel him inside her, seeking the conclusion her desire demanded. Marcus's intensity blistered across her body, fueling her own hunger. His touch was direct, firm and sensual. The rhythm of his desire ground against Jewel and she gasped as if a forest fire had stolen the air from her lungs. Marcus fingers slipped under the laced edges of her drawers, finding the material wet and hot. Deft, deliberate strokes brought Jewel molten flesh to throb, to ache and beg for him. Marcus circled upwards with mounting pressure and Jewel shivered as she ran kisses across his bare powerful chest. His muscles twitched and heaved; he trembled under her caress, Jewel happy she could affect him as much as he tortured her. She pulled Marcus closer only to have him withdraw. Confused she leaned upwards on her elbows, as Marcus knelt at the end of the bed. She admired his bare muscular torso, the divots and valleys sculptured and scarred over the years. His ribbed abdomen and the lines either side that disappeared into his belt line made Jewel's mouth water. He grabbed the heel of one of her boots.

"You know, I dreamed of you coming to me in these boots

and nothing else." Marcus tugged off her boot and let it fall to the floor. "For six months I dreamed of you most nights, just like this." He let the second boot fall.

"And then," Jewel brought herself upwards more, her breasts straining against the sheer fabric.

"And then it changed to the way the morning sun hit your curls, the way you smiled at the crack of a pistol, the color of your eyes after a storm."

Jewel sat upright, Marcus unwound the braid of her hair, pulling her ginger curls into chaotic strands.

"I dreamed of you too Marcus, determined to make me yours, and nothing standing between us."

Marcus smiled, "The boring cowboy trying to tame the wild Ruby?"

"Not Ruby, me. Where one day you would look at me the way I looked at you."

"I can't offer you –"

Jewel put a finger to his lips, she didn't want to hear it. Not some lame gentleman's offer, now was not the time.

"And trust me, there is nothing boring about you Marcus."

Jewel dragged her fingers down his rippled stomach until she tripped over his belt line. With rapid movements she undid his fly, her hand coiled around his thick rock-hard flesh. Marcus groaned his entire body tensed and Jewel licked her lips, "Tonight, are you mine Marcus?"

"All the way," He growled.

"Then show me."

Marcus's desire thundered in Jewel's grip. He rested his palm behind her neck and brought her onto her knees hard against him. Their kiss only broken by her chemise being brought over her head. Jewel pressed her swollen breasts against his bare chest. Her skin like the softest velvet, cupping her breasts in his hands, he gently pinched both nipples, the husky moan wrought from her lips slammed into his groin. Marcus leaned back to enjoy her heavy lidded gaze, her thirst as desperate as his own. He wished for more moonlight to make out every freckle that decorated her creamy white complexion, her supple femininity, so exquisite it hurt. Marcus saw her hesitation, demurely closing her form as if to hide her glorious curves. Jewels shyness only compounded his hunger, his desire to worship her, to possess her in only the way a man could. Jewel may have been married but Marcus would be the one to show her true passion.

He cupped her sex, the fabric wet and hot as he stroked back and forth, her throat exposed, and his lips seized the tender flesh. Jewel arched her back, and Marcus scrapped kisses down her delicate flesh, until he reached the plush curve of her breasts. He seized one hardened center in his mouth and reveled in the whimper that tore from Jewel's lips. With his right hand he slid down the lacy fabric that covered her. His teeth gently grazed her nipple as he stroked the soft ginger curls of her molten core. Marcus shuddered as her tight flesh met him, her slick heat destroying his nerves.

Jewel fumbled with Marcus denim's pushing them past his buttocks. His hardness pulsated in anticipation. Jewel wrapped her hand around his heavy shaft, stroking the entire length upwards to the thick head. She couldn't wait. Her patience was long gone, she ached in all the right places, and now it intensified, needing Marcus like the fields needed the sun. His kisses scalded every inch; his skillful touch brought her to the edge and dangled her above the precipice she demanded. Marcus strength surged and Jewel tightened her grip, she needed him now.

Marcus broke the kiss and withdrew. He stood at the end of the bed and shucked his denims. He stood before Jewel as her eyes raked over his naked form, pausing at each of his scars to run her fingers across the puckered skin. Marcus frowned at Jewels appraisal of the damage, Jewels lips pressed against his left shoulder and his muscles twitched. Her kiss dragged down to the scar across his ribs and Marcus fingers twisted through her hair. Her mouth captured his engorged flesh and Marcus groaned, his entire body trembled, his eyes hooded. Marcus tilted her mouth away and dragged Jewel upwards.

With a single swing of his forearm, Marcus brought her knees out from underneath, Jewel squeaked as she landed on the mattress and Marcus dragged her drawers down her slender legs. Jewel had waited long enough and wrapped her arms around his neck as he descended. Marcus laid a string of kisses between her breasts as he prowled over her, landing his desire firmly between her thighs.

"You could have told me to hold on." Jewel laughed.

"Why? I wasn't letting you go." Marcus said as his mouth clamped over hers.

Their breaths intermingled; his demanding sensual kisses drew tendrils of pleasure from deep within. Jewel didn't want to squeak again, but his intensity created such a rush through her veins, sweeping her up until there was nothing left, but Marcus to hold onto. His thirst for her seemed unchecked, his movements so deliberate and firm, that all her doubts evaporated. Marcus cradled her between his thick arms, as the fine hairs on his chest caressed her bare skin.

The earlier anger at Marcus had evaporated and in its place a fever storm built of carnal delights. Marcus was Jewels' and she relished in his reverence. His tenderness tempered by his eagerness to possess every part of her. Marcus stroked her silken folds, sliding in gently only to retreat and circle to the top. She knew Marcus was enjoying too much of this torture, the fulfilment of her needs, suspended in his adoration. Marcus wrought wave after wave of pleasure and Jewel rocked to his rhythm, she sensed that elusive moment when the pressure would peak and knew Marcus would capture it just like her heart. His strength echoed through his body, cascading through to her, when she was both afraid knowing she was safe, awake and yet drifting aimlessly on the sensual ripples that Marcus orchestrated.

Marcus pressed his flesh against Jewel, her slickness yielding slowly as he entered. Tremors sliced down his tendons, his body begging to be unleashed to ravish the woman beneath. He plunged deeper, responding with Jewel's body. Marcus throat rasped at Jewels gradual release. With nerves strained and muscles bunched waiting for freedom, Marcus's initial thrust forward made Jewel gasp and he froze. A growl thundered through his chest, as Jewels ankles hooked behind his back. His tongue penetrated deep as her purrs multiplied, her breath hot, her mouth moist, as he caught her whimper.

Marcus edges frayed, his control slipping at the maddening delight of her creamy heat tight around his flesh. How did she feel so good, so fiery and supple, engulfing him in all that was Jewel? Marcus buried himself in his woman. He was grateful for the time to mature, to savor this moment, tempering his patience, and not when he was a nineteen year old bronc with too much energy and not enough restraint. Jewel peppered him with tender kisses, constricting, writhing beneath him. He could feel her heart beneath her ribs strumming an impossible cadence in unison with his. Each undulation of their bodies racked him with ecstasy, and shredded his discipline. Heated coils lashed him with each thrust his patience ebbing. She was too tight, too hot and too much.

"You were always like wildfire Jewel."

"Marcus?" Jewel murmured as she nuzzled his neck.

"Everything you touch is consumed, a tornado of vivacity, and it only takes one spark, even me."

Jewel's heart ached as Marcus's words sliced through to the darkest depths of her soul. She had waited for an eternity for Marcus to truly see her. Jewel succumbed. Marcus's rhythm tore tendrils of pleasure through her body intoxicating, blissful and unending, pulsating through her center. Her body peppered with tremors she could no longer anticipate or control. The precipice Marcus promised approached as he plunged deeper.

"Wildfire? Marcus I can't breathe without you."

Marcus kissed her long and deep, his movements deliberately slower, the ecstasy lingering, "Are you saying you need me?"

"Like the tides need the moon, Marcus. That's why I had to leave. If I stayed any longer I would have suffocated being able to see you yet not touch you, not be able to claim you as mine."

"You've always been mine, Jewel."

Marcus thrust forward which sent Jewel's chin upwards, she gasped for air and Marcus ensnared her lips. He massaged her hip, rolling it to match his potent carnal symphony. Jewel's skin ignited as the ripples of pleasure strummed from within. She coiled tighter, sliding her arms around his ribs and digging her nails into his powerful shoulders. Marcus drove forward again and again until Jewel cried out, a crescendo of hellfire surging through her veins. Jewel surrendered to the rhapsody that Marcus had captured.

Jewel's hot flesh constricted around Marcus, her gasps and pants reduced to breathless kisses as she clung to him. Marcus sunk deeper again and again, compounding Jewels release and in turn his own torture. Her adoration no longer bearable, her ecstasy fueling his own, at the last moment, he withdrew spilling his hot seed onto her thigh.

Marcus kissed her deep, his tongue swept across Jewel's as he tried to regain his composure. He didn't want to untangle their knotted limbs, her flushed cheeks, her heavy lidded gaze. Even as her heart thundered against his ribs, Jewel pressed kisses to his neck and jaw. Carefully Marcus sat back and located a washcloth. Gently he cleaned the creamy pale skin of Jewel's inner thigh. When he finished, he rested on his heels, collecting his thoughts as Jewel reclined in front of him.

The moonlight had painted her complexion the fairest of porcelain, her bare slender leg curled around the sheets, puckering around her flat abdomen and bunching under her arm. The wicked curve of her breast exposed in the silvery light. Jewel's curls billowed around her shoulders and down to the small of her back.

Marcus exhaled, his throat constricted, Jewel's form seemed to have been carved from the heavens, just for him. He ran his hand up her dainty ankle, and up to her calf, she laughed husky as the goose-bumps blushed her velvet skin. Marcus felt his arousal harden. He was breathless and exhausted but when he looked at Jewel's languid naked elegance, her provocative gaze, he felt starved, famished, and in dire need of more.

His grip ascended as he stalked over her, laying kiss after kiss up her outer thigh. He reached her plump buttock and gently sunk his teeth. Jewel cupped his chin, dragging him up to her lips. Marcus lay beside her, pulling her thigh over his hip, the tip of his desire like a magnet to her slick molten core. Her breasts glistened with sweat from their previous union and Marcus trailed kisses downwards until he drew her taunt nipple hard against his tongue. Jewel slithered against him until he entered her, his senses erupted; his nerves raw.

Jewel rolled her hips down Marcus's engorged flesh, as he thrust inside her. Their earlier rhythm a ballad compared to this frenzied harmony that strummed invisible chords within. Marcus devoured her, raking his hands across her skin, pulling her down against him to wreck passion deep inside. Her hunger unstated, yearning for his power, she wanted the unrestrained Marcus that had her panting in rapture. His mouth crashed down on hers, the air torn from her lungs and she sunk her teeth into his bottom lip. His growl lost in her throat, as she sought his tongue. The extremities of her body numbed as Marcus bucked, his passion a torrent that consumed her. Marcus gripped her hips, as her cadence outpaced his. Jewel rocked against him, sliding up and down his thick shaft until she could take it no more. Jewel's release came fast and fierce, a savage tempest of a thousand ripples that broke across her skin. Marcus howled a warning as Jewel convulsed around him. In one last surge, Marcus withdrew and spilled his seed again.

Jewel pressed her kisses along his jaw, teasing his tongue, until he nibbled her bottom lip. Their labored breaths mingled into one as Marcus collapsed beside her. Jewel crawled across his chest, her finger tips lazily stroking the fine hair that covered his sculptured form.

Marcus twirled her ginger curls between his fingers, "Wildfire," He chucked as his breaths began to settle.

"If I'm the wildfire, then you are the flashpoint, Marcus Kearby." Jewel added a few more kisses to his chest before she drifted off to sleep.

Jewel awoke to Marcus pressed against her spine, one arm crossed her abdomen and disappeared into the sheets, his left arm wrapped around her shoulder and ended between her bare breasts. The dawn light splintered through the rough hessian curtains that had been strung up in the cabin. She regarded her nightgown strewn across the ground, Marcus's gun belt with duel silver handed pistols still in place. Jewel sighed. Well she had had the best intentions.

Jewel stretched her legs, sparking a rush of sensations as her skin caressed Marcus nakedness. With the barest of touches she melted, feeling the damp heat between her thighs. Who knew Marcus Kearby was a Devil between the sheets? She stifled a laugh. Jewel Daniels knew and she would never forget it.

Jewel felt Marcus stir behind her, his arousal already hard and pressing against her bare buttock. Marcus groaned as he sunk a kiss on the tender skin between her neck and shoulder.

"I feel rested but ruined," He mumbled. "Are you alright?"

Jewel curled backwards, pressing herself closer to him as his palm cupped her breast, "I feel perfectly fine."

He gently massaged her swollen breast until his thumb and forefinger found her pebbled center. A flash of scandalous energy slithered downwards, her body throbbing for him imme-diately. Jewel slinked backwards, Marcus desire slid between her thighs.

"Or I will be soon," Jewel purred as she curled her arm be-hind Marcus's neck, "Unless you'd rather get your rest?"

His groan was lost in the kisses against her neck as he gripped her inner thigh, bringing her leg back, his tip sliding passed her velvet folds, "I never said that."

Jewel's throaty laugh ended as Marcus buried himself deep inside.

Chapter 25

The morning sun splashed down upon Jewel's naked frame. Jewel's slick tight heat had been his undoing. Marcus had lost countless hours fantasying about taking Jewel as his woman and it paled in comparison, like a hastily scrawled drawing of a masterpiece. This morning the fantasies dissolved, the reality embedded in his memory and seared across his heart. Marcus didn't want to tear his eyes away from the golden cream delights, but he had to move.

Marcus rolled over onto his back, and regarded the small vaquero cabin, his gun belt hung in place. What the hell was Jewel doing there last night? Was it another attempt at running? But to where and why? Marcus told her to wait for him. Perhaps he should make her an offer before he left, but what was he offering? Either he returned to clear her name or the Turners would catch them. Or Abe and Theo and then she would hang.

One thing was for certain. Jewel Daniels was Marcus's woman and damn anyone who said otherwise.

Marcus crawled from the bed leaving the bedsheets to cover his love. He pulled on his denims and found a fresh shirt, all loaned from Hamerton. He would have to pay him back somehow. His feet heated on the sun-warmed timber floor and he peered through the rustic curtains. The sun was higher than he expected. If it wasn't for Jewel, Marcus had expected to leave just after dawn.

He heard Jewel stir and he turned back to the bed. She threw her arms overhead, the sheet slipping to obscenity. Suddenly Jewel sat upright with modesty thrown out the window. Marcus couldn't help himself and he leaned over and dropped a sweet kiss on her cheek, and then her neck, her bare breast pressed against his open shirt, as her arms came to rest behind his neck, her skin warm from slumber made him shiver.

Marcus leaned back, "It's long past time I headed south."

"I know," Jewel uncurled her arms from his neck.

"What were you going to do last night?"

"Run to the Crooked K." Jewel brought the sheet up to her neck, "I can't bear you running off to possibly hang or jail time for aiding and abetting. I don't know Quinn, but you thought you could trust Abe and Theo."

"I know Quinn." Marcus ran his finger down her cheek.

Thank God she hadn't gone to his father, she would have discovered Whit and the mess with his fiancé, before Marcus could explain it. Marcus almost blurted out his intentions there and then, but they were empty without resolving all that was stacked against them.

"I know Quinn and more importantly Quinn knows me. We've already started setting the record straight, getting it out there, that Bryce was Baby-face. I can't bet on Abe and Theo heading north to make that official, but I reckon we've got enough distance on the Fort Worth posse and the Turners."

"And I'm supposed to stay here and let you place yourself in danger."

Marcus pressed a gentle kiss to her plump lips, retreating only a fraction to stare into her crystal blue eyes, "It would make matters worse." He kissed her again, this time lingering longer, "Much worse." Marcus tugged her bottom lip with his teeth, "If you were with me. Stay here out of harm's way, and then I can concentrate." Marcus sent his tongue past her lips for the final time before he stood up.

Jewel looked petulant in more ways than one and Marcus relished taunting her, "Could you do me a favor first though?"

"Anything," He stepped back, lest he follow his instincts and bury himself in her again.

"Maybelle washed my clothes."

"I'll fetch them from the line." He buttoned up his shirt one by one, before he buckled his gun belt around his waist, the silver handed pistols in their holsters, "Stay right here."

Jewel smirked at his double layered demand. Until last night she had no intention of staying put. She had given up on Marcus, hoping his father would make him stay in Dew Springs. Jewel hadn't placed any value on the fact that Marcus might be right and Quinn the best option. They were in Texas and the Frontier Battalion was only a day and a half ride. Jewel hadn't contemplated life if her name was cleared. Would she stay in Dew Springs with Marcus? Her heart ached with longing. He had bedded her, but said nothing else. She sat upright as she heard him return. Marcus handed over her clothes, her red checked shirt and denims.

"I'll be packing supplies but I will say goodbye before I leave. I'm begging you Jewel, if you do nothing else, stay put. Dew Springs is the safest place for you right now."

Jewel dressed after he left. She couldn't lie to herself. She wanted Marcus exactly how she had him. Hard, fast and nothing held back. Would she be satisfied with nothing more? Marcus was an honorable man and he had made sure he done everything right. No child would be born of their blissful union and Jewel could be thankful of that. Jewel had allowed herself to hide behind Calvin, using her marriage as a shield. Her heart had already been given to Marcus all those years ago. It was his now forever. Could she settle for being his conquest and nothing else?

Jewel sheepishly wandered over to the homestead picking her saddlebags up from the porch steps and stashing them in Pearl's room. It seemed ridiculous that Jewel worried about her desperate plight for affection from Marcus despite her neck on the line as Ruby Drawers.

Jewel looked in the mirror as she braided her hair. She tucked her red gingham shirt into her beltline and straightened her shoulders. It was really a matter of perspective. After all, the Texas Ranger Marcus Kearby could be seen as Ruby's latest conquest.

Marcus spent his next hour wisely saddling his horse and packing provisions. Maybelle packed him a stash of dried beef and canned beans and peaches. She even saved him two legs of fried chicken tucking them into a handkerchief for him. By the end of his preparations Marcus stood on the porch of the Double E, *Scout* saddled and two pack horses to boot. Hamerton came out from the stable to say farewell, they stood at the last step of the homestead and shook hands.

"Seems you slept in... " Hamerton said as a trail of dust billowed down the drive. Hamerton dashed back to the stable and emerged with a rifle in hand, as Kearby pulled his rifle from *Scout*'s pack.

A group of three horses, led by a pie bold pony pulled up just short of the homestead. On the back of the painted horse, Richard Kline from the Four Star Ranch kicked back his Stetson to take in Marcus and Hamerton both with rifles in hand.

"Well I'll be damned!"

"Just when I think, Hernandez had rid us of all the vermin, you show up." Hamerton said.

"Rick the Tick," Marcus acknowledged the only man in Dew Springs who was shorter than himself.

"Here I was thinking I misheard, Kearby Senior chatting up a storm at Church."

Marcus insides revolved into a solid ball of fire. He could pull Rick out of the saddle and end him before the man could defend himself. Marcus cooled his temper.

"What do you want Rick?" Marcus said.

A rush of feminine voices came around the side of the homestead, Jewel and Pearl side by side.

"Pearl?"

"Jesse!" Pearl gasped.

Hamerton groaned. The younger Kline pushed his horse out from behind his cousin, his eyes stuck on the beauty before him.

"And Miss Jewel Daniels, if I never laid eyes on you again, it would be a fine day indeed." Rick the Tick said.

Marcus got two steps to Kline's horse before Hamerton had him by his shoulders. Marcus's throat constricted. Rick the Tick had been talking to his father!

Jewel stepped down from the porch, crossing her arms as she walked, "You still cross I beat you at calf-roping, Kline? Don't beat yourself up about it Kline, then again, from what I hear you do nothing but beat yourself these days."

Pearl gasped. Hamerton and the other Hands laughed as Marcus coughed at Jewels obscene insult. Marcus was appalled yet deep down admired her poise. Kline shuffled uncomfortable in his saddle.

"Aren't you supposed to teach the help manners, Kearby."

"She doesn't need manners when she's double-backboned, unlike you there Kline."

"My my, Kearby a little hot headed there over this one."

"State your business and get off my land Kline, or I'll drag you out and I won't stop at the gate." Hamerton spat.

"I came to see what all the fuss was about in town."

"What fuss?" Marcus asked.

"A businessman from up north staying at the Bluebell, he's looking for the hometown Texas Ranger. I ain't even made it over to the Crooked K yet, came first here to see if Hamerton had heard."

Marcus froze, his gut filled with lead. How many days had passed since they had left the train? No, Gabriel Turner wasn't on the train. He was in Dodge City. "What does this businessman look like?"

"Whatcha mean, how many businessman up north do you know?"

"Only one that wants to kill you," Jewel murmured from the porch.

Marcus cursed and regarded her poised posture again. She would look Turner in the eye and dare him to take those guns. And then there was Rick the Tick, married to the town's biggest gossip. He heard the news and he had come straight to the

Double E. A small slice of satisfaction worked under Marcus's ribs. He took measured steps to Kline's pie bold and placed his hand on the reins. "I'm afraid I'm going to have to arrest you Richard Kline."

"Arrest me?"

"It's either arrest you or you lend a hand. All of you. I'm authorized under the Texas Penal Code to ask for your help, if you refuse, I'll arrest you instead."

Jesse Kline pushed his mount forward, "Of course we'll help, Ranger Kearby, tell us what you need." The young man said all the while his eyes glued to Pearl.

Jewel stormed up the porch and into the homestead. She stopped inside the warmly furnished lounge room, listening as Marcus gave the orders to the others. She paced back and forth, taking in all that surrounded her. The wonky table with multiple chairs, including a chair built high for Hamerton's son, the settee had embroidered cushions, an array of tiny wooden figurines scattered across the window sill. The screen door squeaked and Marcus strode across the multi-colored rug.

"You can't do this Marcus!" Jewel hissed, her arm on his bicep, "They are Ranchers and cowboys, not Rangers or soldiers."

"I don't need them to be anything but reinforcements here with you, while I ride into Dew and do some reconnaissance around the Bluebell. I have to make sure it's Turner. He's slipped the net so many times. While I'm there I can send a telegram to Quinn."

"Marcus don't do this, please! You'll end up like.... " She couldn't say Calvin's name, "I will not let you do this, not alone. I'll come with you."

"I'm going with him." Hamerton stood over her shoulder, "No-one is better at skulking around Dew Springs."

"Then wait until night fall." Jewel pleaded.

"It'll already be close to noon when we get to town," Marcus said.

"Well what if we both left, dragged the Turners away and headed to Quinn now."

"If it is Gabriel and if Harkin, Brady and Bolt are with him. What if they're not? Say Gabriel sends the others, and he slips through again. Say we can't reach Quinn but McNelly instead. Then we'd both be as good as dead. Let me be sure it's Turner first." Marcus shook his head, "Damn Abe and Theo would kick me if they could, they wanted this all along, to use Ruby Drawers as bait."

Jewel nodded. She could see Abe and Theo's sense. If she managed to draw Gabriel Turner all the way to Dew Springs, surely he would follow her to Quinn? Maybe not. The Frontier Battalion of the Texas Rangers was significantly different than the Nine Lives Saloon.

"Well, who's going to keep an eye on Kline and his bunch?"

Marcus handed Jewel both silver inlaid pistols, "You are."

"Marcus?"

"If I get too close to Turner, they are the only thing that can save me."

Jewel nodded and slid them into her holster, "Make it so I don't have to use them."

Marcus smiled, "I'll try." He quickly dipped his lips to Jewel before rushing to the screen door.

"Marcus just...." Jewel sighed, her words scoring her tight throat, "Don't go doing the right thing."

Marcus halted at the screen door, "I ain't done the right thing for a while now Jewel."

Something about his tone struck a chord within her chest. Jewel closed her eyes for a moment and whispered, "Just be safe."

Marcus climbed onto *Scout* just as Cade returned with a saddled *Maverick*. He didn't like needing to trust Rick, the man was a parasite. But he couldn't risk the man riding off and opening his mouth. He couldn't guarantee his or Jewel's safety riding south not without any of the Turners collared. If Gabriel Turner himself had made it to Dew Springs, then those silver pistols were worth both their lives.

He needed to flush Turner out, to force his hand, if he caught Gabriel Turner or his fraudulent businessman persona Garrett Tanner with the others Jesse, Cooper or Benny Marcus would have a better chance. Marcus had a bevy of Ranchers who could shoot the pip out of a dice at a hundred paces, but facing the Turner Gang was another story. They were cattleman not Rangers.

By the time Marcus and Cade made it to Dew Springs, the sun hung high overhead. They circled around the outskirts, to come in from the far end. The farrier had finished his work for the day as the heat had climbed and Marcus and Cade were able to tie their horses at the rear of his workshop without raising an alarm. There they kept to the rear of the shop fronts, until they reached the laundry of the Bluebell.

Between the gaps of the buildings, Marcus was able to see that Dew Springs hadn't changed in his absence. The timber boardwalk still lined the wide unpaved street. The butcher still advertised his wares on the same blackboard while he sat next door at the tiny cafe, chewing the ear off the lawyer Franklin.

A run of horse lined both sides of the street as patrons hung decorations for the 4th of July celebrations. The Church kept watch over the lot in the center of town, the leafy elm tree shading the immaculate lawn.

Cigar smoke and organ music drifted out from the double doors of the Nine Lives Saloon. The Doves fanned themselves from the heat on the double story balcony. Across the road the Bluebell hotel stood just as tall but instead of soiled Doves, maids beat rugs over the balcony, below the restaurant offered cold sodas and hot meals. For a second Marcus imagined walking in there to arrest Turner and wondered how far he would get. He shook his head.

If Gabriel Turner was there, Irene the housekeeper would

know. She may keep her rooms clean but she knew exactly what soiled the sheets.

Marcus pulled his Stetson low and wandered through to the stables, with Cade behind him. They had to wait several minutes before Irene appeared and sneakily lit a cheroot.

Cade stepped out the shadows of the stable and the hefty grey haired matron jumped.

"What the devil are you doin' in there Hamerton? Don't you be causing trouble?"

"Me? Trouble?"

Marcus listened as Irene answered Cade's questions. Marcus moved down the stalls of the stable, inspecting the horses. No animal stood out as flashy and nothing that indicated they'd ridden hard to reach Dew.

"I know who ya talkin' about, yep, he tips big. Reckons he works with the railways, got some business with a new line from Houston, he's looking at breaking new ground here for a station. But his mate looks like he's been breaking necks more like it, if you catch my drift."

Marcus listened from in the stables, Irene was not known for subtlety.

"Is that so, well where are they now?"

"I dunno left this morning to survey sumthin' affecting the line."

"Which way they headed?"

"South."

"Other than this big fella, who else is traveling with him?"

"Didn't see any, and he didn't say."

"Thanks Irene."

"What's he want with that lovely Marcus?"

"Ah they've got stock in the same shares." Hamerton quipped.

Marcus's mind seemed to grind to a halt. Bonds. Not shares. Turner had been almost bankrupted with shares in the railroads. But if he counterfeited their bonds, he could enact his revenge two fold. Creditors would call on the railroads for their interest, while he had been paid for the bond in full. Smith was simply the counterfeiter, no brains, all thumbs in Emporia. Turner had somehow obtained the plates. From the gold train robbery, the missing manifest! Marcus suddenly wished he had the silver pistols, something about them linked to the counterfeits. He needed to link Turner to the counterfeits. But how?

Hamerton wandered into the darkness of the stable, "What now?"

"You wait here at the Nine Lives Saloon, I'll ride south, see if I can't see what Turners doing."

"What happens if you stumble across Turner and the others? I ain't gonna let you do that Marcus."

"I'm only scouting. Turner is still Garrett Tanner without evidence. I need to know what he's up to."

Cade put his hand on Marcus's shoulder, the taller man's cheeks hardened, his eyes like chipped stone, "Then so do I."

Marcus regarded his options. Calvin swinging from a low limb sprung to mind. He should send Cade back to the Double E. "I've tracked over a hundred horses, and over a thousand cattle. We ride south together."

Marcus should do what was right, send Cade back. He knew it was right by Cade and his family, yet it would leave Marcus exposed. He would been here before, the decision between what was right and what had to be done, only this time Marcus was risking his friend's life.

"I will not rob Evie of her husband or your children of their father. I'm riding south if you follow that's your choice, but you should know, they killed Jewel's husband like they do to all their captives. Hung him and gutted him when he was no doubt still alive."

Cade's expression didn't shift, "We ride south together."

Marcus nodded. He could feel a numbness sneaking into his veins, the same irrational focus, wrapped up in anger that had left enough scars across his body.

Chapter 26

Jewel paced up and down the hallway rug as she rocked Ellie Hamerton in her arms. The pink faced babe had finally stopped squawking and was slowly drifting off to sleep. Evie had almost run Jewel ragged with tasks around the homestead. Jewel had simply offered to lend a hand with laundry, when Evie rattled off a list of jobs that Jewel could fill her time with. Jewel had managed to complete most of them; she wasn't going to skin the vegetables no matter what Maybelle threatened.

Jewel crept into the nursery, the curtains drawn, shutting out the tangerine shades of the afternoon sun. The other twin was already asleep and Jewel pondered the decision to put them to sleep in the same room, but Evie preferred not to separate them. Slowly Jewel lowered the baby into the crib. As Jewel backed out of the room, her heel creaked on a single floorboard. She froze. The baby slept on.

Jewel closed the door slightly and slipped down the stairs. She paused at the bottom looking either side for her blonde taskmaster nowhere to be seen. Maybelle banged pots in the kitchen and Jewel mentally chided the cook for not being more silent. Jewel wandered out the front porch. Opening and closing the door with the utmost caution to prevent the hinges squeaking.

She skirted between the homestead and the main fenced yards, heading towards the stable. It might cool her nerves watching the green broncs settle into the surroundings. Plus she could keep an eye on Rick the Tick, while he nosed around Hamerton's business.

As Jewel crossed the distance to the stables, she spied Pearl leaning over one of the yard rails, her head turned to watch a young cowboy wander towards her. Jesse Kline had a strand of grass in his fingers, his head down as he approached. When he reached the rail, he put his boot on the lowest rung and tilted his hat back from his forehead. The boy was a sight alright, sandy blonde hair, blue eyes, cut from the earth not a single thing in common with his cousin Rick except his surname. Pearl seemed to shift away from Jesse until he said something and suddenly she laughed. Jewel didn't have to watch anymore, Pearl's smile outshined the tiger-eye stripped skyline.

Jewel diverted from the stable yards to the vaquero huts, pausing as she heard Rick the Tick whisper.

"This is horseshit, I don't think there's any Ranger left in Kearby now he's returned home to marry."

Jewel felt the ground tremble under her feet, looking down to realize it was just her knees that had failed her. She flattened her back against the wall of the homestead, missing the Hand's reply. Kline smacked his lips as he chewed something.

"Didn't you hear his father at Church, knocked her up and now has to marry her. Marcus Kearby's days as a Texas Ranger are numbered."

"And nobody is counting them like you?" The Hand replied.

"Thinking he can compel me to help him, shit," Kline spat something on the ground, "Don't get me wrong, I aint in no hurry to return home to Bethany, but my watch is done. Round up the boys, we're heading home."

Jewel stumbled back around the front of the homestead, her legs leaden as she crossed the yard. Pearl and Jesse now stood side by side, their foreheads together, as they watched the sun slide behind the horizon. Jewel's lungs seemed incapable of working. Marcus had a fiancé and a pregnant one at that! He never told her why he was returning to Dew Springs. Jewel knew, deep down she had known that it would have to have been something honorable. She had been right and so very wrong about Marcus. He had bedded Jewel with a pregnant wife in the wings.

No Jewel was wrong, Marcus warned her he had nothing

to offer and now she knew why. Jewel looked up at the white washed homestead. Marcus had still tried to do the right thing by Jewel, risking his life, breaking her out of jail and for what? Because he gave her his word that's why! He had a family waiting for him. His rejections of Jewel seemed to make sense, his reluctance to offer her what he already had.

Jealousy and curiosity collided so fast in Jewel's gut she almost retched. Marcus had some nerve insinuating that Jewel had been shameless and flippant in her affections and here he was, with a secret ready-made family. Her cheeks heated. For all Marcus's standards he clearly didn't apply them to himself; nor his soon to be wife if she was just as unrestrained. Then what made her any better than Jewel? No doubt she came with Kearby Senior's approval. Whoever she was, this woman wasn't the bastard daughter of the Kearby's aging ranch hand.

Jewel couldn't enter the house and decided to circle the tall walls instead. Every part of her wanted to run. Run from Kearby, from this house of happy families, run from the dirt bowl that was Dew Springs. Her tears stung her cheeks as she reached the rear porch. Energy infused in her legs. Jewel dashed to the stables and saddled the beige mare she had ridden from Fort Worth.

Maybelle hollered for dinner, as Evie started shouting at Kline. Jewel peered between the stable doors as Rick the Tick climbed in the saddle of his pie bold and galloped down the drive. Jewel let out a whistle between her teeth as she registered the curse words Evie hollered at Rick's back. The woman was definitely just as ladylike as Jewel remembered.

Where would Jewel run? To Quinn and be hung? To Turner and be gutted? Jewel had run from Dew Springs and look where that got her. Married to a husband who hadn't loved her, she had run from Calvin and landed in the arms of the man who would never love her. She ran from Kearby again and again and nothing changed. In fact, he remained on course to marry a decent girl and settle down. Running solved nothing.

Jewel checked her holsters. She still had the silver pistols.

She didn't need anything else.

She climbed into the saddle of the dainty mare and brought her out into the fading light.

"Miss Daniels?" Jesse called, but it was too late.

Jewel knew where she was headed, "Look after them Jessie." She brought the mare past the front porch of the house, "And don't worry Evie, Cade will find her where I leave her. I ain't no horse thief!" Jewel hollered as the mare leapt the low fence around the house yard and headed across the fields.

Marcus brought *Scout* to a standstill, the tracks of Turner and his heavy comrade had long vanished into dust. Marcus had been careful not to track them too closely but now as they crossed over uneven rocky ground, the horizon exposed them. He surveyed the dips and escarpments, he knew like the back of his hand. Why would Gabriel Turner come this far out of town? Ahead and to the left rose the Ulysses Escarpment lined with the low brittlebushes covered in dainty yellow flowers and the hardy creosote bushes that clung to the arid rock.

Marcus knew from up high on the cliff face, there was at least four caves of a size to conceal several men within them from any onlookers below. He had spent a fair amount of his youth exploring the nooks and crannies when his brothers had discarded him and his father had ignored him. The valley floor was perfect for an ambush. Marcus squinted into the distance. No glow or smoke of camp fire could be seen. The Turners weren't stupid. Marcus felt the hair stand on the back of his neck, a rush of energy surged through his chest. They were up there, he knew it. This time Marcus heeded the warning signs. Marching in there was a death trap. If it had just been him, perhaps he could circle around and try his own ambush. Cade sat astride *Maverick* beside him and the night was already chasing the dusk.

"What do you think?" Cade said.

"I think we head back to the Bluebell for a while." Marcus

said his gaze never lifting from the bands of rock that lined the valley.

Under the cover of darkness they reached the back of the Nine Lives Saloon. A tiny sliver of Marcus wished for the simpler days of himself, Cade, Shelton and Taylor carousing, playing poker and trifling with the dancing girls. Marcus shook his head. He had spent the last two years trifling with girls that resembled the one that had almost escaped him. As soon as he laid hands on the Turners, Jewel would be free to marry him. Marcus ran that thought in his head again. If Marcus hadn't been so stubborn, Jewel had always been free to marry him.

Marcus let Cade speak to the publican who offered him a room facing the hotel. Marcus pulled his hat low over his brow and headed up stairs. The room had a birds eye view over the street, including the front door and the side alley of the Bluebell. Marcus extinguished all but one lamp and waited. A working girl brought them each a cup of coffee just as Jesse Kline burst through the door.

"I looked everywhere for you, Miss Daniels is gone!"

"She what?" Marcus almost dropped his cup of coffee.

"She took that beige filly of Mr Ham –" Jesse looked at Cade and straightened his shoulders, "um of Cade's and tore off across the field."

Marcus closed his eyes, and inhaled slowly hoping the ball of anger would diffuse. He opened his eyes, not surprised the heat still coiled through his abdomen at the blank look Jessie Kline wore across his youthful features. Damn Jewel!

Marcus strode out to the balcony, the noise of the Nine Lives Saloon drifted upwards through the floor boards to assault Marcus's ear drums. Across the street, the lights of the Bluebell cast halos upon the ground, the citizens milled about inside and out, every now and then a gentleman's eye would wander to the doors of the Nine Lives earning him a wolf whistle and then clip over the ear.

"What did she say?" Marcus ground his back teeth.

"She said she ain't no horse thief and that Cade would find

her where she left her."

Marcus cursed. Always running. He had taken a risk giving her the pistols, obviously his trust misplaced, like his affections. Was he mad! Here Marcus was risking his neck for her and she abandoned him. Not only was Marcus risking his life, but that of Cade and his family, Jesse, Kline and half of Dew Springs!

"And another thing, Rick's taken his men and gone."

Marcus shook his head, "Hamerton go home with Jesse."

"I -"

Marcus held his hand up, "I'm not going after the Turners, I know where she's heading." At least he hoped he did. Perhaps Jewel hadn't abandoned him, only hung him out to dry, and there was only one way to do that. "Keep a close eye on your borders Cade, I'm heading home."

"What about the Turners?"

"I have a feeling they're going to be front and center in no time." He should have kept his mouth shut and in the same breath, he should have told her sooner. Jewel was brave, braver than he had been when Abe and Theo suggested it, now he had to catch Jewel before she reached old Sheriff Green.

Jewel tied the dainty beige horse up in the Crooked K stable. The Hands had headed home for the night, only the double story log and stone homestead was illuminated. Through the five bay windows Jewel spied at least three servants rushing about, while the patriarch Pendleton Kearby reclined on the portico. Two spiral columns reached to the second story balcony where no doubt Patricia Kearby dressed for dinner.

Jewel inhaled and straightened her shoulders. Inside the sprawling home, Marcus's bride-to-be was probably preparing herself too, squeezing her full belly into satin and ribbons. Jewel turned away to the tiny farmhouse that leaned precariously to the left. Jewel steeled her nerves as she crossed the field. Somewhere a dog bayed, followed by another and Jewel quickened her steps.

Through the single misted window, Jewel saw a solitary candle, and the man that ate his dinner by the feeble light. His shoulders were hunched, his fingers crooked, but his eyes were still bright. Jewel rapped her knuckles three times.

The door peeled back slowly to reveal the small man, the years had thinned his frame just like his salt and pepper hair.

"Who is it?" he squinted into the darkness.

"It's me Pa," Jewel managed, before the liquid filled her eyes.

Her father clapped his hands together and hooted. Jewel smiled, just as his arms curled around her and dragged her over the threshold.

"I'm not staying Pa," Jewel said, scrubbing the back of her hand across her face.

"Horseshit!! Sit sit!"

Jedidiah Daniels led his daughter over to the single threadbare lounge chair and pushed her into it. He pulled his chair from the small table and sat down, his knees creaking as he did so, "Tell me watcha been up to! Where ya been?"

"I just came to see you. To tell you..."

"Wait!" Jedidiah pushed himself upright and scuffled to the stove, he put a kettle onto a burner and began to blow under the hotplate.

"No Pa, please..." Jewel's voice broke. Her father straightened what he could of his back, and turned around.

"What is it Honey?"

Jewel took a moment. The scent of dusty window sills stirred with the breeze from the open grass fields and the smoldering timber from the stove. It reminded Jewel of all the odors that lead to her wistful dreams; the fresh rawness of the wild. She had been in such a hurry to be away from Marcus Jewel had forgotten why she left in the first place; for the sake of adventure, journeys with an unknown destination and chasing that new horizon with each turning day. Jewel thought being famous would lead to that. How wrong had she been!

"Pa, I came to say goodbye."

"Goodbye, ya just got 'ere!"

"I've got myself into a bit of trouble."

"Trouble," Jedidiah shuffled back to the table, "What kinda trouble? Fella trouble?"

Jewel laughed as she sniffled, "No Pa, but I married a man who was nothing but trouble."

"And his troubles are now y'alls? I'll sort 'im out!" Jedidiah crossed his arms over his chest, his leather vest hung on the back of his chair, his navy shirt was thin with wear, his boots were dusty with the day's work.

"Thanks Pa, but I'm sorting it. I didn't do what they say I did, but I can't get Marcus into any more trouble."

"What's Marcus gotta do with it?"

Jewel leaned back in the chair, "He's been trying to help me, Pa, brought me back to Dew Springs to keep me safe, but I can't let him. Not anymore. I've come to tell his Pa where he is and hand myself in."

Jewel's father rolled his crinkled bottom lip inward, his blue eyes still bright despite the lines that furrowed his brow, "Y'all tellin' me, that ya in trouble and Marcus is helping ya, but ya giving up?"

"Yes. I ain't made nothing of note of myself since I've been gone, I've shot a few shows, gambled some coin and drunk some whiskey, I'm sorry I let you down Pa." Jewel hated the feeling of her stomach twisting and turning, but the moment she said it, a weight lifted from her shoulders.

Jedidiah leaned across the table and pulled down two empty mugs, he pulled out a bottle of whiskey from the door-less sideboard and poured them each a measure.

"Aye got every penny ya sent me, which bought me a bottle of whiskey 'ere and there so ya ain't let me down none. But tell me this Jewel-bug," Jedidiah put the stopper back in the bottle.

Jewel picked up her mug and swilled it around in front of

her nose, the amber liquid omitted the pungent flavor that singed her nostrils, "I didn't find Ma either, I didn't even look for her."

Jewel's father put his hand on her forearm, preventing her taking a sip, "Aye never asked ya to look for ya Ma," He peered into her eyes, his cheeks flat, his brows straight, "Tell me this, did ya have fun Jewel?"

Jewel snorted, "Aye, that I did."

"Then cheers!" Jedidiah lifted his mug to hers and together they threw it back, "Now ya tell old man Kearby what ya need to tell 'im and then we'll fix this fella problem ya got."

Jewel let her father pour her another measure, thinking about what she was going to say to Pendleton and how she hoped the whiskey would provide the bravado.

"Sure," Jewel had no intention of letting her father fight her battles. She had hidden behind Calvin and then Marcus and there was no way she was going to hide behind her Pa. It was time Jewel stopped running and stood on her own.

"Cheers," Jewel clicked her mug with her father's. She finished the contents and stood up. "While the nights still young I suppose."

She bid farewell to her father, holding him tight feigning promises of returning the following day.

Every step Jewel took across the lawn, the whiskey infused in her blood stream. She heard her boots on the portico, her dusty heels echoing off the pristine tiles. A dog bayed somewhere in the distance as Jewel rapped the ornate brass knocker on the double paned door.

A servant opened the door and led Jewel through the wide hallway winding through brick archways to the softly furnished lounge. Long-horn skulls rested along one wall, two large wingback chairs sat in front of an empty stone fireplace. The mantle was stained hardwood, a wagon wheel hung above it. Pendleton Kearby stood to greet his guest with both eyes narrowed. In one wingback chair, a young woman sat, her belly only mildly swelling under the cornflower blue dress.

Marcus's mother wandered into the room ushering them to dinner and paused mid-step. Her lined features suddenly paled, her hands went to her throat.

"Marcus is fine, he's alive and he's at the Double E." Jewel rushed.

Chapter 27

Marcus took *Scout* across the darkened fields, the full moon had passed and now the waning quarter lit his path. He tied *Scout* in the thicket of cedar and elms that lined either side of the main drive and crept wide, the double story homestead lit up like a sunset. He could see people stirring inside the big house. It should stir warm feelings and fond memories of joyous times. Marcus had grown up here and his family was just inside the double paned doors. He thought of his brothers. They had been too old and too many to welcome another younger brother coming along to ruin their fun. Pendleton had never been blessed with a daughter and maybe it would have softened him. As it was, Marcus couldn't remember a kind word the man ever uttered, especially towards Marcus.

Pendleton was almost fond of Robert, his eldest although he looked more like his mother than he liked. Something about Reid's slow almost leisurely approach to life rankled Kearby Senior. But it was Whit Kearby, the third son, who was the apple of his father's eye. With a quick wit, smart mouth, smiles that made any woman swoon and fists that flew fast and often that Kearby Senior championed as taken directly from his own mold.

Marcus, his last child, had been short and dark haired like Robert and his mother and as unhurried like Reid. That was enough to turn Pendleton Kearby's attention away. He hadn't bothered to look deeper, hadn't given him the chance to improve that initial impression. Pendleton had written Marcus off as nothing useful, a dullard, and a waste of good Kearby stock. He had four sons and only one he would rather see grandchildren from. Beyond those log and stone walls, Marcus future wife, held that precious child.

It made Marcus sick that he confirmed his father's low

opinion, that Marcus was dull enough to praise loyalty over his own pride. Despite all that Jewel had put him through, Marcus would rather be chasing Jewel across the arid deserts than spend one minute in his father's company.

Marcus thoughts were disturbed by movement at the rustic shack that leaned too far to the left. Jedidiah. Marcus stormed across the lawn and knocked on the door.

"Jedidiah, open up it's me Marcus."

"Marcus." Jedidiah father pulled open the door and shuffled out of the way, "Watcha doin' 'ere?"

"Come to stop Jewel doing something stupid."

"Ah boy, aye think ya too late. She's up at the big house."

Marcus cursed as he paced in the compact dwelling. Jedidiah had a single table with a single chair, one threadbare lounge chair and a roughly hewn bed with straw mattress. He had lived on the Kearby Ranch for more than all of Marcus's life and his abode had never changed.

Marcus cursed again. Jedidiah rustled behind him.

"Don't ya be leavin' without this..." Jedidiah handed Marcus a mug of whiskey. Marcus accepted it but didn't drink. The old man crouched low he shuffled over to the straw mattress. He lifted one corner and pulled out a sack. Marcus heard the coins clanging against one another. "She sent me all of this, but y'all might need it more than me."

Jedidiah put the sack on the table and opened up the meagre pile, clearly any scrap of Jewel's earnings she had sent her father over the years. Marcus's sighed. His ribs ratcheted another notch tighter, his chest ached.

"I took some for whiskey of course," He smiled, the gaps between his teeth wider than Marcus remembered. The man had more faith in Marcus than Pendleton ever had.

"Keep it Jedidiah,"

"I ain't need it though. I got everythin' right 'ere."

Marcus expected Jedidiah to widen his arms and gesture to his house, the land, or even his whiskey but instead he tapped a gnarled finger to his temple.

"A lifetime of treasures hey?" Marcus smiled.

"Darn right."

Marcus picked up the sack and rewound the neck of the fabric; he pulled out Jedidiah's wrinkled palm and placed the money back in his grasp.

"You keep it as a dowry then, because I want your daughters hand in marriage."

Jedidiah froze. His eyes darted from one side of the narrow room to the other, "Ya sure?"

"Damn sure."

"Well if ya'll sure, I know no finer man than ya'self and I know her heart's been set on ya for a long time."

Marcus picked up his whiskey cup, "Let's hope she say yes then."

"Keep her outta jail and it'd be damn rude of her to refuse ya!" Jedidiah clanged his cup against Marcus's and he threw the dark liquid back.

Marcus did the same, exhaled the fumes that seared his throat. Marcus put the cup down just as he heard boot heels across the tiled portico. He rushed to the door to witness Jewel storming across the lawn headed straight for the barn. Suddenly she broke out into a run. Marcus's veins seared. Jewel ran with her shoulders hunched and her head dipped, it wasn't a run of fear, it was a run of distress. Marcus couldn't move fast enough to cut her off. His boot toe snagged in a divot, his knee buckled and he cartwheeled for half a dozen feet before he regained his balance. She reached the shadows of the stables as Marcus heard Pendleton Kearby shout. Marcus used his hand on a post to sling himself around the doorframe and into the stables.

The last quarter of the moon made the interior almost unnavigable. Marcus paused listening to his own ragged breathing and the snorting of several horses at rest. Then he heard her.

With as much speed as he could manage, Marcus moved down the final stall. Jewel's beige mare pawed the ground.

Kearby senior's voice echoed across the distance, he was in company with at least one of Marcus's brothers and another male. They carried lanterns as they walked, his father completely dressed and rifle in hand.

Marcus didn't waste any time. He rushed up behind Jewel and clamped a hand over her mouth and one around her waist. She squirmed in his grip, her heels coming down to strike his toes.

"It's me Jewel, honey it's me." Marcus relaxed his grip.

"Marcus!"

"Shh! Get up." Marcus half dragged half pushed Jewel to the rear of the stables, they reached the ladder to the hale storage and Marcus lifted Jewel upwards until she grabbed onto the ladder, "Up!" He pushed her buttocks until Jewel climbed.

With hand over hand, and heel after heel, Marcus scaled the lander behind her. The interior of the barn begun to lighten as the lamps neared. Marcus dove forward landing on Jewel and bringing her to the ground. He clamped his hand over her mouth again, compressing her with his frame.

"The nerve!" Pendleton Kearby barked. His voice had not softened over the years. "Bring the mare, we'll take her back to Hamerton."

Underneath him, Jewel squirmed digging her fingernails into the back of his hand, her heels banging on the hay bales. Marcus spread her thighs with his knees. Her hands wriggled to his gun belt and with his left hand Marcus pulled her arm up beyond her head and increased his weight.

"The nerve of that girl, in my own house and under my roof." Pendleton spat as he rushed to saddle his horses. "He's a damn fool."

"Aw you know Marcus Pa," Reid's voice cut through the air.

"That's right I do. Ain't no-one ever called him clever or quick, he's never had a brain in that thick skull of his."

Jewel's movements slowed, she relaxed. The light had filtered up into the rafters and Marcus could see Jewel's moist eyes like bottomless pools of obsidian, he wished he would lose himself deep within them.

"Ease up Pa," Reid cautioned.

"I'll ease up when he shows me some respect. Where's his loyalty to this family? Where's the honor in running off after some bastard of a whore."

Marcus veins engulfed in searing heat, his hand came free from Jewel's soft frame. He raised himself up on to his knees just as Jewel's limbs curled around his. She brought him down and hooked her boot behind his knee. Marcus pushed upright again.

Jewel pressed her lips to his ear, "Leave it Marcus."

"If it weren't for your mother, I'd have sent him to the parish on the day he was born."

"Pa!" Reid hissed.

"I knew that whore would get Marcus into trouble, just not the trouble I expected. Not one word of this to anyone you hear." Pendleton said.

Marcus heard the hooves gallop across the hard packed dirt. Marcus rolled off Jewel. He rested on his back and watched as the light faded from the slats of the stable. They lay side by side in the dark listening to each other's breaths. The straw scratched at Marcus's neck, his gun belt dug into his hip.

"You should have let me set him straight."

"I'm not gonna let you go down there and fight your father over my name." Jewel said.

"He had no right to say what he said." Marcus thanked the darkness hiding his humiliation. Nothing that his father had said about Marcus was wrong. His chest ached but he had Jewel, that's all that mattered, "What did you tell him?"

"I told him you were trying to help me, but it would end up getting you killed."

"And then you were going to hand yourself in?"

Jewel exhaled, "I figured I've done enough running."

Marcus rolled onto his side, his palm reaching for her in the darkness, Marcus found her waist. His fingers slid down into her belt and he dragged Jewel across the timber slats. She curled her fingers behind his neck, "When are you going to start running towards me?"

Jewel snorted, "I've been chasing you long enough Marcus Kearby."

"Then stay still and let yourself be caught."

His lips found hers in the darkness, the flavor of whiskey on her lips just like his. Jewel followed his lead, sinking deep into his kisses, until with both hands Jewel pushed his chest away.

"You're a scoundrel Marcus I don't know why I ever thought of you has honorable."

Marcus laughed and sucked and nipped his way down her neck, as she wriggled to be free.

"I warned you," Marcus tugged her shirt from belt line.

Jewel tried to increase the distance, but Marcus pulled Jewel forward until she lay sprawled across him.

"You're deplorable!" Jewel squeaked as Marcus's teeth sunk into her ear lobe.

Jewel pushed him back but found her own body pressing up against him, seeking his touch, demanding her desire be satiated. She leaned backwards but Marcus followed her again, his grip tight on her buttocks as he pulled her down onto his lap. She sat upright, her knees on the timber floor as Marcus arm snaked around her lower back. He rained kisses down her neck, licking the hollow at the base of her throat. His hot breath scalded her skin as his lips moved lower. Jewel tried to stand. His mouth clamped over her erect nipple, the fabric only dimming the pleasure slightly as his teeth gently grazed her taunt flesh.

"Marcus," she mewed.

Marcus undid her buttons in a flurry, peeling her shirt back to reveal the sheer shift. His mouth dipped to savor the delights as Jewel wound her hand through his hair.

"Every waking minute you'll be thinking of me, every night you'll be remembering these nights we spent together."

Jewel should stop, Marcus's pregnant fiancé was less than a hundred yards away. It wasn't fair. Marcus was supposed to be Jewels!

"I know." Marcus groaned as Jewel writhed across his hard desire.

His callused hand caressed the soft skin across her back. Jewel wanted to revel in Marcus's all consuming passion, despite knowing it was wrong. His ardor was explicit, uncompromising, and intense.

"When you touch her, you'll be thinking of me." Jewel said.

"Huh?" Marcus mumbled as he removed her boots one by one, tossing them somewhere into the hay bales.

"Your soon to be wife!"

Marcus's laugh was muffled by her breasts, he leaned back, his grip on her hips unrelenting, "She's Whit's fiancé and it's his child."

Jewel pushed him back. The faint moonlight filtered through the gaps in the stable roof and Jewel looked down at Marcus's expression. Was he telling the truth?

"What?"

"It's Whit's child, he abandoned her. She's some banker's daughter from Louisiana. My father ordered me to return to take her as my bride. I thought…" Marcus exhaled, it sounded silly in his own mind, but the woman would be without a husband, his father might have been proud of him, the child would be raised with a father. "I thought I was doing the right thing."

Jewel rocked forward and pressed her forehead to his, "Always."

Marcus claimed her lips and she opened for him, her tongue teasing him to advance. Jewel pulled her shirt from her slender arms. Marcus stretched his legs as he felt Jewels fingers fumble with his belt buckle. His pistols fell to the ground and Jewel stood to remove her own. She leaned to the hay bale behind him, her shift angling forward and Marcus couldn't resist.

He drove his hands under the sheer material and cupped both breasts, his thumb dragged across the tight centers and Jewel shuddered. He raked his hands down her soft skin and undid the first button of her denims.

"Beside I haven't even seen her." He teased.

Jewel clicked her tongue.

"What does she look like?" Marcus continued as he popped another button from her denims.

"She's tall, broad and blonde."

Marcus slid Jewel's denims down to her ankles and she stepped out of them. The moonlight caught the frilly edge of her undergarments and it sent tremors through his veins.

"See that's no good," Marcus brought himself closer, and slid the lacy material down to her thighs, "I only like red-heads." He brought her ginger curls to his lips and his tongue tasted the silken folds of her molten core.

Jewel's knees buckled and he held her upright, her creamy thighs pale in the moonlight. Marcus relished her supple velvet, the moist heat that he brought forward, her breathing shallow and fast as her pelvis rocked to the rhythm of his tongue.

Jewel was lost. Her senses overloaded, the edges of her focus were blurred in the rapture that Marcus wrecked upon her. She couldn't restrain the moans anymore she could her body's reaction to the endless pleasure Marcus dealt. He kissed her thighs as he removed his shirt, his fly open, his thick flesh erect and waiting. Marcus kisses ascended her body with rich sensual purpose and hedonistic intent. Jewel clutched his muscular shoulders as his tip entered her without pause. The trembles increased as her slick flesh stretched to accommodate him. Marcus gripped her thighs firmly, as he slowly dragged her down over his thick shaft.

Jewel's instinct took over and she rocked against him. The symphony in her control as Marcus reclined beneath her. Her hands caressed the taunt valleys and ridges that lined his stomach as she slid along his arousal. Jewel's impatience threatened to spoil the rhythm.

She watched his struggle as his wild tempo unleashed, the notes sung in her heart as the pleasure built. Jewel's body responded, her cheeks heated, breasts swollen, the nipples tight and hypersensitive. Her crescendo approached and fragments of pleasure shattered into a cacophony of bliss. Jewel arched her back, gasping for air, her chest so tight her lungs burned.

Marcus rocked beneath her, his hunger not yet satiated. His calloused palm compressed her breast, the roughness of the man barely restrained. His hand slithered upwards to cup her cheek. Jewel bit the fleshy part of his palm and Marcus winced. He sat bolt upright, and brought her hard against him. Jewel coiled around him as his teeth sunk into her shoulder. His cadence increased, thrusting deeper and faster, his hard flesh intensifying her inner turmoil. Jewel's head lolled back, exposing her throat and Marcus suckled the soft flesh, his nips stinging, the growl she tore from his throat, all hers to relish as the rapture took him. Suddenly he shifted her upright and Jewel felt his hot seed splash.

They sat there for a moment, until their breathing settled, Marcus kissing Jewel across her chest, his hands drawing slow circles on her hips. Jewel wished it could end like this. That tomorrow would never come. She rose to find her clothing, dressing in her shift and denims, her shirt she would find in the morning. Marcus shucked on his denims and then descended the ladder, reappearing a short time later with a horse blanket. He laid it out on the timber slats and pulled Jewel down to his bare chest.

"When this is all sorted –" Marcus began to say.

Jewel pushed her hands up to his lips. She didn't want to hear what he had to say. The Turners were out there, she was still wanted for triple murder. And Marcus's father would be demanding his return. Tomorrow she would march into the Sheriff's office and hand herself in. Tomorrow she might never see Marcus again.

"Don't let tomorrow get in the way of tonight, Marcus." Jewel muttered, sleep threatening to steal these last precious hours.

Marcus kissed her on the head, "Fine, tomorrow it is."

Jewel sighed. The wife wasn't his, nor was the child. But it didn't change her fate, only Marcus's. He had a life to live, and Jewel had done her dash. For now she had a good man beneath her, and nothing else mattered.

Chapter 28

Marcus stretched as he awoke in the pre-dawn light. He unwound Jewel from his chest. It was a new day. Today being the first day of his true freedom, he would confront his father before he headed south to Quinn. Marcus stole into the early morning light, the dew on the grass dampening his boots as he reached *Scout* in the cedar grove. He untied his mount and leisurely rode him back to the stable. He should have confronted Kearby Senior last night when his harsh words had been said. Perhaps Jewel was right, Marcus would likely have thumped his father into oblivion. The man was a product of his own ignorance. Didn't mean Marcus had to teach him different. Marcus was his own man, his father could go to his grave thinking his youngest son was useless. Marcus would no longer be burdened by his father's approval.

Marcus led *Scout* into a stall and climbed up the ladder, emitting a sigh of relief that Jewel still slumbered. Her freckled shoulders pale in her thin shift, her bare feet alluring as they rested on the blanket. Her braid had come slightly undone, and it brought a smile to his cheeks as Marcus compared the image to the girl herself. Bright, sometimes brash and always a little bit wild. Jewel was also unable to be restrained at times, yet soft, intoxicating, feminine, captivating and even demure. He lay down beside her, the words unable to be unspoken for much longer.

"Jewel."

She rolled backwards her arm curled around his and brought it around her waist. He inhaled the berry scent of her perfume, the warmth from her skin. He kissed a cluster of freckles on her shoulder and she chuckled.

The sounds of horses thundered down the gravel drive; their speed at odds with the peaceful morning. Had Cade come to check on him? Marcus squinted through the narrow gaps in the timber slats, the pre-dawn light casting the landscape in misty greys and fuzzy silhouettes. He crept to the edge of the hay storage and peered down. Marcus didn't check when he retrieved *Scout* but his father's horse and Reid's were settled in their stalls.

Marcus dashed down the ladder and rushed to the open double doors.

Five horses galloped up the drive, three speared to the left to circle the rear of the homestead, while two pulled up to the front portico. Marcus wiped his hand down his grizzled cheeks, his eyesight betrayed him.

He turned at the sudden pressure on his shoulder, tripping a sleepy Jewel into his arms.

"What is it Marcus?"

He turned back to the big house and watched Gabriel Turner dismount and knock on his front door. Marcus flew into action clambering up the ladder to retrieve his pistols, he threw down Jewel's gun belt with the silver pistols still in holsters. She swung it around her narrow waist by the time he reached the ground again.

They watched as Gabriel Turner pushed his way through the front door. Her father came out from his shack, a pair of overalls on and nothing else, carrying a shotgun. He let one shot off before one of the gang clipped him over the ear. He crumbled like a sack of potatoes. Jewel gasped.

"You ride to get help, I'll -"

Jewel clutched Marcus's forearm, her eyes ringed in red, the tears already welling, "It'll be too late by then." Jewel pulled one of the pistols from her holster and handed it to Marcus. "I'll lead them away, you save your family."

Marcus encircled her waist, holding her spine against his chest. He rested his forehead against her ginger braid. Marcus knew it. He felt it right down to his boots, that Jewel was right.

He pressed a quick kiss to her hair and released her, "The Fox Hole." Marcus scanned the stable, "Take my father's he's the fastest of the lot." He pushed Jewel onto the brown gelding that belonged to Kearby senior.

"I ain't a horse thief Marcus."

"I know but what is mine is yours. Now ride!"

Jewel nodded and changed the single silver pistol onto her right hip. Marcus headed out the doors and circled across the lawn. He crept low over the grass. Jewel let out a wild holler just as the sun broke the horizon.

"Yeehaw!" Jewel fired a single shot into the air, "Gabriel Turner! I hear your looking for me?"

Another man stood on the portico, behind where Turner could be seen.

"Come and get 'em then!"

Jewel let the pistol swing in her fingers, so the silver handle sparkled in the dawn. She booted Pendleton's gelding into action and the horse sped across the fields. The stocky man at the front dashed down the stairs. Raising a rifle to his shoulder he let one shot go. Marcus held his breath as Jewel ducked. The gelding continued. Jewel sat upright and waved her hand in the air, the silver pistol still in her grip.

Three men including Gabriel rushed down the stairs to their mounts. Turner turned to the fourth man, one younger than the others, but tall and broad. Turner grabbed him by the collar and pointed back inside. Marcus recognized the facial features from the wanted posters, and would bet all his coins that it was Cooper Brady had just got put in his place. Brady took a few steps forward and then retreated back inside.

Marcus wanted to rush, to dive in head first, but an ambush was the only way he could be sure that someone would come out of this alive.

It took Marcus several minutes to creep across the open field without being seen; each second taxing his patience. He heard a commotion inside the house just as he reached Jedidiah's shack. He dragged the old man back into his abode and put a rag to his head. He was breathing, but out cold. Marcus scooped up the shot gun rummaging through the crooked sideboard for a handful of shells. Marcus crouched low as he made his way around the rear of the big house, finding the rear kitchen door open and unlocked as usual.

Marcus tiptoed through the wide rooms, the timber ceilings and brick arches echoing every sound he made. He could feel the numbness sinking through his limbs, the urge to run through the hallway to the place where he heard women weeping, and men groaning against bonds. He paused outside his father's study, the sitting room only ten feet away.

"Should we gut this one first?" Someone said, "Your choice this time Benny."

"Wait for Gabriel to get back Cooper."

Marcus craned his neck around the corner, Cooper Brady stood in front of the captives. Marcus's father had a noose around his neck and the rope strung back over his ankles. A pair of boots, Marcus assumed belonged to Reid were visible at the end of the lounge. Marcus's mother, three servants and a pregnant woman knelt in front of Benny who paced behind them.

Marcus placed his shot gun down and pulled out the silver pistol. He balanced it in his hand, the weight unnatural. His thumbnail found a groove in the base of the handle. The pearl and silver inlay suddenly shifted to expose the treasure. Suddenly all the Turner pieces fell into place. The railways, the bonds, even Smith. Marcus didn't have time to dwell on it and slammed the panel shut. Marcus hadn't shot the silver pistol, and couldn't count on the accuracy. He discarded it and pulled out his own. Marcus used his hand to cover the noise of cocking the pistol. He rolled onto his knees, listening as footsteps moved.

"You think Gabriel's coming back? You heard him last night. He wants this over and done with. It's the guns and nothing less. He's rushed off to chase that bitch while we wait here."

"You think he's setting us up?"

"I'm sure of it. Once he has those guns, we're done. I

wouldn't be surprised if after he killed her, and then brought the Sheriff round here. If I'm going down for murder, I might as well have some fun with it."

Marcus heard a horse whiny.

"Shit, Jesse's back!"

Marcus listened as breathless Jesse Harkins thundered up the portico, "He shot me!"

Cooper cursed.

"I almost had her too, reached out and boom!"

Cooper cursed again, "I knew it. To hell with this! Light it up. Gabriel is going to get what's coming to him!"

Marcus listened as the footsteps retreated. Marcus scrambled to his feet and ran down the hallway. Benny howled as Marcus fired. A flash burst from Cooper's pistol and Marcus felt something collide with his shoulder forcing him to the ground. Marcus rolled onto his back as flames licked up the curtains. Marcus rose onto his knees and scrambled to his family.

Coughing as the smoke curled; Marcus unbound his mother and the pregnant woman. Whit's fiancé disappeared as his mother crouched beside him to undo the servants. Marcus reached his father and unhitched the ropes. The haze stung Marcus's eyes and he pulled his shirt up over his nose. He didn't have time. He clutched Reid's ankles and dragged his brother down the hallway as the others rushed to extinguish the flames.

Marcus reached the kitchen and with a butchers knife cut loose Reid's ropes. Reid was breathing but unconscious. His mother wound her arms around Marcus's neck as he sat on the rear porch steps. Bucket after bucket passed him into the sodden lounge room until the fire eventually surrendered.

Pendleton Kearby marched over to Marcus and finger jabbed into his chest, "I warned you about that whore."

Marcus felt his knuckles connect. Inside the adrenaline fueled numbness, he failed to register his actions until his mother screamed. Pendleton lay sprawled across the grass, clutching his nose as blood oozed between his fingers.

"She just saved your life." Marcus spat. He didn't have time for this. "Send for the Sheriff and any man who can hold a rifle. Send them to the Fox Hole."

Marcus sprinted to the stables and clambered onto *Scout*, booting him into a gallop.

The smoke from the smoldering homestead billowed skyward, tarnishing the pale blue sky. The morning sun was rising over the horizon, splashing golden halos around the hoof prints that splattered the fields. Marcus crouched low over the pommel, every nerve strained to breaking point.

Jewel was fast, brave and smart as a whip. He told himself she could out fox and outgun the best of them. And she had for two years. Jewel had to be alright, she had to be safe!

Marcus took *Scout* over the low gully's that crisscrossed the Crooked K land, the trail of his father's gelding shifted left and right but Marcus knew where she was headed and picked up the prints across the gully. Marcus headed for the thicket of red oaks that lined the main river that supplied the Kearby Ranch. The river was fed from a number of other small tributaries including the Double E Ranch. Marcus dipped his head under the branches.

A weight collided with his chest, his head flew backwards and *Scout* continued without him. Marcus throat screamed in agony. The air forced from his lungs as he landed on the hard soil and exposed tree roots. Marcus's finger flew to his throat, digging between his skin and the taught rope. Dust obscured his vision. The ground rushed underneath him, his heels kicking to find purchase. Marcus pulled the rope down and sucked in a shallow breath.

A boot toe landed in his ribs and Marcus snatched at his gun belt. The heel slammed down on his forearm, another landed on his skull.

"Where's she headed!" Cooper spat.

"Well look-sey here!" Jesse howled as his fingers snatched at Marcus's gun belt. The silver pistol snatched; his other one splashed into the creek.

"Where's she goin'?" Cooper wound the rope tighter around his fist.

Black spots appeared in front of Marcus as his throat searing in agony. He would rather die than lead them to Jewel.

"Fine, we'll make her come to us!" Cooper hitched the rope to the pommel of his saddle; his green buffalo checked shirt the last thing that Marcus saw before darkness claimed him.

A shot zipped past Jewel's ear. Kearby Senior's mount was fast but not fast enough. Jewel eyed the shack in the distance; she recognized the shape that had been built into a small escarpment overlooking the river. If Jewel made it, she would be trapped inside. Jewel circled and headed up river hoping to buy some time.

The gelding flagged again, more than likely from Pendleton flogging it to reach the Double E last night. Jewel cursed. She was supposed to be good at running away. Jewel led the horse across the water, hoping to revive it. Turner and his thug turned to chase, not knowing where to cross like she had.

Another shot boomed past her ear. Turner doubled backed to the shallower crossing and Jewel spied her moment. She dug her heels into the horse's flanks and pushed the gelding to its limit. She saw the gully ahead and rose from her saddle. The other thug had reached her side, splashing across the river in a burst of white water. Jewel rose from her saddle and turned to fire. The bullet struck flesh but the man continued. His fingers snatched her stirrup. Jewel tried to fire in his face, but the man leapt across the distance and brought her to the ground.

Jewel's mouth filled with sand and dust and she threw fists and knees into her attacker. Her back scratched across the stone chips as a fist collided with her cheek.

"Pull her up Sampson." Gabriel Turner's voice cut through the double vision.

Jewel focused on his lined face, the sandy brown hair at his temples and the hair lip. Under his Stetson, his steel colored eyes raked over her soiled frame and down to her gun belt.

"Where's the other one?"

Jewels veins seemed entwined with thorns, everything hurt, even her lungs that hacked through the dusty air. Jewel's legs didn't want to support her when Sampson pulled her to her feet. She grabbed his forearm as the fist that had curled through her shirt collar. Jewel spat the mix of blood and mud from her mouth. It landed within an inch of Turner's boot toe. His back hand slammed into her cheek and Jewel fell against Sampson's chest. The bigger man jostled her upright.

"Never mind, we'll head back and ask the family."

Sampson wound a length of rope around Jewel's hands and threw her across her saddle. Jewel kicked out, wriggling until she slipped forward, Sampson caught her by the belt loops and dragged her back.

"This is the girl that killed Francis?" Sampson laughed.

"Other than his enthusiasm, there really was nothing useful about Francis." Gabriel mumbled.

They brought Kearby Senior's gelding with them as they retraced their trail. They hadn't made it far from the river when a single rider waved a hat overhead. Jewel closed her eyes praying that it wasn't Marcus. That he had gotten his family clear.

The rider stopped short of Turner and Sampson.

"Howdy Benny." Sampson called. "How's Jesse?"

"He's a little rattled to say the least." Benny said, "Him and Cooper think y'all waiting for us to die before you claim your treasure." The younger man replied, his voice shaky across the distance. Jewel squinted through her puffy eyes.

"Is that so?" Gabriel answered.

"Well?" Benny prompted.

Gabriel looked at Sampson and then back to the young outlaw, "What do you want Benny?"

Benny spat, his tone thicker, a touch more acidic, "Cooper wants a trade."

Sampson chewed a wad of tobacco and shook his head, "I

told you he was trouble."

Gabriel exhaled, "You shouldn't have missed then."

Sampson smacked Jewel's upper thigh, "Maybe he wants revenge for his Cousin Donny."

"He wants more than that," Gabriel hissed.

Gabriel Turner followed the lone rider back to the shade of the magnificent live oak trees that lined the Crooked K river, the water course that inspired the Ranchers brand. Jewel wiped her eyes on her shirt which only made it worse. In the immense winding limbs of the tree, Jewel deciphered a group of two other gang members and a body twisted out of shape dangling from the branches.

As if Jewel's heart had been ripped from her chest, she screamed at the sight of Marcus. His shirt had been cut from his torso while a fresh injury marred his scarred shoulder and splashed crimson droplets onto the leaf littered ground. A rope wound around his neck and had been looped through his hands and down to his ankles. Jewel sucked in short sharp breaths as she tried to think.

"What do you want Cooper?" Gabriel asked in a tone closely resembling a yawn.

Cooper, the broadest of the three wandered forward, his brown hair slicked back over his skull, the sides shorter than the top. He wore a coffee colored leather vest over a faded black shirt and dark brown denims. He spun a silver handled pistol in his fingers.

"First, I want the whore for Donny's death. You never gave a shit about Francis so you shouldn't give a shit if I take her life for his."

Gabriel looked at Sampson and back to Cooper, "What else?"

"I want half."

Gabriel snorted. "The way I see it -"

"The way I see it," Cooper interrupted, "There's two of you and three of us, and you need those guns to get our treasure."

Jewels mind suddenly spun. There were three. Three.

"I'm done with your posturing all over the countryside, Tanner this and Tanner that while we starve!" Cooper hollered.

"Three of us," Jewel whispered.

Gabriel turned in the saddle to regard Jewel. His steel eyes squinted, his mouth turned down at the corners.

"You want this other pistol -" Cooper continued his rant, but Gabriel wasn't listening, he shifted his horse closer to Jewel's mount.

Jewel didn't have time for this. Marcus eyes were closed but his body remained tensed. Jewel remembered what he told her about the knots. The more Marcus struggled the tighter it would get. His strength would eventually dwindle, leaving him to strangle himself.

All her words came out in a rush, "I beat your brother fair and square for those guns. I'm the fastest gunslinger this side of the Red River."

Sampson's cheeks creased into a thin grin, one of his brown eyes winked at Gabriel.

Now she had his full attention she continued, "You cut him down. Take the guns, just let him live."

"I beg your pardon," Gabriel sneered.

Jewel squared her shoulders and raised her chin, "You know I'm going to win. Three of us against the three of them, we both know you're going to shoot me anyway."

Gabriel's steel colored eyes blazoned at Jewel's audacity. The seconds stretched into moments until suddenly Turner smirked and pushed his mount forward.

"Listen Cooper, this young lady has been chattering all morning about how she beat Francis and how she beat Donnie. She thinks she's the fastest gunslinger this side of the Red River."

Cooper's jaw cinched, his nostrils flared.

"Reckons she heard Donnie squeal when she plugged him."

"That bitch is getting what's owed!"

"That's if you can beat me." Jewel called with only the

slightest tremor. She heard Marcus groan. "Come on, you want this other pistol, win it from me."

Chapter 29

Sampson untied Jewel's hands and pushed her off the saddle, she landed on her feet until Sampson yanked the rope and she tumbled backwards into the leaf litter.

"Don't you know how to treat a lady?" Jewel snapped, hoping her harsh words would bring her courage. Her eyes ran over Marcus's trussed up form, his muscles straining and his veins pulsating under the crimson color of his cheeks.

Gabriel Turner stood beside Jewel and lifted his brothers silver handled pistol up to her eye line and open the barrel, and dropped five bullets into his palm. He pulled out his own golden handled pistol and cocked the hammer.

"Don't go getting any ideas." Gabriel whispered. He spun to face her opponent. "See Cooper she's got one bullet, even better odds for you."

"I'll hang her alongside this one so he can watch. Then we head to Shreveport!"

"Shreveport, yes." Gabriel said.

"Together, but I'm holding the guns."

"Sure Cooper." Gabriel marched Jewel several paces back but in line with Cooper. He put the pistol into her right side holster, "Some would say it's an unfair advantage," he grinned, his pistol levelled at her chest as he stepped back.

"Others would see it as an opportunity." Jewel murmured.

Jewel had one bullet. One.

Jewel didn't have to turn to see where Gabriel stood. She could hear his ornate boots clinking across the hard ground.

Cooper slinked forward, his shoulders raised, a smirk sliced his almost handsome features as he spun his barrel with flair, "Six coming straight at you!"

Jewel inhaled. One bullet. One.

Cooper put his pistol into his holster and rolled his shoulders. He nodded to Sampson. For some reason he trusted Turner's thug and not Turner himself. The older man begin to count. Marcus groaned.

Jewel exhaled, her fingers trembled. She licked her dry split lips.

One bullet. One.

A wind scurried the leaves into soft eddies that rolled across the distance between them. Jewel's heart thundered in her ear drums.

One bullet.

Cooper's shoulder shifted a quarter of an inch. Jewel drew the pistol as her thighs pushed. The tree roots landed in her gut, the air rushed out from her lungs as her finger pulled the trigger. The rope that held Marcus's ankles slithered out. He hit the ground in a heap. Jewel's ears were numb. Sampson's pistol fired into the torso of the one called Benny. He stumbled back as a spurt of blood erupted from his vest. Sounds failed to penetrate Jewel's mind as the seconds ticked by. She felt a sting along her hip as mounds of dirt burst around her. She rolled onto her back. Gabriel stood over her, his finger already on his trigger. Jewel released her grip. The silver pistol cartwheeled through the air. Gabriel's barrel lifted as he tried to catch it. A spout of dirt sent debris into her eyes. Jewel kicked out. Her boot toe landed in Gabriel's gut.

Tuner hunched forward and Jewel dug her fingernails into the dirt, scrambling to get on top of him. The silver pistol tumbled from his grip. A flash of gold raised to Jewel's cheek. She snatched the barrel and twisted. Her forearms strained against Gabriel's power.

Suddenly sound pierced the silence with such ferocity that Jewel cowered, a shot rang out from behind her as she saw Marcus on his feet, wrapping a length of rope around Coopers neck, the bigger man's face turning purple. A string of bullets emptied into Cooper's chest from the other young gunman. Suddenly Cooper slumped, his neck at an unnatural angle. Fingers raked down Jewel's back snagging in her belt loops.

Jewel twisted to the right, releasing her grip on Gabriel's pistol. The retort rang in Jewel's ear, the boom thundering through her skull as behind her she heard Sampson grunt. Jewel winced as a warm liquid splashed across her cheeks. She opened her eyes to see Gabriel's face coated in blood, his eyes wide, nostrils flared. Behind Sampson lagged. She kicked Sampson's dead weight from her legs and crawled upwards. Gabriel aimed a fist to her nose, lacking distance it grazed her cheek and slid off in the blood to collide with her ear. Jewel slammed her hand on the rear of Gabriel's pistol, the webbing between her thumb and forefinger snagged in the hammer.

Gabriel rolled and Jewel squealed as her hand tore from his pistol and she ended up underneath him. She brought her knee up into his groin as his elbows rained down. The hard bone connected with her temple. The lights faded, black spots swum in front of her eyes. A cool metallic ghosted across her fingers.

Gold. Pearl. Mahogany.

Gabriel's weight released from her chest. She opened her eyes to see Gabriel standing above her. His left holster empty, the golden handled pistol in her hand. Jewel squeezed the trigger.

The bullet struck his shoulder. Gabriel levelled his pistol. Jewel dragged her injured hand across the hammer of her pistol, her own blood causing her hand to slip off without reloading. A roar erupted from the right as a weight collided with Turner, sending him reeling into the leaf litter. Jewel sucked in a deep breath, her throat tight, the sound more of a gurgle than a name. Jewel scrambled to her feet as Marcus's fists cascaded over and over into Gabriel's face.

Jewel heard a squeak behind. Instinctively she brought Gabriel's gun level to Jesse's chest as he stumbled, unarmed, and clutching his abdomen. Ribbons of crimson leaked through his fingers.

"Marcus!" Jewel shouted again, just as the sound of a thousand hooves shook the ground. Marcus pulled himself upright, his chest heaving with labored breaths. Turner's face was pulp. Jewel kicked the firearms out of the way as she ran to Marcus. Jewel looked at the far end, to where Cooper lay still, the angle of his head at odds to his body. The third one Benny was crawling towards Cooper dragging his arm behind him. Jewel let off a round just short and he rolled into a ball, one hand trembled above his head.

Jewel's legs began to tremble and then wobble, the ground rushed upwards. Marcus enveloped Jewel in his arms, his forehead coming to rest on hers. She ran her hands over his frame, shivering as her fingers tripped over the deep gouges left by the ropes.

"Are you hurt?" he croaked.

Jewel shook her head, "Not as bad as you," She put her trembling hand over the wound at his shoulder.

"Scar tissue," he mumbled as he pressed a kiss to her hair, his fingers gently clutching her injured left hand.

"God Damn Kearby!" A harsh voice boomed over the sound of curt orders and excited chatter, "Drag me all the way up here and half the job is done!"

Marcus shoulder relaxed as Quinn's brash tones breached the numbness. The Major dismounted and pointed men in different directions. A handful rushed over to Benny throwing iron cuffs over his one good wrist. He howled when they moved his injured arm. A few stopped to check on Cooper and Jesse and Sampson before they shook their heads and moved on. Two men grabbed the arms and shoulders of Gabriel Turner and dragged him to his feet.

"Well we'll never hear the end of it now, Kearby shot Gabriel Turner!"

"No, Sir," Marcus voice rasped through is injured throat, his arm curled around Jewel's waist, "Miss Jewel Daniels did."

"Ah," Quinn ran his brown eyed gaze over Jewel, while he dismounted. He ran his fingers down his thick blonde moustache, "This is the one?" Quinn brought out his water canteen and offered it to Marcus.

He took a careful swig and coughed, "After all she shot Baby-face."

"So my telegrams tell me. Yours, Theo's and Abe's." Quinn winked.

Cade Hamerton galloped up to the grove, before dismounting from *Maverick*. Both man and horse looked like they rode through Hell and back.

"We were only a few miles outside of the town when your man Hamerton intercepted us and told us where to come. I'll tell ya, they y'all got quite a fright when we rode into town, bristling in their britches. Come on get cleaned up, so you can mount up."

Marcus hobbled down to the river with Jewel by his side. He splashed handfuls of water over his face and wiped down his chest and arms. Marcus found a spare shirt in Cooper's belongings and shrugged it on, while Jewel limped over to him. He wanted to kiss her to wrap her in his arms but not surrounded by Rangers. He was supposed to be making an honest woman of her. She rubbed at her hip and Marcus inspected the tiny ricochets that pock-marked her denims and no doubt grazed her soft flesh.

"I might take a closer look at that later," Marcus smiled.

Jewel smiled, "What happens now?"

"I'll need to go with them, to clear up what I can. Quinn believes us, so that's half the battle won. I will have to make it official."

Jewel lowered herself down to the river bank as a man carrying a saddlebag full of medical supplies came rushing over to Marcus. He crouched down in front of Marcus and placed a wad of clean fabric over his weeping shoulder. The medic pulled out a long pair of tweezers and rapidly dug into the wound, Marcus flinched as the tweezer pulled a warped piece of metal from the surface of his flesh. Marcus took a bandage and began to wrap Jewel's injured hand.

"Not deep, doesn't look like there's any bone fragment. I'll stitch it up anyway. Any slower and it might have bounced off you."

"Don't be telling him that Carl, next he'll be wanting to come south with us." Quinn strolled down the river bank.

"No," Marcus shook his head, "Not a chance."

Jewel jumped as the medic pushed her buttock, "Hey!"

"Ma'am if you stay still...."

"Hand me that!" Jewel snatched the cloth and held it to her own buttock, "It's going to be a long ride home." She grumbled.

Marcus snorted.

They took a leisurely pace back to the Crooked K ranch and Jewel was surprised to see the front half of the house scorched. Half the Double E ranch were milling around the house helping move charred furniture while Mrs Kearby fixed people sandwiches.

Jewel limped off her saddle and rushed to meet her father. He sat down on the portico with a cloth to his head and another Ranger checking him over. Jesse Kline tipped his hat to Jewel as he rounded up the others. The boy had grown into a man Jewel noticed. Pearl would be silly to let him go, Jewel thought. Jewel looked at Marcus and shook her head. She should take her own advice.

When the Ranger was finished with Jedidiah he turned on her, demanding to see her injury.

"To prevent infection," he snapped.

Jewel relented and was shown to a room upstairs. She marveled at how she had never actually stepped foot into the big house except into the kitchen to pinch food. She lowered her denims as the medic splashed alcohol across the grazed flesh until it stung. Jewel pressed a clean wad to the tiny divots before the medic sealed it off with a bandage. Jewel listened at Major Quinn greeted Kearby Senior down stairs.

"He's an invaluable member of the Rangers. You'd never have guessed he didn't have military training. More than once he has been the difference between success of an operation or certain death."

Jewel smiled at Quinn's enthusiasm. He was as outrageous as his moustache and Jewel knew why he had earnt Marcus's respect. Kearby Senior grunted and eventually shook the man's hand.

"What happened here?" He pointed to Pendleton's nose, "Turner's men get you too?"

"Yeah something like that," Pendleton grumbled.

Jewel's smile widened.

"You'll have to do without him for a while longer. The young lady too." Quinn continued.

"Who?"

"Miss Daniels."

"Right," Pendleton crossed his arms over his chest as his jaw cinched. "Is that so?"

"Well I suspect she deserve a rest after capturing the West's most wanted man."

Pendleton didn't reply as Quinn took his leave.

Jewel saw Quinn approach Marcus and she pulled up her denims wincing as it covered her wound. She clicked her tongue thinking about Marcus's injuries in comparison. Jewel half rushed half limped down the stairs as quick as her rump would allow.

"Y'all going to tell me what you dragged me out all this way for?" Quinn snorted.

"Get me the guns." Marcus gestured to a younger Ranger who complied. He handed Marcus both the silver pistols and the gold, "He was after these?"

Marcus rolled the pistols over into his hand and dug into the silver inlay, pulling the panel outwards to reveal a weird metal contraption. Quinn turned it over in his thick fingers hands. Marcus then opened the handles on the two golden pistols to reveal more metal pieces. When Marcus was done he handed those to Quinn as well.

"Is this what I think it is? The company seal of the Union

Pacific Railroad?" Quinn turned the other item over in his hands "This is not the company Presidents' signature?"

"From the final gold train robbery in '74..." Jewel mumbled.

"I believe so either of them might have come from the first stage coach robbery. Possibly the specimens accidentally fell into Turner's hands. I doubt it. He's wanted to wreck revenge on the railroads since '73, and he found a way to do it, getting rich in the process." Marcus said.

Quinn turned the stamps over in his hands, "Spectacular, and then with Smiths duplicating the specimens he had a ready fill of bonds for sale and trade."

"Yes, I wired the Pinkerton Detective Agency to find any links to their man Smith and Turner or Tanner as he goes by."

"Turner mentioned Shreveport." Jewel said.

"If Tanner rents an office in Shreveport, I suspect you might find his printers or the like."

Quinn harrumphed and slapped Marcus on his injured shoulder, "You never cease to amaze me Kearby, I don't know how you did it Sir", he addressed Kearby Senior, "Raising such a clever boy with brass ones this size of Texas!"

Jewel scoffed so loudly she held her hand to her lips.

Kearby Senior just grimaced as politely as he could.

Quinn ordered his men about, "We'll make camp just south out of town, Kearby you return with me so we can sort this mess once and for all." Quinn took Jewel's hand and placed a kiss on the back, "My lady," he emphasized.

Marcus waved Cade over, "Can you take Jewel to the Double E?"

"Of course,"

"Jewel, I'm going with Quinn but can I trust you to check for any news from the Pinkerton Agency."

A twang of irritancy stirred within Jewel but she nodded. Marcus was leaving? Gently he lifted her hand and squeezed her fingers. Jewel didn't respond. She tried not to look up to the big house where Marcus's fiancé stood her hand over her swollen belly. Marcus didn't acknowledge her or his father. Jewel limped over to farewell Jedidiah before she rode out with Hamerton.

Two days went past before Jewel felt safe to wander about Dew Springs without fear of Turners or arrest. And still no sign of Kearby. She had heard the First Battalion were a rowdy bunch enjoying their time at the Nine Lives Saloon without Quinn's official approval despite him accompanying them from time to time. Yet still no sign of Marcus. Perhaps he had left to Shreveport as the others were supposed to.

Jewel checked on her father again, and he had handed back her earnings, refusing to keep any more than enough to buy two bottles of whiskey.

Evelyn Hamerton kept her busy with the twins and Lachlan and every other moment her eyes were awake Cade had her helping train the green broncs he brought from Dallas.

Marcus hadn't sent word, but Jewel remained loyal to her task. She was to await the word of the Pinkerton Agent and forward it to Shreveport.

It wasn't until the fourth day that the telegram arrived. The agent complimented Jewel in her downfall of the Turner gang, a comment that perhaps she wasn't meant to see:

Please inform Miss Daniels that if she ever is in need of employment she'd be more than welcome at our agency ~ Helena Ash.

Jewel forwarded the details to Shreveport and hoped it was Kearby who read it. It wasn't until the next day that Jewel sat on Pearl's spare bed at the Double E, turning over the business card of Helena Ash considering her options. Kearby was gone and when he returned he had a wife and child. His father would do his utmost to marry him off. What options did Jewel have? She had told herself before that she wouldn't let another man rule her destiny. Jewel had her likelihood on a wanted poster and now she had unwanted fame as a lawman - or law aider. Jewel tumbled the Pinkerton card again.

Could she live with Marcus married in Dew Springs watching his family blossom knowing her man was out of reach forever. Or Jewel could leave now, leave with her memories filled with their nights of passion and not spoiled by a painful farewell.

Evelyn caught her in one of her morose moods sitting on the rear porch that afternoon, "Thinking about Marcus again?" Evie asked.

"He didn't tell you his father had a wife ready for him?"

Evelyn sighed, "Not me specifically, but I heard all the same."

"I can't give Marcus that" Jewel said in defeat.

"Who said Marcus wants that?" Evelyn wrapped her arm around Jewel's shoulders, "Have you asked him?"

Jewel sighed, "I don't have to, I know Marcus, he's safe, routine, boring...." she stopped talking. Nothing about Marcus matched her words. What the Hell was she supposed to do? Wait for him and suffer being a fool again. Jewel excused herself and went back to her room.

The next morning Evie and Pearl had rushed into town, giving Jewel a quick squeeze in farewell. Evie made Jewel promise she would be here when Evie returned. Jewel just nodded, unsure herself. Just before noon, Hamerton called Jewel to the stables and into the stall with the dainty beige mare.

"She's ruined, won't listen to me anymore," Hamerton handed Jewel the reins.

"Cade, I can't."

"Sure you can. I'm sure when you collect on those rewards for the Turners you'll make payment."

He ran his hand down the rump of the quaint mare. Why would Hamerton gifted her a horse? Marcus. Marcus was trying to do right by Jewel again.

"Have you heard from Marcus?"

Hamerton avoided her eyes, "I have."

"And?" Jewel snapped.

"He said it's been sorted. Your name is cleared and that you knew what to do." Cade said.

Jewel's stomach clenched. The man was sending her away, telling her to run. Marcus had made his decision and Dew Springs was too small for the both of them.

The sun peeked over the fields the sun warming the side of the stable, and Jewel turned her back on Hamerton, returning inside Jewel packed her saddles bags. At least she had her father's savings from her income so Jewel could stop in town briefly and buy new saddle and tack and some supplies. Jewel sighed, perhaps when she reached Houston she would send a telegram to Kearby.

Jewel mounted her new yet unnamed horse in a whirlwind of numbness and kneed the mare's flanks. The coldness of Marcus's final rejection stung more than the tears that spilled. As the Double E Ranch faded from sight, Jewel had made up her mind. Helena Ash had offered a job as a Pinkerton Agent and it wasn't such a bad idea. Damn Kearby, damn the world!

Jewel reached town slowing her new mount to a stroll as she neared the high end of town, the Texas Rangers had congregated around the Bluebell Hotel and a few sat outside the Nine Lives Saloon. Jewel wished to shrink into the saddle as the humiliation built. Instead she straightened her shoulders and raised her chin.

"You leaving again," someone called from across the street.

Jewel ignored the taunt. A shrill whistle cut the air, and the dainty horse stopped.

"I said," a man wandered out from the shade of the giant tree that shaded the Church lawn. "Are you leaving again?"

Jewel clicked her tongue, "I can't stay here Kearby, with you about to be married."

"I supposed I am." Marcus smiled. He wore a pale blue shirt, extremely crisp and clean and tucked in at the waist. Was his new fiancé doing his laundry?

"At least your father will be happy." Jewel spat.

Marcus snorted as he grabbed the reins of her horse, "I'm

not so sure about that. I saw my father just this morning and we had a difference of opinion."

Jewel held her breath, "How different?"

"I told him that by honoring my family I'd be dishonoring the woman I love."

Jewel froze, "You never said that!"

"I did, do you want me to say it again?"

"Yes!"

"Good, I love you Jewel Daniels, now stop messing around and get down here and marry me."

Jewel slid off her saddle and into Marcus's waiting arms. He caught her before her heels hit the ground and pressed his lips to hers. A spray of gunshots erupted with hoots and hollers from the watching Rangers.

"Are you all mine, Marcus Kearby?"

"Forever. Now Evelyn has a selection of dresses waiting for you at the Bluebell if you're so inclined."

"And if I'm not inclined to dresses Marcus?"

"I'll be here waiting to take you as you come." Marcus kissed her again, "So long as you're wearing those boots."

~ THE END ~

Epilogue

Marcus stood inside the Monark Springs post office dictating his latest telegram to Helena Ash in Louisiana; the Pinkerton Agent was still on the trail of Cassidy Smith. It had been six months since Marcus and Jewel had left Dew Springs, Texas following unsuccessful leads the girl might have been in Missouri.

Marcus watched Jewel cross the road from the Liberty Saloon, a smirk brewing across his cheeks at her chosen attire for this afternoon. Her flamboyant hair had been demurely pulled up from her neck as her dress plunged downwards from her throat. The Post Master re-read the telegram but Marcus only half listened. If Jewel was heading his way, she had news.

Jewel scooped up her burgundy frills as she stepped over the threshold, her gaze briefly running over his appearance, her nose twisting at his grizzled cheeks. She approached the counter without a single acknowledgment to Marcus, as agreed.

"I was expecting news today, I saw the stagecoach arrive and I was hoping I could trouble you to look again?"

The withered Post Master looked at Marcus after Jewel's breathless request.

"I don't mind waiting. I'll find something to occupy my time." Marcus grinned.

Jewel lifted her nose in the air, but Marcus caught the slightest blush of her cheeks.

The elderly Post Master nodded and disappeared to the room behind where two hessian sacks were waiting to be sorted.

As soon as the man was out of earshot, Jewel turned to Marcus.

"Marcie's said the liquor delivery man said they had

trouble with a drifter last month, one with protruding ears and a scar from his left ear to his chin. Well Libby spoke to Harriet whose got the same sorta fellow sleeping off a bottle of whiskey in her room right now."

Marcus smiled, Jewel had a way with gossip, "He sounds familiar." Marcus knew exactly which wanted poster matched the man's description.

"At least wait for me to get dressed properly, Kearby, I'm not arresting anyone in hoops!"

Marcus ran his gaze over Jewels exposed décolletage and smirked, "You wearing your boots?"

Jewel lips curled, "Yes."

"Then you're dressed proper fine to me."

The Post Master returned empty handed and Jewel thanked him in a flurry of lashes. Her skirts swished along the boardwalk faster than double struck lightening, hurrying to take her place at the piano as the Liberty Saloon singer. Marcus had enjoyed sitting incognito at the bar these last three days waiting for Howard Davidson to show his face, sipping slowly of his beers while he watched Jewel sing to the crowds.

Marcus thanked the Post Master after the telegram was sent and pocketed the news he had collected from home. Shelton Murphy was chasing silver somewhere in Colorado and Taylor Stone was suffering with cattle rustlers. Marcus had included the information in his telegram to Helena hoping the Pinkerton Agency might lend a hand.

Marcus smiled when he had read Cade's telegram. The Hamerton brood all doing well with the exception of his half-sister Pearl who, against Cade's wishes, had decided to remain in Dew Springs. Marcus would bet all of Jewel's latest reward money that it had less to do with helping Evie and the twins and more to do with a boy named Jesse Kline.

Marcus would expect another wedding on the horizon shortly; whether Cade liked the groom or not.

Marcus gave Jewel a reasonable head start, before crossing the road and entering the Liberty, the smoke haze stung his eyes, the pianist was unaccompanied and Marcus knew he was running out of time to stop Jewel taking matters into her own hands. He caught Jewel at the bar and propositioned her, delighting in the way her eyebrows raised at his words.

"I'd rethink your choices," The muscly bar keep hissed, "Unless you want your fingers down your throat, this one's dance card is full."

Jewel smirked her freckles blushing, "It's okay Leroy, I might make an exception for this one."

"Suit yourself honey," He said and returned to eyeing the crowd.

Jewel led Marcus by the hand upstairs to the Doves rooms letting go when she reached the darkened corridor to pull out a derringer from her skirts.

Jewel pointed to the correct door and Marcus wasted no time in shouldering it open, the hinges splintering from the joists. The man leapt up to his feet, his fists curled with dark hair across his face. Marcus threw his arms around Howard Davidson's waist and brought the double murderer to the ground. The taller man threw a punch towards Marcus, who landed one on Davidson's chin in return. His fist poised over Marcus's face until the cock of the derringer hammer at his temple made him pause.

"Up you get now, real slow." Jewel said with a set of shackles already in the other hand.

They celebrated that night at a camp fire just outside Pleasant Ridge, Davidson's reward adding to their earnings. While Marcus stirred dinner over the coals, Jewel slipped off to the underbrush claiming she needed to tend to *Scout* and her mare Jewel had named *Diamante*. Jewel smirked as the metal spoon cluttered into the tiny pot when she reached the campfire, one of Marcus shirts barely covering down to her bare thighs. Marcus gaze ran down her slender legs to her rose embroidered boots. He reached out and pulled her down to his lap.

Jewel broke his kiss first, "What's next for Marcus Kearby, Pinkerton Agent?"

"I don't mind if we follow Cassidy Smith's trail all the way to Chicago, I'll follow whatever sunset you choose honey." Marcus pressed a string of kisses behind her ear to her throat as he undid her first button.

Jewel shivered in his lap, she hadn't quite gotten used to Marcus's flattery. He was a direct as he was stubborn, his words multiplying the flutters that tickled her ribs. Now how was she going to convince him of her next plan? Jewel undid his top button and pushed her hand through the gap to caress his muscular chest.

Jewel inhaled, "I heard from Evie that Sheriff Green in Dew Springs will hang up his boots next year."

Marcus brought his head up, "Wait you want to return to Dew?"

Jewel stumbled with her words as she traced the scar tissue that decorated his physique, "Not straight away Kearby, but maybe," Jewel nuzzled against his neck, "In a year we might want to have ourselves a little Kearby."

Marcus smiled, "A year?"

Jewel cleared her throat, "Unless something happens along the trail, I thought a year - ."

"I like the thought of having a little Kearby..." Marcus kissed Jewel with force this time his hand running up her shirt to caress her bare breasts, "Or two..."

Jewel's head lolled back exposing her creamy throat, "I never said two."

Helena Ash read the rushed reply from Jewel Kearby, her and Marcus were heading back from Missouri, the search unsuccessful. Where was Cassidy Smith? Helena tossed down the telegram on her cluttered desk and picked up her lamp. Her eyes were sore and she had had no further luck in her searching. Tomorrow she would send a telegram to the Land Titles office, surely there was some record, some detail she had overlooked that would lead her onto the next clue. Smith was too common a surname for any real success.

While her father served his life sentence for fraud, Cassidy was out there somewhere, isolated, unprotected, and alone, bargained off as a condition on a mining lease. When her 'husband' discovered that he had been cheated Cassidy's life would be in jeopardy.

Helena crawled into her single loft bed, and extinguished the lamp. Tomorrow, she would start the search again. Cassidy Smith was out there and Helena would not rest until she found her half-sister.

Cassidy Smith stood on the deck of the steamboat the cool evening breeze speared through her caramel brown hair. Her *'brother'* a street urchin she had befriended in Chicago flipped stones from his pocket into the Brazos River. His sandy brown hair was of a kind to hers, his blues eyes stark compared to her chestnut brown.

"Do you think it'll work Cass?"

"Yes of course. He's supposed to be my husband, remember."

"Yeah that's all well and good for you, what about me?"

"Whoever my husband to be is, he will not be able to refuse to employ his new brides' brother, Jet?"

Jethro Smith tossed his last pebble, "I hope you're right."

Cassidy watched a man stumble down the listing hallway of the steamboat. His blonde hair fell in front his dusty sugar grey eyes; his white shirt unbuttoned at the collar and haphazardly tucked in around his narrow waist. His sandy trousers ran down his long legs into a pair of russet boots scuffed with trail dirt. His shoulders were broad and one of his long arms was wrapped around the neck of a dancing girl.

Her vibrant skirts sashayed down the narrow hallway, the ruffles of her flamboyant dress failing to conceal the scandalous whispers the man muttered into the girl's ear. The dancer eyed Cassidy with a smirk, as she played with the lace choker around her neck. The man's lips sunk to her skin, kissing her between propositions.

"So do I," Cassidy muttered.

What would she do if her husband-to-be turned out like this man; a licentious and salacious man pawing all over her without restraint. The man's eyes met Cassidy's for a brief moment; heat flushed her cheeks until she realized the difference between his gazes. He nodded his head in innocent greeting and continued on his way with his prize. Laughing and giggling they fell into a cabin at the end of the hallway. Would Cassidy count herself lucky?

"Well I'm not so sure Mr Jackson isn't taking us for a ride."

"Who else are we going to find to take us to Colorado? We have enough coin and no sense. Here he is now."

Cassidy neatened her appearance. She was twenty years of age and had taken a gamble that her father's fraudulent deal would land her a good man. A good man with a good heart, and nothing like Mr Jackson.

"Good evening Mr Jackson."

"Aye it is a good evening Miss Smith." the way the man pronounced the 's' made Cassidy cringe. The man edged closer his breath stank of whiskey and tobacco.

Cassidy held her breath trying not to insult the man, after all he was their guide.

Jackson raked a thick finger along his grizzly chin, "I see the dress fits you just right."

"Yes thank you although I don't see the sense in spending our money on such an expense."

"I knew your father Miss Smith. He never wasted a cent for anyone, not even those he owed," Jackson grimaced, "But he'd want his daughter to have the finest of things. Besides " Jackson licks his lips, "First impressions count. Trust me."

Cassidy recoiled further, "It must be nearly supper time in the dining room, did you bring my father's wired funds."

Jackson tapped his top pocket, "I surmise it's almost time for dessert."

Jackson's lips advanced, his fully belly trapping Cassidy against the boats wall. Cassidy turned away, his wet lips met her cheek as his hand slithered around her neck trying to pull her lips towards him.

Cassidy put both hands on his chest and shoved to no avail.

"Mr Jackson!" Cassidy shouted as Jets arms came around Jackson's shoulders.

The malnourished fourteen year old boy was no match for the older man's fist. Jet tumbled back clutching his nose. Cassidy brought her knee up and then her heel down.

Jackson's backhand slammed into her cheek.

Cassidy squealed.

Jackson's hands returned to tug at her pink fluffy dress. Cassidy pushed back and this time Jackson fell back. In fact, he fell all the way back, tumbling backwards over the rail and splashing into the Brazos River.

Cassidy ran to the rail just to see Jackson bob to the surface, stretching arm over arm to reach the bank of the river. A shout was heard overhead just as helpful citizens of Waco, Texas assisted the sodden Jackson to his feet. Cassidy watched the man disappear into the crowd of onlookers as the *Sally-Ann* began to dock.

"Are you alright?" The man with the russet boots and the sandy hair stood in front of her.

Cassidy looked into his sugar grey eyes, the edges ringed in flecks of gold.

"Yes thank you," Cassidy stammered.

The scent of Jackson's whiskey and tobacco was dissipated by the man's cologne of rich plum and cedar wood. An underlying flavor of bruised jasmine tickled her nose. The man stepped back and raked his fingers through his blonde fringe pulling it away from his narrow nose. He opened his palm to Jet who willingly took it and pulled himself off the floor.

"And how about you Champ?" the man slapped Jet on the back.

"I'll be fine." The scamp coughed.

"Good!"

Jet cupped his nose and wriggled it, trying to blink away the liquid that welled in his eyes. "Well not really he had all our -"

"We'll be fine," Cassidy interrupted. Something about the man's languid movements unnerved her. "Thank you Mister...."

The man took Cassidy's out stretched hand, "Murphy, Shelton Murphy."

Cassidy's cheeks drained of color as her lungs raced to catch up with her thoughts. She ran her eyes up and down her savior. He was tall, too tall with straight blonde hair too long for his own good. The honey color of his skin suggested he had spent his fair share in the sun; his calloused hands rough against her palm. Barely dressed, debauched and with a painted lady waiting in his cabin, Cassidy's husband-to-be stood before her.

"Pleasure to meet you, Miss, if you need a hand with any else don't hesitate to holler."

"Shelly!" The dancing girl's head peeped past the door jamb as she twisted a blonde curl around her finger.

Shelton Murphy offered her an awkward smile, dimples pinched his suntanned cheeks. A rush of something forced Cassidy into action.

"Mr Murphy, I'm afraid I will have to impose," Cassidy pulled out a handkerchief from her ruffles and dabbed at her invisible tears. "You see Mr Jackson had all our money..." Cassidy added a tremble to her words for emphasis as she wandered down to his cabin. Jet bounced beside her until Cassidy clicked her fingers and the boy remembered to limp. "And now we're without a guide to take us into Colorado Territory."

About the Author

Louise Crouch loves all genres of fiction mixed with a healthy splash of romance. When she is not writing, Louise spends her time frustrating her wonderful husband and raising their two marvelous children.

Book 3 of the Belles & Boots series *Silver & Smith* will follow Cassidy Smith and Shelton Murphy as they journey to Colorado in 1876.

When Cassidy's father had bargained her off as a condition on a mining lease, she was determined to make the barren mine work for her. It would bring Cassidy her freedom and hopefully a good man to marry. If only Cassidy could stop swindling, she might make an honest life for herself.

Shelton Murphy takes nothing seriously except gold and he had no doubts agreeing to his latest business deal. His partner Hugo James was bankrupt, couldn't raise capital if his life depended on it. He promised Shelton that this latest venture would pay dividends and Shelton hadn't hesitated in signed the mining lease in his name. Shelton had left Dew Springs to carve his place in history and he would rather be dead than broke.

Book 1 of the Belles and Boots series, *Hammer & Lock; a Texas Romance* begins when Evelyn Lockwood returns to her hometown Dew Springs to claim her inheritance, the Double E Ranch. Evie's plans to resume her high society life in New Orleans are suddenly derailed when she discovers her fathers' strange bequeath to the rugged and boorish cowboy Cade Hamerton. With Evie staying on at the Double E, Cade is forced to defend not only his entitlement, but his heart, from invasion.

Louise's debut novel was *Even Spinsters Need Company* which is set in Pennsylvania in the 1870's. Hannah Evans arrives in Franklins Shallows to take up the Headmistress position. She soon finds out not all is as it seems in this quaint town especially the Sherriff, Nicholas Hoffman and his devious family tree.

Louise has also delved into the genre of Space Opera with her soon to be released part one of the Sandes Chronicles, *Under the Light*, with part two *In the Shadow* and the finale *Until the Dawn* to be released later next year.

If you wish to read more of Louise Crouch's books find them here: http://loucrouch.wordpress.com/books

If you want to follow Louise Crouch on Facebook find her here: http://www.facebook.com/LouiseCCrouch/

If you want to follow Louise Crouch on Twitter find her here http://twitter.com/LouiseCCrouch

If you've enjoyed Louise's books please leave a review at your favorite retailer.

Special Thanks

A special thanks to my husband and kids who have put up with me at various stages of the writing journey. Thanks for the support, the encouragement and the late night dinners.

Thanks to my extended family and friends who have provided me with feedback, the good, the bad and the ugly.

A big thanks to my Mum; her avid reading habits led me to develop my own passion for this ever evolving genre.

And finally thanks to the readers for their support! I hope you have enjoyed reading these as much as I have enjoyed writing them.